THREE WHISTLES

An Italian family's love story with America.

Gloria Grillo Barsamian

Is it really feasible to try to live in
a way that runs against the grain of
the moral environment that surrounds us?
Does it really matter that we were here at this time?
Will anyone remember us after we go?

What Really Matters
— Arthur Kleinman

Kindle Direct Publishing
First Edition
Copyright © 2021

ISBN: 9798509615221

To my children and grandchildren who provided
unique inspiration at every turn:
Lisa Green, Stuart Green and Murray Green
Robert Barsamian, Joan Barsamian, Robbie
Barsamian and Michaela Barsamian.

Murray and Stuart listened to my dreams and faithfully
made this book possible.

TABLE OF CONTENTS

INTRODUCTION

Pasquale Foenia grows up in a hardworking family of Italian immigrants in one of America's most famous mill towns. His father, Tony, who works at the local market, yearns to return to the Old Country, but his mother, Maria, though she endures long days as a weaver in one of Lawrence's biggest textile mills, is determined to create a permanent and prosperous life in America for herself and her children; she introduces Pasquale to many of the real-life resistance leaders who fought for workers' rights in Lawrence and Boston. THREE WHISTLES presents a panoramic picture of Pasquale's coming of age and of his family's travels, triumphs, and tribulations. Against the backdrop of the Bread and Roses Strike in 1912, the Sacco and Vanzetti trial in the early 1920s, the Depression, and finally World War II, the novel portrays a family unrelenting in its pursuit of justice and truth, its desire to obtain a good education, and its daily struggle to achieve fair working conditions. Ultimately, this book delves into the challenges and nuances of the universal immigrant experience in the U.S., as Pasquale and his family search for their own version of the American dream. The quest requires courage, persistence, and faith, and as Pasquale experiences hardships, injustice, first love, and the lasting bonds of friendships, he comes to realize how elusive and yet how rewarding that dream can be.

The workday started with whistles. It ended with bells.

The Bread and Roses Strike
— Bruce Watson

CHAPTER 1 – IMMIGRANT CITY

Pasquale Foenia made a promise to himself that he would never go back to Italy with his family. He wanted to stay in Lawrence, Massachusetts, an immigrant city, with people like himself. Men, women, and children similar to his mother, Maria; his father, Tony; and his step-sister, Josephine. Nine million immigrants were lured here by William Madison Wood, a mill baron, and other padrones. Traveling from thirty different nations in Europe to seek a better life, they came to America. Thousands a day, mostly unable to afford first class, were herded through Ellis Island, where government agents asked each person twenty-eight questions. Suspected criminals, strikebreakers, anarchists, and carriers of disease were sent back to Europe.

They settled in mill towns.

Twice a week, Pasquale heard his father's mantra: "When we go back to Italy, Pasquale, you will have fine Italian shoes like mine and work in my groceria; people all over Teano will respect you." In the beginning, Tony's chest swelled with pride.

Maria would hug Tony, cradling his head to her bosom and saying, "We have a good life here; the children are educated in English, and you have a good job at Pettoruto's Market. Why would we leave all of this?"

Tony never gave in. "You would not have to work in the mill like a dog, Maria. You would be respected, and people would come into my store back in Italy and say, 'Good morning, Mrs. Foenia.'"

Maria, Tony, and Josephine had left Teano, Italy, while Maria was pregnant. Tony's first wife had died, and the gossipers in their little town were vulgar and mean. Maria, a beautiful and accomplished harpist from Bari, was much younger than his first wife.

The villagers in Teano would huddle together while drinking black coffee in the outdoor cafés, whispering and giving Maria the evil eye as she walked by.

Sometimes they yelled, pushing themselves shoulder to shoulder, "Hey, Maria, are you gaining weight?"

She felt the evil eye punch her in her stomach, but she ignored their comments, smiled, and remained silent as she rushed by them. She noted that the women were dressed in black over black and looked like *stregas* (witches). She thought to herself, "I do not believe in the evil eye, but if it is true, to protect my unborn I will wear the blessed blue and that golden horn my mother gave me."

By the time she got home, she was sick. She survived the humiliations by saying to herself that they were jealous, silly *chiacehiare* (chatterboxes).

One day, while walking past the gossipers, she came across a colorful poster in the square advertising for workers in Lawrence, Massachusetts. It depicted men and women leaving the mills, carrying sacks of gold. She was wearing her sky-blue dress.

"Are you planning on leaving us, Maria?" They were at it again.

8

She was crying when Tony got home.

"Tony, darling," she said, hugging him close and putting his hand on her belly, "the streets in Lawrence, Massachusetts, in the America, are lined with gold. It is a sign that we could start a new life. You could open a *groceria* in America."

Tony laughed at her interpretation of the bags of gold, but she was pregnant, and determination was in her eyes. "Impossible Maria, I have a business here. *Basta*. We lead a good life. Everyone I love lives in Teano, my brothers and family. The Black Hand has begun showing up in Teano. I need to protect my brothers and my business." Thumping his own chest, he declared, "I am respected." He waved his hands as if talking to a crowd.

What Maria did not know was that Tony had seen the posters too and wanted to start a new life, to start all over again with a new family. It was his business that held him back.

Maria put her hand over her swollen stomach and whispered, "But, sweetheart, we could go, and when you have enough money, we could come back and open a second market in Bari, where my family live. People would travel miles to buy the homemade sausage and the glorious ricotta that only you make. Besides, Tony, I am so unhappy here with no church that needs a harpist. There must be a church in Lawrence that needs a harpist."

Maria was in a delicate way, and Tony did not take a stand. They set sail on the *Amerigo Vespucci* for America in 1900. Maria secretly wished her child would be born in the new world.

When the ship dropped anchor in the Hudson River, Maria was in labor, and a midwife called the steward. "We need a doctor right away. Please help us!"

"Not here, lady, you're not gonna have the baby right here." The steward pulled Tony aside and said, "Maybe there is a doctor on board. If not, I will call an ambulance."

Tony stood by Maria's side, praying to the Blessed Mother, something he had not done for years.

Pasquale Americo Foenia could not wait and was born weighing eight pounds. He was wrapped in Maria's white linen wedding sheet, which had been packed in her knapsack for the occasion.

When Tony saw the Statue of Liberty, he wanted to name his son Americo. Maria, out of respect for tradition, named Pasquale after Tony's father.

After twelve months, Maria went to work in the Wood Mill as a weaver. Josephine, her stepdaughter, was in charge of Pasquale. Tony got a job in Pettoruto's Market on Elm Street in the Plains District.

The lives of people in Lawrence were intertwined with the whistles and bells of the mills, which had strange names. The Pacific Mill, the Washington Mill, the Everett Mill, the Kunhardt Mill, the Arlington Mill. The pride of this community was the Wood Mill, which stretched for one mile of red brick and mortar, perched on the Merrimack River. The building had six stories filled with modern equipment that covered sixteen square miles and produced one million pounds of wool cloth and other textiles a week.

Prior to having the posters put up all over Europe, William Madison Wood, whose parents had been

Portuguese immigrants, had hastily built tenements for the workers in his mills. The apartments were close together; one could not see the sky. They replaced the shanties where the Irish had lived after they came to Lawrence during the Potato Famine. William Wood's dream was to create and erect a new Utopia called Labor, so he created Lawrence.

When the Foenia family arrived, like everyone else in town they were very impressed. They found paved streets, the Boston and Main railroad running through town, a horse-drawn railway, electric streetcars, a pumping station, electricity, and the Oliver School, where Robert Frost, the poet, later graduated.

Everyone who lived in these seven square miles was run by the bells and whistles of the mills and churches. The church bells rang all day long. The whistles blasted their way over the city at 5:30 a.m., again at noon, and finally at 6:00 p.m. During emergencies the bells and whistles screeched at the same time and penetrated the area like one big scream. Children who were asleep covered their ears.

Every morning at the first whistle, Maria put two bowls of milk and Italian bread—with, once in a while, some butter—on the yellow and green kitchen table for Pasquale and Josephine. She also prepared a lunch of soup, sandwiches of escarole, or sometimes a pot of ricotta and pasta.

Like a little sandpiper, she tip-toed into a small cozy bedroom, where two small cots held her sleeping children. It remained dark, with no window to announce the day. She kissed Josephine and Pasquale good-bye. She whispered in Pasquale's ear, "*Caro,* take care of your sister, obey Mrs. Rocco. I left food in the kitchen." Then she ran down two flights of bleach-washed wooden stairs from their third-

11

floor walk-up. She stopped on the first floor and tapped on Mrs. Rocco's door to let her know she was leaving.

Before anyone else awoke, if it was cold, Tony added more coal to the green and yellow stove. He filled a bucket of water and put it on the back burner, so the children could wash. Then he put on black trousers, a starched white shirt, a black tie, and a white apron. His black leather shoes that his brother Paradiso had made for him were as shiny as the black coal. Tony earned $7.00 a week at Pettoruto's Market. At forty-five years old, he was distinguished-looking as he made his way to work.

Maria and the other women and children of Lawrence slaved in the monstrosity of the Wood Mill, which spread like a brick dragon as it crept along the banks of the Merrimack River. They earned $5.40 weekly and worked sixty hours every week.

Maria, a tall, big-boned woman, knew very little about poverty until she came to Lawrence. She was the stronger of the two; Tony always gave in to her.

In spring and summer, Maria's clothing was made of thin cotton because the mills were so hot. From 6:00 a.m. to 6:00 p.m., the machines in the mills poured out heat and dust as they clanged along. The workers got a twenty-minute break. The foremen who watched the workers took whatever time they needed. The air was so bad that the children cut out pieces of cotton and used them as masks.

Today Maria was ironing her mother's linen handkerchief, her mask for the days when she could no longer stand the lint and dust in her eyes and throat at her machine in the Mill.

"Maria." Tony walked over to her and puts his arms around her.

She stopped and put the hot iron back on the stove.

"What are you doing, my love?" His kisses were sweet, and his breath smelled of wine.

"Oh, my darling, I am thinking of my mother back in Italy. Let us have some lunch. We will be alone." Maria served their lunch. "Tony, I heard today that spinners die before they work ten years. The older women look like stooped-over rag dolls, their hair wet from the sweat. We have so little time for lunch in the mill. I cannot go outside. People eat at their machines. I go to a small open window and use the windowsill as a table. It is so inhumane, Tony." She poured two small glasses of Mr. Pettoruto's wine and sat down.

"People do not live long if they work in the mills, Maria. Those mills are responsible for there not being many old people in Lawrence. Those who are alive are the guardians of the sick and small children." Tony stood up, waving his glass. "I heard today that they hire the Italians to work on the spinning floor because they are unruly. Most of them are under thirteen years old. You go outside, Maria!" Tony thought to himself, "We have made a big mistake."

"Caro." Maria's eyes were watery, but she was not in tears. "Me and Mrs. Spinelli tried so many times to go outdoors. If we are only a few minutes late, the *carne da guardia* (watchdogs) start yelling at us. Those men watch over us like *una iena* (hyenas) and keep an eye on the most vulnerable, especially the beautiful young girl children. Slurs and foul language come out of their nicotine mouths. Some of these men give favors to the young beautiful girls. Mrs. Spinelli spits at those snake-in-the-grass men." She

13

sipped her wine and put some biscotti left over from Christmas into a blue and white dish.

It was Sunday. While, the children slept, Maria started washing the escarole and boiling cannellini for the day's meal. "Tony, the foremen, including your friend Joe McLarty, speak English to each other. I sit by the windowsill to have my sandwich, and the window is so covered with lint I cannot see the beautiful river passing by. God forbid, Tony, if we do go out on a beautiful day and do not get back to our stations."

"But, *cara*"—Tony hugged her—"you do not have to work. Soon we will return to Teano, and you will not have to suffer under such terrible conditions. Everyone who comes into my store in Italy will say, '*Bongiorno, Mrs. Foenia.*' I am respected, and you will be too." This year, his chest was not swelling. He wrapped his strong arms around her vulnerable shoulders and whispered, "Everything will be all right, Maria, when we get back home."

As they headed for the bedroom, Maria pulled loose from his arms and sobbed uncontrollably. "Tony, my dearest, Wood is a double-dealing man—not like you, Tony, *sei una persona in gambo*. The poster said no one goes hungry in Lawrence. But every day people go hungry, and children are dying. Mrs. Kiernan told me last year that her son told her that over fifteen hundred people have died here in Lawrence, five hundred of them babies."

Tony wiped her tears and consoled her. "Jack Kiernan is only a clerk, and Mrs. Kiernan likes to exaggerate."

"Her son, who works in the City Hall, can prove it, Tony." Maria took out her braids, and her chestnut hair flowed down her chest.

14

"Darling, innocent Maria, you worry too much about others. Be patient. We will be back to Italy soon."

As he started undressing, Maria turned to him. *"Charismo,* are you not happy at Pettoruto's? Are they not kind to you?"

Tony did not answer.

Maria put his head to her breasts. "We will go back someday, but not now. Italy is plagued by the fascists, and that *schifioso* (disgusting) Mussolini is in power. And besides, dearest, we do not have enough money for all our passages, so we must stay here. Look to the good, Tony, think of the children. Look to the good." And they kissed.

Maria and Tony had made an oath to one another when they got married never to go to bed without a kiss of forgiveness. Maria, however, now made one of her little daily decisions and bargained with herself, so that she and her family would benefit from a new life. She thought to herself while they were making love, "Yes, this is a cruel, senseless world, and I have the luxury of free choice, and for no reason will I take from myself and family the luxury of freedom." They both had tears in their eyes, and before Maria fell asleep she dreamed of a story that her mother had told her when she was Josephine's age.

"In Sicily, where spring comes in February, the almond trees blossom; they signal change, renewal, a rebirth. Everyone greets the day with celebration." Her mother was braiding her hair as she told the story. "In antiquity, Persephone comes back in spring to her mother. In Christian culture, the almond tree is associated with Mary, mother of Jesus, a woman who survived the overwhelming loss of a child. And someday, when you are married, I will survive the fact that you will be lost to me forever."

"Never, mama," and tears flowed from Maria the child, enough to fill an ocean.

Her mother went on, "In time, the blossom of the almond tree becomes a green and fuzzy exquisite fruit, and it takes very hard work to get the fruit to make the milk."

Maria dreamed her own version of the almonds story, in which she imagined a future that would offer her family a chance to be fine upstanding Americans.

In the early morning, she heard Mrs. Kiernan's voice: "Maria, Maria!"

Maria jumped out of bed and went onto her porch. Whistles and bells were slicing through the frigid, icy air. Like children's screams, the Ayer, the Pacific, the Everett, the Atlantic, the Washington, and the imposing Wood Mill whistles shrieked.

"Maria!" Mrs. Kiernan on the second floor was yelling at the top of her lungs. Maria hung over the rail to hear her. "Father O'Reilly got the permit to build a steeple on our church. They would not allow a Catholic church on the common. My son told me that the steeple will be so high, it will be visible for miles around. The man is the cock of the walk, and pretty handsome too."

"Finalmente, Bridget! You Irish run the city, so how about getting us Italians a church on the Common?"

"Ha! Maria! Wishing you the luck of the Irish. Come down for a cup of tea, and we will talk."

Maria let Tony know she was going to the first floor.

Mrs. Kiernan had come to Lawrence during the Potato Famine in Ireland. She had lots of power in the city,

16

not because she was smarter than all the other women who lived in the Plains but because she spoke English.

The tea was steaming from a teapot adorned with little pink roses, and a group of little shortbreads was in a saucer. The linen tablecloth was glistening and starched. The sewing machine took a prime place in her kitchen. In the corner, a basket held the work she took in. The starched white lace curtains decorated the two windows. Hanging on the door to the bedroom was a beautiful blue dress.

Maria eyed the dress and almost touched it, but pulled back. "How beautiful this is."

Mrs. Kiernan understood her shyness and said, "Such a beautiful fabric and color, Maria—the blue of angelic clouds. It belongs to Mr. Wood's daughter. My daughter Rose works as a maid for the Woods in Andover and often brings me her clothes to mend. Sit down, my sweet. Tell me, how do you like working in the Wood Mill?"

"Thank you, Bridget, for helping me get the job on the weaving floor. I will get used to it, as time passes."

When Maria had first moved to the third floor, Mrs. Kiernan was the first person to welcome her. They had soon became special friends. Maria would have trusted Bridget Kiernan with anything.

Maria sat on a wooden chair adorned with a lace cushion. As she patted the lace, she transformed herself into a woman having tea. She was back home in the splendor of Italy with her mother. "Bridget, I have to ask you something," she whispered. "Do you ever think of going back to Ireland?" She picked up a raisin scone and put it on her dish.

17

"Why do you ask, my sweet? The answer is no." Bridget got up from her chair, went over to Maria, poured out some more tea, and put a hand on her shoulder. "Maria, Lawrence is a mill town with schools for the children, churches. There is life here; not far from here is hope for our children. In Ireland there is no hope, only the sun that comes up every day over rolling hills and stone walls and the *seamrog* (shamrock) held by St. Patrick, who drove the snakes out of Ireland. I want more for my children and will get it here in America."

Outside, the bells and whistles were silent, as silent as Maria's thoughts: "Thank you, dear Lord, for showing me that I am not the only one who thinks like this." Her admiration for Bridget McKiernan turned into love as she whispered, "I want to stay to raise my children as Americans. Not so much Josephine, because she does not seem to care—but my Pasqualino gets so sad when Tony says we are going back to Teano. I am afraid he will run away." Maria's mouth twitched. It was the first time she had voiced what she was thinking.

Lately Mrs. Kiernan had been calling Pasquale Paddy. "Maria, Paddy is a very nice, strong young boy. He is already an American. He needs to stay in school. Let Tony go back himself." A yellow and black tin box sat on the end of the table, and she reached over to spoon out more tea into the teapot before going on. "If it is all right with you, I will have my son show Paddy how to collect the coal that drops from the Boston and Main Railroad onto Pine Street. The cars' last stop is in front of the Cross Coal Company. Plenty of coal drops when they fill the bins at Cross's."

18

Maria took a deep breath, and blood warmed her cheeks. "How safe is it?"

"Very, very safe. Do not worry, you have a smart boy, and Mathew made a lot of money selling the coal, with never a problem."

She put on her woolen coat and handed Maria a fur jacket, a hand-me-down from the Woods. "My son works full-time now in Mayor Scanlon's office and does not have the time to collect the coal. Come for one minute, and I will show you the place."

Bridget handed Maria a woolen hat and gloves, and off they went, arm in arm. They took an electric trolley that ran through the center of town. They waved as they passed old Mr. Stein and his old tired horse, traveling in the same direction; his cart was filled with pots, pans, and rags. They passed the business section, the Oliver School, the city hall, and the public library. The trolley stopped across the street from the railroad station, in front of the coal company. "Lawrence itself is alive," Maria thought to herself.

That day the two women became friends forever.

From then on, Maria looked forward to Sundays. For the immigrant women and children in Lawrence, Sunday was a special day, for church, cooking, playing, and catching up on gossip.

Everyone made fried dough using Maria's recipe. "So easy," she told Mrs. DeFusco. "Get your flour, milk, and eggs. Shape the flour like a large donut with a hole in the center, then add the eggs, milk, and yeast. Knead and knead the mixture until it forms into a ball. Wrap it in a cotton cloth and put it in a bowl to rest overnight. Sunday morning, put your small finger on top of the dough and push in. If the hole in the dough stays there, knead it once

19

more and then cut it into pieces, sprinkle each one with flour, and shape it round or square. Fry them in good oil until they are brown and crispy. Finally, you can sprinkle them with sugar."

She never said "delicious"—she just put her thumb and forefinger together and pinched her cheek. Mrs. Kiernan and the other women picked up the expression.

She put two golden pieces of fried dough on a plate for Tony and the children, and smiled as she said, "It is so funny how each woman adds her own touch to my recipe. Mrs. Kiberstis adds chopped vegetables, Mrs. Yazey puts raisins in hers, and Mrs. DeFusco adds lots of spices and hot pepper."

"Sweetheart, you look so happy today." Tony's chest swelled. "The whole neighborhood smells like one big kitchen."

Eventually Maria's raviolis began to resemble Mrs. Kiberstis's pirogues. While getting ready for church, Pasquale asked his mother, "Why do you all talk about food so much, Mama?"

"Pasqualino, *caro,* food and smells remind me of the magical days I spent with my parents in Bari, and I miss them. Here we have no parents, but we do have one another and we have our food, and in that way we belong to each other."

"And best of all, Mama"—he jumped up and down—"I am the luckiest kid on the block because Joey DeAngelo and his cousin Rocco live here too, and we belong to Lawrence."

Before 1912, Lawrence had been a city unnoticed, and Pasquale's mother made him think that he was living in

20

luxury. Years passed, and Maria was still ironing Tony's white shirts and her handkerchief.

Pasquale sat by her side to keep warm. "Someday I would be like Mr. Wood and have lots of money, Mama, and you would not have to work in the mill. You would have lots of beautiful blue dresses."

She told him stories of the Irish and other immigrants who lived on Cross Street and elsewhere, neighborhoods that were filled with boarding houses and cluttered with garbage. These people were less fortunate than they were, and he came to understand that they were better off than many people, and he felt sad.

She moved the hot iron back and forth and looked down. "Mrs. Yazey told me that you have a beautiful soprano voice and that she has been encouraging you to sing and play the banjo. Your father and I are so proud of you. Soon you will have your own banjo."

Pasquale looked up at her tears and said, "Why are you crying, Mama?" He hugged her waist, and her tears disappeared. "I practice on the stage at the Broadway Theater when my friend Louie works there, and he sneaks me in when the theater is closed. Someday, Mama, I will win a prize and sing at weddings, and I will buy you a beautiful woolen coat so you can skate on the Merrimack River. Can we go today to see the sled race, Mama, please?"

"*Caro,*" Maria said. She finished ironing and cooling off the iron, and took his face in her hands. "Pasquale, dearest, I want you to bring a bucket of coal tomorrow to the widow Mary on Cross Street. My soul weeps for this family. Your father told me he saw her in the alley searching for scraps, and Mrs. Pettoruto gave her a

21

bag of warm clothes and a sack of food. We must always be grateful for all we have. Including the Merrimack River. Now dress warmly, and wear your woolen scarf and mittens, and bring the skates Guy Pettoruto gave you."

"Mama, I too weep, but to me Lawrence is like a kettle filled with people—you know, all together and making something. You said that to make something good, things have to ferment. We are all the same, and someday I will help people be happy."

They all bundled up in their warmest clothes, and when Josephine noticed that Pasquale did not have any mittens, she shared hers. They crossed the Falls Bridge, flushed from the cold, and reached the Merrimack River feeling very excited.

The Lawrence brothers and Daniel Saunders had secretly bought the land on both sides of the Merrimack River as an investment, and to gain the water rights. They knew how to make money. First they built a great dam across the Merrimack River. Soon mills began springing up and the best and latest equipment started arriving, filling the brick buildings with machinery. These Yankee investors developed and annexed seven square miles of farmland from Andover to Methuen. Among the investors, it was known as an "Industrial Experiment."

The Merrimack River runs through the middle of Lawrence. In winter, families could skate on it and buy ice from an ice company perched on the shore. The iceman traveled in a buggy to deliver square chunks for the neighborhood iceboxes. People who lived in Andover ran horse races on the shiny frozen river. Everyone from Lawrence lined up on the left side of the river. On the right side the rich and privileged people of Andover dressed in furs and warm clothing. The people of Lawrence thought they looked silly and, as they nudged each other, called them "cockamamie feathered hats."

Red sleds slid down the ice over a wintry rainbow. Pasquale did not put his skates on. The snow was piled up on the left side of the river, leaving the right side for the horse races. Pasquale's fingers ached in his gloves. His cheeks were numb, and he pulled down on his cap to keep them warm. Disappointed, he gave his parents and sister a history lesson. "Can you picture corn growing in the farmlands, and the smoke signals the Indians sent to their neighbors up the river? They were peaceful farmers and fishermen. Someday I will buy a canoe and travel for one hundred and seventeen miles. I will begin in New Hampshire, go through Lawrence, and follow the Merrimac into the Atlantic Ocean."

Tony waited until they had returned home and had hot milk and biscotti before providing his own history lesson: "The Irish immigrants built a canal in the middle of the Mill District so that the water from the Merrimack River could be delivered straight to the mills. Look at the river now—it's a pitiful sight. Nowhere in Italy has there ever been such an abuse of nature." He picked up a mug of steaming espresso and went on. "Back in 1860, after the Pemberton Mill collapsed and burned down, Billy Wood and many of his backers purchased tracts of farmland in Andover and Methuen; they had a master plan in mind. They enlisted the labor of immigrants, luring them with promises of work and food for all. The first labor force consisted mostly of Irish men who had fled the Potato Famine and were looking for work. Stone by stone, these Irishmen created a man-made island, digging a one-and-a-

23

half-mile canal with great locks and dams that would propel the water from the Merrimack River for steam power to be used in the mills. Earning seventy to eighty cents a day, the Irish also erected shanties for themselves. Wood and his cronies tore them down, and we live here now in the Plains, where once lived the poorer than poor." Tony moved closer to the stove to keep warm. "That master plan was to create a new Utopia called Labor. One of the mill owners was heard saying, 'I regard my work people just as I regard my machinery.'"

The wind was swirling. The window panes were covered with ice. Maria put chestnuts on the stove, and they forgot about the darkness and the bitter cold of the Plains and huddled together. They could hear Mrs. Yazey playing a recording of Caruso and cooking her favorite Kibbe. Saturday was special. Pasquale was invited up to the fourth floor and listened to music on Mrs. Yazey's phonograph. "I will become a great singer and a successful American," he said, "and you and all the people in Lawrence can come for free to hear me sing." He bit into the hot Kibbe snack Mrs. Yazey gave him and felt happy and secure.

Poles, Jews, Irish, Syrians, Germans, Armenians, and Lithuanians lived in the Plains, but it was called the Italian district. What Pasquale loved about Lawrence was Broadway, the longest street in the city, and the second brightest after Broadway in New York. It had four movie theaters: the Broadway, the Empire, the Star, and the Victoria. There were also an Opera house, candy stores, a barber shop, and Louie Pearls. His friend Louie Scanlon worked as an usher at the Broadway, so he got in to see the movies and live shows that all the people from Andover attended. Pasquale's dream was to sing on the Broadway stage to a full house of people who lived in Lawrence.

Little did he know that a plan was in place to cut out the core of the immigrants who, to Wood, were mere "machines"— particularly the Italians inside the Italian District.

*The weaver God, he weaves and by that weaving,
he is deafened that he hears no mortal voice: and
that humming, we, too, who look at on the loom
are deafened and only when we escape it shall we
hear the thousand voices that speak through it.*

Bread and Roses
— Bruce Watson

CHAPTER 2 – A CITY OF BROKEN DREAMS

The Wood Mill covered thirty acres and was one mile long.
The 230 spindles and 1,470 looms produced the largest
number of textiles in the world. Underground tunnels
connected it to its sister mills: Ayer Mill and others. It was
the crown of Lawrence. Its enormous tower loomed toward
the sky; its weathervane was perched 267 feet above street-
level. The tower boasted the largest four-sided mill clock in
the world, its bells sounding every hour, pealing across the
Merrimack River Valley. The tower held 20,000 gallons of
water. No matter where you lived in Lawrence, there was
no escaping the mills, and there was certainly no escaping
the bells and whistles. Everyone who lived in The Plains
could walk to the Wood Mill, but no one could see the
whole building at once.

By the time the second whistle roared, Maria was on
Common Street with the other mill workers, lunch-pail in
hand, marching on the cobblestone streets. Women and
children walked in unison, arm in arm, while chatting and
visiting with each other. They dodged around dung from
the horses that pulled carts laden with ice, fish, and pots
and pans, as vendors lined the streets in hopes of selling

their goods. In the good days before the strike, they laughed and sang and told stories about their lives back home. Soon the farmers scooped up the dung for their farms in Methuen, and the merchants begin washing the streets with water and bleach. The air was always damp and pungent, filled with anticipation, the smell of garlic, and the sound of singing.

Once the throngs of people entered the mill, the huge iron gates were locked. Maria took the stairs to the fourth floor, walked past the rows of whitewashed windows shut tight so that a little filtered light could sneak in, and found her place at the weaving machine. Once the engines were turned on, the clack-clack-rat-tat and roaring began. The various sounds from the machines melted into a single noise was that was deafening, like a loud protest.

This was the timetable that all the workers received once they were employed:

Commence Work 6:45 A.M.
Leave off work (except Saturdays) 6:00 P.M.
Leave off work on Saturday 4:30 P.M.

First morning bell 4:30 A.M.
Second bell 5:30 A.M.
Third bell 6:35 A.M.
Lunch bells ring out 12 P.M.
Ring in 12:50 P.M.

The gates will be opened at the first bell and will close one minute before the machines start up.
Machines must run 60 hours per week.

One night, Tony was having a glass of wine while Maria cooked pasta for supper. Tony dipped a wooden spoon into the sauce and said, "Maria, why are you making so much tonight?"

"Tony, Mrs. Ippolito has been deaf for many years because of those machines that crack your soul. We keep her deafness a secret because her husband is a scoundrel and crazy, and because there are three children to feed. Pasqualino will bring the family some pasta."

"Such a sad thing to think about, Maria dear. Soon you will be back in Italy, and, instead of a machine, you will have a harp. I promise you that, my darling *piccolina*." He had said the words so many times that Pasquale could visualize the harp. "I know how you miss your family and the music, Maria." Tony put his hand under her chin. "We have half the money for our passage, and, without your help, we would not be able to leave soon. I love you so much, and my only wish is to make you a happy *principessa*."

Tony took a deep breath but could not keep speaking; it was the first time Maria had seen his sad hazel eyes fill with tears. She prayed in her soul, telling God that that she would do anything for him, and then she embraced his face and kissed away the salty tears.

Maria did not leave her job as a weaver. She took Pasquale into the mill during the week he turned twelve. "Pasqualino, you will never have to work here, I promise, even if I have to go back to Teano."

"Oh, Mama, please do not go back. We will stay in Lawrence, and I promise I won't work in the mills and will go to school." Pasquale watched his mother twine the threads on hooks attached to three pulleys. Back and forth,

28

the click and the clack never stopped, intermixing the threads until they were woven into a beautiful fabric admired all over the world. Lint, dust, and fumes from the chemicals and dyes made his eyes water, and he had a hard time breathing.

Any woman who worked on the fourth floor had to be strong and sturdy. Maria was such a woman, and, since she had been an excellent quilt-maker in Italy, she was quite well-suited for the job. The truth is she worked on the spinning floor because it paid fifty cents more a week. And now Mrs. Rocco's husband had been transferred to her floor, and she felt more comfortable. Maria was certain that Mr. Pettoruto had something to do with the change of supers on her floor.

Each week Maria spent fifty-four hours spinning, weaving, and sweating and got paid $5.40. Tony worked forty hours and earned $6.00 a week.

Mr. Pettoruto owned the small *groceria* on Elm Street, in the Italian part of town where Tony worked. In the evenings, men from the neighborhood congregated in the small back room of the store for a glass of wine, a shot of anisette, or a cordial. Lots of talk went on there about Italy, the mills, and going home to Italy and Mussolini. Lucia Pettoruto was the rock behind the store's success. She and her husband had two daughters and four sons. In spite of all the mouths to feed, she always managed to give Tony a bag of food that was "too ripe to sell" to take home.

Tonight, Tony had something on his mind. "Watch yourself, Maria," he said, "the Polish are getting angry about their pay. Joe Toscano told us yesterday that they are fed up. They are a strong, hard-headed group, those Poles. Something is going to happen. We think they are planning

29

a strike. Do not go to the mills, Maria, I beg you. We can manage on what money I earn at Pettoruto's Market. Things are heating up every day. Mr. Wood plans on fighting back if a strike happens. Maria, stay home, darling—you have endured enough in the mill. A strike is not a place for women and children."

"Oh, Tony," Maria answered. She was folding clothes and ironing close to the stove. "Mrs. Kiberstis is the kindest, gentlest lady on my floor, and she is Polish. I have not heard anything. I will ask her tomorrow if that is true. And if it is true, a strike is good. It is time that we do something for the good of all of us, my darling." She went closer to him, in her blue apron made from scraps of cloth picked up off the floor at the mill. "Tony, please understand me now, at this moment. Strange as it may seem, I love the people in our community deeply. I love them for their simplicity, their courage, and their strength. The children, through no fault of their own, are working, but they are still lighthearted, despite their circumstances. Their sweet voices and baby hearts know their unrealized yearnings. They long for something they do not know. And the women, they are lonelier without their roots. The men are like you, putting up a brave battle to support their families under the tyrants who steal the playtime of children for thirteen cents an hour. Italians like us, we have no access to beautiful communities, to the capitalists' social life— except to clean their homes, tend their children, and iron their clothes, like Mrs. Kelley's daughter Colleen. But America is our country, Tony, and the fault is ours if we do not strike."

"Maria, you do know about the strike?" Tony's head bobbed, and he looked at her, startled. "Be careful, my

30

sweet innocent one, and mind your own business. Keep your head straight. Do not ask too many questions." His jaw clenched, and he turned away.

Maria was skilled at changing the subject, and she went over and hugged Tony. "Tony dearest, I would like you to take Pasquale to Pettoruto's on Saturday, so he can help you and meet the Pettoruto children."

Her plan was hatched.

Pasquale loved going to the groceria with his father. At the store there was always something going on. Customers spoke in many Italian dialects. He listened to their hardships, their debates over the Catholic Church, and their love of cooking and singing. The latest gossip was that Mussolini was headed for war. Pasquale became fluent in many dialects. Mr. Pettoruto read newspapers in English and Italian, and Pasquale took them home and read them.

One day Mr. Pettoruto asked him to stay behind the counter with his son Lawrence. "You speak well and are like your father—you show respect. Lawrence tells me you are good at addition. He will show you how to post in the black book."

Later Pasquale ran all the way home. He flew up three flights of stairs and could not wait to tell his mother. "Mama, Mr. Pettoruto asked me to come in on Saturdays, and he will pay me!"

"Good, Pasqualino!" Maria hugged him and pulled his ear. "What do you do there?"

"Weeping women come to the counter begging for credit for food, Mama. I am allowed to give certain ladies credit and write it in a little black book. Mr. Pettoruto gave me five black books for free."

31

Pasquale had his black notebooks filled in no time with names and places. *A way to remember everyone,* he thought. He became an eavesdropper and also grew skilled in addition. No one had money, and he was filling the books with entries of five and ten cents. One Saturday Mrs. Pettoruto whispered, "Pasquale, charge the widow Mrs. Arno one cent instead of two cents when she comes in."

It was a cold winter, and Pasquale asked Joey to help him in his coal business. They were the first ones to arrive at Cross Coal Company. "Guess who came into Pettoruto's on Saturday, Joey?"

"How would I know, Pat? I wasn't there." Joey threw a large piece of coal in the air, and it landed in the pail.

"Mr. Pittochelli, the undertaker, with Mr. DiAdamo, the Captain at the police department. They walked in to ask for a donation for the Columbus Day parade and celebration. I thought they were bigshots, wearing black suits and the uniform. Mr. DiAdamo had ribbons on his uniform and said, 'All the Italians will be marching, Dom. We can thank Father O'Riley, he spearheaded the parade, and he has donated a hundred dollars for prizes. Great man, that priest.' Mr. Pettoruto handed him twenty-five dollars. And then, Joey, the officer turned to my father and said, 'How are you, Mr. Foenia? Is that your son behind the counter?' My father is a man of few words, when he wants to be. He said, 'Yes.' The cop turns to me and says, 'What is your name?' 'Pasquale, sir,' I say, and salute him. The guy says to me, 'Pasquale, you come on Saturday, and I will let you carry a flag in the parade."

Pasquale gave Joey a slap in the back. "You can come with me and carry a flag too, Joey. And, Joey, guess what—Betty Pettoruto came out with a bag of books that she and her brothers no longer need, and she asked me if I wanted them."

Joey's pail was full, and he was about to leave. "You're always talking about her. Do you work at the store just to see her?"

"Betty Pettoruto is the most beautiful girl I know. Her black hair is always shiny, like my mother's. I'm going to marry her someday, Joey."

Joey was a cold and distant person. He had a hard time making friends. His life was different from Pasquale's, and often he felt jealous of the other boy. His only remark as they walked home was "Not if you go back to Italy, Pat. Betty likes Americans."

Pasquale's parents saved all they could from the $12.80 they earned each week. Pasquale figured it would take them years to save enough for the passage back to Italy. So, for now, he felt safe. Going to Pettoruto's made him feel part of Lawrence, and there he could see Betty Pettoruto.

Every Saturday evening, Pasquale gave an account of his day at the groceria. "Do you know Mrs. Bacigalupo?"

"Yes," Maria answered, "she works on the sorting floor."

Tony did not say anything. He got up and put more coal in the stove, giving the cover a good bang.

"She came in crying because her daughter, Assunta, came home from kindergarten crying. Miss McSweeney, her teacher, put hot mustard in her mouth for whispering." Pasquale went on, his face flustered, "If I were older, I would collect all the lint that the workers carry on their

33

clothes when they come home from work, and all the sawdust from Pettoruto's, and I would throw it all over Miss McSweeney's classroom. Joey has a name for her."

Maria stood in the middle of the kitchen, arms folded, and looked at Pasquale and Josephine. "You must watch yourselves at school. I know that some teachers like McSweeney are very strict. No talking out loud, understand?" She walked over to Tony and whispered, "For whispering a child is abused? Tony, it is disgraceful! Ask Albert Pettoruto to do something—he is studying the law."

Tony agreed to talk to Albert.

The wind was howling over Lawrence. It was the winter of 1912, and the river and dams were frozen. Pasquale had figured out a short-cut to the Boston and Main Railroad station tracks to collect the coal that fell from the coal cars. He was early today and warmed his hands in the little shack, talking to the gatekeeper.

"What time do the cars come by, Mr. Kelly?"

"The trains come through several times a day, Patty, on their way to Boston." The man's eyes didn't stray from the clock on the wall and the list on the small table. "They will be here in five minutes."

Pasquale stood in front of the shack to avoid the strong winds and the snow. As the trains hooted by, the clouds of smoke from the engines resembled ice puffs. The engineers waved to Pasquale. They called him Patsy and, often, Paddy. Sometimes they purposely dropped coal on the tracks. If they didn't stop, they still drove by very slowly.

Once they passed and he had enough coal, he went back into the little shack and asked Mr. Kelley if he wanted any coal.

34

"No, I get enough every day. Come warm yourself before you go home."

Pasquale never charged Mrs. Rocco or Mrs. Yazey for coal. Mrs. Rocco checked on Pasquale and Josephine several times a day. If it was raining or snowing, the Rocco and Foenia children played together. Out of her six children, Joey was closest in age to Pasquale, so they became friends. Once a week Mrs. Rocco took them to the Common on the other side of town.

Mrs. Yazey lived on the top floor. She was young, tall, and quiet. Pasquale thought to himself, *She is not stooped over like all the factory girls.* He never charged her for the coal. It was his way of paying her back for the wonderful music that came from her Victrola all day long. She worked at night at the *Lawrence Eagle Tribune* as a typesetter. Her husband worked in the Everett Mill. One day Pasquale told her how much he loved singing and sang *O Solo Mio* for her. After that, she gave Pasquale singing lessons and taught him about famous opera singers.

The tenements were so close together, one could not see the sky. Many apartments had more than one family living in them. On Mondays the makeshift clotheslines that connected the buildings were heavy with just-washed laundry. The rooftops were covered with ropes hung with clean clothes flapping in the breeze. During the winter of 1912, the sheets turned to glimmering sheets of ice and children would crush the panels and watch the shadows of the clothes while they told stories to each other. The clotheslines were communication stations for the women, and that was how Maria heard about Pasquale singing. "Pasquale, everyone says they can hear you singing at Mrs. Yazey's house. Tell me why you go there, dear." Maria

35

was stirring the Sunday spaghetti sauce, and she gave Pasquale a spoonful to taste.

"Mrs. Yazey appreciates the coal, Mama, and I think she is very lonely, because Mr. Yazey works during the day and she works at night. They do not have any children. She is very religious, Mama, and is always praying and has candles burning in front of a statue. She also plays records for me, and I have been learning some Italian songs so that I can sing them to you and Papa. Sometime Josephine comes and plays with a doll Mrs. Yazey bought for her called Dolly."

Maria looked at her son and smiled to herself. He is no longer a child and has a fine strong Roman nose like his father, a strong chin, and green eyes like my mother. Soon he will be taller than me. She let out a soft sigh. Thank God that he is working at Pettoruto's, where he will learn what reciprocity really means. She wiped the stove clean of splashes of tomato sauce, realizing that Pasquale made friends wherever he went. "I hear you have been singing at the Palace Theater on talent night."

"Oh, yes, Mama. Louie Scanlon helped me get a spot to sing, so I can practice. I want you and everyone to come when I get better, Mama." Pasquale stood tall over his mother and kissed her forehead.

"Mrs. Yazey said to me the other day, 'Pasquale's smooth skin is beginning to show a beard.' Pasqualino, someday you will be a great tenor, so always take care of your voice. These are very difficult times for all of us, but someday you will be a man. Always remember to be true to yourself and never sell your soul. Practice your singing like prayers, and sing every day."

Maria's heart jumped into her throat. She knew then that Pasquale would never leave America or Lawrence.

Lawrence was a city made alive by its emotions, its hopes, its passions, its prayers, and the relationships of all its inhabitants. Pasquale loved every mile of it. The largest mills in the whole world, bridges that linked South Lawrence with North Lawrence, the Merrimack River, underground tunnels connecting the mills, fire stations, and a downtown like no other in the world, where at 8 p.m. every Tuesday evening huge crowds promenaded down Essex Street, no matter the weather. This was Pasquale's world.

"The Wood Mill reminds me of a brick fortress," he said to Joey one day. "Let's count the bricks. How many do your think there are? A million?"

"Pasquale, it would take us a trillion years to count those damn bricks."

The windows were so dusty they could not see inside. The younger and prettier girls who worked in the mill got the best spots, near the windows. Joey liked girls. In the summertime, if the windows were open, he and Pat would take mandolins and sing outside, hoping the girls would look at them. Winters were cold in Lawrence: everyone wore woolen skullcaps and gloves in the factories to keep warm. While the women huddled together during a break or for lunch, the men smoked cigarettes and stogies. The mills were smoke-filled, dreary, noisy places.

The rambling river that provided the steam and electricity for the mills, called the Merrimack River, rambled down 110 miles from the White Mountains in New Hampshire. It was Lawrence's greatest gift, visible from every window located on the west side of the mill. Once the

37

river had been lined with meadows and farms and swarmed with shade and sturgeon. The Pawtucket and Algonquin nations paddled their canoes and rowboats up and down the river, fishing and traveling. The Pawtucket named it "Merrimack," meaning "Rapid Waters." In 1912, however, it was loaded with debris pumped out from the mills' basements. The water from the mills took on a rainbow hue from the dyes that stained the textiles. Men, thinking they were superior to nature, tamed the river. But the immigrant women who came to Lawrence in the early 1900s would not be tamed. Rapid Waters, once beautiful and dignified, heard the sighs that came from the mills, and the wind carried the women's despair out to the Atlantic Ocean. Maria called her floor the Floor of Sighs.

Pasquale heard them too. "Why do you sigh so much, Mama?"

"I feel better after a good sigh." She took a deep breath and, feeling a deep yearning for her own mother, told him a story. "As a little girl, I went to Venice and walked over the Bridge of Sighs, an enclosed bridge with bars across its windows, just like the windows in the mills. The Bridge connected the old prisons to the interrogation rooms in the Doge's Palace. Lord Byron gave the bridge its name because the Venetians said they could hear the sighs of the prisoners as they took in their final view of Venice before being executed."

The sighs in the mills in Lawrence were the workers' way of expressing their exhaustion and longings. How ironic that, resonating throughout the mills, mingled with the loud noise of the machines, were the voices of thousands of women and children, the cries of souls propelled by the dream of a better life. These sighs were a

38

release from their exhaustion and sadness. Of course, no one forced these women and children who crossed the ocean to work in the mills, but in the beginning it was a way of survival.

Although Pasquale promised his mother every single day that he would not end up in the mills, he worked on the twisting floor for one week. It was summer, and school was out. He told the overseer that someone would be sending to Italy for his papers to prove his age, and that he was thirteen years old— crossing his fingers behind his back in the hope that his lie would not be found out.

Children like Pasquale who were under twelve years old often worked in the mill with their parents for several weeks without pay, learning the job. The basement of the mill was the worst place. There they took apart the compressed cotton, removing dirt and fibers, and then fluffed the substance from the seeds. A vacuum tube blew the cotton to the pickers, who were mostly black men and children, and they organized the cotton into sheets. The sheets of cotton traveled to the carding machines. Then the cotton traveled to the Spinning Room, where Pasquale was put next to Giuseppe. Giuseppe taught him how to run up and down a line of machines and look for snags. If they found a tear in the cotton threads, they had to repair it before the threads went to the spoolers. The clacking, the squeaky sounds, the blasts, and the shouting were unbearable. A constant trail of cigar smoke filled the air. There was laughter from the left side of the floor, the windows rattled, and the children acted like adults.

On his second day in the mill, Pasquale shouted to Giuseppe, "You can work here, but I'm quitting. I hate it!"

Giuseppe, who was older, yelled back, "Listen Pat, I have to work here so we can eat. My father died when the old Pemberton Mill collapsed, and there are five mouths to feed in my house."

"There are better ways to get food," Pasquale said, never taking his eyes off the spindles weaving threads.

"Not in Lawrence," Giuseppe replied, "and my mother said that in Italy it wasn't much better."

For a week, Pasquale watches people marching to their places. The older men looked like conquered creatures, well-trodden beasts. During their breaks, all they talked about was the good "Old Country." Yet when they were not being observed, Pasquale detected a sense of familiarity among them that he missed later, in his old age.

And the sighs—Pasquale never forgot the sighs of the women and children as he walked through the second and third floors on his way out for air.

In the mills, the Overseers would encourage the workers' bickering while the machines thundered over their name-calling. When they turned their backs or went to a corner to light up stogies and talk, Giuseppe and Pasquale would switch or tangle the thread, creating a slug in the material. It was their way of expressing the boredom and anger they felt. It was also fun, since neither of them ever got caught.

At lunch one day Giuseppe told Pasquale what had happened on July 10, 1909. "I heard screaming sounds, like a loud screech. Carmela Teloi's blood was streaming down her face and body. Her scalp had been torn off her head— her hair got caught in the rollers of a twisting machine. When she fainted, Assunta ran over, pulled the lever, and turned off the twisting machine. Carmela's black hair hung from the machine like a wig. It was as if someone had split her head open with an ax. The Super pulled the emergency switch. Once it went off the place shook with the terror, and people took out their rosary beads, praying for something they couldn't even see. Women tried to help, whispering '*Dio mio*' under their breath. 'Mary, Mother of God. Help us.' Many people just froze. Assunta wrapped her apron around Carmela's head. The dusty air was filled with moaning. Women fainted, and children started crying. The Supers raised a sheet of fabric so the workers couldn't see her. The other machines roared on. Dr. Calitri came with his black bag, and Carmela was carried out, her head wrapped in cloth. Two pieces of her scalp were wrapped in newspaper and rushed to the hospital with her. I was close to the stretcher, Pasquale, and I saw the skin of her eyelids turning black." Giuseppe couldn't stop his hands from shaking. "I thought she was dead."

When the accident happened, Carmela Teoli was thirteen years old.

"Mama," Pat said to his parents that night, "he thought she was dead, but she was alive. Papa, once I couldn't work because a kid caught his finger in the machine, but Giuseppe didn't stop spinning, and he yelled over to me, 'Get back or you will get into trouble.' Giuseppe didn't stop working, but the fear that entered my soul melted it. Papa, I will never go back."

Maria and Tony talked and comforted him, and since it was Friday, they promised to take him to the river the next day so that he could learn how to skate. Mrs. Pettoruto gave Tony a pair of skates that Marco had outgrown.

41

Before going to bed, Pasquale opened his first pay check: four dollars for sixty hours of work. He handed over the money to his father and promised that he would go back to school. He felt relieved that his father understood.

There was an intense rivalry between the Neapolitans and the Sicilians workers in the mills. Giuseppe was Sicilian and Pasquale Neapolitan, but it made no difference to them. Nevertheless, in the factories there was no love lost, and the rivalry never relaxed. The rows of machines and workers resembled a sport, Sicilians versus Neapolitans.

Wood's bonus system made it worse, for he rewarded the laborers with production quotas, called piecework. The weavers, who were mostly Sicilian, depended on the work of the spinners, who were mostly Neapolitan, and the spinners in turn depended on the doffers, and so on. This kind of piecework made everyone dependent on everyone else for work. Later, as the work began to grow, the interdependence was not enough for Wood. If a worker missed one day a month, the wages for that day would be deducted from her paycheck. Maria talked about this at every chance she could. Tony would roll his eyes, shake his head, and stomp out of the kitchen.

The rivalry between Neapolitans and Sicilians extended to the neighborhoods. Neapolitans would not shop at stores owned by Sicilians, and Sicilians would not shop at the Neapolitans' stores. If a couple intermarried, the families might disown their children. Only on Essex Street did it not matter—there people of all kinds window-shopped and promenaded.

Pasquale was fluent in Sicilian and Neapolitan, and this gave him a great advantage. He was accepted by both

42

the Sicilians and the Neapolitans and escaped their hot-blooded tempers when they were arguing.

Italians in Lawrence were unable to find employment except in the mills. They learned quickly that the better-paying jobs were wool-sorting, dyeing, bleaching fabrics, spinning, and operating the largest machines. Wool-sorting, a skilled job, was back-breaking work. The average worker's pay was eight dollars a week. Young children, many of whom lied about their age, worked at wool-sorting and earned less. The average weekly rent for a tenement apartment was five dollars a week. Unable to get jobs in post offices, fire departments, police departments, or any white-collar positions, Italians learned that an education wouldn't help them. Many stopped applying for those jobs and didn't bother to go to school. But at Pettoruto's Market, Mr. Pettoruto encouraged everyone who complained. "Try again," he would say. "Always try again and learn good English."

The newspapers gave an account of Carmela, who lived to tell her story. She testified at a hearing before Congress. When questioned by the committee, she said, "Well, I used to go to school, and then a man came up to my house and asked my father why I didn't go to work, so my father says, 'I don't know whether she is thirteen or fourteen years old.' So, the man says, 'You give me four dollars, and I will make the paper come from the old country'—the paper saying I was fourteen. So my father gave him the four dollars, and in one month came the papers saying that I was fourteen. I went to work, and about two weeks later I got hurt in my head." Mrs. William Howard Taft, who was sitting in the front row, cried openly. Carmela Teoli spurred the struggle for Federal laws against child labor in the United States and all over the world.

On July 11, 1911, her father's birthday, Maria read an article in the newspaper that changed her life. Ten thousand women had marched in the second annual parade for women's rights in New York. The reporter commented on the women's hats and clothing. But Maria observed something else. She began hatching another one of her plans to stay in Lawrence.

People like Mrs. Arabella sighed and said, "Oh, what's the use? We are not light enough, and our clothes are ragged." Mrs. Pettoruto folded her arms and in her sweet Italian voice reminded Mrs. Arabella to "be brave and look for the best in everything." As a result of being turned away, and often not even trying, the Italians found it necessary to form societies of mutual help in the event of death, illness, or unemployment.

At 6:00 p.m., every work day, the third whistle gave a lonesome shriek. After a long, ten-hour day, Maria and the other workers would march home with weary faces, dim and ghostly white, their clothing and bodies covered in dust and lint from the machines and worsted cloth. Tired as they were, they still managed to cook, sew, wash, and pray every night. In good weather they sat on the stoops outside, talking and gossiping while knitting and crocheting. The men disappeared into their clubs.

For the children of Lawrence, who felt like prisoners in their small apartments, the whistle was a happy sound, one they waited for every day. It meant their parents would be home soon and they could go out and play.

By the time Pasquale was seven years old, he knew every street, alley, and railroad track in Lawrence. His best

44

friend, Louie Scanlon, lived on Tower Hill and worked in the movie houses. Josephine helped to scrub the tenements' steps and hang out clothes. The bleach smell was everywhere. The clotheslines looked like the sails of ships flapping in the wind. Every Saturday Giovanni the fisherman came around selling dried bakala, eels, and sardines.

One summer before the strike, Mr. Ferrara and his sons purchased land in Methuen, five miles from Lawrence. They planted vegetables, and a farm was born. Pasquale helped them, and in return he was allowed to take fresh vegetables. It took them one weekend to build an outdoor garden. They carried the pipes and equipment from home. They called it Pleasant Valley.

In the winter of 1912, Pasquale kept his promise to his parents and stayed in school. Joey hated Miss McSweeney, their teacher, and while walking to school one morning he turned to Pasquale. "Miss McSweeney hates Mortadella, Pat." (He called their classmate "Mortadella" because he was fat and round like a ham; Joey had a nickname for everyone.) "Watch how she picks on him. But better him than me, eh, Pat? She's always yakking on, telling us how lucky we are to have Mr. Wood as our parents' employer. I hope she gets married and goes to live in Andover with the Woods."

Pasquale did not tell Joey that he planned to escape from the Oliver School. He found the schoolroom suffocating. The O'Brien brothers were always fast asleep. Pat would tune out and dream about singing like Caruso. Once Miss McSweeney walked to the back of the room. Rita Teoli was sitting quietly, alongside the other children fiddling at their desks. The teacher's voice filled the classroom as she picked up Rita's braids. "Your hair is like a rat's nest. You go home and have it washed." Rita left with tears of humiliation and shame. Miss McSweeney looked over at the O'Brien boys and said, "I have great expectations for you boys, so stay alert."

Powerless Italian children like Rita were victims of teachers who themselves were humiliated and shamed. Pasquale went home and told his parents, but they did not have the tools to combat the shame in spite of their love and affection.

One day in class Joey whispered to Pasquale, "*La Strega,*" (witch). Miss McSweeney turned to Pasquale and snapped, "What did you say you, little dago?" He could not rat on his friend Joey. She hurled more words at Pasquale, then picked up the pointer and went to the black board. Class resumed, the students' eyes on the pointer in her hand, and Pasquale wrote in his notebook, "I cried to save Joey. I have learned to keep things to myself, so my soul will not disappear." Pasquale was figuring out how to weave himself into his own cocoon while the harshness of life surrounded him.

Joey belonged to a gang. Pasquale was a hero that day, but he did not join the gang. Seven boys followed him as he made his way home, and he heard them say, "Don't believe that Irish witch—Billy Wood lives in a huge house in Andover and has ten cars, Italian gardeners, Irish cleaning ladies, and French cooks." Then they left him alone, and he walked to the Star Theater instead of going home and saw *Yankee Doodle Dandy*. Like many young immigrants scattered across America, he viewed the movies as a refuge from an abusive, scornful, and careless culture.

46

Louie Pearl ran the candy store between the buildings on Broadway called Theater Row. On special days Mrs. Pearl stood outside and handed out free candy. It was the happiest street in Lawrence. Both sides of the street were lined with lights that danced on the neon marquees. The area was filled with music, organ-grinders, and photographers equipped with ponies—for five cents, a picture became an heirloom. Before 1912, there was a parade for everything and every nationality had its feats and fiestas.

In 1912, Lawrence housed three hundred to six hundred people per square mile and competed with Harlem as one of the most densely populated areas in the country. Italians in Lawrence had strong village-based loyalties and did not comprehend the prejudices they faced. Many of them clung together, lured by the American Industrialists who posted signs in small communities in Italy reading, "Always Work! No Padrone. COME TO LAWRENCE, MASSACHUSETTS." When they arrived, they found themselves referred to as the "dagos" of the lower classes, in a city built specifically for what Billy Wood called "LABOR." Wood's planned industrial community was a dream that had become a nightmare. In their plot to maintain control, the owners of the mills exercised a tyrannical power over their workers, mainly by pitting one ethnic group against another, in rivalries that played out primarily in the Irish and Italian communities.

Pasquale and Maria realized that the lives they were living were just ordinary to them and others. For a long time no one asked questions, and some pretended nothing was happening. But life for the Italian textile workers and their families became more and more difficult, as they

47

became victims and scapegoats for the powerful. They had been lured by promises of a better life but found themselves in a city where the costs of food and rent outpaced their wages.

The Italians resented the Irish immigrants, who had at one time been weak and powerless themselves. The Irish solidified their position in 1911 by electing an Irish Catholic mayor. The Lawrence government became a miniature Tammany Hall that dominated nearly every sector of the city. The police and fire departments, the school system, the sanitation department, and, most importantly, the Roman Catholic Church were all under the control of the Irish. Their networks touched everyone's daily life. The Italians, who were outside the clan, could never be accepted for jobs in any of the sectors where the Irish ruled, and they knew it.

It's not surprising, then, that in 1912 the powder-keg erupted.

*No trumpets sound when the
Important decisions of our
life are made. Destiny is made
known slowly.*

— Agnes De Mille

CHAPTER 3 – THE RAILROAD CARS WAILED AND RUMBLED ALONG

January 9, 1912. The wind whistled in the freezing weather. Snowflakes were coming down and chasing themselves, and Pasquale hoped it would snow all day. He went back to the Oliver School after lunch, and as he left the tenement his hands stuck to the door handle. His mother had asked him that day to accompany Carmela Teoli for her first day back at school. Over her headscarf she was wearing a woolen scarf that Maria had made specifically for the day.

As they walked along side by side, avoiding snow mounds, Pasquale turned to Carmela and said, "Where are your mittens that my mother made for you?"

Her shoes were wet from the snow, and her lunch-bag was oil-stained. Her huge brown eyes said it all. "I am so ashamed, but my brother Marco, who is six years old, did not have mittens or a hat, so I gave him the mittens. I wanted him to be warm when he went to the nursery school run by the Venereni Nuns. He has to climb a big hill to get to the building." Her lips quivered as she spoke. "Forgive me, Pasquale."

"Carmela, do this." He rubbed his hands together and put them under his sweater. The image of her scalp

49

hanging from the weaving machine rose in his mind, just as it did so often in his dreams. It was the kind of fear that clings to one's soul.

Carmela's brothers were Cosmo, the oldest, a mule-spinner; Julio, who ran a twisting machine on his mother's floor; and Tony, the youngest, who sorted cotton. Her sister, Assunta, was a maid. Her family had had no idea how cold it can get in New England and were not prepared for the deep freeze of that year. The wind was brutal, and Pasquale and Carmela wrapped his long woolen scarf around themselves, blowing on their hands while they ran.

As they moved swiftly, holding onto each other so they wouldn't fall, Pat thought to himself, How lucky I am, with pockets in my jacket and a scarf that my grandmother sent me from Italy. It is large enough to keep us both warm. "Carmela," he said, "always thank God and say 'Lawrence, pray for us' whenever you pass any church. Prayer and thanks help us to remember our faith and feel free. It will not grant you wishes that you don't deserve, or bring you money or even material things. But prayer will soothe your soul, Carmelita." Pasqualino opened the door to the school. "When you cannot fight back, it will help you to remember and feel free." At that moment he seemed to hear the sweet voice of his mother: "But best of all, Pasquale, prayer can help mend a broken heart or will." Today he understood what she meant.

The classroom was cold as the kids huddled together to feel each other's warmth before the teacher came in. The next several hours passed slowly. Joey squirmed in his seat as Miss McSweeney took up the long pointer she used to beat the palms of their hands in

50

punishment, continuing until they cried. The children became like statues frozen in their seats.

After school the little children of Lawrence slid on the Merrimack River. The Boston and Maine Railroad never missed a stop to drop coal. And outside the Oliver School and the mills, the splashing rain turned to snow, hitting the huge windows of the brick textile mills, with their hums and shuttles, where everyone knew they would die young.

As we go marching, marching in the beauty of the day,
A million darkened kitchens, a thousand-mill lofts gray,
Are touched with all the radiance that a sudden sun discloses,
For the people hear us singing "Bread & roses! Bread and roses!
As we go marching, marching we battle too for men,
For they are women's children and we mother them again.
Our lives shall not be sweated from birth until life closes;
Hearts starve as well as bodies; give us bread but give us roses.

— James Oppenheim

CHAPTER 4 – THE BREAD AND ROSES STRIKE

The gossip started on Thursday, January 10, 1912, and word spread quickly throughout the neighborhoods, up the stairs, and into the alleyways, the markets, and the mills. Two hundred Polish women had stopped the looms at the Everett Mill and refused to go back to work. The supervisors of each floor kept after the women mercilessly: "Get to work, you whores, start up those machines!" When the women refused, the supervisors ordered everyone out of the mill. Men, women, and children stood like statues near their stations while some machines were left running. The overseers grew tenser, running around shouting, "Why? Why?" A roar filled the building: "Not enough pay!" Then the women began walking out, urging others to join them. "Short pay, short pay!" The words echoed through the mill. A thousand looms shut down.

During that night, in dark meeting halls, Italian

people served coffee and huddled together, waiting for some word on what to do. Every post and building in The Plains displayed a poster: "MEETING FOR ALL ITALIANS TONIGHT – COME TO PAUL CHABLIS HALL, 108 OAK STREET, AT 8:00 P.M. EVERYONE WELCOME – HOT COFFEE."

At home, Tony was adding coal to the stove. In a loud thunderous voice that trembled, he said, "Maria, you are crazy—you have a family, and it is very dangerous. I do not want you to go to that meeting tonight, and please do not go to the mill today."

"Tony, you just worry too much. Believe me, nothing is going to happen today. It is all talk, and I do not want to miss my pay this week. We have half the money for tickets back to Italy. I earned two more dollars from the piecework."

Pasquale could hear them talking softly now, as his father banged covers on the stove. He whispered to Josephine, "All Mama talks about these days are the conditions at the mills." And the children covered their heads and went back to sleep.

Before leaving for Pettoruto's, Tony took Maria into his arms and told her again not to go. "Mrs. Rocco's nephew Angelo is a stupid troublemaker. The boy is responsible for getting everyone grumbling about a strike. I tell you, Maria, Angelo Rocco is a socialist. He is a noisy Americanized brat."

Angelo Rocco lived in Lawrence. When he wasn't in school, he was running meetings
in churches, clubs, and basements all over town. His mind was always on his future goal of becoming a lawyer.

Maria pulled out of Tony's arms and put her hands

on her hips. "Then, my dear Tony, you can call me loud and Americanized too."

Pasquale woke up, and his mother's voice came through the bedroom door like a radio.

"It is we who are stupid, Tony, we work like dogs, and for what, just enough to feed ourselves and pay the rent? Shame on you for calling Angelo Rocco such a name! His mother works next to me at the mill—one of my best friends. She told me that her son is twenty-eight years old, and last year he made so much progress in the fifth grade that he was advanced to Lawrence High School. He is a self-made student, Tony. His story is our story."

Pasquale visualized his father closing his eyes and putting his hands over his ears.

Maria talked louder. "When the Governor reduced the number of working hours for women and children from fifty-eight to fifty-six, and then fifty-four hours starting next year, Wood said we would not lose any wages. Now Wood has announced that wages will be reduced. We do not even know when, or how much. This means starvation for all of us, Tony. Do you not understand? All you talk about is going back to Italy. We are white slaves."

"I too love this community, Maria. Every day at Pettoruto's I listen to people who are putting up a brave battle, breaking beneath their load. The price we will pay is too high for bread, Maria."

"We do not want only bread, Tony *caro*, we want roses too." Maria looked at Tony, knowing it would be all right as long as she kept him talking.

"Such silliness," Tony barked. "How will roses help you in the mills?"

54

"Roses are the sweetest-smelling flowers in the world. We need them to remind us how sweet we really are. We are treated like cattle, Tony, and I heard today that the owners of the mills refuse to employ Jews. Next year they might say the same about us. Remember, 'Do unto others as you would have them do unto yourself.' Mrs. Gold could not get a job, so her husband is riding around in a horse and buggy, picking up rags."

"Better for him." Tony's voice was shaking now. "He does not have to work in those sweat shops." The cover of the coal stove made such a loud sound that Maria's voice became softer so that he would pay attention to her.

"The Italians have the least money in their paychecks." Her lips curled in anger. "We do not have drawing rooms, literary clubs, and fashionable hats like they have in Andover." Maria was crying now.

"Is that what you want, drawing rooms and fashionable hats?" Tony was talking gently. "You will have all these things and more when we go back to Italy." He hugged her, and her tears made his black vest wet.

"This is not right, Tony. We are not animals." Maria pulled away and poured out two glasses of demitasse. They tipped the glasses as if to celebrate.

Maria was thinking to herself, He is understanding me. It will be okay.

Instead, Tony moved over to Maria and took her hands. "Mr. Pettoruto's wife does not talk like you do. She is a quiet mother and listens to her husband. You know, Maria, as long as I work in the store, we will always have enough to eat. You and the children will never go hungry. We are not malnourished. So give up this foolishness."

55

"Neither Mrs. Pettoruto nor any of her children work in the mill. Besides, *caro,* it is not foolishness to want to be respected, as people. I want the right to have our children educated like those people who live in Andover. The ladies from only three miles away look down their snooty noses under their fur hats and snicker whenever they come to Lawrence to buy things cheap and Italian. The social workers want to see how we live. *Basta,* Tony. *Basta* (Enough)." Maria got up, touched his shoulder, and went into the children's room.

Pasquale turned his body to the wall as she went over to him.

"Good morning. There is no need to afraid, *caro.* Take care of your sister and please go to school. You will be safe there, no matter what happens." She stroked his brown hair and talked into his ear. "Now you are thirteen years old, and if you are good, I will take you to the meeting tonight. Stay warm, Pasqualino, it is very cold." She kissed Josephine's forehead. "Good morning, *cara.* Stay home with Mrs. Rocco today—it is snowing."

Pasquale poked his head from under the blanket. "What is going to happen, Mama?"

She did not answer him.

The bells and whistles rang on time. Pasquale walked into the kitchen, making lots of noise. Maria was draped in black—a black dress, black shawl, black stockings, and black shoes, just like hundreds of other Italian women in Lawrence. Pasquale noted to himself, *Oh, something is really going to happen today.*

His mother was getting in the last word, acting child-like and whispering to Tony, "Most of the people in Lawrence are immigrants, Tony, just like you and me."

56

Tony threw up his hands and went into the icy blast of winter to work.

As promised, that night Maria and Mr. and Mrs. Rocco took Joey and Pasquale to Chablis Hall on Oak Street. The Hall was vibrating with excitement, packed with men, women, and children uncertain about what would happen. Joey and Pasquale tried to act like older guys.

Angelo Rocco jumped on the stage. Pasquale leaned over to Joey and said, "Holy Mother of Mercy, there must be hundreds of men and women here, Joey." Maria's strong hand went over his mouth. She did not say a word; her piercing eyes were enough. He knew she meant business.

The crowd cheered and howled, sometime in English, sometime in Italian. "*Sciopero! Sciopero!*" and in English, "Strike!" It sounded like one huge word: "Scioperostrikero."

Angelo was of medium height, with black curly hair, a strong Roman nose, and very dark, sad eyes. His clothes looked as if he had outgrown them—unlike Tony, who was always well-dressed. Once Angelo had raised his hands and crossed himself, the room went quiet. Like a silent breath, the Hall took on a church-like atmosphere. Angelo Rocco was ready to speak.

"*Me, Io* (I) am one of you." Slowly at first, he spoke while gesturing with his hands, and everyone seemed to understand. As his voice got louder, his passion filled the air like the smoke from the cigar that Joey's father was puffing. His first words were "To fight for workers' rights is an art, not a profession."

Maria thought to herself, We are not here to listen to theatrics.

57

Peter Romano leaned over to Patsy Amante and whispered, "He is a follower of Troublemaker Number 1, the anarchist Carlo Tresca."

Amante sent him the old Neapolitan gesture—thumb up, fingers closed.

Angelo's voice rose to a screech. "We will be tested tomorrow. You will survive, but first I implore you, in the name of God—no violence. Give the mill owners any sign of violence, and they will kill us. *Capishe? Capishe?* (Do you understand?)"

Everyone waved their hands, throwing insults about the mill owners and floor managers.

"*Basta, basta!*" Angelo screamed, and put out his right hand with two fingers raised. The crowd went silent. Everyone's silence saluted the air. "Like you, I kissed the ground when I came to America from Roccamonfina. Is anyone here from Roccamonfina?"

The crowd screeched, and this time Angelo waved his arms along with them. The children jumped up and down.

"I came to l'America because I wanted to do better. I have worked in mills in Rhode Island and Maine, and nowhere are Italians treated the way they are here in Lawrence. I, like you, made worsted for rich men's suits, which men in high places, like Wood, wear as they insult and degrade us. Italians do the dirtiest work in America for the least money. We have a reputation, because we went to work during the last strike and they called us scabs. We were fooled then, but not anymore—we must get organized." Rocco stared at the women. "If tomorrow your pay is cut, do not go back to work. *Capishe?* Whether you are young or old, married or single, just refuse to go back to work if they cut the pay. *Capishe?*"

Helen Scalera, a church-going woman, spoke up: "Who will feed our children for us?" Her husband, Guido, put his hand over her mouth, but it was too late.

"Do not be crazy!" Rocco leaped off the platform and went over to her. "Do not think this way!" He raised both hands as if praying. "What do you have now—water, molasses, and bread? Not enough heat to keep you warm. Only enough food to keep you working like slaves. Do your children go to school, or do they work in the mills? Do they live to be adults, or do they die before the age of twenty-five? We shall organize, help is on its way, and there will be food. I promise you that you and your children will not starve." Like a son, Angelo Rocco gave her a hug and a kiss on her cheek.

The echo of his Italian boots as he jumped back onto the stage made Pasquale like him more. Everyone raised their hands in a traditional Italian salute. Rocco was pacing back and forth. "Last night, the Craft Unions voted to strike. If the Polish, the Germans, the French, and the English go on strike, we need to join them. *Capishe?*"

The crowd became more subdued, waiting to hear more. While talking, Rocco took a step back. "There will be a meeting for men tomorrow. Others will be there who will help us. I beg you, *paesani* (relatives), keep your heads. No violence, and keep your ears and eyes open. Tonight, I will introduce you to my best friend. I cannot tell you his name, and all of you must never tell anyone he came here tonight. *Capishe?*"

"It is Nicola Sacco," Peter whispered. "I would know him anywhere."

59

Amante barked, "For Chrissake, Pete, shut up."

Out of the shadows, a thin man of medium height stepped out onto the platform. The room fell silent. Dressed in a black serge coat with a velvet collar and a white shirt, he looked like one of the mill owners. Pasquale had never seen a bow-tie; he punched Joey and laughed.

Maria turned to Mrs. Rocco. "Is he one of us? He looks rich."

Mrs. Rocco nodded. "Wait—you will see. I knew his mother in Italy. He comes from the humblest people you will ever meet. With him with us, we will win this strike."

Pasquale's gaze was fixed on the man's beautiful black leather shoes, just like his father's.

The mystery man's first words were in English, mixed with the Barese and Sicilian dialects. "I *coma* here because I have an *interesta* in you and want to help you. *Io, lika* you, have left those things you loved dearly behind to *maka* a new life in l'America. I was born in Torremagiore, and my father wanted me to work in his olive garden and vineyards, but I chose l'America. I work in a shoe factory now and like my job. I have worked for a construction gang, carrying water like a *ciuco* (donkey), and in a foundry room carrying granite. I have a family. Your families must survive here in l'America, and you must be strong. You and I have eaten of each other's bread and know how hard the road has been. The owners of the mills have lied and turned on you. Every day of your lives, the noise of the machines in the mills rings in your ears. You must erase the ringing of the machines and hear our music. You and your children need to survive this *Purgatorio* (hell) that has befallen you. Your path to a better life has

60

been cut off. We have reached our limit, and yet, deep in our hearts, we pray for a better future for our children. The time for a future is now, and we must let the mill owners understand that we will never be satisfied until we are treated like human beings and not like animals. Their cheeks, not yours, will have to blush for this shame they have thrust upon you with deceit and promises of a better life. You and your children will bear witness—we must survive. But to do so we must protest for the right to live like human beings and be free. Sacrifice now everything that is dear and sacred to the human heart and soul, so that the day will come when your children will be proud of you and know that you were not cowards and hypocrites."

"Is he an anarchist or a socialist?" Amante asked, nudging Peter.

"My father told me this guy is a socialist. My father hates anarchists and socialists." But Peter, who never made a quick decision, added, "Let's wait and see."

Whispering and hissing went around the hall, and when the mystery man raised his hands, silence echoed in every corner of the building. "They tell you I am an anarchist," Sacco said with a smile. "It is not a sin to be an anarchist, but I am not one, or a socialist. You work hard for Wood, and yet, like all Italians across this country, you will never get a chance to go to Harvard or live in Andover. I tell you that I am for freedom and peaceful protest. I am here in Lawrence to support you in your strike, which will be called The Bread and Roses Strike—bread because it is the staff of life, roses because the women will each carry a rose, the sweetest-smelling flowers in the garden." He took a crushed rose from his coat pocket and waved it. "Tomorrow, all of you will make a big decision. Your decision to go in peace during this strike will ring throughout this land as the savior of justice for all!"

"*Sciopero, sciopero!*" The roar went on for five minutes, shaking every wall as if an earthquake had hit Lawrence.

Sacco stretched his arms as if he were on the cross and said, "No, no." From his pocket, he took out a small American flag. "You must shout 'Short Pay, Walk Out.' *Parla, parla* (say it)."

The sing-song chanting filled the room. "Shorta a pay, walka out."

"You will carry the American flags that Rocco will give you."

Joey and Pasquale jumped up and down, their hearts beating to the rhythm of the song. Pasquale thought to himself, *I am the man with the bow-tie now, filled with compassion and honor.* His eyes swelled up with tears. He blew his nose to hide his face from Joey.

Rocco, with arms raised, stepped up next to Sacco. The audience strained to listen as he spoke. "I came to l'America for a better life and to fulfill a dream. There are two Americas, and Italians are the other America. From Boston to San Francisco to Mexico, I have worked in mills, and in no place in this fine country except here are Italian people treated like the black people who pick the cotton for the fabric you make. This strike is a cry for help, not only for Italians but for the black people as well. We are the weakest because we are not organized. I have witnessed legions of the human oppressed. I worked the worst jobs and earned as little as $1.33 a week. I worked for a *padrone*. Thank God, you are not subjected to a *padrone*."

The voices of the crowd pierced Pasquale's ears:

"*Mai, mai* (never)."

Peter smiled eagerly and gave Nunzio a push. "The guy is all right."

Pasquale tapped his mother's hand. "What is a *padrone?*"

"Shh, shh, I will tell you later." The blue in her eyes had become translucent, and her eyes were filled with fire. Pasquale was proud to have such an intelligent mother, who stood erect and absorbed. He wanted to be the same himself.

Rocco moved toward Sacco and put his right hand on the man's shoulder. His voice rocketed upward, and with his left hand outstretched he said, "Send your children to school, not to the mills. Capitalism is evil; government is slavery; war is a crime against humanity; freedom and education are essential for human development." He crossed his hands over his heart and said, "*This is my religion.*"

Pasquale started to clap his cold hands, and before he knew it, the whole crowd had started clapping with him. When the applause died down, Rocco continued, "Hear me, listen! Do not be divided— women and men, Neapolitan and Sicilian, children and parents, business owners and workers. For all who will come after you in this land of opportunity, for your mothers and fathers and children, you will find your rightful place in the Rose of Paradise."

"*Viva L America!*" Side by side, a pair of shiny black leather shoes and a pair of scuffed worn-out leather boots stood together like marble statues.

Pat said to himself, "Amen," and he knew that he was not only himself but also Rocco and the man with the bowtie and shiny Italian leather shoes. The beacon of hope

63

from these humble men allowed a people who had lost hope to wish again.

Then, like lightning that catches your eye and then goes black, the mystery man with the bowtie vanished, and Rocco again reminded everyone, "A meeting for men will be held tomorrow night at the Ford's Hall, at 8:00 p.m." Rocco asked Joey and Pasquale to help pass out stacks of pamphlets written by Luigi Galleani, a lawyer, several newspapers, and a pamphlet by Emma Goldman. Then he said, "*Buona sera* (good night)," and jumped off the platform, waving the American and Italian flags as he walked out the back door.

***

Tony was waiting for them when they got home. "Tony," Maria said, noticing that the dinner was still on the stove, untouched. "I made Tiella, with escarole and the anchovies, your favorite food from Gaeta. It is still warm. Here, eat, my dearest."

Pasquale took a small slice and went to his room. He read the pamphlet by Emma Goldman to Josephine, who was still awake. The pamphlet was about the emancipation of woman and the unhampered development of children. Josephine fell asleep while listening.

Tony was eager to hear about what had gone on at Chablis Hall. Maria sat down with him while he ate the Tiella. She waited before telling him anything. She did not want the children to wake up. When he started drinking the homemade red wine, she began.

"*Caro*, it would have been better if you had come with us. We missed your strength, and you would have understood the men who spoke. And a good sign, dear—as we were leaving the hall, snow flurries started falling.

64

Lawrence will be clean tomorrow."

Tony took a sip of wine and stopped eating.

Maria, sensing his impatience, thought, *He too must be unsure of what is going to happen.* In her most positive voice, she said as she picked up her glass of wine, "Tony, everything is going to be all right. We are going to get help to stay alive and have a better life. Angelo Rocco is one of us—he *is* us. Join us with him."

"What are you talking about, Maria? Tell me who was there." Tony finished his wine.

"The whole Italian community, that is who was there." She poured him more wine.

"The Pettorutos?" His eyes shot a skeptical glance at her, his lips pursed.

"No, Tony, I do not think so. Maybe their son Albert, but I could not be sure." For the next ten minutes Maria described the event. She added more drama and her own ideas. "The mystery man left Torremagiore when he was seventeen, in 1908. He was a shoemaker, and now he is a man who wants freedom for all of us. He asked us to make a peaceful protest. Mrs. Rocco said his name is Nicola. She knew his family in Italy. He told us we must sing and wave flags and carry roses as a way out of this horrendous business."

Tony stood up and looked at Maria, his eyes narrowing. "Sing and carry roses! What nonsense. Roses for what?" His soft hands went up in the air, and he shook them as if he were leading a symphony. "Stay away, I tell you!"

Maria was startled and blocked him as he headed to the bedroom. "No, Tony, I will go. I wish you would come. We have brains in our heads. You know I am right, and,

65

besides, a rose has the most perfume and makes you sing. Tomorrow will be a day to remember, Tony, and I plan on being part of it."

Pasquale, still awake, realized that his mother was adding things to the story to make it more pleasing for his father. Before falling asleep, he gave Josephine, who was fast asleep, a kiss and whispered, "Sweet dreams, Jo." Then he fell asleep and dreamed about the rat story.

Earlier that week, Maria had stood watch at the wake of Guido Scalera, who had died unexpectedly, and when she came home Pasquale asked her, "Why do you go to so many wakes and pray and stay with the body? Mama, the person is dead. He does not know you are there."

Maria took his small hands in hers. "Because, *caro*, our custom is not to leave the dead person alone. We do not want any rats from the alleys snooping around to get in the casket. We do not want the family to be alone. We bring the food to the family to provide comfort and nourishment."

"Why does everyone stay in the kitchen and eat and talk to each other while the dead person is in the house, Mama?"

"To us it is a means of breaking bread and supporting the family." She poured him a glass of milk with a dash of coffee.

"Why do you wear black?"

She turned away and did not answer.

"But, Mama," he went on, picking up a piece of bread, "I was afraid yesterday when you asked me to kiss *Zio's* forehead in the casket. His skin was all brown."

"He is your adopted uncle, Pasquale, and you will never see him again. Enough now. It is our tradition to

66

show respect; it is the Italian way."

Pasquale looked up at her. "To be afraid, Mama?"

"No, *caro,* but enough, *basta, basta.*" Maria took him in her arms, and the tears that were in her heart tumbled down on him as she said, "Never, never be afraid. Always have hope."

That night Pasquale dreamed of dying and of rats eating his flesh. Whenever Pasquale was frightened, he would dream of those rats. They always wore black suits, white shirts, and shiny black shoes, and the faces kept changing with every event.

***

Conditions in Wood's mills had been miserable for years. Poor wages, long hours, accidents, poor nutrition, and child labor were all rampant. In Lawrence people were fighting for their lives.

January 11, pay day. The women who worked in the weaving room were waiting to see if their pay would be cut, and it was, by fifty-four cents. "Short Pay, Walk Out!" became the new chant that blocked out the bells and whistles.

On that bitterly cold day in 1912, Lawrence, Massachusetts, the greatest worsted center in the world, became a stage for the rest of the world to watch. The Bread and Roses Strike began, and the city was locked down. Twenty-seven thousand women and children sang, "We want three loaves of bread and roses too," to the melody of "God Bless America," as a bitter snowstorm swirled around the workers forming picket lines by the gates of the mills.

When the cut in wages was announced, it was not a surprise. Not only Italians were involved—fanning the flames of the strike were people from dozens of nationalities. But the Italian word for strike, *sciopero,* circulated through the gathering crowds. For two hours' pay, the most important and dramatic strike in U.S. history began to foment. The new law reduced the work week from fifty-six to fifty-four hours. In most cases, it amounted to thirty-two cents less in each pay check, the cost of three loaves of bread.

Annie Basile was going door to door with a petition for the strike, handing out small flags and red roses. Patting children on the head, she handed them small flags and pieces of candy donated by Pearl Candy Store on Broadway. "Hey, kids, keep the faith. Go out and give everyone you see a flag. When I come back, I will bring you more candy. Now get going." Annie was known to the men in town as "the Battleax" because she talked like them and ran her own dry-cleaning business.

The streets were filled with people shouting, "Short pay! Strike! Strike!" Pandemonium took hold on Common Street, and the crowd, like a snake, wound itself down every block and street. Annie led the charge on Elm Street, barking at Connie, Lisa, Rita, Helen, Grace, and Marie, going door to door, climbing narrow dark stairwells, slipping petitions for the strike under doors, and asking anyone who was home to sign a petition. "Victory is near. Don't stop, girls, we have a job to finish! Do not go to work—carry your flag and rose tomorrow."

At home, Maria was outraged. 'Thirty-two cents they cut from our pay! *Non-e giusto* (not right). It is the cost of three loaves of bread."
Pasquale did not know who she was talking to until he saw Mrs. Kiernan entering the kitchen. She was carrying a

68

pamphlet she had torn from a post on Elm Street and handed it to Maria. "They are everywhere."

SCIOPERO – come to a meeting tonight at Ford Hall (men only).

Maria was angry and outraged. "No women are invited?" She tossed the flyer onto the table. "Vergonia, it is a slow death for all of us." She turned to Pasquale. "I want you to go to Ford Hall with Joey, *caro*, and be very careful. Do not tell your father."

Mrs. Kiernan patted Pasquale on his head and ran down to her apartment to tell Joey.

The seeds of the strike had been planted in 1911, when the Massachusetts Legislature ordered the mills to cut women's and children's work hours. Many people were malnourished and fainted from the poor air, which was filled with dust and sawdust like bits of cotton flying all over the place. Others succumbed to consumption, anthrax, tuberculosis, and pneumonia. Every day the women in Lawrence went to a wake for someone they knew.

Before the strike, the mill owners, driven by greed and eager to make up for lost profits, had sped up the machines and cut the pay, forcing everyone to work even harder. The work was so demanding and dangerous that when people fainted the machines were left running, and people had to continue working while the floor manager called for help. Every mill had hundreds of accidents a year, and though sometimes the mill owners did help a worker's family, if the person who was the primary breadwinner got disabled, most of the time the neighbors, the churches, and business leaders gave what they could to keep families from starving. The Everett Mill was known worldwide for the high quality of its gingham and denim fabrics. Yet many of the women who worked there, after they used their weekly income for food, rent, and fuel, had only thirteen cents left and wore clothing that was shabby and ragged. Mrs. Scalera often hid scraps of gingham in her bosom and shared those pieces with women in The Plains, who made quilts out of the scraps to give as wedding presents.

***

Pasquale met Joey at Ford Hall. He was writing in one of his black notebooks. "Ford Hall January 11, 1912." It took nearly a whole page.

Joey was annoyed. "What the hell are you writing in that book for?"

"Well Joey, I want to remember everything so I can report back to my mother." Pasquale did not tell Joey that he had been writing names and places in the notebooks for some time.

"You are *pazzo*, Pat, *molto pazzo*." Joey gave him a shove. "But you're a good fellow."

After the meeting Maria and Mrs. Kiernan were waiting for Pasquale at the kitchen table, having tea. Joey went home to sleep. Pasquale was out of breath because he had run home. His eyes were red and watery from being in a smoke-filled room. Maria poured him a cup of tea, and Mrs. Kiernan put several biscotti on a dish. She was tatting a handkerchief, and she looked up and asked, "How many people were there?"

"I heard Patsy Amante say nine hundred men, all workers. They gathered in small groups, talking and smoking. Most of the men were older, and Joey and me, we tried to blend in by holding cigarettes in our fingers. Then Joey said to me, 'Let's get out of here.' The smoke made our eyes tear up. And Joey tried to leave. I was a little scared, Mama, but Joey came back when I called him. After that we stayed close to the door, in case we had to run out. A group of men near us were talking revolution." Pasquale dunked the biscotti in his tea. "They were anarchists, preaching and gabbing. I said to Joey, 'These guys are not like the people we heard last night. They look like terrorists. But Joey said they were not terrorists, they were just trying to scare us. I said to Joey, Mama, 'I don't like these guys as much as I liked the speaker last night.'" He turned to Mrs. Kiernan. "They looked different from the guys who live here in Lawrence. They look like they're from the big city."

Mrs. Kiernan, who knew everything, poured out more tea. "Those must be the trouble-makers from the Lawrence Local 20 of the Industrial Workers of the World. I heard they might show up."

Then Pasquale got really animated. "Rocco was there. He stood up and took the stand. He always looks tired and shabby. This is what he told us, Mrs. Kiernan. The craft unions—the Germans, the French, and the English—are organized, and if the mill owners cut their pay, they will go on strike. He begged everyone not to be scabs and break the lines. He was shouting, and it was cold in the hall, so he put his hands in his pockets, and he told us, 'The strike committee has tried to find out for days now if the wages were to be cut or readjusted. Yesterday we sent them a special-delivery letter. The mill owners are too busy to answer. Are we as replaceable as bobbins that they just ignore us? Do you understand me? *Capishe? Capishe?*' Everyone loves that word, Mama. A cheer went up from the crowd. Angelo went on and told us that they were not

71

asking for a pay raise. They just asked the mill owners not to cut workers' pay. But they never received any answer."

Pasquale looked down at his notes and went on. "This is what he said. 'Like you, *paesani,* I work in the Wood Mill and have lived in Lawrence for two years. I have no family, and I take classes at night school. Send your children to school and not the mills. Education is not from Mr. Wood or the owners of the mills. It is a gift that America offers all of us.' He pointed at me, Mama, and said, 'If you plan on going back to Italy, then work and have your children work. If you stay, *education* for your children is the key. I have received word that we will have outside help and will not be alone in this strike. I am in touch with people from New York, and they will be here tomorrow. Most of all be peaceful, watch over each other, and no fighting. *Capishe?*' Everyone yelled, 'Yes Angelo! We *capishe.*' Then, Mama, Joey brought me over to his cousin Rocco, who hugged him and tussled his hair. When he tussled my hair, Mama, I felt his strength enter my body. I was so impressed that the will to follow him grew stronger in me. An Italian man, telling others to be brave and proud and to fight for what is right!"

Pasquale looked at his mother. "Mama, Papa seems so weak to me."

Maria got up from the table and stood over him. "Your father is not weak. He is a good man. You must understand that he wants us all to go back to Italy, where we would not have to fight to live. Have respect for your father, Pasqualino, and never let me hear you call him weak. How do you think you got here? It is a good thing he is not here to hear his son talk like that."

(During the meeting, Tony was at the store, where

72

men were congregating each other and drinking shots.)

"I love Papa, Mama, but I will stay in Lawrence." Pasquale hugged his mother and turned a page in his notebook. He brought it over to his mother and Mrs. Kiernan. "I wrote this, Mama, so I will remember it forever. 'There is something better down the road, and you must be strong and ready to receive it.' Mr. Rocco said that, Mama. He looked at us with such sincerity, and I liked him right away."

It was the beginning of a relationship that lasted until Angelo Rocco left Lawrence.

Pasquale went to bed and opened a new notebook. While in bed, he thought, Somehow, my mother must approve of me going to the meeting, because she wanted to know everything that went on. She did not tell Papa that I did not go to school. It was an education that I could never get in Miss McSweeney's class, that's for sure.

He dreamed of the last time he had been in class. Miss McSweeney had held the pointer in her hand and gone up and down the rows of desks, repeating, "We weave the world's worsteds." She wrote it on the blackboard and said that she was going to give them a test on it the next day and that they should memorize the words. Pasquale woke up sweating before he could see again the pointer coming down on Joey's hands because he had laughed. Suffering children and abusive teachers were not enough. Pointers would be a memory forever.

***

For the mill workers, the cut in hours went into effect on January 11, 1912. It blew the lid off a smoking city. Close to fifty thousand employees were affected.

"Maria," Mrs. Baci said, so close that she could kiss

73

her. "The mill owners conducted secret meetings with the supers, executives, and floor managers. My husband went and told me that there was talk of a possible pay cut. Mr. Wood and the others said they did not expect that people would not show up for work. And he also told them to watch for any signs of a walk-out, and they would be well-rewarded."

"The scoundrel! I heard that his family have so much food left over that they feed it to their dogs and horses." Maria was whispering because she thought her children were asleep. But Pasquale was not asleep.

That morning he did not know if he was hearing bells or whistles. At 6:00 a.m. he usually did not get up. Today, however, penetrating and intense, the factory whistles, driven by the compression of the steam from the mills, sounded like ship horns. The emergency alarm was heard for ten miles over the smokestacks and tenements of Lawrence, Methuen, and Andover.

"Loud enough to wake the dead." Tony was shaving and opened the frosted window to see what was going on. The bells melted into the whistles, producing a whooshing sound. Tony ran out to Maria, who was setting the table. "Maria, get the children dressed—those are the sounds of the riot alarm!"

While thousands of families were preparing their bread and molasses for breakfast, stamping their feet to stay warm or melting frozen pipes, they heard the word *sciopero* echoing over the rooftops. Others were running in the streets and shouting in their own language.

A ripple turned into a thunderbolt. The women and men of Lawrence stormed the mills, shouting, "Short pay! Short pay! Everyone out!" That morning, when women

74

opened their paychecks and found their pay cut, they threw off their aprons. They grabbed picks and sticks from their lunch boxes and marched out of the mills. The men carried knives and slashed the machines' belts on their way out. The machines come to a stop.

In the Wood Mill Maria followed the children, who were crying. When they came to the gatekeeper, he would not unlock the doors for them to get out. "Have pity on these children," Maria cried. She was surrounded by children, crying and frightened. Many had soiled their clothes. She raised both hand, begging. "Open the gates, please. These are children!" Then the workers stormed the gates, shouting curses and names that the gatekeeper had been calling them for years. They lifted the gates out of the cement.

Joey and Pasquale skipped school that day and stood outside the gate on the bridge over the canal. Pasquale cried out "Mama!" but she did not hear him. She and a group of workers were running toward the Washington Mill. Maria drifted away from workers, keeping the children with her, and Pasquale lost sight of her. She turned up Jackson Street with a group of the frozen, ragged, frightened children, some of whom did not have warm clothing on, and hid them in The Capital Theater, where it was warm.

Pasquale's mind froze. The next sounds he heard were three quick gongs going off every few seconds. The sirens tore through the wind-swept city, carrying the riot alarm and whistles into the quiet neighborhoods of Andover, Methuen, and North Andover again and again.

Joey grabbed Pasquale's shoulders and shook him. "You are not going to find your mother, Pat. She probably

75

is in some house. We're about to be trampled to death. Follow me."

They hid out in an abandoned car at the railroad track until the riot alarm stopped. From there they could see everything. Mr. Berry at the Pacific Mill tried to lock the gates, but the mob lifted the grill right off of the hinges, and people flooded in. Joey was panic-stricken. "Pat, the workers are smashing things—this is bad!"

The bridges were covered with ice. Polish, Lithuanian, Yiddish, Greek, Syrian, Italian, and English workers all kept slipping and sliding, howling *Sciopero!* When things quieted down, Pasquale and Joey went to Angelo Rocco's room for flyers to place in every stairway or business in The Plains that night.

Angelo was reading the *Lawrence Evening Tribune*. He read the headline: "'Radicals and Lawless Foreigners.' That is what they think of us."

Pasquale felt a pang in his chest. Here he is, a single man with no family of his own, living in a rooming house with six other Italian men. He combs long strands of fibers from short ones, making wool for suits that men all over the world wear. He wears tattered clothes that are not warm. Every night, he goes to night school. Pasquale noticed stacks of books under Rocco's bed and thought, He is the leader here in Lawrence, and people trust and listen to him.

It was at this moment that Pasquale committed to memory what Angelo Rocco had said the day before: "We Italians will always carry the burden of blame for the riot of 1912." Pasquale made a decision then to be part of this fight, not for the money but for dignity and respect, for Italians and for all of mankind.

"Make sure, boys," Angelo said, getting up and

putting his hands on their heads, "to blend in and be careful. No bragging and no trouble, especially you, Joey." He pointed to Pasquale. "You make sure you keep an eye on Joey." Then he sat down on his bed and waved them over. He looked serious, and Pasquale thought they had done something wrong. "Keep your heads on straight and up." Rocco put his arms around both boys. "Do you know who Amerigo Vespucci is?"

"Who?" Joey and Pasquale said together.

"Well, boys, he was born in Florence, Italy, and he was a great Italian explorer. America is named after him. And tell your mothers that, instead of calling it *Americo*, they used a woman's form of the name and called this wonderful country America. Never forget"—he was on a roll now—"that Getulio Piccerilli carved the Statue of Liberty from Massa Carrera, from Italy, and the Abraham Lincoln statue out of twenty-eight blocks of Georgia Marble. Always remember those facts, because you won't get them in school in Lawrence. Tomorrow night we are expecting help for the strike, so keep your ears open." Before they left he handed Pasquale a worn and tattered book and said, "Joe Ettor is coming to Lawrence tomorrow. Go to the Common and hear him speak."

On Friday night, Joe Ettor arrived in Lawrence.

"We have a leader now," Maria said at the table while they were having dinner, "and his name is Smiling Joe. Angelo Rocco sent Joe the telegram. He is the President of the Industrial Workers of the World. Tony, come with us tomorrow morning and hear him speak."

"No, I will not go." Tony always spoke more softly when he was at the table with his family. "And why is Pasqualino going? He needs to listen to a troublemaker?

77

Maria, you are turning our son into a rabble-rouser. I hear about all the things he is doing. Pasquale," he added, shifting into his imploring mood, "these union workers are all from other states and do not know what it is like here in Lawrence. You are too young and do not understand the game of these troublemakers. Do not listen to them." He turned to Maria. "Maria, please, if you go, let the children stay home." His red wine rippled in his glass, and he thought, *I must do all I can to get my family out of here.*

"The children cannot stay home," Maria said. As though she had read her husband's mind, she went over and poured out more wine. "Dearest one, do you have to go to Pettoruto's tonight? I want Pasquale to come with us, because it will be dark and he is a good protector. Josephine can stay home with you. It is important that we know what is going on, you know that. We do not have enough money yet for our passage home."

Tony gave in and stayed home.

The Common was overflowing with a weary, exhausted crowd of workers. When Joe Ettor got on the podium, Angelo Rocco was behind him. The church bells from Saint Mary's stopped ringing. Smiling Joe Ettor was well-dressed, wearing a fur-collared woolen black coat and a scarf that hid his stoutness. A small flag was pinned on his lapel.

It was so cold that people clung together, and their breaths blew out clouds of cold hope.

"How old is he?" Maria asked Mrs. Baci.

"Rocco said he is twenty-six years old. His father was gravely injured during a strike, and the boy is now a man, a leader for the people. He studying to be a lawyer." She whispered to Maria, "We have a leader here."

78

Maria answered, "He looks like a baby and has such a huge smile."

Smiling Joe Ettor's voice screeched across the snow-filled park. He spoke in English, Italian, Syrian, Polish, and Hebrew. "You are the most important people in the mills. You matter. *Capisci?* You matter!"

The people had never heard that they were the most important people in the mills before, and a roar went up. "We matter! We matter!"

He quieted the workers by raising his hands. "Your labor, your sweat and toil built these mills of brick and stone. Women and children's hands made the cloth that Billy Wood and millions of men in this country wear every day. If there is blood to be shed, it is up to the strikers to decide whether it shall be the blood of the working classes or of your employers."

The crowd was uneasy. They started hissing and jeering and clamoring, "No violence! No blood!"

Pasquale did not understand what Ettor was talking about. As the man continued, his voice rose to a pitch so high that it roared across a silent, exhausted people.

Ettor was relentless. He pointed his finger at them. "This is what Billy Wood told his fellow capitalists at a meeting." Ettor took a dollar from his jacket and waved it. "Take a dollar and place it on a shelf, look upon that shelf, and at the end of six months you will find it still there. But take the working man or woman and place that person on a shelf for six months, and you will find a skeleton. *Capisci?* Do you understand? *Capisci?*"

Mrs. Baci turned to Maria. "Mayor Scanlon has a frightened look on his face. Wait, it looks as if Joe has more to say."

79

"They will starve you into submission, and you are not equipped physically, mentally, or emotionally to do this alone. But you will have help, I promise you that. Fifty cents buys ten loaves of bread. Every one of you has that much invested in this struggle. It is a question whether you will get more or less bread then." This time he talked more softly and put his hands in his pockets. "Always smile." Ettor had a grin as large as a fava bean pod. As he raised his hands to praise heaven, in a pleading voice he said, "Give me a smile!" Everyone smiled, and he went on. "My mother says, no matter how hard you work, always smile. Keep a shining smile always on your face. And always sing and carry a flower. Do not let them insult your soul. Have courage and sing for the roses you will carry."

He jumped off the platform and left with Angelo Rocco and other men dressed in black coats and hats. As the crowds dispersed, sparkling white snowflakes fell to them, soothing the very soul of Lawrence.

Tony had hot cocoa waiting for them; he was anxious to hear about the crowd. Pasquale slurped down his cocoa and went to bed. Maria told the story, adding some drama: "Ettor said that Monday morning we must cause the mills to shut down even tighter than they are now. We must not cause any violence, because all the blood we will spill will be our blood. We cannot win by fighting with our fists against armed men or the militia, but we have one weapon that they do not have. We have the weapon of labor, and we can beat them down. We must stick together. *Capisci?* Tony, *capisci?* Tony, Ettor spoke in Italian and then repeated his words in French, Polish, and Lithuanian."

Tony answered, "Maria, I *capisci* that the man is a trouble-maker and irresponsible."

80

Maria ignored his remark. "He formed a committee of many nationalities, and these are the demands they will present to Wood." Maria read aloud the demands and handed the paper to Tony. "Angelo Rocco wrote them down and passed them out."

1 – A fifteen-percent increase in wages on the fifty-four-hour basis. ("This means one dollar and five cents for many of us," explained Maria.)
2 – Double pay for overtime work
3 – The abolition of all bonus or premium systems
4 – No discrimination against the strikers for activity during strike

"These demands are not much to ask for are they, Tony?" Maria took out a bottle of wine. Tony began to listen, and Maria thought, *I have finally won him over—for now, anyway.*

"These are reasonable demands of a reasonable people, Maria," Tony said, "but be careful what you do. You have a family, and your first obligation is to Pasqualino and Josephina. Committees usually do not win, and then they go on with their lives and leave the people behind. *Capisci?*" He took a large gulp of wine. "This is what I picked up at Pettoruto's today. Tonight, the strike committee met with Mayor Scanlon and the Board of Aldermen and presented their demands. These men have only been in office for a few weeks, so we do not to expect too much from them. When they come to the groceria to buy Mr. Pettoruto's Italian sausage, they asked lots of questions and were very nosy. Mr. Pettoruto is a very smart man. He said to me today, 'Be careful, Tony, how you act

81

and what you say. There may be good men in Lawrence, but people think that there is something funny about them.' We didn't know then that 'the good men' had petitioned Governor Eugene Foss for help. Mr. Pettoruto whispered to me, 'The fear of pay-back never goes away in Lawrence, Tony, so be careful.' He told me to tell you to watch your step, Maria."

"Oh, *caro.*" Maria wrapped her arms around him. "Tony, you are so careful about everything. Let's be happy for today. A parade is coming, and the children can have some fun, my darling!"

Tony sighed and put his arms around her. "My dear Maria, you are so innocent, and you believe all that you hear. But I will come to the parade with you on Saturday."

The most chauvinistic of patriots, the most
optimistic of optimists, the immigrant was
more American than the native born…This
was the truth about Lawrence which observers
in 1912 were unable to detect…poor and
frightened immigrants sought security and
found it in their clubs, in the mills, and in
a desperate effort to be Americans.

Immigrant City
— Donald B. Cole

CHAPTER 5 – FOR GOD AND COUNTRY

Ettor organized the Parade. Pasquale and Joey were allowed to carry the American flag while marching in the procession. Pasquale felt his heart swell when people cheered, shouted, and sang *God Bless America*. The American flag floated in the freezing wind. Pasquale felt that he was part of something he believed in.

As crowds gathered, the parade grew to ten thousand men, women, and children, all singing and waving flags. Then, suddenly, they were confronted by descendants of the Minutemen, carrying rifles and bayonets, ready to disperse the workers. Joey and Pasquale were carrying a stack of pamphlets, and when they saw the flashing bayonets, they ran for cover into a tenement on Amesbury Street, where they looked out from the third-floor window.

"Hide those pamphlets, Pat, just in case they come in," said Joey.

They put them in Mrs. Balducci's washing machine.

Mrs. Testa was at the window too, ready with buckets of ice-cold water to dump on the men who were pushing and shoving the crowd toward the bridges.

"God," Pasquale whispered to Joey, "she dumped water over the captain! He'll be sure to come in."

Instead, the captain, no older than Joey, ordered the marchers to retreat or disperse. The crowd started jeering, hissing, and hurling sticks and insults at them. He stepped back and ordered his men to fix their bayonets and charge.

Allesandro Rapasari's shoulder was pierced. He fell forward, his blood rippling over the cobblestones. The crowd was noisy and running toward the bridge. Women were praying and children crying. Joe Rapasari, Allesandro's son, used his coat to stop his father's bleeding, then put him in a grocery cart and pushed him toward the hospital. Screaming women and children raced across the bridge into the freight yard.

Pasquale turned to Joey. "For Christ's sake, that's my mother out there! She's wearing a blue scarf—I know it's her."

Joey held onto him to stop him from jumping out the window. "Keep your head. Your mother can take care of herself, Pat."

Pasquale punched him in the stomach and ran down to the street, searching for Maria. He prayed that his mother would not get shot or bayonetted. He found her on the bridge, guiding the children to safety, and helped them to a safe place. Walking home arm in arm, they decided not to tell Tony.

Every day people watched more militia barge into Lawrence, wearing leather boots, carrying bayonets and revolvers. The farmers were not allowed into the city with

84

their carts to collect the horse manure, and the streets stank. Mrs. Balducci shouted from her window, "There is no one to clean it up, you fools!" She dumped more water down and at the top of her elderly lungs called out, "*Pagliaccio!*" As the weeks passed, people heeded Joe Ettor's advice: "Keep your hands in your pockets and do not be afraid of the bayonets." Flags were flying from every tenement window and all the business storefronts. When food got scarce, women who lived in Methuen brought in provisions for hundreds of soup kitchens.

In the meantime, the newspapers reported that "people who live in Lawrence live in squalor and are ignorant, lawless Immigrants."

Joe Ettor was everywhere, preaching to the crowds wherever he found them. Angelo was always with him; he was even starting to act and talk like him.

That night Maria told Tony about the militia who had turned hoses on the marchers. "Angelo went right up to their horses and looked at them and said, 'You may turn on your hoses, but there is a flame being kindled—a flame in the heart of the workers, a flame of proletarian revolt that no fire-hose in the world can ever extinguish.' The horses whinnied, and some of the men pointed their weapons." Tony never missed a chance to scold Maria. "Were you there? How do you know that? Where is the help Ettor promised everyone, Maria?"

She did not answer, because the help had never come.

Tony sat close to her and held her hand. "Maria, Mr. Pettoruto is worried because Ettor was firing up the Italians. He's meeting with them more than once a day."

85

Maria frowned and raised her eyebrows.

"Yesterday he came into the groceria, and Mrs. Pettoruto gave him her famous spaghetti and sausage plate that she was making for her family. When he complimented her, she offered him a glass of our homemade wine."

Maria put on her Mona Lisa smile and relaxed.

He went on, "Lucia handed him the wine, looked him straight in the eye, and said, 'Tell me, Mr. Ettor, you tell us to keep calm, but it is like a war zone out in the streets. I will not send my children to school for fear for their safety.' The bastard gave her a big smile, looked at all of us, and said, 'Keep faith, and you will survive.'" Before Maria could say a word, Tony continued, "He is the most radical man I ever met. You keep Pasqualino away from him. Do you not understand what is going on in this house? Josephine has started to stutter, and I know she is wetting herself. You must stop going to these radical meetings."

Maria was very calm. She picked up his hands and held them in hers. "Josephine told me she was afraid to go to school because her teacher kept saying mean things about the strikers. The teachers praise Mr. Wood and tell the children that Wood is responsible for putting food on our tables. They are educating our children to go against us, Tony. *Caro,* please understand."

Maria got up and started putting dinner on the table. She placed her hands on her hips and said in perfect English, "Peaceful persuasion is the weapon we have, *caro.* We must stick together—Poles, Germans, Greeks, Turks, Armenians, French, Canadians, Russians, and Jews. Men, women, and children. One race, one creed. We need to reach down and pull ourselves up."

"That is Joe Ettor's talk." Tony got up from the

table and tried to hug her, but she pulled away. "All I ever see in the march are women, Maria. Where are the men? Do you not see the riots in the streets, Maria? Are you blind?"

"Tony"—she was crying now—"you are a man, and you do not see what I see or hear what I hear. They are saying that the Italians started the riots; they blame us for inciting the strike. But this is not true: it was the Poles, God bless them, and you know that, Tony." When she cried, Tony always stopped his rages and hugged her.

***

Maria, the other women, and their children all stood beside each other in the marches, to keep their heads above water and to help each other. Rocco showed up daily with a little saying. Today he was talking about reciprocity: "Do unto others as you would have them do unto you."

Pat thought to himself, I bet he is practicing his law homework.

Everyone stopped and listened.

"The Bible says it differently, but that is what it means. In Ecclesiastes it is written, 'Cast your bread on the waters, and you will find it in many days.' I know this to be true." Rocco turned to Joey and Pasquale and beckoned for them to follow him. Later Pasquale wrote the word *reciprocity* in his notebook; he lived his life by its philosophy.

While Joey and Pasquale were stacking pamphlets, Rocco said, "A long time ago, I thought things would get better, so I started going to night school. By the time I was twenty-three, I had worked my way up through the fifth grade. I kept educating myself, and I was twenty-five years old and in the eighth grade. And wouldn't you know it? I

87

was the only Italian kid in the high school. After the strike, I want the two of you to stay in school. *Capisci?*"

Angelo started lifting the heavy boxes of pamphlets and in a gentle, strong voice said, "There is a mountain near Naples called Mount Vesuvius. One day it started to erupt, and the lava was headed directly to Naples. The Neapolitans believed in their patron Saint Gennaro and placed a statue of Saint Gennaro in the river, and they shouted to the statue, 'You can die, or you can save us.' The saint, whose two fingers were raised, raised two more fingers in response and performed a miracle, causing the hot lava to change directions and go into the sea. Well, we can change the direction for our workers. I do not believe in miracles but in hard work and reciprocity." He raised four fingers. "Go to school, *caro,*" he said to Pat. "You're a very smart boy. Don't waste your life."

Pasquale thought, my mother always calls me "caro," but no one ever called me smart before.

Angelo turned to both of them and said, "Always remember these days in Lawrence!" Then he stormed out. The next few days were terrifying. People stormed through the mills yelling, "Shut down the machines! Short pay!" It was utter chaos.

"Rioting gone bad," Rocco said, upset. He was helping Pasquale hide more pamphlets in the cellar of the apartment building.

Maria was carrying the American flag and the Italian flag in the demonstrations. After the third day of rioting, Tony said to her, "Maria, you are crazy. You have a family! Stop this nonsense. This group of hooligans is unorganized. We'll be going back to Italy soon."

"No, Tony, I have an obligation to all the people I

88

work with. I have to stand alongside them. This strike will shut down the mills—all of them. The committee has Joe Ettor with them. They are forming twenty-seven different groups based on nationality, and I am going to stick with my Italian patriots. We have eleven soup kitchens and over a hundred investigators, and people are raising money outside of Lawrence. The strike committees voted on giving two to five dollars a week to each family every two weeks, for fuel and clothes. Dr. Calitri, who was against us striking, has volunteered with Dr. Hindman to give medical aid. Mrs. Annie Weizenbach is on the committee. The woman earns twenty dollars a week and is going around telling the skilled workers to stay on that picket line. Does that sound like we are not organized, Tony?"

"It is a strange way you think, Maria. Not like an Italian woman." This was Tony's only comment.

The next day Maria was at it again. She always began while she was cooking and talked throughout their dinner. "Ettor addressed us again today. He said the skilled workers are paid more than the others so as to create jealousy between us and the different nationalities." The kitchen's aromas and the wine made it a perfect platform for her pitch. As she circled the room, her voice was low like a man's. "Reach down and help each other, or all of you will be pulled down together. The owners will show no mercy."

Pasquale and Josephine came hungrily out of their room.

"My dear, do you remember what brought us to the United States?" She put down a plate of pasta and went on. "The signs in our village read, 'NO ONE GOES HUNGRY IN LAWRENCE.' You had a sign up in our groceria, Tony.

89

And now look around you. There are hundreds of people starving in Lawrence today. Thank goodness our women's club is able to offer them a little food every day."

Unable to tolerate her speeches any longer, Tony looked up. "Now you belong to a women's club? Are you crazy, Maria? You do not have an obligation to anyone but your family."

Maria did not miss this moment to explain. "No, Tony, it is not a real club—it is just like a fellowship, you know. Mrs. Sanders from Methuen helped us get organized. We are learning how to be more helpful to each other. Hundreds of women—like Mrs. Szostak, who lets women use her washing machine every week, and Bridget Kiernan, who does our sewing and ironing while we demonstrate in peace."

Tony answered her in Italian. "Maria, listen, you chose to go to work; you do not have to work. You will be a *principessa* when we get back to Italy. And, my dear rebel, this is not a peaceful strike, as I hear about it."

She answered in a quiet voice. "How can we save the money for our passage to Italy? That is your dream. Besides, it is my duty."

"Your duty is to your family and no one else," Tony insisted.

Pasquale spoke up at the table for the first time in his life. "I am not going to Italy, Papa. I will stay here with Angelo Rocco."

"That is the talk of a boy, Pasqualino. You are a man now. You will have a good life in Teano. The groceria will be yours. You will be able to go to college in Naples. You are too young to stay behind. So no more talk—you cannot make this decision."

90

Pasquale got up from the table and looked at his father. "I do not want to work in a store. I want to stay in Lawrence. I want to see America and go to school and help people live lives of respect and dignity. It is my duty. *Capishe,* Papa?"

Maria poured the wine and changed the subject. But "my duty" became Pasquale's secret slogan for the rest of his life.

Tony shook his head. "And this is what it has come to—my own son disobeys me." He gave Pasquale a backhanded slap that landed him on the floor.

Maria went over to Tony and calmed him down. "Your anger cannot change his mind, darling. Please, peace—he is just a boy."

Pasquale marched into his bedroom.

Tony was homesick, and because Maria worked so many hours he was lonely. He yearned for his small town of Teano, his friends and relatives, even for the smell of the olives and garlic he sold in his store. "What do you want, Maria?" he went on. "I cannot do anymore."

Maria understood his pain. She went over to him, and he whispered through his tears, "I am lonely, and what have I done, Maria? Help me understand my son."

"Just be patient with us, and I promise I will be ready to go back. But not now. I am worried about you. Make sure you do not insult anyone with your anger, or you will be hurt, Tony. People are saying that some store-keepers will not wait on the scabs."

"But how do you know so much, Maria sweetheart?" He thought, *she is wise.*

"Simple" she said. "What all of us long for is respect, compassion, and recognition. And that, my dearest,

91

leads to action."

As a young boy Pasquale did not understand his parents' longings, but he understood his mother's plea for respect, compassion, and recognition in his soul—he longed for the same thing.

Today she was really being lofty and prepared black demitasse. "When we used to go to the mills, it was dark and so cold that my girlfriends and I huddled together to keep warm. *Caro*, we talked about these things. Even though we cannot speak good English, we understood each other. We talked and compared our pay. My friends are Lithuanians, Syrians, Poles, and some Jewish women whose husbands cannot work in the mills. We now can cook each other's food. We talk about everything. Mrs. Baci works in the mills and is the only breadwinner, and they have six mouths to feed. The lentils I gave her last week were the only protein they had. In summer she is able to get some chicory or dandelions, but not in winter. They are worse off than us, Tony. Please, *caro,* be a humanitarian, like the Good Samaritan."

"Some Samaritans are terrorists," Tony said. In these moments he was driven by his own sad odyssey. "You are too trustful, Maria."

"Listen, Tony, we try to keep away from the troublemakers—they are the terrorists. In the mills, the Supers tried to separate the women who were friends, and we said to each other, we are sisters. We are the sisterhood, and no one can ever break our bond."

Yet, because she had left her own family behind, Maria knew about abandonment, and she made one of her decisions now not to abandon Tony. "*Caro,* try to have the faith in me and trust that I can make the right decision."

92

She took his hands and her children's hands into her large work-torn hands as if she were praying. Pasquale understood it as begging.

"Listen to me," Tony said, scowling. "I am right. I hear many things in the grocery store, and we must be very careful, because of the Black Hand. Mr. Pettoruto wants me to be neutral or else people will not come to shop. It is a risky thing you are doing, Maria."

"What is the Black Hand, Papa?"

"The Black Hand (*Mano Nero*) are a group of thugs and criminals, and what you must know now is that you are never to mix with them. And stay away from people like Angelo Rocco, or you will never make it back to Italy."

Maria relaxed when Tony and Pasquale spoke to each other.
***

Pasquale was so intrigued by the *Mano Nero* that the next night he went to Rocco's
room. Rocco was reading by the light of one lightbulb, and the room was covered with pamphlets, papers, and books. Maria had sent over some lentil soup for "that poor boy," and Pasquale waited until he finished it. Then he said, "Please tell me everything about the Black Hand. I need to know."

Rocco smiled, and his eyes lit up. They both sat on the bed. Rocco was at his best when telling stories. "Once upon a time, Spanish anarchists invented the phrase, and it spread throughout Europe. The Black Hand is not an organization. It consists of a band of lawless criminals who use an imprint of a black hand to spread fear. In New York, their chief targets are successful men. If a victim turns to the police for help, they pay him back by trying to blow up

93

his house with bombs. Some Italian immigrants are known to be part of it."

Pasquale took out his black notebook and started writing, but Rocco closed the book.

"Remember this in your soul, and do not believe what people will tell you. Pasqualino, these guys come into the city of Lawrence and try to shake down anyone who owns a business. They are criminals and have formed syndicates, and some of them live right here in Lawrence among us. They tell me these guys came from Naples, but I do not believe that, since I heard that some of them are other nationalities, trying to get money from rich people. They are not Good Samaritans, I'll tell you that. Many are uneducated immigrants. What they did to Caruso—you know, the singer—they sent him a letter with a Black Hand and dagger on it and asked for two thousand dollars. He paid it, and then he got another letter demanding fifteen thousand. So he went to the police, and at a prearranged spot the police arrested two Italian-Americans, businessmen. They were our own kind, Pat, our own kind. Caruso will come here soon. The *Lawrence Evening Tribune* reported in the paper that Enrico Caruso supports the strike and will give a concert in Italian at the Star in a few weeks. I will make sure you're there, Pat. Now, Pasqualino, you must promise to go back to school after the strike."

"Not me, Mr. Rocco. My mother and father need the money I make from the coal I pick up on the railroad tracks, so they can buy tickets to go back to Teano. My father owns a beautiful groceria like Pettoruto's; right now, one of his two brothers is running it for him. You know he is a winemaker and makes all the wine Mr. Pettoruto sells

94

in his groceria. He does not get extra money for making the wine, just food that is not fit to sell. My mother makes a feast out of the food he brings home and also gives some to Mrs. Baci and Mrs. Kiberstis, a widow with six kids. He will someday go back, but me, I'm staying in Lawrence."

"Pat"—Angelo Rocco put his hands on his head—"think about going back to school. You will not have a chance in this country unless you are educated. It is the American way. *Capisci?*"

Pasquale left with Caruso's voice in his head and could not wait for Enrico Caruso to come to Lawrence.
***

Every day now Tony had a new mantra: *"E'il Purgatoire per me lei; torero a Paradise."* (It is Purgatory here for me; I will go back to Paradise.)

Maria always told him, "Tony, it is not so bad here; let us stay. Josephine goes to school, and Pasqualino loves it here." She knew, though, that they would return to Italy and that it would be right for him.

Pasquale, in an effort to understand his father's ways, tried to engage him. Every day after the strike, he told Tony pieces of American history. Tony responded with Italian history.

Pasquale did not tell him that he was responsible for posting flyers on all the posts in The Plains, whenever a meeting was called. But one night Tony said, "I hear you are hanging around with that anarchist Angelo Rocco. What has he been telling you, Pasqualino?"

"Well, Papa, did you know that the Merrimack River, where the mills dump their trash and pollute it, is one hundred and ten miles long and runs from the White Mountains to Boston? Do you know what Merrimack

95

means?"

"No," he said. "Tell me, Pasqualino."

"The Algonquin and Pawtucket Indian nations named it Merrimack, and it means 'rapid water.' It was clear and pure then, but now it is lined with factories, colored by dyes, and choked with waste. Papa, someday I want to take a canoe like the Indians did and go up to the White Mountains in New Hampshire. Mr. Rocco gave me a book from the library about an American Indian called Hiawatha, by Henry Longfellow. Hiawatha was a hero. He ran along the river in his bare feet and fished in it, Papa."

Tony looked pleased. He touched Pasquale's head in approval.

"Angelo Rocco read that to me, Papa, from his book *Hiawatha*."

Tony did not know what to say. He talked instead about the feast of San Gennaro, and how he remembered as a child participating in the festival—the men carrying the saint, the women pinning money on the Madonna, the food and the music. "You will be part of that someday, dear son."

Pasquale thought, My father is the only one who believes all the propaganda about Rocco. I love Rocco like an uncle, and he is not an anarchist. He asked his father, "What is an anarchist?"

Tony muttered, "Why do you care?" He sipped a glass of wine and looked away. Pasquale noticed that there was fear in his father's eyes.

The next day Pasquale asked Angelo Rocco, "What is an anarchist?"

"Well, Pat, an anarchist wants to be free, but most of all he wants everyone else to be free. The slaves who

96

were brought here against their will and picked the cotton that is processed in the mills—the people who owned the cotton farms owned those slaves. Pat, your mother and the other people in Lawrence are paid, but they are still slaves."

"Are the black boys who work as wool-sorters in the mills slaves or anarchists? I would rather shoot myself than be a slave."

"No, Pasquale, because President Lincoln freed the slaves, and if you were in school, young man, you might be reading about what happened in the Civil War."

"Are you an anarchist?"

"No, Pat, I am not an anarchist." Angelo took him by the shoulders. "You do not have the heart of an anarchist or *mafioso;* you are too sensitive. In order for a sensitive man to survive in America, he must first know his own history and know and listen to his own people. I want to tell you that we in Lawrence are not the only Italians persecuted in America. In the Southern part of this country, Italians have been lynched, then hung on trees and used as targets. In Tallulah, Louisiana, Italian children were not permitted to attend white schools because their parents, storekeepers and business people, were friendly toward black people. The anger against Italians in Louisiana was mostly because we staged a parade to protest taking away the vote from black people. Italians were called landless and illiterate."

In that moment that Pasquale felt that he truly understood Rocco and his great desire to be educated.

Angelo picked up an issue of *The New York Times* from 1911 that was lying on his bed.

The Abominable Wop

Negroid features polishing American shoes
accompanied by the following qualities
A pound of spaghetti and a red bandana
A stile and a corduroy suit
add garlic what make for him
a strong damu
and a talent for black a-da-boot

"Take this, Pat, and write it in your notebook and soul."
The next week, Rocco brought him a book called *Uncle Tom's Cabin: Life among the Lowly* from the library. It was written by Harriet Beecher Stowe. One line that struck Pasquale was "Treat 'em like dogs, and you'll have dogs' works and dogs' actions. Treat 'em like men, and you'll have men's works." He wrote these words down, since at first he did not understand them. Much later in his life, the words became very meaningful to him.

When he brought the book back to the library, he asked for his own library card, and his mother was so proud. His father ignored his happiness.
***

Monday, January 15, 1912. The marchers were peacefully protesting when they ran into the militia again. The bayonets were carried this time by a thousand young Harvard students on foot and horseback, who had arrived to intimidate the workers. Harvard University gave credit on midterm exams for boys who went to Lawrence to break the strike.

The strikers threw ice in protest. The citizen-soldiers disbanded. They could not contain the marches that snaked through the streets and alleys.

Farris Marad led the Syrian Drum Corps in a peaceful parade, with no incident.

That night ten thousand people welcomed the poet Arturo Giovannitti and Bill Haywood; with them was "The Red Flame," Elizabeth Gurley Flynn.

The next day Mayor Scanlon suspended parades for ten days. But the people kept up their tempo.

Rocco was reading headlines again. "Heads Broken When Battery Holds up Mob." He turned to Pasquale and Joey. "We will force the nation to face the question of community and immigration. Now deliver those pamphlets tonight."

Friday, January 19, 1912. The police, following a tip given to them by John Breen, an undertaker, discovered dynamite at three locations. Breen, the son of an old party boss, had mapped out where the dynamite was planted and given the map to police. One place was next door to Antonio Colombo's printing store. Mr. Colombo had printed some of the flyers that Pasquale and others gave out. The printing office was also where Ettor got his mail.

That night Maria was all revved up. Mrs. Kiernan was with the family in the kitchen, having hot tea, and Maria said to her, "They arrested Ettor for the dynamite bombing. He was booked and is now in jail. The *Tribune* blamed the Italians for planting the dynamite." Without stopping for breath, Maria went on, "And the mystery man who spoke at the rally—remember him, Pasquale? Sacco, the one with the bowtie. He is a friend of Bartolomeo Vanzetti. Well, I know for a fact he has been collecting money and providing food to the food kitchen and is a friend of Angelo Rocco. I went to a meeting yesterday at the Progressive Women's Club, held by two teachers at

99

Wellesley College. Elizabeth Gurley Flynn collected five hundred and fifty dollars at a rally for us in Pennsylvania, and as she was speaking the riot call sounded and over two thousand of us women ran out into the streets singing. The police were outside, though, threatening us, so we broke up."

Tony looked mournfully at his family. "Let me tell you once and for all, Maria. People at the store are reporting that Ettor and his crowd are extremists, but we all know he did not plant the dynamite. The newspapers are blaming the Italians for planting the dynamite." Tony took the *Lawrence Evening Tribune* from his coat pocket and read the headlines, which said that Wood had made an offer and was asking everyone to go back to work. "The strike will soon be over."

Maria, unable to control her anger, stopped him. "For your information, Tony, Ettor is calling the offer from Wood and his guys a bunch of lies, spread around so that we will give up. Today that poor woman Miss Flynn with the red hair was taken to a psychiatrist, and Wood and his cronies are trying to declare her insane so that she can be institutionalized and put out of the strike. She is one of the smartest women here. She knows all about strikes and is helping the women out here in Lawrence."

Tony burst out, "She must be crazy, sleeping with Joe Ettor!"

Pasquale and Josephine knew it was time to go to bed. Mrs. Kiernan bid them all good night.

In the darkness of their bedroom Maria whispered, "That is not true. In Lawrence, Tony, courage is mistaken for insanity. *Dio mio,* what are we coming to?" She said nothing about Flynn sleeping with Ettor, because that was

100

true.

"Be careful, Maria." Tony tiptoed out of their dark room and went to kiss his children good night. He whispered to them, "Do not worry—we have enough money saved for tickets to get us out of here soon. We will be back in sunny Italy, and you will be safe."
***

That same night, Arturo Giovannitti, a twenty-seven-year-old poet, orator, and editor of the Italian newspaper *Il Proletario,* came to Lawrence to help with the relief efforts.

That morning the temperature was below zero. Families and children waiting in line for soup and bread found the cold unbearable. Steam coming from the kitchen-tents melted the tears frozen on the faces of the children, who had given their energy in the mills. Italian bread with soup warmed their hope.

Pasquale and Mrs. Rocco were handing out bowls of the hot soup. "Look, Pat." She pointed to a man who looked like a monk. "That is the poet, Arturo Giovannitti."

Giovannitti was warming the children's hands, saying gentle and kind words like *courageo.* He turned to the crowd. "This is a humiliation that I have seen before, and I can offer you all only prayers and hope." He shed tears of sadness and blessed them. "Come to the Common, and I will give you a piece of bread with my poem."

Pasquale went to hear him speak the next day. Thousands of people came, and Mrs. Axelrod was passing out warm gloves. Workers showed up for bread and got a poem called "The Sermon on the Common" and a piece of cheese.

His arms raised to heaven, his voice like thunder,

101

he began: "Blessed are the rebels, for they shall reconquer the earth." In the blink of an eye, Giovannitti had them. The strikers cheered and clapped.

There is no destiny that the will of man cannot break;
There are no chains of iron that other iron cannot destroy
There is nothing that the power of your arms, lighted by power of your mind, cannot transform and recast and remake.
Arise then, ye men of the plough and the hammer, the helm and the lever, and send forth to the four winds of the earth your new proclamation of freedom which shall be the last and shall abide forever more

Angelo Rocco jumped on the platform and led the crowd in singing *God Bless America*. The two men, one young and one old, stood together with raised hands and ended with "God bless America, and God bless Lawrence. God bless you all!"

The news spread quickly that night—there would be no more formal gatherings. The Star Theater, a popular vaudeville house, locked its doors. Caruso would not be coming to Lawrence. Mrs. Yazey played Caruso on her Victrola so loudly that the whole building could hear.

Joe Caruso, Ettor, and Giovannitti all landed in jail for "creating a disturbance."

Pasquale ran up the stairs, out of breath. "Mama, Rocco went to visit Ettor and Giovannitti in jail today, and Marshall O'Connor recognized him and shouted, 'Lock him up, lock him up,' and they charged him with disturbing the peace."

Maria went over and put her arms around him. "I

102

heard about it, and they are calling on Bill Hayward, who will be here tomorrow. Angelo will be out tomorrow. Do not worry, *caro.*"

Tony was staring into his glass of wine as though he were viewing something. His mind in a rage, he thought, *He sounds like his mother. We must get out before it is too late.*

Bill Hayward arrived in Lawrence and got Rocco out of jail. At once Angelo began putting the word out, and the Lawrence Bread and Roses Strike started garnering national attention. Pasquale overheard Rocco and Hayward talking while he was picking up pamphlets.

"Listen, Angelo. Peter Kelley—you know, Fabrizio Pittochelli—is a big banker here in Lawrence and a good friend. We can ask him for help. Those Franco-Belgians are in the forefront here and operate Local 20 of the I.W.W. They'll allow us to use their cooperative. They are a tough group."

Pasquale thought, *why did Fabrizio Pittochelli change his name?* He slowed down as he packaged the pamphlets in order to hear more.

"You're right, Bill, but the Syrians are making a big contribution. Farris Mara, James Brox, a grocer, and Doctor Hajjar are on the strike committee." Rocco put on his coat, then stopped in front of Pasquale. "This young man is writing down what's happening here and is a big help."

Bill Hayward put out his hand and shook Pat's. "Keep the writing going, kid."

Rocco was talking while walking. "Bill, in the beginning Father Milanese supported the strike and said the coins put in the collection basket were for the strike. But in secret he didn't support us. William Wood gave the Holy

Rosary Church fifty thousand dollars to build a school and, in a letter, asked him not to support us. From the pulpit he has openly asked parishioners to go back to work."

Pasquale heard them whisper as they left the building, "Exodus," but he did not understand what that meant. Later, he found out. While the other American children were reading *The Adventures of Pinocchio, The Wizard of Oz, and Peter Rabbit,* Lawrence children, neither foreigners nor Americans, were preparing for an Exodus.
***

A knock on the Foenia door found them by the stove, eating chestnuts. Angelo Rocco greeted everyone and went to the pot of coffee to heat his hands. "Please hear me, as I am about to ask of you that which I would ask only of myself."

Pasquale thought, My mother and father are up to something.

Maria filled some cups of hot coffee and asked everyone to sit around the table.

Angelo's voice was weary but clear. "We are sending some children to families in New York and Vermont, so that they will be out of harm's way during the strike. Margaret Sanger and her people want to help. They met with hundreds of families who will take good care of the children. The plan is to have Italian children with Italian-American families, and the other nationalities will do the same. Your daughter, Josephine, will go with a wonderful family, the Grillos, who live on Park Avenue. They have three daughters."

Josephine began crying, and Maria pulled her onto her lap.

Angelo spread an article on the table that had

104

appeared in a magazine. "'The Fangs of the Monster in Lawrence,'" he read to them. "'When you get to Lawrence, on every corner are soldiers with guns bayoneted, ready to plunge this deadly instrument into the living flesh of working men and women…who have rebelled against wage slavery.'" He put his arm around Pasquale. "I have talked to your parents, and they agreed that you will not join those children. You are of great help to the strikers. You will not be able to go to school, but if you have to hide out, Mr. Pettoruto will hide you in the cellar of the groceria."

Tony put his glass down and stood up. "One thing I heard today, Angelo—that this is all a way to gain attention for the strike. The children are being used as pawns. Is that true?"

Angelo jumped up from his chair. "Mr. Foenia, no, it is not true. This is what I know is true, sir. When the immigrants came to Lawrence, they were disappointed but worked hard. Some wanted to become Americans. Some wanted to earn enough money to go home. They were unwilling to face reality. It is not the Italian way, but somehow that is what they learned. We are all afraid, but we find hope in our desperate need to be American, in our families, our clubs, and even the mills. Others outside of Lawrence may not be able to understand, because they do not live in this hell hole. Some of the children, Mr. Foenia, like your son, Pasquale, will remember this and will let everyone know what happened here. I want you to know that I will protect your son as if he were my own during this time."

Tony sat down. "I believe you, so my word is my honor. Go and be safe. God speed."

Maria sobbed and put her arms around Tony, and he

105

felt he would cry.

Pasquale looked at his parents and said, "I want to stay."   The first Exodus included one hundred and nineteen children and was carried out with no incident. Margaret Sanger coordinated it and helped the children get on a train to New York. Maria accompanied Josephine, who finally let go of her mother and got on the train with the other children, along with Margaret Sanger and some social workers from New York.

Pasquale was hiding out at Mrs. Yazey's house, listening to Caruso. She was cooking rice and lighting candles in front of a statue. "Have you heard from Josephine, Pasquale?" She gave him a taste of the rice.

"Not yet. I hope she will be all right. When she left she was so thin and always crying. The family she is going to in New York have three daughters. She will attend Saint Theresa of Avila Catholic School. She promises to write."

Mrs. Yazey's tears rolled down her cheek. "Your mother tells me she will go tomorrow with Mrs. Baci and her three children to the train station, to send off the second group of children. Will you go, Pasqualino?"

"No, I am supposed to stay out of sight for a while." Pasquale was relishing the rice with tomato sauce. He looked up at her and said, "You are as good as this piece of bread. Thank you."

One hundred and fifty children, accompanied by their mothers, arrived at the train station the next day. But two hundred militia carrying guns, as well as police on horseback, closed in on the children, keeping them from boarding the trains. They beat the mothers, who were resisting them, and dragged all of them to a military truck that brought them to the jail. Maria ended up in a cell with the other women and children. The children were locked up alongside thieves and murderers. Margaret Sanger and the social workers, however, stayed with the children and later helped them get on another train.

Maria and all the mothers were charged with child neglect.

Albert Pettoruto and Tony rushed to the jail and got the women and children out. Maria and the other women were more resolved than ever to "fight the abuse of women and children."

The replacement train arrived at 7:30 P.M., and the girls and boys of Lawrence, many of whom had been neglected and worked in mills, headed for New Hampshire and Vermont.

This second Exodus created a national scandal, and Rocco took advantage of the incident. Lawrence was now on the world stage again, but this time the President of the United States, William Howard Taft, intervened. The Rules and Means Committee listened to the stories of the Exodus, while Mrs. Taft sat there with tears in her eyes.
***

Back in Lawrence, Maria found more places for the women to meet in secret. "Let's meet at the soup kitchens. They are open day and night, and it will be safe to gather there." Elizabeth Gurley Flynn continued to lead the women protesters and met with them one night. Her red hair, which was usually pulled back, hung down, and she looked young. "Link your arms together tomorrow, all of you. Maria, you will carry Mrs. Bravo's baby."

Maria and the other women looked at her, puzzled, and said, "Carry the baby?"

107

Elizabeth explained, "The committee believes that if pregnant women and women holding babies are in the front line, the militia won't fire."

The next day the men on the bridges were drenched with firehoses.

In the streets, Elizabeth Flynn led the women protesters. "Link your arms to protect each other, and avoid arrest! Maria"—she handed Mrs. Bravo's baby to her—"carry the baby." It was so cold that Maria used her scarf to cover the baby's mouth as they sang.

"*Dio mio!*" Terrified, Maria covered Baby Bravo and stared at the militia's guns.

Mrs. Sara Axelrod was hauling a wagon of provisions for the strikers. She did not flinch as the militia tried to stop her; she just kept flicking the reins of the horse as he moved steadily ahead. The women and children walked in unison, circling her wagon as she delivered potatoes, sugar, bread, chickens, pigs, and eggs to the soup kitchens. Without Mrs. Axelrod, the strikers would have been starved into submission.

Women like Sadie Zamon, Annie Basil, and the girls from Elm Street kept watch for scabs from their third-floor windows. Buckets of cold water sat by their sides to pour over them. Pearl Shinbers and Josephine Lis opened their houses as gathering places. The Jewish strikers formed a club that sponsored leftist speakers as well as social events. Maria, a very social person, went to the meetings often. She felt comfortable there, even though she could not understand Yiddish.

Whether it was good or bad, Lawrence was on the world stage. The city's people were tested beyond anyone's imagination. Pasquale and Joey nailed copies of an article

108

from *The New York Times* on every post in The Plains and placed hundreds more around the city.

The well-known axiomatic truism, "A virtue if carried to excess becomes a vice," again finds exemplification in the tearing away of the Lawrence strike children from their homes and their natural protectors under the plea of helping them. Thus, while it is a virtue to help underpaid wage workers to improve their condition, it becomes a vice—in some case becomes a vice—in this case almost a crime for labor leaders, or misleaders, to keep wage workers from earning a living to a point where they can no longer care for their families and are obliged or advised to send their children away among strangers, and worse yet, to exploit these impoverished innocents in order to extract a few more dollars from possible sympathizers by exhibiting them at their parades and mass meetings.

J. Schuyler, New York, Feb. 21, 1912

On February 25, 1912, following the third attempted Exodus, rumors flew that the Italians would go back to work. Ettor advised Angelo from jail on what the Italians should do.

Maria was trying to convince Tony that things were going well. "Angelo is helping us to stay calm, and above all he tells us every day to stay put, use no violence, never attempt to fight back. They have no intention of giving us anything but false promises, and we must get Ettor and Giovannitti out of jail. They are rotting there."

Maria was exhausted. Tony was listening, but he was also drinking more wine these days. "Maria, we all know that Ettor and Giovannitti are innocent and did not murder that woman, but we must be careful. The strike will be over soon."

On Friday, March 1, 1912, the American Woolen Company issued a notice that they were offering a five-percent wage increase. All the other mills issued a similar offering. The strike was over, but Ettor and Giovannitti were still in jail, fighting for their lives.

The next day, March 2, Margaret Sanger led a group of sixteen children, of four nationalities, to give testimonies in Congress. The hearing had been called because of the interference with civil rights during the riots at the Lawrence railroad station.

At Pettoruto's, everyone was telling their own version of the incident. Newspapers all over the country printed her story. Margaret Sanger was preaching all over New England about children's rights. Tony read a portion of the testimony.

Carmela Teoli sat in a witness chair in the grand marble Congressional Chamber of the United States of America. Teoli's voice, small but clear, was a symbol of injustice in Industrialization. Mrs. Robert Taft, wife of President William Howard Taft, sat listening.

The chairman asked Carmela, "How old are you, Miss Teoli?"

Carmela answered, "Fourteen years and eight months."

"Where do you work?"

"I work in the woolen mill," she answered.

"Do you work for the American Woolen Company?"

110

"Yes," Carmela replied.

"What sort of work do you do, Miss Teoli?"

"Twisting wool into yarn," she answered timidly.

"Now, tell us how you got hurt, and where were you hurt. In your own words," the chairman said softly.

Carmela took off her headscarf in answer.

The chamber went silent. Mrs. Taft, President Taft's wife, cried.

"Explain this to the committee," the chairman said, staring at Carmela's bald head and scar.

With her chin up high, Carmela looked at Mrs. Taft and said with doleful eyes, "The machine pulled my scalp off."

Mrs. Taft cried through the whole interrogation.

Rosario Contarino testified that he was sixteen years old, worked sixty hours a week, and earned $5.10 per week.

The testimonies were the talk of the country. In the Foenia home, Pasquale told his own version. "I know Rosario, Papa. He is my friend. I met him at the railroad yard." Pasquale was about to say more, but he noticed that Maria, who was clearing dinner away, was crying.

"We have not won yet, Tony." Maria held up her hand as tears rolled down her face. "Caruso, Ettor, and Giovannitti are rotting in jail for something they did not do. Yesterday we received a letter from the poet at the soup kitchens, telling us to take heart. Imagine, he and Ettor are facing execution for a crime they did not commit, and he is praying for us. *Dio mio!*"

"*Basta!*" Tony punched the table. "We are going back to Italy. It is impossible to have a normal life here

111

anymore. The strike is over—do you understand?"

Maria shook her head in defeat; she knew they were getting close to having enough money for tickets back to Italy.

***

April to September, the transition period in Lawrence, passed quickly. Many families went back to their country of origin, but the Foenias stayed. Like others who had hope, they went window-shopping ion Essex Street, saw movies, listened to radios. Pasquale and Josephine loved "The Shadow Knows" and like most kids told their own stories about The Shadow.

By October of 1912, the trial of the three Italian men was still raging on. Maria and Mrs. Rosa Caruso, carrying her three-month-old son, went to the courthouse, walking back and forth while praying. Joe Caruso, Smiling Joe Ettor, and the poet Arturo Giovannitti were in a cage, waiting and waiting for a death sentence for the murder of Anna LoPizzo.

Maria came home late that evening from the trial. Tony gave the children dinner, and then he and his wife went out onto the street.

"Tony." Maria was flushed. "I met the man. Do you remember him? Sacco. He is raising money to help the lawyers. He told me that people all over the world are upset. Tony, I told him we know who shot Anna LoPizzo. It was the policeman, Oscar Benoit. Sacco said something to me about 'No God, No Masters.' Do you know what he meant, Tony?"

Tony did not answer, and without having supper they went to bed. Maria feared that soon the trip to Italy would be a reality.

On Wednesday, October 2,1912, with the trial in Boston postponed, Mayor Scanlon issued an appeal to the people of Lawrence.

Mrs. Pettoruto was preparing for her weekend of cooking, putting food ready to be cooked in her basket, when Mrs. Rocco barged into the groceria, out of breath. "Louis Scanlon is out to run the I.W.W. out of town. More riots to come! Watch out for your store, Mrs. Pettoruto."

What happened in Lawrence on the next day was the most spontaneous outburst of peacetime patriotism in American history. Every building in Lawrence was covered in red, white, and blue. Cars, horse-carts, fire engines, and storefronts were all adorned with flags. Every millworker carried a small flag to work, and when they entered the mills the walls were covered with flags and balloons. Lawrence was in a burst of color. *The Eagle Tribune*'s headline, "Lawrence Is Back," was followed by the Pledge of Allegiance.

On the date that celebrates Christopher Columbus, a parade of all parades was held, and a banner made by Father O'Reilly spanned Essex Street:

For God and Country
The Stars and Stripes Forever, The Red Flag Forever!
A Protest Forever against The I.W.W.
Its Principles and Its Methods

For Maria and Pasquale, the parade was a distraction. They were focused on what was happening in Boston at the trial.

On Thanksgiving Day, November 25, 1912, at 7:00 A.M., the bells rang. At noon they rang again, and at 6:00

113

P.M. the bells chimed with whistles while crowds gathered everywhere, singing *America, the Beautiful* and *The Star-Spangled Banner*. Pasquale, marching and singing with the crowd, passed the church, shouted, "God bless Lawrence!" and continued marching.

The Bread and Roses Strike was over, but the discrimination against the Italians and Italian-Americans had been a drama of major proportions. It affected how Pasquale and all Italian-Americans behaved and lived for the rest of their lives.

During this time poor and frightened immigrants sought security and found it in their families and clubs, in the mills, and in desperate efforts to be American. The strike was a paradox.
To an unseeing. It revealed an un-American city where security was utterly lacking. To those who knew it, it marked the emergence of Lawrence as an American city with the security that the term American implied.

Immigrant City
— Donald Cole

CHAPTER 6 – AN AMERICAN CITY

The bells started ringing again, but, in spite of the spring weather and the children returning from the Exodus, unrest hung over the city like a ghost. At Pettoruto's market, the word was out that there was a plan to run the I.W.W. out of town.

Mrs. Rocco, who never went unnoticed these days, was picking her green beans and talking about the struggle of the union to keep workers loyal. "My son Angelo tells me that mill agents, overseers, detectives, and the police formed a committee to run the unions out of town." She looked around before whispering, "Father Milanese and Father O'Reilly should go also."

Mrs. Pettoruto frowned and raised her head. "Why is that, Mrs. Rocco?" Then, because she knew enough about gossipers, she returned to the newspaper.

"Because he never stopped helping Wood to end the strike. I am so worried today and mixed up. My head hurts." Mrs. Rocco picked out a Sicilian black olive from

115

the olive barrel.

Mrs. Pettoruto, not one for idle talk, opened the newspaper but, while reading, inched closer to Mrs. Rocco.

"The unions are running out of money and have only forty-nine cents in their fund. Those fellows are more dangerous in the mills now than before the strike. They are a bad bunch."

Lucia Pettoruto usually did not talk about politics in her store. Now, with fire in her eyes, she moved even closer to Mrs. Rocco, almost in her face. "Mr. Kirby was crushed in the elevator at the Everett Mill last night. Did you know that Guy Torrisi was oiling a carding machine in the Wood Mill and had an accident? He died at the Lawrence General Hospital." She re-tied the string of her white apron. "Let's see what we can do to help these fatherless families. We need to help those children, or they will starve. Let's get some women together to cook for them for now, until they get on their feet."

"Listen to me, Mrs. Pettoruto, it's a plot. The owners and scabs are paying us back for the strike. When people like Bill Haywood and the Gurley woman leave Lawrence, we're all going to suffer. All the women in my tenement are worried." Mrs. Rocco was no longer whispering.

Tony was sweeping the floor and put in his two cents. "Do not be surprised, Mrs. Rocco, if Bill Hayward and that rebel of a woman skip town after all the damage they have done." He surprised himself, for he never gave his opinion while working.

"*Dio mio!*" Mrs. Rocco looked faint.

"Now, now, Mrs. Rocco, be patient. Everything will be fine in

116

Lawrence. My son Albert tells me not to worry about those people. What we really need to worry about is the bad virus in the Andover area; we must be vigilant if it hits Lawrence. Albert is home from college and is meeting with some health officials at City Hall. I heard of two cases in North Andover, and that is not far from us." Mrs. Pettoruto looked worried, but she spoke calmly, and no one in the store could dismiss what she said.

Mrs. Axelrod opened the screen door, and the bells on the door jingled. She looked tired, and her clothes were rumpled.

Mrs. Pettoruto went to stand next to her. "What's the matter, Sara?"

Everyone drew together as Mrs. Axelrod turned to Mr. Pettoruto, who was writing in his credit book. He laid down his pencil.

"I came here to help. Someone in Lawrence has the Spanish Flu."

Mrs. Rocco wailed, "*Dio mio,* what are we going to do? Who is it?"

"First of all," Albert Pettoruto said in a calm voice as he walked in from the back of the store, "you must all calm down. The Spanish Flu is at our doorstep. Sammy Canasta died this morning. We need to close down, Pa. The city of Boston has ordered that all stores and businesses be closed."

The ravages of this flu hit the world like a ton of bricks. It sickened millions globally. In the United States, 675,000 people died.

In October of 1918, while Lawrence was awaiting the return of its heroes who had served in World War I, instead of planning a homecoming they were in full

117

quarantine. It was a full-blown epidemic.

October 2, a rainy gloomy night. Tony and others gathered their families around them.

"I want you all to eat lots of garlic. Each of you will have two masks that Mrs. Axelrod brought in today. God bless her; she takes a chance every time she enters this city with her wagon. Wash your hands as much as you can. And stay away from the houses that are quarantined. Every business in Lawrence has been ordered to close, and tomorrow all public places will be sanitized. One good thing—we have a bleach factory on Canal Street and they are giving it out free, so use it. Cover your face if you breathe in toxic fumes from the bleach or the smoke. They are burning lots of clothes and blankets. Be careful and stay home."

The two doctors who lived in Lawrence were still in the Army, and so the Federal government set up a tent hospital. On October 9, Major Charles Durant of the U.S. Army medical team announced, "We are woefully undermanned at the tent hospital. We need people who are not afraid of facing this situation. There is a tremendous amount of work to be done, and we have not enough people to do it."

Josephine, Betty Pettoruto, and her sister Rita joined the hundreds of nuns who were the first to volunteer at the tents. By the end of October, the Army and Navy had piled into Lawrence with food and opened kitchens. Children stood in lines to get food for their families.

Joey turned to Pasquale and said, "This is like the old days of the strike again, only with a smell of death."

"Yeah." Pasquale was by his side, his hands shaking. "Mr. Pettoruto came to my house last night and

118

asked my father to help him open the store. He wants to give everything away before it goes bad. Let's go over there and help out."

They ran for dear life, dodging quarantined homes and heading toward Pettoruto's. They passed men, women, and children washing streets, sheets, store fronts—everything in sight. Mrs. Axelrod was on Elm Street; her cart was filled with masks, provisions, and whatever she could get from the government-operated stores in South Lawrence, Andover, Methuen, and North Andover. People from Tower Hill and Prospect Hill were bringing in cooked food.

When the boys got to the market, they took out every bit of stored food and placed it on the curb in front of the store. Barrels of olives, pickled peppers, bakala, and rice were all on the curb for the taking. Betty used the remaining flour and added more semolina with the yeast to make as many loaves of bread as possible. There was no olive oil or meat to put out.

After a few hours, the militia stormed in and ordered the store to close.

"Lorenzo, Albert, Gaetano, Marco—come down!" Mr. Pettoruto called for his sons as the militia came in. Betty was covered with flour, and Mrs. Pettoruto was handing out the bread. The food did not last long. The militia left as quickly as they came, for fear of getting infected.

On October 5, Joey, Louie Scanlon, and Pasquale, with two boys from Phillips Academy in Andover, sprayed and sterilized the trolley cars and boxcars as they stopped at the train station. The nurses at the tent hospital taught the city's women how to care for those who could not get into

119

hospitals. Doctors and nurses came from Pennsylvania to help. They brought some bleach from a factory in California for disinfecting everything.

When the bleach was getting low, Betty went over to Dr. N., an older man from Italy, and told him about the bleach factory on Short Street. She offered to take him there.

On the way, Dr. N., kind, exhausted, and unshaven, looked at her. "What are you doing here, Betty? You would make a smart and wonderful nurse. I will be happy to sponsor you when you're ready."

Her eyes lit up. Secretly she wanted to get out of the town, but instead she said, "Thank you so much, but you see, I have a big family here in Lawrence and could never leave them. I bake bread for my father's store, and my brothers depend on me to go to college."

"Do not waste your life here, Betty. Any time you change your mind, please let me know."

They met Patsy Amante, who gave them as much bleach as they could carry. Amante made frequent trips to the tents, delivering all the bleach that they needed.

Mrs. Shala hid the fact that her son Julio was sick, and he died at home. Some neighbors were angry at her because her family was allowed to come and go as they pleased. Maria and Mrs. Pettoruto carried his body to the church. Corpses lay on the alter, pews, and floor. There were no caskets for the dead.

At the Foenias' house, Tony was exhausted from working in the churches, wrapping the dead in sheets. "Fifty new cases this week. Promise me you will wash your hands as much as you can, and stay away from the houses that are quarantined."

120

Josephine came home one night worn out, her face ashen. "Pasqualino, the nurses and doctors at the tent hospital treat the sickest children. Giovanni, Mario, Patrick, Coleen, the black boy Noel—they all died today. The whole of Lawrence is in mourning. The Red Cross is coming in and taking things over; they're using Ayer Mill as a warehouse and headquarters. The funeral parlors have run out of caskets to bury the dead."

Pasquale's mind was racing; all he could think of were rats running around in the churches among the bodies. He put his arms around his sister, who was sobbing.

"We're running short of blankets. People just don't have enough bedding and clothing to keep them warm." She kept wailing and shaking.

"What do the people look like, and what do you have to do, Josephine?" Pat asked, though he didn't really want to know.

Josephine said, "The treatment is called fomentation. I treated an old person today. First you have to heat up white towels with hot water, and then put the hot towels on the person's back. Dr. Sam said it soothes the nerves. He said it takes all the bad body wastes from the body."

"And they get better?" Pasquale was full of hope.

"No, Pasqualino. Sometimes they die." She hugged him because he looked sick.

She never told him that the bodies had purple spots all over them before they died.

"Where does all the water come from—the river?" Pasquale knew how to change the subject, just like his mother.

"No, the government sent in tanks of water, and

121

portable stoves, and huge pans that we use to boil the water. After the hot water, we pour cold water and put warm blankets over them. It will be a good idea, Pasqualino, if I teach you how to boil water to keep at home for drinking."

"*Dio mio,* Josephine, I hope I never have to undergo that treatment, and that no one in our family does either. You are the bravest woman I know. Do Betty and Rita do the same thing?"

"Yes, they do more than most sometimes, because their mother is trying to keep her family from getting sick. They help out at home. Rita is younger, but she is very smart and quick. Betty is getting to be a good friend of mine. Pat, she asked for you the other day."

"She did? What did she say?"

"Oh, she just asked if you were all right."

Pat thought, *I will marry Betty Pettoruto someday.* "Have you heard anything about Boston, Josie? The *Tribune*'s headlines today said that Boston has an even worse crisis on their hands, and Angelo Rocco is there."

"No, but Dr. Sam goes to Boston on Sunday, and I'll ask him about it. He's a bright man, and maybe he can find Angelo." Josephine looked up to Dr. Sam and respected him for his great wisdom and fearlessness. "I want you to meet him, Pasquale—you'll like him as much as I do."

Pasquale gulped and hugged his sister. "So what's going on with Dominic Nicolosi, the guy from North Andover?" He thought, *This is too much sadness, and I cannot hear anymore. She may die, and I need to help her have some happiness.*

Josephine had gone to New York during the

Exodus. She had left as a shivering child and came back a robust inquiring girl. She was as tall as her mother now, and was Maria's constant companion. At Pasquale's question she opened her large brown eyes and said, "I have seen him several times, and we talked a lot about our families. He was one of the children in the Exodus during the strike. He stayed with stonecutters in Vermont, a wonderful family. He said he just wasn't cut out to work in the quarry, like the men in the family. He's a very kind fellow, Pat, and I think you'll like him." It was the first time in weeks he had seen her face light up with a smile.

"Do you like him? How old is he?" Pat sensed that she more than liked him. "When will I meet him, Jo?"

"Not yet, Pat. He works a lot. He is three years older than me, and before the epidemic he took me to see 'Rebecca of Sunny Book Farms.' He said Rebecca reminds him of me." Josephine was that kind of person, with a cheerful and generous temperament. "Betty Pettoruto was at the movie with her friends."

"Did you tell Mama and Papa you went to the movies with him?"

"Mama knows everything, and I think she might be telling Papa. You know he's about to buy tickets back to Italy. I told her I wanted to stay here with you." Then Josephine changed the subject: "Anyway, Dominic lives with his parents and eight brothers and sisters in their own house on the Shawsheen River in North Andover. I haven't met them yet. He hopes to build a house someday on the river, because he loves to hunt and fish."

"North Andover, Josephine—that's so far away. How does he get to Lawrence? And you saw Betty there, at the movies?"

123

She nodded and went to bed. She had grown thin again during the epidemic, and he worried about her.

In the middle of October, Josephine woke Pasquale up. "Pasqualino, the flu is getting better! There were no new cases tonight."

Suddenly she began sobbing, and all Pasquale could do was try to stay calm. "Let's go out on Elm Street and celebrate," he suggested.

Out into the deserted street they ran, and on to the Merrimack River. Brother and sister sat on the bank, giving thanks that they had survived one of the worst epidemics in the world. On the way home, they went into the Holy Rosary Church to pray.

The tent hospital was closed in late October, and all the medical workers left Lawrence. But the city was never the same. Seventy-five thousand people had died in two months.

CHAPTER 7 – ON NOVEMBER 27 – THE BELLS RANG AGAIN

Mrs. Pettoruto seemed happy again. The groceria was full of food piled on the shelves, and people were happy to be alive. Today, there was something different in the air as she was talking to Mrs. Rocco. "Albert is home from college, Guy has a New York girlfriend named Rose, and Larry has a Polish girlfriend named Nella. We miss my husband, but we know he is in a better place." Mrs. Pettoruto nibbled on the almonds she kept in her pocket.

"What better place to be in, proud as a peacock, Lucia, than in heaven looking down at your fine upstanding children? Do you think there will be a wedding in the Pettoruto family?" Mrs. Rocco had played her part so well during the strike, amid all the angry gossip, that now there was no longer any talk of her being a foolish bore.

Suddenly the door opened. Pasquale looked up in surprise when Maria walked into the store. Mrs. Pettoruto recognized her and said at once, "Mrs. Foenia, you have a fine son. He will be a mathematician someday, like Leonardo da Vinci."

Maria blushed with pride. "Thank you, and how are you and your fine family?" She walked over to the stacks of long, crispy loaves of bread that were still hot from the oven, glancing as she did so at Pasqualino, who was waiting on Mrs. Romano.

There was a long silence. Tony came up from the basement, where he was making wine from the grapes that had been delivered that morning.

Mrs. Pettoruto turned to address both Tony and Maria. "I would like you and your family to be with us on

125

the next holiday. Rita and Betty are the only ones home. It will be a Sunday, and we will arrange it soon. Is that fine with you, Maria?" She handed Maria a box of Perugia candy. "For your family." Then Mrs. Pettoruto went on piling tomatoes into a bin next to the potatoes.
***

Larry and Nella took Pasquale, Rita, Betty, and Joey to a concert in Boston the next Friday. All the way to the concert everyone joined in singing, telling jokes, and laughing. Pasquale noticed how different Nella was from the girls on Elm Street. She sang, told jokes, had red hair, and was a lot of fun. Her favorite saying was "Do you think the rain will hurt the rhubarb?" But when Betty laughed, he remembered that someday he would marry her.

People were coming and going back to the old country, and the talk around town was that a war was coming. The mills were operating at full steam, receiving every day more orders for khaki wool for uniforms. People were back at work, but something was wrong. The machines were speeding up.

Back home on Common Street things started up again. Maria hurried up the stairs, out of breath. "There were no checks for us today. The women had a meeting and are worried. Something bad is going on, Tony."

Tony guffawed, waving his finger and shouting. "What are you doing, Maria? The strike is over. Why did you have a meeting? Was that *strosha* Elizabeth Gurley Flynn at the meeting?"

They always seemed to talk this way in the kitchen. Pasquale rolled his eyes, while Josephine just shook her head. They headed for their bedroom rather than go outdoors. Lately Josephine had been hanging around Maria

126

in a protective way.

"Mama is not one to hold things back," Pasquale whispered to Josephine.

"Papa is too controlling," she answered.

My sister thinks she is quite a big-shot, Pasquale thought, *since she came back from New York.*

"Pat, can you keep a secret?" Before he could answer, Josephine blurted out, "Dominic Nicolosi asked me to go to a movie."

All of a sudden they heard their parents' voices. They went back into the kitchen to make sure they were not hitting each other.

Maria was on a tirade. "Elizabeth Gurley Flynn is not a *strosha* like that one who sits by her window all day! You know who I mean. If it were not for the Flynn woman, Joe Caruso, Giovannitti, and Ettor would be still rotting in jail. 'That woman! that woman!'" She was out of breath again; her face was scarlet. "*Caro mio,* she raised more money than anyone else for our soup kitchens during the strike. She was the one who arranged to have all the children taken out of town. The children came back healthy—look at Josephine, the picture of health. She wants to go to college someday, and Mrs. Grillo from New York will pay for her tuition. Tony," she continued, "do not be like all the newspapers and lazy men who call Elizabeth Gurley Flynn the Rebel Girl. She is a precious woman, Tony, and brings pride and joy to us."

Before she could go on, Toney raised his fist, like Flynn did in her speeches, and said, "She is a socialist, and I heard today she is a communist. I will not allow you to be in her presence! *Capisci?* Maria, *capisci?*"

Pasquale whispered to Josephine, "His face is as red

as a ripe tomato." He heard Maria whisper, "No, *caro, never.*"

In support, Josephine went over to Maria and hugged her. In a child-like voice she said, "Mama, I liked Miss Flynn. At the party she gave for the children of the exodus at Chablis Hall, she talked to me. She said a girl like me should go to school and wait to get married. She said I could be a doctor if I worked hard—a doctor, Mama, just like Dr. DeCesare. Even Betty Pettoruto talked to her. Did you know they have the same blue eyes?"

Pasquale thought his father made no sense. Like many other men from Italy, he was very old-fashioned in many ways.

Later he went into Josephine's room. "How is that Dominic Nicolosi?"

"I think he likes me, Pasqualino. He is a hard worker. He told me that sometimes he gets in the boxcars on the train and rides in them. Then sometimes he walks, and it takes a long time. I hope to see him next week. But please, please keep it a secret. Only Mama knows." She got closer to him. "Pasqualino, Papa is like an Italian immigrant bird, who must migrate back to Italy. Sometimes he reminds me of a soul in purgatory."

"Josephine, what are you talking about? We are better than most people here. It certainly is no purgatory."

"Pasquale, you are a fine son, but please be patient with Papa. I love you so much."

Pasquale reminded her about the parade on the week end. Nothing would ever match the parade that Mayor Scanlon had sponsored with banners covering Lawrence: *God and Country*, and *The Stars and Stripes Forever*. The strike and the Spanish Flu were both over. In

128

fact, however, the parade was more political than anyone understood or realized. Louie Scanlon wanted his voters back.

On Columbus Day, every building and shop in Lawrence was covered with American flags. The mills were cloaked with red, white, and blue banners. Mayor Scanlon ordered thirty-thousand flags and flag pins. Mr. Pettoruto cut out the Pledge of Allegiance from the newspaper and pinned it on the wall in his store. The mill-workers forgot about everything that had gone on during the strike and were happy, singing and carrying the flags and wearing the pins. Mrs. Rocco and other women representing every nationality came dressed in Statue of Liberty costumes—Angelo had gotten the costumes from the Boston Costume Factory. Mrs. Kiernan whipped up pioneer dresses for herself and Maria.

Father O'Reilly, who had stretched the banner across Essex Street, said he hoped the I.W.W. and their band of pirates would get out of Lawrence and that all the anarchists should be expelled and driven out of Massachusetts, or they would get what was coming to them.

The next night Pasquale and Louie were at the Broadway, watching *Uncle Tom's Cabin*. Topsy reminded Pasquale of Betty—brave and adventurous.

Louis poked Pasquale and whispered, "Be on Essex Street at nine o'clock sharp tomorrow morning. Be careful, though, because if anyone shows up from the Industrial Workers, they're going to be run out of town."

During the intermission Pasquale leaned over to Louie. "Why throw the I.W. workers out? Those guys are trying to help free Ettor, Giovannitti, and Caruso, who are

129

in jail for a crime they didn't commit. You know they didn't kill Anna LoPizzo—a cop killed her. They were miles away from the strike that day. The cops have been brutal to the Italians, Louie, and now this craziness is keeping innocent men in jail too long."

"How do you know they're not guilty, Pat? Anyway, the cops will never let one of their own be convicted. They're all Irish, and you know there's no love lost between them and the Italians."

Pasquale murmured, "Ettor and Giovannitti have been in jail since January, and the trial starts this week. I know all about it, Louie, because Albert Pettoruto wants to be a lawyer. He goes to trials whenever he can, with Rocco."

Pasquale and Louie thought very differently. Pasquale was feeling sad, and Topsy in the movie now reminded him of his mother. He turned to Louie. "Please ask your father to help get them out of jail. They are innocent."

But Louie ignored his request, and Pasquale didn't want to lose a friend. That week he added Giovannitti and Caruso to his list of names. He had written Ettor's name on the list when he first came to Lawrence. He said to himself, "What good would it do? Someday they will leave Lawrence if they get out of jail, just like the rest of the guys."

At Pettoruto's, the word was out. Since the parade, the outsiders were lying low and conducting their speeches and meetings secretly. While Mrs. Pettoruto was cutting up the pork for her famous sausage, Mrs. Rocco walked in. "Lucy," she whispered. "Did you know that a hit man was hired by those scoundrels to knock off Hayward?"

130

Mrs. Pettoruto did know, yet she acted surprised. Without missing a sausage, she said, "My son was talking to Judge Bacigalupo last night when he came in for some sausage. Seven martyrs were sentenced to death in Haymarket Square in Chicago many years ago. Albert found out in his law books that that incident is going to set the precedent for the trial of Ettor and Giovannitti in Boston."

Mrs. Rocco was in one of her *can you top this* moods. "Lucy, those two are smart, but let's face it, all of Lawrence is really upset over one of our own, Joe Caruso. The man is a saint, and evidently he went to one I.W.W. meeting and didn't know what was going on. My son Angelo said the mayor is out to get any I.W.W. members still in town." Mrs. Rocco was screeching now. "On October 19, Jonás Smolskaski, a Lithuanian man who lived in The Plains, went into a saloon, and someone pointed him out as an I.W.W. member, and he walked out. He fell and hit his head on a rock. It was a very suspicious incident. Rumors say that an Irish gang that followed him."

Mrs. Pettoruto gave her some sausage, but she was happy to see Mrs. Rocco leave the grocery store.

At the last minute she popped back in. "Maria was at the funeral and at dinner, and I saw her sniffling. Thank God Bill Haywood was there—he helped everyone get to the cemetery. And all the while the trial of Ettor, Giovannitti, and Caruso is going on in Boston." Then she strutted out, in her old way as the town gossip.
***

Maria and a group of women led by Elizabeth Gurley Flynn drove to Boston to picket the courtrooms when the trial was in its last day.

On the way Miss Flynn gave a lecture. "Listen to me!" She tooted the horn. "When we get to the courthouse, do not say a word. I know the barrister who allows people in. He is a friend of Bill. Three of us will be allowed in, and the rest of you, just roll your eyes and fold your hands as if you were praying."

Annie Basile, dressed in black, looked over at Maria and said, "Okay. Maria, you will be one of the ones who go in, and make sure we get the whole story."

Maria knew what had been going on from Tony, who listened to Albert when he was in the store. "Money was raised by some of the leaders of the strike for some of the best lawyers in Massachusetts, so we must listen to them. These innocent men are up for murder and could be in jail for life, or even executed!"

It turned out that seven women from Lawrence were allowed into the courtroom.

That night Mrs. Kiernan, her son, and the Foenia family all waited for the news. Maria began her story in a soft voice. Pasquale listened with concentrated devotion. Tony was sitting with them.

"Ettor took the stand and talked for over two hours. But the best one was Giovannitti. All of us sat and cried—I could not help it." Her eyes glassed over as she went on. "The three of them were in iron cages." Everyone in the kitchen felt a rush of emotion. "Giovannitti never flinched, and through the iron bars he looked around, and such silence—you could not hear a pin drop." Maria waited and then read from a newspaper article. "'Do you gentlemen believe for one single moment that we ever preached violence? A man like me, as I stand with my naked heart before you, do you believe I could kill a human being?

132

Gentlemen, if you think that there has ever been a spark of malice in my heart, that I ever said others should break heads and prowl around and look for blood, then send me to the chair, because it is right and just."

Then Maria said, "Guess what he did? He turned to Caruso, who was sitting next to him, and he begged the jury to consider poor Mr. Caruso and his wife and family. In a pleading voice he told the jury that Mr. Caruso should be home having dinner with his family. Do you understand—Mr. Caruso does not understand English, and the people in the jury and the journalists started to cry." Maria lowered her head as if in prayer and waited before she went on. "The man is a poet, one of the greatest of our times. 'I am twenty-nine years old,' he said. 'I have a woman who loves me, and I love her. I have a mother and father who are waiting for me in Italy. I have an ideal that is dearer to me than can be experienced or understood. And life has so many allurements, and it is so nice and bright and so wonderful, that I feel the passion of living in my heart.'"

Mrs. Kiernan said, "He is a hero, that man, and all he wanted to do was help the workers. I love that he is a poet. I will go to the library and ask them for a book of his poems. Did you know he is writing a book while he is in jail?"

Just then there was a knock at the door. Elizabeth Gurley Flynn walked in, waving a paper in her hand. Tony was white with rage, but Maria knew he would never blow up at a guest in his own home.

Everyone turned to listen as Miss Flynn told them that her friend, a journalist, was going to publish word for word what had gone on in the courtroom. He had given her

133

a copy to edit. "It will be in the *Tribune* tomorrow."

Maria chimed in while Mrs. Kiernan put on water for tea: "I told them the first part, Elizabeth, but please continue." Maria was in charge in her own home.

There was a long pause. *The woman is best with an audience,* Tony thought as she read from her notes.

She looked at everyone, and they were mesmerized by her beauty. "Never forget what I will read to you, word for word," she said, and read what Giovannitti had said in court. "'Set me free, and I promise you that the first strike that breaks again in this Commonwealth, or any other place in America, where the work and the intelligence of Joseph J. Ettor and Arturo Giovannitti will be needed and necessary, there we shall go again, regardless of any fear and of any threat. We shall return again to our humble efforts, obscure, humble, misunderstood soldiers of this mighty army of the working class of the world, which, out of the shadows and darkness of the past, is striving towards the destined goal, which is the emancipation of human kind, which is the establishment of love and brotherhood and justice for every man and every woman in this earth. And, if we are convicted and condemned, then tomorrow we shall go forth from your presence, where history shall give us the last word to us. Whichever way you judge, men of the jury, I thank you.'"

Tony stomped out of the house, growling, "Every time has it martyrs."

There was much chatter and tea and wine-drinking before everyone left for the night. Pasquale went to his room and wrote in his book. He would go to the library to find out what *martyr* meant.

The next morning, Pasquale joined a group from

134

Lawrence in Pettoruto's van-wagon and went to the courthouse in Boston to await the verdict. A peaceful crowd filled the block. Elizabeth Flynn passed out a poem that Giovannitti had written called "The Walker" and disappeared into the assembly. Pasquale kept his autographed copy, written in English and Italian.

One by one, each wearing a red rose in his lapel, Caruso, then Ettor, and then Giovannitti were released from their cages. They walked through the huge court doors with Elizabeth Gurley Flynn behind them. The three of them had been found NOT GUILTY.

The crowd sang and clapped, hugging one another while singing "La Marseillaise."

> *God of mercy and justice*
> *To arm, to arm, be brave!*
> *The avenging sword unsheathes*
> *March on, march on...*

On Thanksgiving Day, November 25, 1912, at 7:00 A.M., the bells of Lawrence rang, and again they rang in the evening. Groups gathered everywhere, singing "America The Beautiful" and the "Star Spangled Banner." Pasquale and hundreds of others who commemorated Thanksgiving that year also celebrated the fact that Ettor, Giovannitti, and Caruso were free, and that the strike was over.

Pat passed the church on the march and thanked God. *God bless Lawrence,* he said to himself.

Again, and again, insight is dramatized by showing the conflict between what is ordinarily seen, ordinarily understood and what is now experienced as real. Cracking the shell of the world is finding that the shell of the world is cracking under you. The unrealizable ideal is to write as if the earth opened and spoke.

In the Western Night
— Frank Bidart

CHAPTER 8 – LIFE AFTER A STRIKE – PAYBACK

"One of the worst winters since the strike, Pasqualino," Mr. Pettoruto said, scraping off the store windows. "We appreciate the coal you brought us last week. Fuel is scarce here in Lawrence these days. How do you manage to get such good coal?"

Spreading sawdust on the clean floor, Pasquale looked up. These days he was trying to impress the Pettorutos one by one. "I have been going to the railroad yard to collect the coal that falls off the trains, and sometimes, since I know the guys on the trains now, they drop some off just for me. The Cross-Coal Company is across the street from the rails where the trains stop. I pick up the coal that falls in between the tracks as they dump the coal in the bins. That is the best coal. I shovel snow these days too, Mr. Pettoruto, if you need me."

"Don't you go to school, Pasqualino?"

"Oh, yes, I go to the train station early in the morning and then again after school." Pat crossed two fingers behind his back and thought, *It's only a lie for a short time—I will go back to school this week.*

136

As he had promised himself, Pasquale did go back to school. Joey was still there.

"Is it just me?" Pasquale asked Joey at recess, "or is this Miss Finch worse than Miss McSweeney? Joey, I am going to quit." They were climbing a snow mountain to decide who would be King of the Mountain. The snow was hard-packed and resembled marble.

Joey did not answer. From the top, he looked down at Pasquale and declared himself King. "Listen, Pat, the woman has a heart of stone, but I figure it is the best way to get through this winter. You can do it—you're a smart kid. Besides, there's not much doing now that the strike is over. My hours were cut, so we have less money to do things. How about getting me into one of the movie houses where your friend Louie Scanlon works?"

Pat kept his promise.

***

Wood gave orders for the machinery in the mills to speed up.

"We are very confused," Mrs. Kiernan said. She was having coffee with Maria in her kitchen. "The mill owners never replaced the machinery, and yet they have ordered the machines to speed up."

"That is not all, Bridget. The foremen are singling out those of us who were in the strike and shouting slurs if we do not produce more every day. Tony has been very quiet lately about going back to Teano, and I am worried that he is up to something."

"Oh, Maria, you cannot go back to Italy now. I will miss you so much."

Mrs. Kiernan was not an emotional woman, but they hugged each other. Still, Maria did not say she would

137

not go back to Italy.

"If you do go back," said Mrs. Kiernan, "I must have the recipe for your *zuppa inglese*."

People who did not go back to their countries had a ray of hope: Broadway and Essex Street. On Essex Street there was a fashion show every Tuesday night. In spite of the need to conserve energy, the merchants lit up their windows. The men gravitated to Kap's Men's Store, where they could always find something to wear to church. Broadway was like New York, with bright lights, popcorn smells, candy, and peddlers selling their wares. People there could act cheerful. Vaudeville Night was held every week at the Broadway Theater.

Pasquale's dream was to sing on Vaudeville Night. Tommy Catalano, Louie's best friend, operated the lights, sound, and projectors. Pat's key to his kingdom was a place to practice singing. Pasquale paid Louie back by cleaning up twice a week.

Whenever he visited Don Pietro they sang Italian songs together. "A voice like Enrico Caruso," he told Pat after one session. Don Pietro played the violin. He had been burned when the Pemberton Mill burned down, and he lived with his daughter, Angelica, in a four-room apartment that had been converted from a store. In spite of being a sparsely furnished home, it was colorful, with a washing machine and lots of appliances. Don Pietro had played at La Scala in Milan before coming to Lawrence. In winter, Pasquale always brought coal to their apartment, and he visited once a week for his singing lessons.

Angelica, Don Pietro's daughter, had been left with a neighbor when her father and mother went back to Italy. But when her mother died, Don Pietro returned to

138

Lawrence. She was his sole support and was now twenty years old. "You are a picture of the Mona Lisa," he told her each morning. She had flaming red hair, gray eyes, and a complexion as smooth as mozzarella. Men in Lawrence called her "La Scala," and everyone knew who she was. She was part of Lawrence and The Plains family. During the day, she worked in the spinning room at the Wood Mill. Whenever she walked onto the third floor, as proud as a peacock, women under their breaths would whisper to each other, "*Putana*" (prostitute).

During the Bread and Roses strike, Angela hid Pat under her father's bed when the police were looking for "those little Wop bastards." Like many others, she called him Pat.

It was a warm Sunday, and Pat was visiting Don Pietro, as he did often, just to chat and sing Italian songs. Before tinkling the tiny bell, he picked up a bowl of pasta from the stoop that Mrs. Rocco left there once a week. The door was never locked.

"Who is there?"

"Good morning, Don Pietro, it is me."

"Ah, Pasqualino." He was fully dressed and sitting in his stuffed green chair. His eyes were bloodshot and half closed. "I could feel your footsteps. Come closer. Stay a while—my Angelica is at church and will be home soon."

The touch of intimacy between the two, a ninety-year-old blind man and a young boy, was sweet and beautiful.

"How are you, my boy?"

"I am fine, Mr. Pietro. Mrs. Rocco left pasta, and my mother made you some fava-bean soup and sent some grapes and an apple." Pat put the food on the table, washed

139

the grapes, and brought them to Don Pietro.

"I am waiting to go back to Viggiano. Angelica says it will be soon." Pietro's face showed contentment as he spoke. "Have I told you about my beautiful city?" His old voice, usually cracked, was now mellow and happy.

Pasquale had heard the story many times, but he always listened because each time the story was different, and usually it was about music.

"You know, some day I will play at La Scala again, Pasquale. I have my violin under the bed." He laughed, and Pasquale sensed his yearning and took his hands in his. "If you only knew how beautiful it is there, Pasquale. Flowers are everywhere, and in the evening the whole city sits and sings outside their white-washed homes." He reached inside the seam of his green chair and pulled out a deck of cards. "How about playing a game of Brisco before singing today?"

The homemade cards were large enough for him to see, and after two games the violin came out. Together they formed a pair that brought happiness to the home. Today they sang a Neapolitan love song.

A tingling bell announced Angelica.

Angelica, her voice like a bird's, flitted past them into her bedroom. With her door open, she undressed. Her flowing red hair reached down to her waist. She was looking in the mirror, and Pasquale turned his head so as not to see her naked.

She put on a bright yellow robe and came out of her room, touched the top of his head, and said, "Patsy, thank you for delivering the coal and for taking good care of Papa." She handed him five dollars.

The washing machine was humming and shaking.

140

Two neighbors walked in with bags of laundry. Pasquale left the five dollars on the old man's table and bid them good-bye.

***

Before going to work, several of the women in The Plains would go over and use Angelica's machine and talk to her father. Some brought cooked food. In return, the women would take turns hanging out Angelica's sheets and ironing them. They gossiped about her whenever they got together.

This Monday, when Angelica arrived at her spinning machine at the mill, Mrs. Cleary and Mrs. Malico, sisters-in-law, ran onto the floor screaming, "*Putana, Putana!*" All the chitchat stopped, and Julio, the Super, ran into the bathroom and locked the door. The echoes of their name-calling carried throughout the floor. Then someone turned on the spinning machines, and the two women spat at her and walked out.

For three nights, Mrs. Cleary and Mrs. Malico, disguised as men, followed Julio Malico to Angelica's front door. They watched him leave, and on the third night of their sting, they knocked on the door. "Julio? Julio? Come out, we know you are in there!" The neighborhood stood quiet as their voices echoed through the alleys. No one came out, and the women tried to smash the door in and failed. Those same women went to Angelica's apartment every day and used her washing machine and talked to her father.

On a balmy night in July, a full moon lit up The Plains. Three women in disguise knocked on Angelica's door to coax her out of her house. Her father was fast asleep. She cracked the door and then tried to bang it shut,

141

but they were stronger than she was. Angelica bolted past them, and they chased her into the alley between Elm and Oak Streets.

The men playing craps in the alley scampered away and disappeared. Pasquale and Joey raced down the nearest cellar stairs, where they could be out of the way.

"It looks like the battle-ax," Joey whispered.

"Who is that fat woman?" Pasquale crawled up the steps.

Joey was not moving. He mumbled, "She is not from The Plains. She speaks perfect English. Someone who looks like a man."

The fat woman cut off Angela's red hair, walked up to a trash barrel, and flung it in.

They held Angelica down. "Help me! Please help me!" Angelica's cry rang through The Plains as loud as the whistles.

A window closed. Pasquale climbed one step further, and the English-speaking woman screamed, "Now you won't be fucking my husband again!" She struck Angelica's legs with a huge club.

Pasquale crawled all the way up the stairs and saw the attackers flee. Joey ran home.

"*Aiuto mi! Aiuto mi!*" (Help me!)

The dark alley was illuminated by the moon. Angelica looked up, dazed. "Pasquale, help me. I think my legs are broken."

He tried to lift her up. "Hold onto me and try to stand." She fell forward. "Please, Angelica, stay still. I hear Mr. Pettoruto closing his store." He bolted over. "Help, Mr. Pettorutto! Angelica's legs are broken."

142

She was sobbing in pain.

"Don't hold her up. Go over and get the pushcart from the front of the store, and then get Mrs. Pettoruto."

Mrs. Pettoruto was putting the meat in the icebox and cried out, "*Dio mio!*"

They pushed Angelica in the wooden cart through the streets. Not a sound rang through the neighborhood except her whimpering and crying. When they got to her home, her father was fast asleep and snoring.

Mrs. Pettoruto never left her side until the next morning, when she called out to Patrolman O'Malley. "Please, Mr. O'Malley, help me get Angelica to the Lawrence General Hospital."

In the end Angelica's father was brought to Bessie Burke, a hospital for the poor. He died in six months. Angelica still lived in her apartment and remained as beautiful as ever. The women in Lawrence still used her washing machine.

***

Pasquale got home late that night, while a glaring moon beamed on a small group wheeling a wailing woman in a pushcart. He heard music coming from a Victrola.

Maria was waiting for him, as she always did before locking the door. His mouth was quivering as he told her what happened. "We tried to get a doctor, Mama, but we could not find one."

Maria started thinking that it was time for them to go back to Italy. At that moment she made one of her decisions.

Some time later, Josephine married Dominic Nicolosi. It was a small wedding. Every weekend, the

143

Nicolosis invited the Foenias over for rabbit or pigeon dinner. Rose, Dominic's sister, played the piano and sang duets with Pasquale, and everyone clapped.

Pasquale wondered if Josephine had gotten married so that she would not have to go back to Italy, if their father ever kept his word.

It was the best of times, it was the worst of times,
it was the age of wisdom, it was the age of foolishness,
it was the epoch of belief, it was the epoch of incredulity.

A Tale of Two Cities
— Charles Dickens

CHAPTER 9 – BIRDS OF PASSAGE

Years passed. Work started to pick up in the mills. The demand for labor in the factories and businesses brought people from other cities, like Lowell and Merrimac, looking for employment. Families were living on top of each other in the tenements. The rooming houses were choked for space. Waves of immigrants were becoming Americanized. The immigrant children were exposed to a different culture.

During this time, Lawrence was trying to recapture the time of its "Gilded Age." Leonard Bernstein was born, the speed limit was six miles an hour, electric cars finally got equipped with a stove in each car, and the Kimball Brothers and Segal manufacturing companies sold shoes all over the U.S. and Cuba. Pettoruto's Groceria sold Cuban cigars. Betty drove their new truck. Children who had once earned money shoveling snow, putting up vegetables, and hawking news were now adults who opened their own businesses: Sullivan's furniture store, Durso's Chicken Store, a five-and-ten. Automobiles and trucks were in demand. For men it meant working outside the city. Salisbury Beach was more accessible—a trolley-ride away for fifty cents.

Yet there was a silence over the city, like the silence

145

before a hurricane.

The first hints of decay came when the mills did not replace their equipment. The Atlantic Mill moved to South Carolina, and there was talk of the other mills moving out of Lawrence to the South too, where wages were cheaper.

On a weekend in May, Maria cooked lasagna. She was wearing her beautiful blue dress that she wore to church. It was Tony's birthday. She had invited everyone from the tenement for a surprise birthday cake. "The Pettoruto are coming," she casually mentioned to Pasquale.

Pasquale had no hint of what was to come; he went into his room to change his shirt.

Suddenly the tenement was echoing. Mrs. Spinelli was screaming at Constanza at the top of her lungs. Pasquale thought, *It is becoming a weekly thing with Mrs. Spinelli.*

"You will speak Italiana and no Americana, Constanza. *Capisci?*" The Spinellis were at it again.

"No, Mama! I do not understand. Do you think I want to be called a *dago* and have people making fun of me for my escarole sandwiches? I want to learn everything and talk English, so I can do all the interpreting for you. Why do you deny me this? And from now on, my name is Connie. *Capisci,* Mama? Connie!"

Mrs. Spinelli answered, "This is what you learn in America, to disrespect your Mama?"

Pasquale thought he heard the slap.

That night, while celebrating Tony's birthday, Pasquale learned he would be going back to Italy. They were to be birds of passage. "The Spinellis will be going with us," Tony said, pouring out wine for the celebration. Pasquale had his own beaker.

146

The lasagna got cold, and the huge cake had five candles waiting to be lit.

Maria did not respond in any way; she just kept on setting the table. Pasquale told himself that she must have known something. He stood up, and Maria noticed that he was almost as tall as his father.

"I am not coming with you, Papa. I will stay here with Josephine and Dominic. You cannot drag me with you. I will run away." He turned to Maria. "Mama, say something."

Maria said nothing.

"The tickets are bought." Tony, all of a sudden the boss in the family, went over and stood by Maria. "*Che e la parola finale.*" (This is the final word.)

Pasquale went to his room.

People arrived, and the candles were blown out. Within five minutes there were congratulations and pats on the back. The going-away party was in full swing. Everyone was happy except Pasquale.

Betty did not come with her parents. Pasquale never had a chance to say good-bye to her.

***

After a week of excitement, packing, and saying good-bye to their neighbors, the two families piled into the Pettoruto van. Larry Pettoruto drove them to New York.

As they boarded the *Vespucius*, Pasquale turned to Connie. "This is the saddest day of my life. He took her hand. "Let's stay together." Then he declared, "I am coming back."

Connie, her eyes watery and red, stopped on the gangway and turned to him. "I will never get back. For me, a girl—I will be stuck in Italy until I get married."

147

"Do not give up, Connie." The two of them clasped their baby fingers together in a promise to stick with each other until they were able to get back to Lawrence.

They would enter a world as foreign to them as the worlds that countless other children of immigrants have endured. As they pushed through the crowd of passengers, Connie started chattering: "Pasquale, I counted the questions the guy asked us. Twenty in all. The guy was from Teano, and he said they are used to keeping track of returning emigrants from everywhere."

Pasquale answered, "Sometimes you're too friendly with people, Connie."

They ignored their parents, who were shouting to them, "Stay together!"

On the gangway, a man and a woman dressed in uniforms gave them a red card: "Good for one ration, a horse blanket, a tin cup, a tin spoon, a tin fork, and a tiny tin pan."

"We are passing through the luggage, Pasquale— see if you can find ours." Connie stopped. "Oh, *Dio mio,* Pasquale, I never saw such fine leather suitcases—and the hatboxes, they must have beautiful hats—and look, that suitcase is as large as a car!" Connie's eyes were popping. She never noticed the colorful blankets, baskets, boxes, and shawls filled and tied, chock-full of a life on the other side of the rope fence. A small American flag waved in the wind, tied to an Indian blanket.

They were to be neither in steerage nor in first class. Pasquale, pressing his way through, thought, *It's a barricade that separates two different worlds.*

Connie whined about getting back to her parents. "My father gave the person who sells the tickets an extra hundred dollars, and he promised that we would get a closed compartment. We will not be in steerage, thank God. It will be a sort of superior steerage, near a bathroom, so we'd better find them. Otherwise they'll kill us."

They nosed around, looking for their parents and the room, and came across a Mr. Berio, an olive-oil dealer from California. He was wearing a white linen suit and spoke perfect English. He walked over to Connie.

"No Italian—I speak only English." He stepped closer to her and took her chin in his hands.

Connie brushed her hair back and thought, *I should have put my lipstick on.* He was tall, tanned, and handsome. "Where are you going, sir?"

He let go of her face. "I am going back to Calabria, Italy, to my farm. I will bring back some of my olive trees to California and will produce fine California olive oil, the Italian way." Now he tried to smell Connie. Pasquale saw his long mustache move and his nose pucker.

"What is the Italian way?" Connie fluttered her eyelids like Mary Pickford in the movies.

Pasquale said to himself, *This son of a bitch likes young girls. He is as old as my father.*

The man ignored Pasquale and started talking about olives. "Olives are a fruit. Did you know that, dearest one?" Now he was so close to her that he could touch her body.

"No, what are they used for?" She put her hand on his shoulder.

To break their spell, Pasquale grimaced and stepped between them. "Mr. Pettoruto has barrels of them in the grocery store. Green and black crinkly ones with oil. We sell many of them. Maybe they come from your farm, Mr. Berio."

149

Annoyed, Mr. Berio went on, "Oil comes from olives. There are hundreds of different varieties. Italy started growing them twenty-five hundred years before Christ. They grow on trees, and the trees can grow as high as fifty feet. But to make good olive oil we have to keep the olives small. Olive trees are as beautiful as you, my dear, and have feathery leaves that blow in the wind and cast shadows in the shade."

"Sort of like a silent movie?" Connie was at it again. Pasquale gave her his *stop it* look. "Why can't you grow them in America?"

"Olives need a warm climate, and the winters have to be cold but not freezing. In Italy, my olive grove grows two kinds of blossoms. One has a perfect flower that has beautiful petals, like you, Constanza, and the other does not have any petals. That is called stamina. Male and female elements—that is how they pollinate." His groin swelled. "My olives will be hand-picked in October. The best oil comes pressing the olives within four hours of picking. If you have ever watched wine being made, it is similar. We grind and press the olives, and then pour the oil into vats and age it."

"Will you build an olive farm in America?" Pasquale asked the questions, showing interest now.

"There are some farms in California. I hope to bring some trees back, and I shall call my oil 'Philippa,' after my mother. Now I must go to my cabin." Mr. Berio ran off, and they never saw him again.

"The guy must be in first class. Let's go." Pasquale pulled Connie toward a bulkhead door. "We don't have anywhere to sleep, but we have plenty of time. I want to go down below, Connie, to see what is happening in steerage."

150

"Pasquale, our parents will be looking for us, and I do not want to see what those people are like down there." Connie was whining as Pasquale pulled her forward. She stumbled down the iron stairs into a small opening filled with people.

An older woman noticed her crying. "Are you hungry, *piccolina?*" She took Connie's arm and guided them toward a narrow hall.

Pasquale was holding onto Connie as they passed two levels of iron beds flanking both sides of many narrow rooms. Rows of straw mats were stacked up neatly against another wall. Everywhere he looked, luggage, bags, and baskets of food were piled on top of each other.

They were in line for food with the steerage passengers. They slipped and moved along. Pasquale felt Connie's fear himself.

"I can't eat this awful-looking macaroni. The bread is soft, and the water smells." Connie dropped her plate started heading for the stairs.

"Hold on." Pasquale grabbed her arm. "We will never get through. Eat some bread at least, until I can find a path out of here."

She looked sick and cried out, "My mother is going to kill me!"

Pasquale realized that the place was overcrowded, poorly ventilated, and unsanitary. "Do not worry, Connie, I'll tell her that we got lost, and she'll be glad to see us." Pasquale led her up a spiral staircase, and the air and sunshine revived them.

On deck, they could see Tony waving his arms and calling out, "Constanza, Pasquale!" His voice cut across the deck. It could be heard all the way to Ellis Island. When he reached them, he grabbed Pasquale by his shirt, and for the first time in his life he shook him until he pulled away.

Pasquale's hatred for his father was swallowed in his anger.

When they got to the room, Mrs. Spinelli gave Connie a slap that spun her to the floor. "Americana! Americana!" she yelled. Maria watched motionless.

The room had six bunk beds and a tiny round window that could not be opened. A cross hung on the only wall space.

"Papa, we are six people. This is worse than steerage." Pasquale felt like Connie now, who always managed to let the cat out of the bag.

"This is Paradise, compared to steerage!" Tony was agitated, and Mr. Spinelli hollered out, "And how do you know what steerage is like?"

Pasquale stared at Connie and hoped she would not spill the beans.

Maria came between them. "Where are the bathrooms, Tony?"

Tony opened the door. "There are two bathrooms not far from our room, with a toilet and a sink for washing. I guarantee you the food is better here than in steerage." He walked out onto the deck and left the women to unpack.

Connie and Pasquale took the top beds. Pasquale left early every morning and wandered around the ship.

The first day was beautiful, and the ocean was calm. Pasquale went over to a young man hanging over the rail. "Are you okay?"

Jack was seasick; he looked as yellow as a banana.

152

He told Pasquale that he was going back to Italy to die with his family. "I worked in the coal mines since I came to America, when I was fourteen years old, and now I have consumption or, as some say, black lung." He took a deep breath. "Maybe the Italian air might help me live a little while longer. I want to see the Bay of Naples for the last time." Jack said urgently to Pasquale, "Never work in the coal mines! It is voluntary slavery. It took me six years to send a thousand dollars back home. My family, they are now comfortable, so I will be with them when I die." Jack was twenty-four years old.

Pasquale walked to the end of the ship to clear his mind. He noticed six people sitting in a circle, eating crackers. A young man stood up and motioned him over to share their food.

An older man stood up. "Where are you going, young man? What is your name?"

"My name is Pasquale Foenia, and I am going to Teano, Italy, where my father owns a groceria." He bent over to shake everyone's hand and motioned for them to stay seated.

The spokesperson handed Pasquale a flat cracker. "Why are you going back to Italy? You sound like an American, Pasquale."

"My father insisted that I go back with him. But I will be going back to Lawrence soon." Pasquale changed the subject and told them about the strike. Then he asked, "Where are you going?"

The young man looked like Tony. He said, "My name is Dr. David Steinberg; these people are my uncle and his children. I am taking them back to Ukraine." He reached into his pocket and took out a folded page from

153

The New York Times.

Pasquale stepped closer and stared at the picture. "It's the same poster that was pasted on a storefront in Teano, that my mother told me about. What country was this one posted in, Dr. Steinberg? Why do you carry it with you?"

"The poster was in Odessa, and in hundreds of villages throughout Eastern Europe. In spite of this, the courts have deemed that my family, who came to New York for a better life, must be sent back. I sent for them, and now I want to be assured that they get home safely. I have been told that the people who were responsible for the posters were agents from factories in New York and other cities."

"So what is going to happen to them, Dr. Steinberg?" Pasquale thought that the doctor was the most intelligent man he had ever met.

"I would like to get them back to Odessa, but we are on our way to London, to a center for poor Jews." He took Pasquale aside and said, "Remember this: money is what talks with these people. I have enough to make sure some of it passes hands in London, and I hope we will soon be on our way to Odessa."

Pasquale thought that they would be friends for life, but they saw each other only when the sea was calm and the days were sunny.

The seas started rocking and rolling. Back in their room, Maria and Mrs. Spinelli were sea-sick. Connie and a woman from steerage were taking care of them.

The people in steerage got the worst of it; they stayed in their cots, throwing up. They had nothing to make them feel better.

Tony kept looking for Pasquale. "Where are you always going?"

"Papa, I need to stay on deck and talk to people, so I won't get sick."

"Why do you carry that book with you, Pasqualino? Are you writing a book?"

"I help the stewards sometimes, Papa, and they give me their names, in case I meet them again in Italy one day. Papa, they give me extra water for helping them, to give to Mama and Mrs. Spinelli, so that they'll feel better."

Tony was proud of his son and put his arms around him, saying, "That's my boy."

The truth of the matter was that Pasqualino just wanted to write down names in his notebook. He also wanted to learn all he could about steerage. He was planning to go back to Lawrence on steerage.
***

The ship docked in the Bay of Naples while it was still light. As soon as they got off the ship, the Italian spirit was all around them. Brothers, wives, and children met them with hugs, kisses, wine, and fruit. To Pasquale, Naples did not look much different from Lawrence. As he bid Connie good-bye, he whispered, "I heard from some of the sailors that Naples is the City of Thieves, so be careful, okay?" Connie disappeared into the arms of her relatives.

Life in Italy began with a party on the streets of Caserta, which melts into the town of Teano. Saint Antonio's church bells were ringing as if the Pope had arrived. When the mass ended, the whole village marched out into the streets. The sounds of music from the shoemaker, the café, the ironsmith, and the tailor echoed throughout the village. The churchgoers went to the square

155

and started dancing. The town elders with canes, walkers, and wheelchairs appeared from the hills.

Tony put his arm around Maria. "Show them how you dance the tarantella, my darling." He led her into a dancing circle.

Pasquale watched his mother dance the tarantella with ease and grace. When his father entered the circle, he and Maria flew into each other's arms, and Pasquale whispered to the air, "This is where their love will survive. I can go back to home now."

Teano is a village surrounded by hills. If you stare at it long enough, it looks as if the buildings are climbing the mountains in the distance. Like all the structures in the walled city, the first level needs some means of support. Next to the Foenia groceria there was a shoemaker, a few buildings down there was a barber, and at the end of the cobblestone street there was a tobacco store.

The Foenias' apartment had two floors. White marble covered the floors throughout. Pasquale's room was as large as their whole apartment in Lawrence: there was a bathroom on each floor, with as much hot water as they could use, and a housekeeper arrived every day.

Maria felt overwhelmed, going into her kitchen that was equipped with everything she had missed while in Lawrence. A faint smell of food that the cook had prepared filled the room. Only for a moment did she feel a longing for Lawrence. Then it was over—enough. She thought she heard the faint sound of a harp. She embraced Tony, who was at the window. "My darling, I insist on cooking dinner from now on. This is my kitchen."

The sunshine poured down on the concrete, and the walled city was lit from within.

156

The next morning Tony took his son to the Foenia groceria. He raised his arms and hugged the air. He thought, *The unhappiness I felt in Lawrence was just a dream.* He devoured everything with his eyes and kissed the pristine wooden counter. Behind it were cases filled with different shapes of pasta. A cold box was filled with an assortment of salamis, hams, and cheeses. A sign over an open doorway read "Fresh Ricotta and Mozzarella every day," and beyond was a room filled with huge tin buckets, sieves, and stoves.

Tony turned to Pasquale. "This will be all yours, Pasqualino. Your uncles have grown the business since we left. We will have a good life here; your mother is happy."

Pasquale understood, for the first time, how much his father had needed to come back to his homeland. "Papa, this is where you belong. I will be happy for you and Mama. But tell me, Papa, how much money do you make?"

Tony believed in his heart that his son would remain with him. "Ah, Pasqualino, enough to feed our family and the families of my three brothers, who will be working with me. They will be going to the markets to pick the food, instead of having the vendors deliver their specialties. We pay more to the vendors than for the food."

Paradiso was cutting meat. He was the worrier of the three brothers and chimed in now: "We are tortured by the Black Hand and must be very careful, since they make money from the deliveries. If we start our own delivery system, we will have to pay them."

Tony's eyebrows went up, and his skin turned red. A blue vein popped up over his right eye. "They are scoundrels and robbers! We will not bow to their demands. Mr. Pettoruto and his sons are going to put them all in jail

157

someday in Lawrence, and we shall do the same thing here."

Pasquale's heart beat fast; his fear was like nothing he had felt before. He thought, *My father is valiant.* He had won his position by his ability to be honest and to work hard. Pasquale rejoiced, and a tear dropped onto his new sweater.

Relatives took Pasquale every day to places where he basked in the glory of history. Once, when Maria was with him in Verona, Pasquale asked if she could help him go back to America, since he was unable to say anything to his father.

"Mama, Italy is a huge museum. You belong here. The people, no matter how poor, live in the midst of art and sculpture, beautiful flowers and sweetness—so art is not a big thing for them. Italians live in art's midst, Mama. Mr. Bill Wood, and others who live in Andover, make a big deal about buying a painting or a sculpture for their homes. Why, then, are we so despised in America? I have a mission in America, Mama. I do not know what it is, but I feel it in my soul." He begged her to help him go back to Lawrence.
***

Paradiso began going to Naples to purchase supplies for the groceria. Others in the town started to follow.

One Sunday at sunset, three men, one with a mandolin, another with a flute, and another with an accordion, began playing in the street. Within five minutes, women and girls appeared from everywhere and formed a circle. Pasquale and his family were leaving church and stopped to watch. Hands came from nowhere, and he was pushed into the middle of the circle. The girls began dancing, passing a small Italian flag to each other over their heads, under their legs, round and round until in the end it was tossed to him. The tarantella for young people is for a single boy or girl to dance until, exhausted, he or she falls to the ground. As Pasquale crawled out of the circle, all he could think of was Betty Pettoruto. Pasquale thought, *I know I am here, but my soul is in Lawrence, Massachusetts.* It was Maria's last chance for her to keep her son in Italy.

Pasquale insisted on going via steerage. When he boarded the *Amerigo Vespucci*, he noticed that the men in steerage were wearing shiny black shoes like his. Pasquale realized that he had a mission, and that his plan that might work.

In steerage, among the walls and the people, he felt the space closing in on him; he could not breathe. Greeks, Spaniards, Syrians, Hungarians, and Jews were all chattering and trying to hold onto a spot. He could not understand anyone. Families were packed in like *bakala* (dried cod). He climbed a ladder. On the quarter deck the hatches were about to close. He slid through them like an eel and took a deep breath. He thought to himself, *These people are caged cattle.*

Near the stern, a man dressed in white pants, a white jacket, and a white hat was smoking. "Hey, what is your name, *Rigazzo*?" He looked like Gaetano at Pettoruto's.

Homesickness crawled over him, and Pasquale started to cry. "My name is Pasquale Foenia. I was supposed to have a job in the kitchen, but I cannot find it. Do you know where it is on this ship? What is your name?"

159

The man cocked his head and peered at him. "Enzo is my name. Where is your family?" Enzo got a little closer. Pasquale noticed that he had kind eyes like Mr. Pettoruto.

"They are in Caserta, and I am going back to Lawrence, Massachusetts, in America."

"Why?" he said. "Do you not love your family?"

Pasquale's eyes started watering. "Oh, Mr. Enzo, I love them so, but I want to be American and to be like Mr. Wood, who was a Portuguese immigrant and now owns all the mills in Lawrence."

"What makes you think you are so smart? You want to be an entrepreneur? You are a cry-baby, no? Cry-babies do not get anywhere in America, or on Italian ships. Do you not know that, Pasqualino?"

Pasquale liked him right away. "Are you Italian, Mr. Enzo?"

"Yes, Pasqualino, I was born in Genoa and learned all about ships from my father. Genoa is the largest seaport in the world. My father, like Christopher Columbus, was a navigator of the sea."

"Is that where Christopher Columbus was born?"

"Of course. You live in America and you do not know that? Shame on you!" Pasquale's eyes filled with excitement, and Enzo went over to him. "I have been on the sea for over twenty years, all over the world. I have worked all sorts of jobs, and now I am the head cook here."

Pasquale's eyes teared up. "Please, let me work for you, Mr. Enzo, and I promise you will never be sorry. I cannot go down to that purgatory. I'll sleep on deck."

Enzo's brows furrowed. "I spent five years in New

160

York on Mulberry Street. When I arrived at Ellis Island, the consul said to me, 'For you a shovel or a brush, and you will survive.' So, Pasquale, do you want to wash pans, scrub floors, boil food, and survive this journey to America?"

"You can count on me."

The response took Enzo by surprise, and he thought, *A fine boy.* He went on, "In New York I could not speak good English and became a boot-black. I shined the shoes of the richest men in New York. In Italy, I was a first-class shoe-maker. So I went from shoe-designer to boot-black. I shared a room with an organ-grinder, a barber, and a cook. The only thing we had in common was our Italian ancestry. It was the life, but I saw and heard many things as a boot-black. To those men who live in high places in New York, we Italians are lower than the poor blacks who live in the South. Giulio, the organ-grinder, told me that one man asked him if he was the father of the monkey, and the barber told me he wanted to cut a banker's throat when he said, 'You speaka the English, boy.' After a while, I learned English pretty good. The stockbrokers did not know that I understood them and talked a lot about stocks. This guy, whose name I will never forget, Theodore, said to his companion, 'Lots of dagos coming over these days.' The other guy, called Gerry, said, 'Yeah, for sure they are not going to buy any stock. Keep 'em down polishing shoes.' I gave them the *mal occh* (evil eye)—*capisci?* And I got lucky: I learned to cook from the head chef in the finest restaurant in New York. In that atmosphere, I met the finest and the best of America."

Enzo handed Pasquale a clean white handkerchief from his back pocket. Pasquale wiped away his tears.

"Only if you are not a cry-baby, Pasqualino can you come down to my kitchen."

The sea was calm, and the mist covered the boy and the big-hearted cook like a soft blanket.

The kitchen was massive. Huge pots, tin pans, knives, and wooden spoons hung from the ceiling. Flames from the stoves made the room warm. The sailors cooking the food for the steerage passengers looked haggard. Their white sailors' uniforms were stained with food. In another section the cooks were talking and measuring; the counters were sterile.

Pasquale was calm. He looked straight ahead, and like Rocco he noticed everything.

Enzo brought him to a cot. "This cot is yours. You will sleep next to Stupido."

But it was not time to sleep. Pasquale listened in as he had done at home. Some of the men hadn't gotten off the ship or seen their families for five years. Spiro, the Greek cook, walked over to Pasquale, saying, "Tell us about America, kid."

Pasquale told them about the Bread and Roses Strike and narrated the flu epidemic. He made up so many stories that eventually he believed them too. He got to know the cook's helpers, and he asked questions. They liked him. Some of the cooks did not speak English, yet they got along.

One day a furious storm hit, and Pasquale was worried that he would be sea-sick. The cook almost got cooked himself when a vat of soup boiled over. He scooped up the soup and put it back in the pot. "Keep those pots steady—the soup is almost ready." Then he thundered,

162

"Pasqualino and Stupido, I want you to go down to steerage and bring the food today."

So Stupido, a boy who usually cleaned up in the kitchen and never talked much, and Pasquale picked up the huge vat that held the soup, which was made from food scraps left over from first class. The waves were over fifty feet high. The deck was flooded as they balanced themselves and the vat so as not to waste the food.

The bottom of the ship was worse than anything Pasquale had ever faced in his life. But Stupido was steady. They dropped the soup off and fled back to the kitchen.

"From now on," Enzo ordered, "you did such a good job that you two will be responsible for cooking and delivering the food to the people in steerage."

The next morning was calm. "What is your real name?" Pasquale asked his partner as they made a breakfast of porridge and coffee.

"My name is Santo Gallo."

"Why do you let those guys call you Stupido? I don't think you are stupid; in fact, you are very smart."

"Listen, Pasquale, I just want to survive. I am a stowaway, and Enzo put me to work to pay for my passage. I plan on jumping ship when I get to New York and making my way to Pittsburg, where my brother is living."

"Does he work in the coal mines, Santo?"

"I don't know. *Dio mio,* you ask too many questions, Pasqualino."

They now occupied a corner of the kitchen, where they were allowed to cook. They slipped good stuff meant for the first-class passengers into the evening meals they made. Partners in crime, they become the food mafia for the people in steerage. Pasquale convinced Santo to get

163

good scraps and food from the real cooks, who felt sorry for him and would excuse his stealing.

Once when they were up on deck for some fresh air, a group of sailors from the upper decks strutted over to them and yelled, "Hey, cook-boys, we dare you to jump in the ocean. You jump first, Stupido!"

Pasquale was scared and wet his pants. So as not to embarrass himself, he jumped in. Stupido followed. A small buoy was close, so Pat hung onto it. Stupido was treading water. The sailors put down a small raft and shouted, "Good-bye! We are putting you out to sea, and you can paddle to America!"

People from steerage ganged up on the sailors. Screams echoed over the ship. The people in first class were unaware. Enzo and the Captain arrived, and a rescue took place. The sailors apologized. Everyone in steerage told a different story about it, and everybody had something to talk about.

Pasquale made friends with the Italians in steerage, and when he was not cooking or cleaning, he went to their deck and joined in the singing. His notebooks were filled with Italian songs like *E'La Luna Messa Mari*. Since Pasquale's notebooks were almost full and he did not have more paper, he often memorized the words so that he would be able to sing them to Betty when he got back to Lawrence. Whenever the weather was not so good, the Italian people hugged their children and sang. Their songs echoed all over the ship, right into the Atlantic Ocean: *O Solo Mio, Finichio li Finicula, Timepe Felice.*

One day, when Enzo was in a good mood and the ship echoed with songs, he joined them. Later, he took Pasquale and Stupido aside. "Did you ever hear of

164

Giuseppe Petrosino, a famous police officer in New York?"

Stupido said, "No," walked to the edge of ship, and started looking for flying fish.

Pasquale got closer to Enzo, who was smoking. "How do you know about him, Enzo?"

"Pasquale, it is a sad story. I hope you will remember his name."

Pasquale asked to go to the bathroom and ran to the kitchen. He took out two pieces of sailcloth, pasted them together, and wrote down "Giuseppe Petrosino." He folded the sailcloth notebook and hid it under his cot.

Enzo was annoyed. "Why did you not use the toilet on deck?" When Pasquale shrugged, Enzo rubbed his head, as Angelo had done in Lawrence, and went on. "Mr. Petrosino came to Italy on a mission for the United States government. The rumor on the ship was that he was the descendent of Christopher Columbus, but that is not true."

"Who was he?" Pasquale was curious.

Enzo stomped out his cigarette. "He was the first Italian-American police officer in New York City, the head of the "Italian Branch," hunting down the Black Hand in America—a good friend of President Theodore Roosevelt. The United States government awarded him the Medal of Honor for tracking down over three thousand Italians and other thugs operating in New York. He declared war on the Black Hand. He was born in Padula, in Sicily. But eventually the Black Hand assassinated him. I know this to be true because when his family was aboard ship, bringing his body back to America, I became friendly with them. They were good Sicilians, and I understand that the United States paid Mr. Petrosino a great tribute." Suddenly he added, "Have you heard of Enrico Caruso, Pasquale?"

165

Pasquale nodded, confused. He cocked his head and answered, "Yes, he is an opera singer, and I heard him sing in America."

"Well, Enrico Caruso got a Black Hand letter signed with a hand and dagger, asking him to pay two thousand dollars. He paid the ransom, but then more letters came asking for more money. Petrosino and his Italian officers uncovered the guys, and the scoundrels turned out to be Italian businessmen."

Pat thought, *The Black Hand keeps coming up, and everyone has a different explanation.* He asked, "Who is the Black Hand?"

"I will tell you later, but let me finish my story. You ask too many questions. Petrosino received a message from the mayor of a town in Italy to meet him at the Café Orto in Palermo. Petrosino went there by himself. While he was sitting there, having a glass of wine, he was shot to death by two men. They were never found. The family believes that Italian-American gangsters informed the Sicilians that Petrosino was undercover."

"Enzo," Pasquale said, turning his head to check on Stupido, "was Petrosino an informer?"

"No, Pasqualino, he was a patsy for the United States of America. Never be a patsy for anyone unless you understand why you're doing it."

"But, Enzo, what is a patsy? I do not understand."

"In Italian we call him a *paccii,* a fool, a sucker—you understand. Petrosino was a scapegoat for the Black Hand and for the United States of America. But enough about Petrosino, Pasqualino. Tomorrow, before we reach New York, I will tell you about the Black Hand, okay?"

"Please, Enzo, can you tell me now? I will be so

166

excited when we reach New York."

"You will not stop until I tell you." Enzo was worn out from talking, but he said, "So, now I will tell you."

Pat thought to himself, *I like this man as much as I like Angelo Rocco.*

Enzo looked into the vast open space. "The Black Hand is a secret society of very violent men, *furfanti* (scoundrels), who are well-organized for terror and blackmail. In Italy, they are dreaded because they threaten people of wealth and high position. They are feared and respected only out of that fear. In America, people think they are anarchists, but that is not true. Maybe a few stragglers are, men who are not educated and do not belong to the organizations, but most of these guys pretend to live good lives. They thrive in America because the people think they are from Sicily, but most of them are not. Pasqualino, they are violent men, terrorists, murderers, and they will stop at nothing to make people afraid of them. Never fear them, Pasqualino." He turned to Pasquale. "Before tomorrow, when you disappear into your family, I want to thank you for all your hard work. I probably will never see you again, but set your own compass and follow your dreams."

Before the ship docked in New York, Pasquale went to say good-bye to his friends in steerage and to the guys in the kitchen. Stupido was gone, and he never saw or heard from him again. But Enzo and Stupido were recorded in his notebook, along with *Set Your Own Compass and Follow Your Dreams*. His third book, made of sailcloth, was filled.

*The crowning experience all, for the
homecoming of man, is the wonderful
feeling that, after all he has suffered,
there is nothing he need fear any more—
except his God.*

Man's Search for Meaning
— Victor E. Frankl

CHAPTER 10 – PASQUALE'S WORLD

Josephine and her husband, Dominic, met Pasquale in New York. Josephine beamed her Mona Lisa smile. "Welcome home!" Dominic wrapped his soft arms around both of them.

Pasquale kissed her. "You did the right thing, Josephine," he whispered in her ear. "I thought you married Dominic so you would not have to go back to Italy, but I was wrong."

Once in the car, Dominic said, "How about seeing the sights? I have never been to New York, and I would like to see Mulberry Street, where most of the Italians live."

Pasquale and Josphine agreed, and they made their way to Little Italy. "I can't believe how colorful this place is," Josephine said, opening the window. They chatted about how clean the city was and how much it was like Lawrence.

"Stop the car, Dominic, I think I see someone I know." It turned out not to be Stupido after all, but Pasquale told them the story of the kitchen and steerage. Then, suddenly, Pasquale leaned over to the front seat. "Let's get out of here." This was where the Black Hand survived.

The car sped up like an attacking bull, and when they got to Lawrence they felt safe.

The apartment on Oak Street where the newly married couple lived was bulging with people cheering, singing, and drinking wine. The table was piled high with food. Broccoli rabe with lots roasted garlic, stewed rabbit, a huge platter of spaghetti. Pasquale took the plate that Dominic handed him and dug in. It was a feast to Pasquale's eyes, and he re-filled his plate and walked around the front room. Men were smoking and talking. He stole a glance into the kitchen, where all the women were chatting and filling plates. Betty Pettoruto was not there.

He leaned against a wall, and women asked him about the people back home. The baker Squatrito pushed a plate of cannoli in his face. "Today I baked these special for your homecoming. Do you like vanilla or chocolate? How is your father? I miss him now when I go to Pettoruto's to deliver my pastries. A fine man, your father, a man of honor and a good Italian. Send him my regards."

"Thanks." Pasquale could not remember the man's name and thought, *I will go by the bakery tomorrow, since his name is on the store window.*

Pasquale opened a bag filled with red horns, and everyone left with a token of remembrance from his mother.

Josephine hugged him and showed him to a cot in the living room, where he would sleep. Pasquale dreamed about caskets and rats and men in black suits.

Early the next morning Dominic took him aside. "We are happy to have you with us. Josephine is going to have our first baby soon (a boy, I hope), but don't worry,

169

we will manage. First of all, I want you to go to school and see if you can get a job on weekends. I have a big surprise for everyone. Josephine and I have saved enough money to buy a little place in North Andover on the Shawsheen River, with lots of wildlife. It is close to my family, and Josephine will have lots of help with the baby. We want you to live with us."

"How far is North Andover, Dominic?" Pasquale's heart sank.

"I walk there all the time. The owner has allowed me to hunt on his property for some time now, and I give him lots of rabbits and birds for his family. We will fix up the little place for all of us. We will raise a few chickens, all our own vegetables. You know, I love hunting. That is where I shot the rabbits and squirrels for your Welcome Home. Did you like them? Josephine can make a feast for a hundred people with just rabbits, tomatoes, flour, and water. It will be a happy home. The owner left us a piano, and we will have music."

Pasquale's joy for his sister and her husband's news came out of love and respect, yet he started planning immediately how he would stay in Lawrence.

Winter bore down on them with a blast of snow. The milk bottles on the window-sills had snow cupcakes piled high. Pasquale went to school during the day and picked up coal at night.

On a clean bright day after a huge snowfall, Pasquale and Joey decided to skip school and shovel snow.

"Let's go to the churches—maybe they'll pay more than the storekeepers." Joey handed over a shovel. "How are you doing, pal?"

"Not as good as I want, Joey. I've got to get a job

170

fast. I don't want to work in the mills." The desire for hope and dignity swept over him. "I need to contribute something to my sister, Josephine; she's pregnant. Joey, people can't pay for the coal I collect every morning and night, except for a few cents. Let's go to Essex Street—there are more stores and sidewalks there."

"Pasquale, when you were gone Wood's son died in a car crash and Wood had a stroke. Some of the mills are closing and moving south. You were lucky to get back to America. The government has imposed quotas on the people coming in, and the Italians have been hit hard. Many businesses were hit hard too."

They were running to keep warm, and Pasquale yelled, "I am an American citizen, and they could not keep me out. I would swim across the ocean if I had to."

They got to Essex Street only to find that the stores were closed.

"Priests pay a few cents more—didn't I tell you?"

When they reached the sacristy at St. Mary's church, Joey ran the other way, pulled his hat over his ears, and ran up a snow embankment. "King of the Mountain, Pasquale, and then we will knock on the door." Joey climbed to the top of the pile. Pasquale followed, and then they slid down onto the steps of the priest's home.

Joey tapped the cross-shaped knocker. Mrs. Bacigalupo, the housekeeper, opened the door. The scent from the cooking inside entered Joey's frail body. He opened his mouth as if he could taste the smell. "Can we shovel the paths, Mrs. Bacigalupo?"

Pasquale was impressed that Joey knew the housekeeper. The beautiful marble flooring in the front hall reminded him of his mother and father, and he took a deep

171

breath.

Joey was about to ask for fifty cents when Father O'Reilley came to the door. "You know these boys, Mrs. Bacigalupo?"

His stare frightened Joey. Pasquale stared back, shrugged, and put on a big smile, showing all his teeth.

"Yes, Father, I know them both. They come from good families." She smiled, wiping her hands on her apron, which had a dusting of flour.

Father O'Reilley's eyes raked over them. "When you're finished shoveling the walks and the path that leads to the church, come back, and Mrs. Bacigalupo will make you some hot chocolate." He nodded and disappeared into the house.

Pasquale could taste the hot chocolate already. "Don't ask for the price, Joey—let's just shovel."

They finished shoveling the snow. The kitchen was filled with the smell of chocolate and cookies. Pasquale whispered, "Joey, how come they have so much food and good stuff?"

Joey put his finger to his lips and looked around to make sure Mrs. Bacigalupo was not in sight. "Priests depend on whatever people put in the basket on Sundays. But dimes and nickels add up. It's nice and warm in here."

They finished the hot chocolate and cookies and thanked the housekeeper. Joey and Pasquale felt full of food and full of pride for the dollar bill they'd gotten for shoveling.

"Let's look for another job, Pat. There is a baking company on Mill and Methuen Streets, and we might be able to get some bread or leftover donuts."

They cut through Essex Street and come to a

clearing with a huge brick building that had several garage doors and a large sign that read, "THE MOREHOUSE BAKING COMPANY. SUNLIGHT BAKERY."

"Joey, they shoveled already!" Pasquale climbed to the top of a snow hill. Joey followed.

As they slid down the hill, a side door of the building opened and a robust, red-haired man shook his fist. "Get out of here, you little bastards!"

Joey shouted back, "We came here to shovel your walkways. Do you need any help?"

The guy yelled back, "It's too cold today, go home. Come back tomorrow."

They got two jobs shoveling doorways on Essex Street and then went back to the Morehouse Bakery. Trucks filled the parking lot, and the garage doors were open. Five delivery wagons were stuck in the snow. The same man shouted, "Beat it, kids, and don't come back, or I'll call the cops."

Joey grabbed Pasquale's arm. "Let's get out of here before we get into trouble."

"We didn't do anything, Joey." Pasquale stopped him from running. "I like this place. The smell of bread, the white snow that looks like flour—they remind me of my mother and our house on Oak Street."

Joey and Pasquale had always had the power of communication without words. Sometimes Pasquale thought he knew what Joey was thinking. They punched each other in the shoulder and started running.

"I'm going to come back tomorrow to see if I can get a job."

Pasquale was serious, but Joey cried out, "Are you crazy? There are a bunch of Irishers working there; you

173

will never fit in."

"I need the job, Joey, and besides, I don't want to live in North Andover with my sister. I want to stay in Lawrence. I'm going to try, anyway. Do you want to come, Joey? People always have to eat bread."

"No, Pat, you'll have a better chance by yourself. If you get a job, then you can talk for me." They bounced shoulders, and the snow formed white stars.

Pasquale climbed the stairs to the apartment that night in such deep thought that he ended up on the fourth floor. As he ran down, he heard a small sigh, then a voice that whispered, "Go in peace, Pasquale, and if it is what you truly want, just be yourself. St. Anthony will look after you."

"Okay," he said, and his mind started churning. *Tomorrow is Monday, the trucks will all be out on the road. Maybe if I dress up like Rocco told me and wear the pants that my mother had me save for Sunday mass, someone might let me in. It is a good place to work, and no matter what happens, everyone has to buy bread.*

Josephine and Dominic were busy packing, ready to move to their new home. The apartment, usually tidy, was unrecognizable. Their happiness filled the air. They were laughing and playing with each other. A haze of bliss filled the atmosphere.

After Pasquale had carried their possessions down to the entrance, he asked Dominic if he could borrow a jacket. Dominic did not ask why, and Pasquale went to bed to continue planning how he could land a job at the Morehouse Baking Company.
***

Everyone was at work. Pasquale washed his hair

174

and bathed in a small amount of water. He thought, *January 13, 1916. A day to remember—so, Saint Anthony, do your job.* He put a gold horn in his sock for luck. Dominic's jacket lay on a chair.

Dressed in his Sunday best, he stood in front of the sliding garage doors of the Morehouse Baking Company, wondering how to get in.

Then a side door opened. A tall man wearing a dark suit and tie came out. "What do you want, young man?" Pasquale liked him immediately for calling him a man. He was holding onto his vest. "What do you want, and why did you come here today?" He opened the door wider and stepped back from the icy wind. "What is your name?"

"My name is Pasquale Foenia, and I am looking for a job." Pasquale was trembling.

"I am Mr. Morehouse." A strong wind pushed itself into the building, and he stepped back even further. "Do you go to school?" Mr. Morehouse was now totally in the building, and Pasquale was halfway in.

"I go to school at night and have to work during the day, so I can help support my sister and my mother, who is in Teano, Italy."

"Where is your father?" Mr. Morehouse lowered his head, peering at him.   "My father went back to Italy last year and was murdered because he would not pay ransom to the Black Hand. Now I live with my sister, Josephine, and her family on Oak Street. I want to work to help them. Someday, I will send for my mother. I am strong, Mr. Morehouse, and I need a job." Pasquale's hazel eyes started filling up. He held the tears back and turned pale as he stepped one more foot into the building.

Mr. Morehouse's countenance changed. His eyes

175

grew sad. For a year he had been in a deep depression over the death of his own son. Thoughts flitted quickly through his mind as he ushered Pasquale in. *He could be my son.*

Mr. Morehouse shut the door. Pasquale felt the warmth of the building, and it smelled like home and bread. They dodged a worker dressed in white work-clothes that were covered in flour, getting off an elevator and wheeling a metal cart filled with bread.

Mr. Morehouse nodded and raised his hand, a sign that they would talk later. "Have you eaten today?" he asked.

Pasquale could not believe his ears, and though he was not hungry he said, "My cousin ate all the food my sister left before going to work." He had his fingers crossed behind his back and told himself it was part truth and part lie.

Mr. Morehouse walked over to the bread racks and opened a loaf. The bread was wrapped in white wax paper, and a large red label, BETSY ROSS BREAD, covered the loaf. Unlike Betty Pettoruto's bread, it felt soft and squishy.

Drivers were rolling carts filled with bread, donuts, and black moons toward the delivery trucks. The men tipped their caps in salute when they walk by.

Mr. Morehouse nodded as they walked on. "This is the main garage; our trucks delivering bread to stores and people go out from here with the bread and cakes, every day. When they return, they check in here. The bread that isn't sold is unloaded here and put on the racks."

"Where are they now, Mr. Morehouse?"

"The trucks are out on the road, delivering bread."

"What do they do with the old bread, Mr. Morehouse?"

"We have a store here that sells it. The bread in the store is old, and the pastries are not perfect products, so we cannot sell them to grocery stores."

"Where do you deliver in Lawrence?" Pasquale remembered Angelo Rocco's words: "Always ask questions, and do not be a *bumbalooka*."

"They do not buy much Betsy Ross bread in Lawrence, because the people can come to the store here and buy the not-so-perfect loaves for half price. We deliver to Andover, Methuen, and all over Boston. If the salesmen see a new store, they stop because they always have extra bread."

Pasquale thought, *Wouldn't that be nice, seeing everybody and maybe getting some leftover Betsy Ross bread to bring home.*

"Are you afraid of elevators, Pasquale?" Mr. Morehouse opened sliding doors into a wooden elevator.

"No." Pasquale took a big step inside. "I worked in the Wood Mill before the strike for one week."

"Really? I opened the first bread-line for the strikers, Pasquale. Were you there?"

"Yes, Mr. Morehouse. I helped my mother, who was very active in the strike, and I promised her that I would never work in the mill. I worked for one week and was on the floor the day Carmela Teoli got scalped. I never went back again."

Mr. Morehouse understood something about Pasquale and himself. Both of them had been through much that was serious, too serious for tears. Because he felt this strong emotion, he
decided to have one of the foremen show Pasquale around for the rest of the time. He himself was too close to tears.

Pasquale resembled his dead son. "Want to see more?" he asked.

"Yes, sir." Pasquale followed him and looked up toward the elevator. He thought, *I want to work for him for the rest of my life.*

The room was filled with sacks of flour. "This is the storage room," Mr. Morehouse said, "and it must always be absolutely clean. Bread-making is an art, Pat, and it is important to keep this floor spotless. Here at Betsy Ross, we use spring wheat and soft wheat flour, and yeast as fresh as possible."

"I know about yeast, Mr. Morehouse. My mother and the Pettorutos made Italian bread and pizza dough every day during the strike." He noticed the flour in white sacks, piled on platforms.

What stood out later in Pasquale's memory was that Mr. Morehouse knew everything about his bread company. He also called every person who worked for him by his first name. "Hello, Joe. Hello, Luke. Hello, Mario!" Pasquale thought, *No Stupido here, like there was on the ship.* He felt safer here than any other place in the world.

Mr. Morehouse kept talking as they get off the elevator on the second floor. He called over to a burly, red-haired man. "Jack, please show this young man around, and then, when you are done, come on down to my office."

"So what's your name, laddie?"

Pasquale felt like a midget next to Jack. "Pasquale Foenia," he answered, and he held out his hand for a handshake.

"Just call me Jack, and I'll call you Pat." Jack went right to the point. "The big bins in the racks above the flour

178

sacks hold seventy-five pounds of flour. These mixing bins must always be very clean. This is what happens to the flour, Pat."

They walked over to mixing machines that were swishing and grinding. Two funnels—*as large as a weaving machine,* Pasquale thought—hung above the machines, sifting the flour from the third floor through the funnel. When the flour reached a scale, it was weighed and put into another mixer. Then a faucet poured a certain amount of water into the flour.

"The yeast is here in the big square boxes. Sometimes we use milk or potato water, or both, for the liquid. And we add salt, sugar, and shortening." Jack turned to Pasquale. "How old are you?"

Pat repeated the story he had told to Mr. Morehouse.

"Mr. Morehouse had a son your age who died last year."

Pasquale thought, *No wonder Mr. Morehouse had such a sad face.* He felt sorry and sad and thought about his own father's murder.

A huge chunk of yeast was lowered into the mixer, which started up grinding and swishing. A man dressed in a white uniform put in a thermometer. When the machine reached a certain degree, the noise stopped and the machine spun. Another worker came when the machine stopped spinning. He removed the dough and put it in big tin pans to rise.

Jack signaled to the worker operating the machine. The worker explained to Pasquale, "After the dough rises it is weighed, and then it goes through this machine."

Pasquale noticed that it had a square door. "Where

179

does it go from here?"

Pasquale was showing interest, and Jack smiled and said, "The dough goes down to the donut girls."

"What are donut girls?" Pasquale's eyes lit up into a smile.

"Follow me, young man. I will show you."

The smell of bleach on the stairs accompanied them. The first floor had rooms bigger than the garage. The space was filled with sliding wooden racks that faced doors leading out to the street. Pasquale pointed to them. "What are those racks for, Jack?"

"For the donuts, Pat. Have you ever had one?"

"No, I haven't."

Jack led him to a room filled with cheery voices and laughter, and he thought, *Wow, what a place to work.* The room fell silent as they walked in.

Girls were wrapping cakes and donuts. On one side a man was turning the wheel of a donut machine. As the donuts come out, they landed on a rack to cool. "Give Pat a donut, Louie." The room smelled of sugar and spice as Pasquale devoured the donut. The frying donuts reminded him of Sunday morning and fried dough.

Everything was weighed and then sent to another table, where men were ready with a block of wood with a hole in the center large enough to hold six doughnuts at a time. They put wax paper over the block, and with a quick jerk sent six doughnuts to the girls at the end of the table, who filled the boxes.

Next door to the donut room was the seconds store. Pasquale noticed Mrs. Bacigalupo buying bread.

As they passed through the oven room, Pasquale looked up and said, "You could fit a whole building in

180

here, Jack." Several men were taking loaves of bread out of one oven with a long paddle. The bread-catcher grasped the loaves as they flew out of pan; they were cooled before being forced through a machine that had knives as sharp as Mr. Pettoruto's meat knives. The bread was sliced and put on racks, cooled, and then sent to the wrapping machine. A special belt carried the bread to the boxes, and a man piled the boxes onto the trucks.

The huge clock over the office read 3:30. "Will someone be looking for you, Pasquale?" It was Mr. Morehouse.

"Oh, no, everyone is at work in my house."

Mr. Morehouse opened the door to the office. A sign on the door read "NO HELP WANTED." Pasquale's heart sank. The place was filled with tables and machines and paper, and everyone's head was bent low over their writing. No one looked up.

Mr. Morehouse's office was at the end of the space, and they went in.

"Now, Pat, here is a loaf of Betsy Ross bread and a bag of donuts (not perfect ones) that you can bring home." He led him to the door.

Pasquale's heart started pounding as they shook hands.

Mr. Morehouse looked at Pasquale. "Would you like a job, Pat?"

"Yes, sir, Mr. Morehouse." Pasquale felt faint.

"Come back on Thursday morning, and bring your sister or brother-in-law. We will find something for you. And, Pat," he added, "we will give you work-clothes when you get here, okay? And a white cap."
***

181

Pasquale went to the Holy Rosary Church to give thanks. He said to God, "I think Mr. Morehouse heard my heart sink and my soul quiver." He loved Lawrence so much that it meant everything to him.

Early Thursday morning, Dominic and Pasquale met with Mr. Morehouse and Mr. Smith, the bakery manager. They sat in Mr. Smith's office, and Mr. Smith turned to Dominic. "I hear you have a fine brother here."

They shook hands, and Dominic smiled. "He is my brother-in-law."

Pasquale was holding onto his chair. His eyes began to burn, and he could feel his lip tremble. His feet gripped the oriental carpet in his black Italian leather shoes.

"Mr. Smith has come up with two options, Pasquale. What you think you could handle? One is in the basement, helping Struofolo keep it clean. The other would be in the garage."

Pasquale thought, *Joey told me that Struofolo works catching rats and that there is water everywhere in the basement. Struofolo is the son of Mrs. Stromboli, and he is always sick.* "I would like to work in the garage," Pasquale answered, without a quiver in body. He thought, *Please, God, help me get the garage. I can never work catching rats.*

"I need a man to check in the trucks when they come in and register what goes out and what comes in. Do you think you could do this?"

"Yes, I can," Pasquale answered, so fast that Mr. Smith seemed surprised.

"You will start on Monday morning at 6:00 A.M. You will meet with Jack O'Loughlin, whom you already know."

182

Mr. Smith would now be his employer. Pasquale never asked how much he would get for salary, and Dominic said nothing; he seemed to be in shock. Eventually Mr. Morehouse showed them to the door.

Once they were out of the building, Dominic turned to him and said, "Pasquale, how come you didn't ask how much you are going to get paid?"

"I don't know. I need the job, I like the place, and Dom, I need to pay you and Josephine back for everything you've done for me since I came back from Italy." Pasquale didn't mention his obsession with Lawrence. He put his hand on Dom's shoulder. "Your jacket did it, Dom. Thanks so much."

Pasquale went to Pettoruto's grocerio to tell them that he could work there now only on Saturday and Sundays. He hoped to see Betty. But Mrs. Pettoruto was making Italian sausages in the back room. She stopped the sausage machine to greet him and ask about his parents. "And when will your father come back?" She did not ask for his mother.

Albert came in and went to shake Pat's hand. "Glad to see you back. How was Italy?"

Before he could answer, Mrs. Pettoruto hugged both of them.

"My father was murdered, Mrs. Pettoruto, by the Black Hand."

"*Dio mio*, Pasquale, what happened?" She sobbed uncontrollably.

Pasquale explained the murder and described how his father had died from gangrene in the gash on his head. He held back his tears. "Three men from the Black Hand hit him with a hammer when he tried to stop them from

183

taking cash from the cash register."

"We loved your father, Pasquale. How is your mother?" Mrs. Pettoruto was crying. "We want to help you get her back to Lawrence, Pasquale. Albert will help you; he knows the ropes."

"I am very sorry, Pat." Albert shook his hand, and his two brothers expressed their sympathy too. "Your father was a gentleman of all seasons, and we shall miss him very much, especially since my father died from a severe stroke."

Pat placed a kiss on Mrs. Pettoruto's cheek. "Accept our condolences to you all." He turned to Albert. "Can you help me get a work permit? I just got a new job."

On his way to the grocery store, Pasquale had practiced in his head what he wanted to tell them about his job at the Morehouse Bakery. He wanted desperately to impress them and blurted out now, "I have a job at the Morehouse Baking Company, Mrs. Pettoruto."

Mrs. Pettoruto seemed interested and asked lots of questions. Albert disappeared while they were talking.

"I will soon have enough money to send for my mother and find an apartment in Lawrence. Will you let me know as soon an apartment that you think is good comes up?"

While they were talking, the sausage machine started humming. Mrs. Pettoruto jumped up and went to the counter. Albert was putting the washed sausage casing on the nose of the machine, while also putting pieces of pork into the funnel on top. She did not say anything but kept watching to make sure he was doing it right.

Pasquale thought, *Al is just showing off, like me with the job story.*

184

Then everybody in Lawrence heard Al's scream. Blood was suddenly spurting from his hand like an abstract painting; the blood splattered over the white wall behind the counter. He had been putting the pork into the machine when three of his fingers were caught in the motor with the pork.

Pasquale ran over and shut the machine off. He grabbed a white flour sack and wrapped it around Albert's hand. He had seen one of the cooks do this for a kitchen helper on the ship from Italy, when the helper sliced off his finger.

Gaetano Pettoruto came up from making wine in the cellar. He ran over and held the sack covered in blood tightly.

"Pasquale, do you know where Dr. DeCesare's office is on Oak Street?" Albert was talking, and everyone relaxed a little.

"I pass it on the way to work."

He ran past Elm Street and down Chestnut and knocked on the door of 30 Oak Street.

Mary-Ann, the nurse, let Pasquale in. "Lucky he is not at the hospital, Patsy." She got the doctor's black bag, and the three of them ran to Pettoruto's.

Albert lost his thumb, index finger, and middle finger at the knuckle. He was rushed to Lawrence General, and Mrs. Pettoruto asked Pasquale to stay in the store. Betty had been there all the while.

"You are my hero for saving my brother Albert, Pasquale." When Betty hugged him, he was so embarrassed he bit his lip.

People kept running over to see what happened. Later everyone started talking about whether Albert would

185

be able to go to Dartmouth College. Mrs. Pettoruto remarked, "It is a blessing he is going to college because he could never work in the store. Now," she went on, "it will be up to Lawrence and Gaetano to learn how to cut meat and make sausages. Betty will be in charge of making bread, and young Rita will go to school." Mrs. Pettoruto looked pale and seemed ill.

Marco ran in through the back door. "What happened, Ma?"

Marco had graduated from high school and was planning to be a lawyer. Usually he popped into the store when he was out of money. Everyone called him "Tricky King" because he had gone on a "lost weekend" of dancing and won first prize for staying up all night tripping the light fantastic. He looked like a movie star: six feet tall, thin, with black hair, a thin black mustache, and hazel eyes.

Betty, who was his main source of cash, ran over and hugged him. "Marco, if it had not been for Pasqualino, Albert might have died!" Betty was crying.

Marco shook and hugged Pasquale, who was thinking, *He is so smart, and I should read the books that Betty gives me when he does not need them anymore.*

That night, Pasquale began educating himself. A few days later he returned to night school. Writing names, dates, and reading became his focus in life. Mrs. Pettoruto found a small apartment for him, and he shared it with three other men until he could bring his mother back to Lawrence. In his room, he hid ten filled notebooks packed in an old valise under his bed. Before closing the valise, he opened the first page of one of the books. Betty Pettoruto's name stood out. "I am going to marry Betty," he said to himself.

186

Albert went to to Dartmouth College, and Marco enlisted as an officer in the Army; he still planned on going to school to be a lawyer. Betty graduated from Lawrence High School with Great Distinction.

***

It wasn't until he had been working at the Morehouse Bakery for one year, learning how to work with the salesmen, that Pasquale opened his notebooks again and once more saw "Elizabeth Betty Pettoruto" written in pencil. Again he said to himself, "I wish my mother were here so that she could tell me what to do. All I know is that I have the same feeling about Betty as I do about Lawrence."

He dreamed of her every night, and every Saturday while he was working at Pettoruto's he could not take his eyes off her. He wanted to see her more often.

One night, while walking home, he saw a tiny light shining in the store. He was wearing his white uniform, and through the door he could see Mrs. Pettoruto counting money.

"Ah, Pasquale come in, come in. Have you eaten anything?" She looked tired and was still wearing her apron, her pocket filled with almonds.

She shoved the day's earnings into her other pocket. Her father was sleeping in a rocking chair, smiling and rocking next to the sink. The pork casings had been washed, ready for the next day's sausages. Gaetano was at the butcher-block counter, cleaning the surface and sharpening the knives after a day of cutting meat.

Pasquale walked over to the old man. "How are you feeling, *nonno?*" The man's breath smelled of wine. *Probably drunk,* Pat thought. Nothing annoyed him more

187

than a drunken old man sleeping. The old man was rocking, smiling and sleeping.

Gaetano said, "He is hard of hearing; we think he is going deaf. So speak up, Pat. What is happening at your bakery? How is the job?"

"The work is good, Guy." He made sure Mrs. Pettoruto was in hearing distance. "Between working and going to school, I don't have much time. I like the work, and last
week I got a raise and a small promotion." Pasquale walked over to the bread rack, which was empty. "How come you don't sell Betsy Ross Bread and donuts in the store? I think people would like it. We also make black moons."

"Betty's breads sell out fast, Pat, and that helps us with all the bills here. I do not think Italian people would like white sliced bread. But what is a black moon?"

"Two black cakes put together, with a white filling in between. We make them every day at the Morehouse. I will talk to the driver who has this route and ask him to stop by here. Is that okay with you?"

"We will see," Mrs. Pettoruto answered, a phrase that he always took as yes.

The next night Pasquale dropped by, and she was friendly and smiling. "How are you, Pasqualino?"

"I'm good, Mrs. Pettoruto. I brought you some Betsy Ross bread and black moons that I bought from the company store at the Morehouse. Try them, and if you like them a salesman will drop off some more. You know, if you do not sell their products after three days, they take them back and sell them in their own store."

"Really?" She looked interested. "Thank you, though I still do not think people will buy them here."

188

"Have them drop by, and we will see."

"What do you do there?"

Pat looked at her face. Her eyes had turned the color of a blue ocean, shiny and full of praise. She looked impressed.

"Well, I am learning how the place is run, and someday Mr. Morehouse said I could work my way up to foreman."

The old man groaned and said he was hungry, so he left.

Pasquale stopped by the next night and bought meat and bread for Josephine. Mrs. Pettoruto was very friendly and offered fruit to bring to his sister. He got up the courage to ask her if he could ask Betty to go to the movies with him over the weekend.

She stared at him through her thick glasses. She was not happy. She put her hand in her apron pocket and nibbled on almonds.

Gaetano overheard them. "Oh, Ma, let Betty go with Pat. She has been working so hard, making bread every morning before she goes to school. Pat is an honest boy."

She edged over to the counter and picked another almond from her pocket, unsure of what to say. "We will see, Pasquale."

Hope flickered into his life, and as he left he thought, *These Pettorutos like the phrase "we will see."*

The next night Betty was filling drawers with freshly made pasta. Her blue eyes met his. "How is your new job, Pasquale?" Her black hair was pulled back with a bow, and her eyes were bluer than he'd realized. She was wearing lipstick.

189

He walked over to lift up a basket filled with gnocchi.

She handed him a bag. "For you and Josephine, Pasquale."

The knot in his throat weakened. Words came tumbling out of him. "Would you go to the movies on Sunday afternoon, Betty?"

Mrs. Pettoruto, washing pork casings, shut off the water. Betty screwed up her eyes and continued filling the drawers with pasta. She knew what was coming.

"As long as you take Connie, America, Rita, and Annie Basile, you can go. You will all walk." Mrs. Pettoruto, finally, had not said, "We will see."

Betty turned to him, and he asked them both if Sunday afternoon was okay. Mrs. Pettoruto gave her permission, and he dreamed of clouds and angels all night.

That Sunday, Louie Scanlon was at the ticket office and let them all in for twenty-five cents. He winked at Pasquale and brought them to the middle row. The girls filed in, allowing Betty to sit next to Pasquale. They laughed and giggled as they watched Charlie Chaplin play with two potatoes at the dinner table. Betty was glued to the screen in awe. Beautiful women dressed in 1920s fashions were smoking and drinking.

Once out of the theater, Annie said, "Let's have a secret code for when Pasquale comes around the neighborhood."

The girls all agreed. Mrs. Pettoruto had a reputation for being strict with her two daughters regarding dating. Betty went along with it but did not seem overly enthused.

"Swell!" Annie was on a roll. "If anyone sees Pasquale in the neighborhood, just call out from the

190

window and yell over to Betty, 'P.G. is here, never fear.'"

Betty did not resist. She had her head in the clouds over the beautiful women's clothes in the movies.

Pasquale walked everyone to their doors. Alone with Betty at last, he took her hand. She withdrew it and then offered it back, her blue eyes letting him know it was okay.

"Can I come by soon and go for a walk with you, Elizabeth?"

They were in front of the cigar store, where a tall statue of an American Indian stared at them.

"I will ask my mother. We will see. Thank you, Pasquale, for treating all of us to the movie."

On his way home that night, he decided that he would have to please Mrs. Pettoruto more. While passing the groceria the next day, he tipped his hat but did not go in. Betty was looking sidelong at him as she filled the pasta drawer. The girls' secret code was working.

***

Pasquale asked his roommate, Sergio, to teach him to play the mandolin. Sergio was something of a gigolo, and Pasquale told him about Betty during practice.

"You're ready now. I will come with you to the back of the store where Betty is baking bread. We will play and sing."

That night Pasquale dreamed that Mrs. Pettoruto warned him that there was danger ahead. He woke up, and his legs felt weak.

"Okay, Pat, you are ready?" Sergio asked. He said that they should go to the back door of the groceria later that morning.

A light was on, and they could see Betty covered in

191

flour. The first thin ropes of dough were ready to go into a gigantic oven. The door squeaked as she opened it, and hot air filled the space. She did not hear the knock on the window.

Sergio tapped Pat on the shoulder. "Start singing. I will play. You just sing." He himself could not sing.

Betty appeared at the window and smiled, but she did not open the door.

"You know, Pat, that girl is very shy. I could tell by her face. So go slow. Wait a few weeks before you go back."

Pasquale turned to Sergio. "I must think of something to do that will make a shy girl love me as much as I love her."

"Buy her a present, Pasquale. You don't know what love is yet."

The next day Pasquale went to Jennie Giusti's Dry Goods Store. Jennie recommended buying a pair of nylon stockings. While wrapping them, she smiled, nodding her head up and down. "So, my dear, you are interested in Betty Pettoruto?" She could spread stories like no one else in The Plains.

He ignored her question, and she shook her head. He gave the nylons to his sister for Christmas.
***

A year passed, and he was promoted to manager of the garage and delivery trucks.

He had more confidence now and went into Mr. Morehouse's office. "I noticed that we get a few buckets of stale bread back every week. I know a Mr. Bonnano who owns a farm in Pleasant Valley. He raises many pigs that he sells to Pettoruto and other markets that make Italian and

192

German sausages. I asked him on Saturday what he feeds his pigs, and he told me whatever he can find. So I was thinking, rather than throwing our old products away, we could sell it to him cheap. He would love all the really stale bread that no one else can use, to feed to his pigs."

Mr. Morehouse did not say anything right away. "Mmm. Let me think about it, Pat. It sounds like a good idea."

Soon afterward Pat, who had not made much headway with Betty, began his new ventures. He got his driver's license so that he could drive one of the bakery trucks.

One Sunday he filled the truck with old bread and pastry and delivered it to Bonnano's farm. "No charge, Mr. Bonnano. Mr. Morehouse was glad to get rid of it."

The farmer patted him on the head and every two weeks gave him "the fattest pig I got."

Before bringing it to Pettoruto's, Pasquale would stop at Josephine's house, and Dominic would come down with a butcher knife and slice off what he wanted. "Cover the inside of the truck with heavy paper, Pat, so that it won't stink." Dominic showed him how to cover the floor of the truck. He would wash the truck out afterward with the hose in the garage of the bakery.

Gaetano Pettoruto gave Mr. Morehouse some sausages every time he delivered a pig, and that is how Pettoruto's sausages became famous.

Betty never knew about it until one day she stopped Pasquale when he was bringing in the pig. "My brother Guy told me what you are doing. We really appreciate the pigs, Pasquale. We have customers from nearby cities coming to buy our sausages."

She offered him a pie (as she called it) with thick red tomato sauce, mozzarella cheese, and sprinkles of sausage. "I made it out of the bread dough that I whip up every morning. Do you like it?" she asked, as she cut him another piece. "Here." She wrapped up the other half. "Bring this home to Josephine."

Licking his fingers, Pasquale thought that this was really something no one had made before. He looked at her and said, "Betty, you can sell this in your father's store, it is so good—and you could make some money."

Betty laughed. "My mother said it is not like the pizza in Naples. I am only allowed to make it for the family. She was the one who told me to give you a piece."

He looked around. No one was in sight. "You could do it, Betty. Call it Betty's Pizza." He went home carrying the pizza and decided that he would ask Betty to go to another movie with him. He dreamed all night of red wine spilling out, coins, and pizza, all mixed up, and of flying all over Lawrence, trying to catch the pizza.

Since little Tony had been born, Pasquale often walked to North Andover to visit. Today he was bringing Betty's pizza and a wooden rattle for the baby.

"Do you believe in dreams, Josephine?"

"Oh, yes, I believe in dreams. The night before Aunt Filomena died in Italy, I dreamed of her, and she was waving and smiling and happy. I know she went to heaven. What was your dream?"

Now Pat had to tell her his dream, and he worried about what she would cook up.

"*Caro*," she said, "that is a good-luck dream. The spilling of the wine and the gold coins are excellent. Silver coins are good luck too, but both are good fortune. About

194

the pizza, I don't know, but let's pretend it means your marrying Betty someday."

Pasquale yawned, and she said, "*Crisce sante* (grow holy), Pasqualino and my baby Tony."

"Una ragazza per bene non lascia il petto paterno prima ch si sposi."
A good girl does not leave the parental nest before she is married.

— Italian proverb

CHAPTER 11 – AN ITALIAN LOVE STORY

Connie and the girls were looking out of their windows, watching Betty and Pat, who were out walking. When they were out of sight, Pasquale took hold of her hand. They were gone for over one and a half hours. Excitement spilled out of the open windows.

The next day, Mrs. Lucia Pettoruto arrived at Josephine's, wearing her straw hat with blue flowers, which she wore only to church and wakes. "My dear Josephine, have you heard from your mother?" Before Josephine could answer, she added, "And please, my dear, call me Lucia." Lucia never wasted time. "Josephine, I am here to ask your permission to set the wedding date between my daughter Betty and your brother, Pasquale."

The first thing that came to Josephine's mind was that maybe Betty was pregnant. "How wonderful, Mrs. Pettoruto! But I must talk to my brother first."

Betty heard about it and made contact with Pasquale through Annie, who knew how to get out of these things. "I will go to the bakery and tell him you want to see him right away. Do not let her get away with that, Betty, unless you want to." She arrived at the bakery out of breath.

Pat waited to go to the Pettorutos until it was time

196

to go home. On the way over to see Betty, he stopped at the Dry Goods store and bought a silk scarf as a present for her.

When he got to the market, they were waiting for him. Betty was upset and began sobbing. "Pasquale, I do not want to get married. It has nothing to do with you. I like you very much, and if we were older I would marry you. But I am only eighteen years old. I just want to have some fun and go out with more people." She turned to her mother. "Mama please, *per piacere!*"

Two weeks later, the Pettorutos invited Pasquale's family to dinner and served *mezzo-ziti*, signaling that they were half-engaged. "The store will be closed on Thanksgiving Day. Betty, darling, we hope that you and Pasquale will make that your wedding day." The family agreed.

"Come on, Betty, we are going to buy the dress." Rita gathered Connie, Annie, and America, and they all went to Boston to buy the bride's and bridesmaids' gowns. Betty picked out a silk white dress with a six-foot train and a crowned veil. Timidly she agreed to wear it.

As happy as he was, Pasquale thought, *What have I done?* He went to his sister, Josephine, and asked her how he would know if he was in love.

"*Caro*, love is different from sex. Everyone is different, but once I read a letter by Rilke, who wrote that to love another person is our ultimate task, and there is no preparation for that, Pasqualino. I found that to be true with Dominic. Once you find someone you love and marry her, in our religion you are married for life. You say that you love Betty, but are you sure it is not loneliness or sexual desire?"

Pasquale thought, *What the hell is she talking about? All I know is I want to be with Betty for the rest of my life and have a family and live in Lawrence.*

"Pasqualino, you are young, and getting married to a woman includes not only passion but bodily love as well."

"What do you mean by bodily love? Like kissing? Betty allowed me to kiss her once, but as good as it felt, I was just bewildered."

"The physical part, I mean. You must speak to Dominic about this soon. *Capisci?* He is a fine man and husband, and a devoted father. When Mama and Papa left for Italy, I did not want to go, so the matchmaker and Mama arranged for me to marry Dominic, since he was also from our village in Italy. They served a beautiful Italian meal, and I noticed he had fine manners. He was not what you would call handsome, and he is a little shorter than I am. But something deep inside me said, he will do; he will be a fine father and husband. I did not know what love was. I could never imagine someone being so nice to me. He is filled with respect, kindness, and gentleness. I love him dearly and want to be with him until I die. From him I learned commitment and devotion. So that is the Italian *amore,* Pasqualino. Now go and talk to him."

Instead Pasquale went to his best friend, Rocco. "Tell me what love is, Rocco."

"What?" he said. "You have never had been with a girl? I mean a naked girl, Pat."

"The only body I have ever seen naked was Angelica's, the *putana* with her red hair, and I felt sorry for her with her two broken legs. I wanted to respect her, so I did not get closer, Angelo."

"What the hell do you think the *putana* does with the men who pay her? Sit and talk? They have *sesso fiasco* (sex). I will take you to Boston next week, and we will go to a bordello. The women are very nice and beautiful, and they will teach you what to do."

"No, I cannot go. I am going to marry Betty on Thanksgiving, and that would be unfaithful."

"*Che se pazzo,* Pat? Going into a woman body is the most beautiful thing you will feel in this world."

"What about marriage? Do I have to marry the woman?"

"Oh, Christ, I would never marry anyone I have sex with. Why, I have no respect or love for them, it's only a release. Think about it, Pat, and I will take you next week. I will pay."

On his way home, Pasquale stopped by the church. While talking to the statue of the Blessed Mother, as his mother used to do, he whispered, "Now that the wedding date is set, we will find out about love together."

Angelo made another attempt to take him to the bordello. When his patience was tested to the limit, he called Pasquale "*Test tostai*" (hard head), but after that he let him be.

Pasquale went to the library and looked for the poet's book that had taught his sister about love. But that did not help either, so he went to Louie Scanlon and learned about the sacredness of love and sex in his own way.

Mr. and Mrs. Morehouse and some friends from the Morehouse Bakery went to the wedding, even though it was on Thanksgiving Day. They sat with the Pettoruto family as honored guests. The wedding dinner was an

Italian feast. The seven bridesmaids and Rita, Betty's sister, and the girls from Elm Street wrapped a hundred and fifty sugared-almond candies in white tulle, with pink and blue satin ribbons, as favors to give to the guests. Betty looked beautiful. Pasquale was now part of one of the most respected families in Lawrence. It was a dream come true. The Pettorutos had Loring the photographer document the marriage. Mr. Kapelson, now a friend, lent Pasquale a tuxedo and some shiny new shoes with tassels.

From that moment on, his lonely life was over.

***

Betty did not understand his yearning to belong and be respected. She became more involved in her family and spent every spare moment at the movies.

Now everything started happening at once. Holding his first child, Pasquale fall in love. "Let's name her Glory, after Mr. Morehouse's daughter." Eleven months later, Pasqualino (Betty insisted on calling him Little Pat) arrived, with his father's reddish-brown hazel eyes. Lucia, named after Betty's mother, came eleven months after him, with the greenest eyes like a cat. A still-born came next.

Five years went by. Then Anthony arrived with a broken arm—eventually he would go on to become a winning baseball player. Their last child was born on St. John's Day and was named Joannella; she had blue eyes like her grandmother.

Pasquale sent for his mother from Italy. His notebooks were still filed away in a box, hidden from his family.

***

Pasquale kept busy at his job. The Superintendent of Maintenance called to him one day. "Come on, Patsy. I

200

want to show you the deepest part of building. The stairway is dangerous but clean. Here we set rat traps, and Silvio's job is to get those animals and dispose of them."

"Didn't he just die?"

"Yeah, the poor bastard fell in a sewer."

They trapped two monstrous rats. Pasquale threw up and ran out.

The next day, Mr. Morehouse went over to him. "I understand you have no stomach for catching rats, Pat. Since this building is close to the canal, those critters get in often, so we have to catch them. Try it again some time."

The thought of Betty and what she would think if he became a rat-catcher flashed through his mind. "Mr. Morehouse, you know I would do anything for you, but I got very sick last time and cannot do it. But I know someone who could."

Mr. Morehouse did not ask who the person was; he just took Pasquale aside. "Pat, I want you to keep quiet about what I am going to ask of you. None of the workers must find out, do you understand?"

"I would do anything for you but catch rats. You can count on me, Mr. Morehouse."

On Thursday, Pasquale went to Kap's Men's Store, and Mr. Kapelson, the owner, said to him, "Well, my young man, Mr. Morehouse ordered a nice brown suit, a white shirt, a tie, and shoes for you. Come with me, and Nunzio the tailor will get you fixed up."

Pat did not understand how Mr. Kapelson knew about him. But he liked the feel of the woolen fabric on his skin.

The first thing Nunzio noticed about Pasquale were

201

his shoes. "Fine shoes you have. From Italy, no?" When the measuring was complete, he went on, "You are a perfect size 34. Pick out a tie and socks."

Pasquale walked out of the store the next week looking like James Cagney in the movie *The Public Enemy*.

That same week, Mr. Morehouse asked Pat to get in the front seat his car, a 1922 Ford. "You get to drive." Pasquale took the shiny wheel and stepped on the gas. They went around the Common, up and down Essex Street, and along Oak Street before he heard Mr. Morehouse say, "Stop the car, Pat." Mr. Morehouse got out, they changed places, and Mr. Morehouse drove up to Clover Hill and onto a long driveway flanked by white geraniums and yellow daisies. He stopped in front of a fine yellow two-story house.

Pasquale could hear the trees swaying and birds singing.

A maid came to the door and took Mr. Morehouse's hat. A very tall woman was watching them and smiling. She descended the stairs, dressed in a dark dress with a white collar. Pasquale notices her sparkling diamond earrings; his mother had always loved fine gold earrings.

"This is Mrs. Morehouse, Pat."

She was the most elegant-looking woman he had ever seen. She asked him about his family. Pasquale fell deeply in love with her refinement and beauty. And so began an adventure that lasted until the Betsy Ross Bakery closed its doors.

Every Thursday, Pasquale would pick Mrs. Morehouse up in the 1922 Ford and drive her to the Rockingham Race Track in Salem, New Hampshire. She talked all the way to the grounds. "It is the finest stable in

202

the world, Pat and, the best thoroughbreds are raised here. I was brought up on a horse farm and had my own horses, and I love to watch the races." He enjoyed her stories and her boldness.

Rockingham had a hundred-mile track. Prior to horse-racing, the tracks had been used for car and motorcycle racing. The track raced the best thoroughbreds in the country. Rockingham was once the finest racecourse in the world. Gambling was illegal, but Pasquale came to love to watch the horses race.

Eventually he found out that Mrs. Morehouse and other gamblers placed their bets in an underground room known only to them. The chauffeurs had their own special room in the clubhouse, where they played cards and gossiped. They played their card games every Thursday, and Pasquale became an expert.

On the way home she would ask, "How do you like the other drivers, Pasquale?"

"The finest men in the world, Mrs. Morehouse."

Every week she handed him two dollars. "Good luck, and don't lose it. Remember, you will someday have a family to feed." Then she flitted away.

The money Pasquale made from her gambling went right into the bank on Common Street. This was his secret. He gave Josephine five dollars a week. The Italian teller would raise his left eyebrow when he made a deposit.

Now that Pasquale and Mrs. Morehouse had become friends and confidants, the conversation went both ways. When she found out that Pasquale could sing, she made arrangements for him to sing at the Broadway Theater. Everyone from Elm Street, Oak Street, Chestnut Street, and the Morehouse Bakery came to see him. He won

203

first prize. Mrs. Morehouse was in the crowd. The next week she told him that he sounded like Enrico Caruso. One Christmas, she gave him his own record player and a record of Caruso. He memorized every song. Soon everyone was asking him to sing at weddings and christenings. At his own wedding he sang "Roses Are Shining in Picardy" and won Betty's heart.

One day Mrs. Morehouse asked him to stop on Main Street in Andover to see her doctor. Their new Thursday plan was to stop at the psychiatrist one week and go to the racetrack the other week. Her life became an open book to him, since she talked all the way to her home about her addiction to gambling. Her suffering became his suffering.

He thought, *Here I am in the happiest days of my life, and as much as I want to help, I can't offer any words of wisdom. All I can do is listen.*

The strange names and people she spoke of he did not understand, and he wrote them down in his notebook. Later he would go to the library and talk to the librarian. The librarian would search out the people whose names were in his notebook.

One Thursday Pasquale handed Mrs. Morehouse a hand-written card:

"You gain strength and confidence by every experience in which you really stop to look fear in the face... Do the thing you cannot do." — *Eleanor Roosevelt*

His last words before she got out of the car were "I wrote that in my notebook, Mrs. Morehouse. I copied it from the library. I wish I were that smart, but I am not."

Bartolomeo Vanzetti and Nicola Sacco, you shall suffer the punishment of death by the passage of electricity through your body on Sunday.
— Judge Thayer, July 27, 1927

And life has so many allurements and it is so nice and bright and so wonderful that I feel the passion living in my heart and I do want to live… But I say this, that there is something dearer and nobler and holier and grander, something I could never come to terms with, and that is my conscience.
— Arturo Giovannitti

Everything should be done to keep alive the tragic affair of Sacco and Vanzetti in the conscience of mankind.
— Albert Einstein

CHAPTER 12 – THE PASSIONS OF SACCO AND VANZETTI

After seven years, four months, and seventeen days, on August 23, 1927, at 12:03 A.M. in a room at Charlestown Prison in Boston, Massachusetts, a tall skinny electrician from the Bronx pulled two switches on a white panel. First came Celestino Medeiros, who had confessed to the crime, and then Nicola Sacco, while his friend Bartolomeo Vanzetti, gaunt and pale, watched. When it was his turn to die, the guards fitted the skull cap and clamped electrodes on his head, while Vanzetti spoke these words: "I wish to tell you, I am innocent." Before the mask was put over his head, he said, "I wish to forgive some people for what they are now doing to me." Two thousand volts went through his body, and then his smoldering corpse collapsed in the huge electric chair.

It was a day in history when everything ceased. Tanks had to hold off angry mobs in Paris and London; there were walk-outs in South America; protests erupted in Australia, Bucharest, Berlin, Amsterdam, Rome, Tokyo, Athens, Prague, and Johannesburg.

It was the "Jazz Age."

Outside the Charlestown Prison in Boston, Pasquale was with Angelo Rocco and hundreds of others who believed that the two Italians were innocent. Huge floodlights lit up a watchtower overlooking the crowd, who were waiting for a reprieve.

Angelo turned to Pasquale. "As long as the floodlights are lit and steady, they are alive, Pasquale." He slipped in and out of the crowd.

Boston was an armed camp, and all over the world protestors were clashing with police. Attorney Albert Pettoruto was with Herbert Ehrmann, who shouted to the crowd, "This behavior is much broader than strictly a political one."

Pasquale felt a yearning unrealized. "Albert is with us."

He turned to Mary Donovan, who was next to him and wanted to say something, but the lights flickered. A hushed silence turned to fear. The world was listening to radios. The airways and telegraphs were clogged. The lights flickered again. The silent crowd and the earth wept. Pasquale's nose started to run, and he held back tears.

"Does America have no passion for people who have passion?" The poet Edna St. Vincent Millay was weeping. She yelled out to the crowd, "This is a murder we

206

shall not forget." Earlier that week, she had been arrested for picketing and ended up in jail for a few nights. Her passion was unyielding.

Mary Donovan was sobbing uncontrollably. She shouted, "I cannot believe it!" and fell into a faint.

Rocco, unfamiliar with motions of affection, held Pasquale in his arms. "So many passionate pleas, Pasquale, and this is the way it ends. Here—Edna Millay's poem. It was published in *The New York Times* today. You read it to Stevie Piscatano; he cannot read English. Have him pass it around." Angelo disappeared into the crowd.

> *What from the splendid dead*
> *We have inherited—*
> *Furrows sweet to the grain, and the weed subdued*
> *See now the slug and the mildew plunder*
> *Evil does overwhelm*
> *The larkspur and the corn*
> *We have seen them go under*

Stevie did not understand the poem and gave it to a man in front of him, Herbert Ehrmann, whose eyes blazed with tears.

The Italian Newspaper wrote an article about Sacco and Vanzetti, and in it they printed a note found in Vanzetti's pocket. Mr. Pettoruto cut out the article about Sacco and Vanzetti one day and hung it on the back wall behind the counter in the groceria. This is what it said:

> *Fellow Workers, you have fought all the wars, you*
> *have worked for all the capitalists. You have*
> *wandered over the countries. Have you harvested*

the fruits of your labors? the price of your
victories? Does the past comfort you? Does the
present smile on you? Does the future promise you
anything? Have you found a piece of land where
you can live like a human being and die like a
human being? On these questions, on this I argue,
and on this theme, the struggle for existence,
Bartolomeo Vanzetti will speak. Admission Free.
Freedom of discussion to all. TAKE THE LADIES
WITH YOU.

On the evening of the execution, it rained all night in Boston. A bystander was overheard saying, "I'm glad that those wops are dead and the damned thing is over with." A storm hit Governor Thayer's home in Worcester. Sewers backed up. A new storm was just about to begin.

Pasquale wondered if Mr. Pettoruto was turning into an anarchist as he watched him pin the article on the bulletin board. Out of respect for his father-in-law, he said nothing.

"What are you thinking, Pasquale?" Mr. Pettoruto did not give him a chance to answer. "Read the article, and I will give you a copy to send to your mother. I, like others, believe they were executed because they were Italians. Not only that, though; my son Albert has convinced me that the real reason was that Ettor and Giovannitti were acquitted after being charged with Anna LoPizzo's death in 1912."

Pasquale asked, "Was it payback, Pa?"

"The biggest payback, which someday will be forgotten." He walked over to the cash register and slid out a folder filled with newspaper clippings. "Read this, Pasquale. It is from the *Eagle Tribune,* published in Ettor's

208

and Giovannitti's defense. It's what Helen Keller said in court: 'This is of course a legal fiction devised by the mill owners and their agents.' It took eight years for the mill owners and society to pay back the Italians."

Pasquale went home and opened a shriveled notebook labeled "1912 – Bread and Roses Strike." He found "Sacco" written in a child's script. He remembered that Sacco had come to Lawrence to speak at the rally for the Bread and Roses Strike and wore a bow-tie.

He thought back to the day years after that when it had all begun, on April 15, 1920, in Braintree, Massachusetts. Braintree was an industrial village where everyone knew everyone else. The start-up whistles brought thousands of workers into the shoe factories. By mid-afternoon, at 2:45, paymaster Frederick Parmenter and his guard Alessandro Berardelli picked up five hundred envelopes, containing $15,776.52. The afternoon was sunny and warm. Two strangers hiding in the shadow of an empty building uncoiled like snakes and shot and killed Parmenter and Berardelli. One stranger, wearing a felt hat, grabbed the moneyboxes and raised his hand in a signal. A black Buick slowly approached the crime scene and picked up the men and money, then sped down toward the railroad tracks. At 3:15 the gatekeeper hobbled out on one leg to lower the gate. Just then the Buick reached the crossing. "Put them up or we'll shoot!" The gates rose, and the gunman fired anyway and missed. One witness heard men in the Buick talking "foreign gibberish."

Sacco was in Boston applying for a passport for his wife and son, Dante, so that they could return to Italy for his mother's funeral. Vanzetti was in Plymouth on Cape Cod, selling eels for the Catholic holidays. He was living and working in Plymouth.

After seven years and seven trials, Sacco and Vanzetti were convicted and sentenced to death.
***

Rocco visited the Pontiac Club, Pasquale's club in Lawrence, periodically. He lived in New York and worked for a law firm. He kept reminding everyone about the murder. Tonight he came for a reason, and everyone listened to him. It was Wednesday, spaghetti and meatball day.

Pasquale had asked Glory, his daughter, to help him cook that day, since he was expecting a crowd. When Rocco arrived, he asked his daughter to go home for the night.

Rocco began with his usual history lesson: "Sacco worked in Boston, hauling paving stones for the streets of Boston; he also worked in a shoe factory. He was a man who believed in dignity, freedom, and justice. He did not have a fighting chance. He was a freedom fighter at heart but also a family man like all of us. Nicola Sacco was from Torremagiore in Italy. So am I, and many of you are also. We are getting paid back because of the strike. Never forget that."

Many of the men, longing for some peace in their lives, blurted out, "Forget about it, Rocco, it is over."

Angelo Rocco never faltered; he carried on: "Sacco worked all over the place before he came to Needham, Massachusetts. He knew what it is like to be looked down on as a *dago*. The guy was smart enough to get a fellow worker to teach him the trade in the shoe factory. He had to pay the Irish bastard two weeks' worth of his salary. He is known in the trade as one of the best edge-trimmers. He is not a murderer. He is an Italian who was murdered for a crime he did not commit."

"Rocco is talking as if Sacco were still alive," Phil DeFusco whispered to Gaetano. "And the anarchists supported the labor movement in the 1912 strike."

"So what?" Gaetano piped up. "He supported the strike in 1915 in Hopedale, and participated in the picket line on weekends, and went to rallies at night. That does not make him an anarchist, Phil. While Sacco and Vanzetti were in jail, he became a father to Dante, Sacco's son, and worked very hard so that he could go to school and be an American."

Rocco heard the conversation and leaned over to Pasquale, who was handing out plates of spaghetti. "Like you, eh, Pasquale, to be an American?" And then the old Rocco returned to his old way of educating Pasquale. "Always remember, Pat, just because I believe in some of the same principles, such as being able to have a different opinion from others, speaking openly about it does not make me an anarchist. We have a right as Americans to express radical views and diverse cultural practices without fear of persecution."

Pasquale thought, *Angelo is practicing his speech for law school.* He was glad he didn't have to give him a test about what he had just said.

Rocco went on, "The Constitution of the United States guarantees freedom of religion, freedom of speech, freedom to assemble peacefully, and freedom of the press. We were not given that right during the strike."

The younger men were losing interest and squirming. Angelo did not falter. "There is a man, Felix Frankfurter, we should all revere." He jumped up on a chair

211

and waved his hands. "For six years, Sacco and Vanzetti waited to be free. In the meantime, a small-time criminal, Celestino Medeiros, confessed to the robbery and murder. But the judge considered Medeiros mad and would not consider the confession." Rocco turned to Pasquale. "Write Frankfurter's name down in your book, Pat. He is a Harvard Law professor, and he was the leading guy in this campaign to help Sacco and Vanzetti."

Phil DeFusco said, "Yeah, and we heard you are a member of the committee he established, the Citizens National Committee. What's that all about?"

Angelo did not answer him. "Felix Frankfurter. And you"—his hands circled the room—"should always remember him. He jeopardized his job at Harvard and was threatened with dismissal. They not only call us dagos and wops, they called him a kike because he was a Jew."

Pasquale did not have his notebook, so he wrote "Felix Frankfurter" on a piece of wrapping paper.

Prior to the execution, Rocco picked up Pasquale and took him to a meeting at the Boston Headquarters. The hall was packed. Pasquale sat next to Jane Addams, who reminded him of his mother. *My mother would have been here with me, as I was with her during the Bread and Roses Strike*, he thought. His mind went back to the days before the trial.

Herbert Ehrmann was the first one to speak. "Celestine Medeiros has confessed to the murder and robbery of Frederick Parameter and Alessandro Bertarelli in Braintree." A cheer went up. "Do not cheer!" Ehrmann waved his arms. "Judge Thayer and others have concluded that Medeiros, who is a petty thief and a murderer, is also a liar." A howl went up and melted into a scream. "This guy

212

was part of the Morelli gang and is in the same jail as Sacco and Vanzetti. A small-time criminal and convicted murderer, he confessed that it was the Morelli gang from Providence who committed the crime."

Elizabeth Gurley Flynn and Emma Goldman shouted, "This case is a frame-up!" A burly guy shouted, "Take those goddamn hats off!"

Ehrmann went on, "The jury is biased. No foreigner in Dedham, Massachusetts, could receive fair trial with a prejudiced Angelo-Saxon jury. Judge Thayer said, 'The facts of life do not penetrate to the sphere in which our beliefs are cherished.'"

"What does that mean?" Pasquale tapped Miss Flynn's shoulder. He admired her forthrightness during the strike.

"Tell you later," she answered, standing up. Everyone heard her. "The case is a frame-up, and we all know that Thayer is prejudiced against foreigners. Herbert Ehrmann worked the hardest of anyone for Sacco and Vanzetti. He has been relentless in his quest for the truth. He believes that the Morelli brothers committed the robbery and murder. It was only after F. Laurelton Bullard wrote an article called 'We Submit,' which won the Pulitzer Prize, that Ehrmann and others were granted a new trial for Sacco and Vanzetti. He did a great job." The crowd was full of praise.

Moore, who was the defense counsel for Sacco and Vanzetti, stood up. Emma Goldman turned to Elizabeth Flynn. "Oh, him again. I do not like him. The S.O.B. will take all the credit."

"All is not lost. Felix Frankfurter and Garner Jackson, a reporter for the *Globe,* will be with us. Felix

213

Frankfurter is an Austrian immigrant and a Harvard Law School professor. There is more at stake than just the lives of two men. The evidence is unreliable, the eyewitnesses gave unreliable testimony, and we have proof of collusive efforts by many in the court. Frankfurter and Jackson have a plan that will get millions of people to support us. We can all give a round of applause and thank Ladino Feliciana and Mary Donovan, who pleaded with them to join us. For us, on this day in 1927, everyone in the world will be involved, waiting on a request for a new hearing. We will give them free access to everything we have and know."

Elizabeth Gurley Flynn turned to Pasquale and whispered, "I hate that son of a bitch."

That night, when Pasquale got home, Albert was helping his mother close the store. Pasquale went to help move the fruit and vegetables that were out on the sidewalk into the store.

"How was the meeting, Pasquale?" Albert asked, interested.

"Al, I and others believe that Medeiros was part of the Morelli gang and that he pulled the trigger."

"Medeiros had a lot to gain by making the confession, Pasquale." Albert dragged in the cart filled with dried fish.

"But Medeiros said that he drove a Hudson—that was the car spotted at the murder scene. He even talked about switching cars and getting into a Buick. Then they stopped at a speakeasy a few miles from Braintree and waited until it was time for the hold-up. They drove back to some woods in Randolph and changed from the Buick to the Hudson and drove back to Providence, Rhode Island. Julie Kelleher saw them; because the Hudson was swerving

214

and driving recklessly, she wrote down the number. It is the same number that was spotted on the robbers' car in South Braintree. Al, I believe that makes Sacco and Vanzetti innocent. These two men are innocent, I am sure."

"Pat, don't let anyone hear you talk like that—this subject is not for you to discuss. I think the guys might be anarchists stirring up trouble. We don't want trouble at Pettoruto's Market."

"Well, I want to know what you think about it, Al." Pasquale always looked up to attorney Albert.

"Probably Vanzetti is innocent, and Sacco is a fanatic. So that's it, Pat. Stay out of trouble. We at Pettoruto's want you to stay alive. You have a family to think about."

"You know, Al"—Pasquale walked over to him—"there is nothing proven against them. They were framed because they are Italian, and even though you may want to side with the Anglo-Saxon views, as an American I have the right to think and say what I want. All of us have parents and relatives who were strangers to America and did the best they could so that we could live in peace and harmony, and so our children could have a better life."

Albert gave him a sarcastic glance.

"Al, I don't think Felix Frankfurter would be defending them if they were not innocent."

On the way home, Pasquale thought, *I stood up to him, and nothing happened.* He was surprised.

Felix Frankfurter, a Harvard professor and a member of the Defense Committee, lobbied for his colleagues at Harvard to help. He was convinced of Sacco and Vanzetti's innocence. The backlash he got from supporting two Italian men innocent of a crime was

215

incomprehensible. Judge Thayer, the judge on the case, called Frankfurter "Professor Frankenstein." Judge Thayer also colluded with the Ku Klux Clan to convict the two innocent "dagos."

Mrs. Morehouse was wrapped up in the trial. Today she was telling Pasquale what her club ladies thought about it. "Everyone is talking about it. Did you know that Mary Donovan, Mrs. Evans, and many others are making telephone calls, putting up posters, and mailing out ten thousand copies of John Dos Passos' pamphlet called *Facing the Chair*? Have you seen it?"

"No, I have not."

"Here is a copy; you can read it later. Last week, eight thousand people filled Union Square in New York, cheering for Sacco and Vanzetti. What do you think about that, Pasquale?" She'd been talking all the way to the track. Pasquale bit back an answer and kept his eyes on the road. He thought, *I do not want to lose my job.*

The next Thursday she asked him if he had seen the article in *The Atlantic* by Felix Frankfurter called "The Case of Sacco and Vanzetti." "Readers everywhere are reading and talking about it, Pat. Even President J. Edgar Hoover and U.S. Supreme Court Chief Justice William Howard Taft called it propaganda. Not only did the President of Harvard Law School, Lawrence Lowell, condemn Frankfurter, but Frankfurter almost lost his job because he wrote it."

"Was Lawrence named after Lawrence Lowell?" Pasquale asked, deciding that he'd better say something.

"I have no idea," she answered.

He thought it was a silly, stupid question, and he didn't know why he'd asked it.   Pasquale read

216

the article while Mrs. Morehouse was at the races. He thought, *The whole world must have read this article, and all I can hope for is that one man, a Jew, breaks down the barriers that prevent Italian-Americans from having a place in a new world named after an Italian explorer, Amerigo Vespucci.*

At work, Mr. Morehouse asked him if he had read the article. It seemed that everyone was talking about it. "It is a fine article, and all of you should read it."

Pasquale wondered what he meant by "all of you" and answered, "Yes, we all have read it. I admire Felix Frankfurter for speaking his mind and trying to help innocent men. He is a hero to Italian-Americans all over this country."

Mr. Morehouse had a stern look on his face. He went on, "The establishment, including Governor Fuller, will kill Felix Frankfurter's reputation, Pasquale. Thayer said publicly that Sacco and Vanzetti are Bolsheviks, and one of the newspaper articles said this morning that they are waiting to see if he will side with the sob-sister Mary Donovan."

Pasquale was writing on a ledger in the garage and said, "I understand Mary Donovan has started a petition that they will present to him, asking for a pardon. Over two thousand people have signed it. That is a lot of names. Incredible, isn't it, Mr. Morehouse? Incredible."
***

It had been six years, and Sacco and Vanzetti were still in jail. Pasquale and Betty had three children by that time and still lived over the groceria in a six-room apartment. Betty was even more beautiful when she got pregnant. The babies had many aunties and uncles.

Pasquale still worked at the Morehouse Bakery. Mr. Smith was now the head and treated him like a son. "Pasquale, I want you to know that I think Sacco and Vanzetti are innocent and have been railroaded. The gossip around my circle is that Governor Fuller is going to sentence them to death in order to end all the protests. Last year the defense lawyers squashed the protesters and urged restraint. Many of the women in Mrs. Smith's circle have been visiting them in jail, and Mrs. Smith told me that they do not understand why Mrs. Sacco has remained silent."

"I am hoping they will be pardoned tomorrow, Mr. Smith. Six years in jail, and they are still waiting to be free. You should tell Mrs. Smith that maybe if she or another woman befriended Mrs. Sacco, she might gain the confidence to speak out. She is so frightened and has a small child. I heard she has no family here, but Sacco's sister is coming, so things may change."

"If you want the day off, Pasquale, you can go with the rest of the people who believe in justice and await the sentence in Boston."

Pasquale told Betty he was going with Phil DeFusco.

"Pasquale, I do not think you should go, but I know you will not be able to work or do anything unless you do. So go, my darling. The children will pray that you stay safe."

Betty and the children hugged him. Pasquale felt their love and pride. He hugged Betty and whispered, "It's always safe to go with Phil, because he is one of the strongest guys I know. So don't worry."

By some fluke, they were able to get into the courtroom, thanks to Phil, who wasn't always forthcoming with the truth. "After all, Pat, we are distant relatives."

"Hear ye, hear ye." Judge Thayer took his place on the bench and spoke. "Bartolomeo Vanzetti and Nicola Sacco, you shall suffer the punishment of death by the passage of electricity through your body on Sunday, July 27, 1927."

The court was silent as the clerk asked Sacco and Vanzetti, "Do you have anything to say?"

Sacco looked sick and worn out. He apologized for his English and told Judge Thayer that he felt he was in the oppressed class. "I never knew, never heard, never even read in history anything so cruel as this court. After seven years of prosecuting, they still consider us guilty. This sentence is between two classes, the oppressed class and the rich class, and there will be always collision between one and the other, and I am in the oppressed class. You know, judge, I am never guilty, never—not yesterday, nor today, nor forever." Then he stood up straight.

Pasquale knew he was the man he had seen years ago in the bowtie, yet he did not look the same. Pasquale felt deep inside his soul that he did not want to end up like him.

Vanzetti was different because he could speak like any American judge or lawyer. He looked robust and had sharp eyes. He wore his moustache like a crown, revealing a strong roman nose and square chin. "I am not only innocent of these two crimes, but in all my life I have never stolen, and I have never killed, and I have never spilled blood. Is it possible that the jury could be right when the whole world says it is wrong? Seven years we are in jail. What we have suffered during these seven years no human tongue can say, and yet you see us before you, not

219

trembling. You see me looking you in your eyes straight, not blushing, not changing color, not ashamed or in fear."

He was in a cage. Emma Goldman was crying, and as she wiped her tears she said, "Pasquale, never forget these words; they shall ring out all over the world."

"This is what I say," Vanzetti went on. "I would not wish to a dog or to a snake what I have to suffer for things that I am not guilty of. My conviction is that I have suffered for things that I am guilty of. I am suffering because I am a radical, and indeed I am a radical. I have suffered because I am an Italian, and indeed I am an Italian. I have suffered more for my family and my beloved than for myself, but I am so persuaded to be right that if you could execute me two times, and if I could be reborn two other times, I would live again to do what I have done already. I am finished. Thank you."

A reporter wrote that the tears people were shedding in that courtroom could fill an ocean.

Pasquale could not talk to anyone until he got home. Then he said, "Betty, for me, deep down, something died." And they hugged each other and cried. The names of Emma Goldman, Felix Frankfurter, Mary Donovan, and Justice Brandeis, with so many others, had a special page in his book of names. That was all he could do that night.

On the next Thursday, Mrs. Morehouse asked him what he thought.

"I believe they have been railroaded because they are Italians. I believe in my heart that they are innocent. This history may be forgotten by the next generation, but I can tell you the next generation will have this travesty of justice written in their genes. They will be very cautious about speaking their minds or running for office. Judge

220

Thayer and others have accomplished their goals. They believe Italians do not matter, but let me tell you, they do." Pasquale was shocked by his own words, but also proud.

Mrs. Morehouse was silent on the trip to the track the next Thursday. Then, out of the blue, she asked him the same question. Pasquale was ready and gave the same comment.
***

In August of 1927 Italian-Americans had every reason to believe that if they raised their voices as a group, someone would be executed. Like Pasquale, many of them still believed the myth of heredity that held them together, common souls looking for the yeast to allow them to grow.

Before Angelo went off to New York, he took Pasquale to the North End in Boston for lunch at Luigi Pastene's spaghetti restaurant. The long tables were covered with red, white, and green paper, and people sat in groups, chatting, eating, and laughing. Pasquale wanted to sing.

"Have you heard of Fiorello LaGuardia, Pat?"

Some men stopped eating to listen.

"No, who is he?"

"In New York he is loved by all the Italians, and he is still called a dago and an anarchist, in spite of the fact that he ran for the House of Representatives and was a hero in World War I. He is a good friend of Arturo Giovannitti, so I will be with the two of them when I go to New York. The scoop is that Fiorello might run for mayor of New York. I will need your advice, so learn all you can about politics—this is big." And he got up to leave.

"Wow, Angelo! Good luck and God speed. I hope you get married and are as happy as Betty and I are. I love

221

you and respect you as a person. I shall never forget you."

"Well, Pat, don't forget to write 'Fiorello LaGuardia' in your book." He gave Pasquale a love punch on his arm. "Perhaps we will meet again, and maybe if he runs for mayor I will call on you for help."

After he had said good-bye, Pasquale wept.

"There are things in the world that cannot be brought about. There are mistakes that cannot be repaired. But there is one thing sure -- that loyalty and friendship are the most precious possessions a man can have."

— Herbert Hoover

CHAPTER 13 – THE DEPRESSION YEARS

After the execution of Sacco and Vanzetti, Mary Donovan was arrested and dragged off a platform carrying a sign from a newspaper, which said, "DID YOU SEE WHAT I DID TO THOSE ANARCHISTIC BASTARDS?" She was dragged by her feet and ended up in jail for two nights.

Pasquale lost track of her once she got out of jail. His life was getting very full. In spite of the Depression of the 1930s, it was a happy time in his life. He started the Pontiac Political and Social Club, in an empty store right next to Pettoruto's, at 120 Elm Street. Louie Scanlon helped him get some funding, and he applied for a charter, and Governor Paul Dever signed it.

When he went to the Governor's office, he brought some of his now famous spaghetti sauce that Betty had bottled in a Ball canning jar.

Governor Dever said, "Thank you very much, Patsy." He looked up as he signed the charter, his eyes as cold as stone. "I want you to help me win the Italian vote in Lawrence when I run for my second term at the end of the year, Patsy."

"Sure, thing, Governor." They clasped hands.

As the Governor led him out of the office, he put his

223

arm around his shoulder and said, "Bring me sauce anytime. My family loves Italian food."

Weeks later, Pasquale received Paul Dever posters and several stacks of wood for the signs. He made a sign for the charter and hung it in the club.

Although he had a beautiful family and was part of one of the most influential Italian- American families in Lawrence, Pasquale always considered himself lonely and not good enough. Betty would try to pep him up, saying, "Be grateful, Pat, and look at what we have. Always look for the best."

"I know you mean well, sweetheart, but loneliness is something I cannot help or explain." Pasquale frowned, and his eyelids were half-closed.

"Darling, your mother will be here soon. She will be a great help with the children. You will be able to go to the movies with me. Look forward to it, sweetheart."

Betty did not know what she was getting into; she was shocked when Maria brought her stepdaughter with her. She returned to baking bread and helping out in the market.

The Great Depression of 1931 came with a crash and hit Lawrence very hard. Pasquale kept busy to ward off a deep sadness that he could not control. He began involving his family and friends in his collection of names.

"Daddy, whenever you want to learn the name of an important person, date, or event, call the Lawrence Library," Glory told him; she was grown now and becoming an activist.

Pasquale called the library so often that Mary, the librarian, knew him by the sound of his voice. Today he asked Mary the name of the Vice President who had served on President Taft's team in 1913.

"Pat, I'll have to look it up. Not many people ask for that information." He waited, and eventually Mary said, "It was James Sherman, Pat, and just for your information, President Taft was the tenth Chief Justice of the Supreme Court." Pat was happy with this unsolicited history.

Pat brought Mary his tomato sauce, and they became friends for the rest of his life. The situation at Pettoruto's got worse by the day during the Depression. Mrs. Pettoruto could not let anyone leave the store without giving them something to eat. No one saw it coming.

Pasquale, after a long day's work at the Morehouse Bakery and driving Mrs. Morehouse around, was always tired. Once, when he opened the door to his home, he found Betty sobbing. "What is wrong Lisa?" (He often called her Lisa, now that he knew about the *Mona Lisa*.)

"Pat, the city is going to put the white flag up on the store." Her tears were as large as her blue eyes. "It means bankruptcy and losing everything. It means our lives. My mother, Larry, Marco, Albert, Gaetano, and Rita all depend on the store. Marco and Albert are in College and cannot help. They will not be able to finish school."

"How could this happen? Where is your brother Albert the *Advacato?*"

Betty was beside herself, unable to speak.

"Lisa dearest, please, we can fix this." He went over and lifted her limp body from the chair.

"*Caro,* my mother is at Lawrence General Hospital. The doctors told us she fainted from the stress. Rita, Albert, and Gaetano are there with her. I came home to be with the children. I felt safe here, Pasquale. Oh, my god!" She let out a sound that woke the sleeping children.

225

Pasquale was not surprised about the possible take-over from the bank. Mrs. Pettoruto could not refuse food to anyone. The family devised a credit system. They gave a little black book to all the customers who could not pay for all the food they needed. After they paid what they could, the balance was noted in the black book. "To be paid back when things get better." Betty improvised, adding more water to the bread and pasta. Larry made cordials for the Italian men who had lost jobs and wanted to meet at back of the store over a pot-bellied stove to keep warm and talk.

"Do not worry, Lisa, I will speak to Mr. Smith, who is now part owner of the Morehouse, and he will advise me. Maybe he could lend money on my pay. I will go to see him tomorrow. Mr. Smith is a smart man, and he will help, I am sure of this."

"Please, Pat, can you go now?"

"Tomorrow will be fine, Lisa. I'll go to the club now and find out what is going on, that it has come to this."

Mr. Smith beckoned Pasquale into his office when he arrived the next day. "I was working all night on a plan to make the flour go further for our bread. We will have to cut out making black moons, Pat, and use that flour for bread."

"I will ask my wife how she makes Italian bread go further. I think she adds less semolina."

"If the market stays under, we will have to cut more. Maybe the donuts, but not now—some people live on them. Pat, you will always have a job here. You have proven to be a trustworthy family man who is able to do almost anything here, from chasing rats to delivering bread. But these are tough times. We will have to cut people's pay to keep afloat. You understand? Now, what can I do for

226

you, Pat?"

Here he was in his office, asking for a favor for the Pettorutos when Mr. Morehouse and Mr. Smith had their own major problems. "Mr. Smith, I apologize for asking this favor. That is, if it is possible. My in-laws, who run Pettoruto's Market, are being threatened by the bank; the bank is going to foreclose on the store because they have not kept up with their mortgage payments. Is it possible for me to use part of my pay every week to keep the bank satisfied, until things get better and people are able to pay what they owe to the Pettorutos? Right now, from what I understand from my wife, Betty, no one leaves the store without some food on credit. The Italians have these little black books and keep records of what customers owe. But they are good people and will pay it back. I promise you on my father's grave."

Mr. Smith put his head down. "Come and see me on your lunch hour, and I will see what I can do."

At twelve noon, the office was as quiet as a funeral home before a wake.

"Well, Pat, I spoke to Mr. Murphy, who is the president of the bank where the Pettorutos have their mortgage. He would like to meet with us on Thursday. No proceedings for bankruptcy will go on until after the meeting. He can see us at twelve noon. You can bring your brother-in-law Albert, the lawyer."

Mrs. Lucia Pettoruto, out of the hospital, Guy Pettoruto, and Pasquale went to the Essex Street bank. Mr. Murphy met them at the door and brought them to his office. Unlike Mr. Smith's office, his was grandiose: beautiful paneling, a huge mahogany desk with gold etchings, and leather chairs. Three telephones sat on his

227

desk.

"Thank you, Mr. Murphy, for taking the time to meet with us." Pasquale shook his hand.

He looked like Clark Gable. "Mrs. Pettoruto, sit here," he said, pointing to the finest chair, nearest to his desk.

Except for Sunday mass, Mrs. Lucia Pettoruto always wore a black dress, black stockings, a white apron with pockets, and black lace-up shoes. Today, however, she had on a black dress with a white lace collar and a blue hat with two floppy flowers on it. She was not wearing her stern look.

Mr. Murphy addressed her first, which Pasquale thought was a good sign. "Well, Mrs. Pettoruto, how are you today, and how is your son Albert?"

She answered in a very soft, sweet tone. "We are in good health. My son Albert could not get home for this meeting, Mr. Murphy, so I am sorry."

"My son, John, is at Dartmouth College, and has good things to say about him, Mrs. Pettoruto. You should be proud. How many children do you have, Mrs. Pettoruto?"

"I have two daughters, Elizabeth and Rita, and four sons, Albert, Marco, Lawrence, and Gaetano. Lawrence was named after Lawrence, Massachusetts."

This woman is quite a businesswoman; her English is perfect, Pat thought.

"What about you, Guy, what do you do?" Mr. Murphy was using "Guy," a good American name for Gaetano.

"I am a butcher in the grocery, and I am now learning to make wine."

228

Uh-oh, Prohibition. Pasquale's mind went blank.

"Well, I make the wine for our family and friends. We do not sell it, sir."

Smart. Pasquale relaxed.

"Now, Pat," Mr. Murphy went on. "Mr. Smith here tells me you are one of his best workers. So you are married to Elizabeth, Mrs. Pettoruto's daughter?"

"Yes," Pasquale said, deciding to keep it simple.

"I understand you have a growing family, including your mother and sister. Your sister works in the Wood Mill, Pat?"

"Yes, Mr. Murphy. We all support our mother, who is a widow, and we sent for her because she was alone."

Pat could not figure out what he was doing, but a soft velvet voice in his head murmured, *Tell the truth. No exaggerations.*

Mr. Smith leaned forward. "Mr. Murphy, these are good hardworking people." He went on and on.

Thoughts started up again in Pat's mind. *He probably already knew about us. There is no way he will give us the money unless we work, and not many people have jobs these days.*

Mr. Murphy turned to Mrs. Pettoruto. "You also have a son named Larry? What does Larry do, Mrs. Pettoruto?"

"Well, Larry is married to Nella, and he works for Nabisco Crackers and has a huge route all over Massachusetts. These days he is gone most of the day, and his wife works in a place where they make javel water (bleach)." She stared at him went on, "My son Marco, he wants to be a lawyer, and my daughters work in the store. Betty gets up at 5:30 to make dough for bread and pizza.

229

Rita is in high school and works in the afternoon at Maugeri's fruit and produce, and she gets paid two dollars a week."

"Well, Mrs. Pettoruto, I am very impressed by your family." He turned to all of them. "I am going to help you out during this time. This is my plan. We will not put your store up for bankruptcy. If you can pay the bank at least ten dollars a month until this horrible Depression calms down, then you will start paying the regular mortgage monthly, when things get better." He turned to her. "Mrs. Pettoruto, are you in agreement with this?"

Out of the mouth of an immigrant, her voice became business-like again: "Will we be paying any interest, Mr. Murphy?"

"No, Mrs. Pettoruto, you will not be paying interest."

Then she nodded, and her watery blue eyes filled with tears. Not a drop fell. She looked at Mr. Murphy with such gratitude that Pasquale did not recognize her.

They were on their way home. Their dreams had survived the weight of the day.

"Guy," said Pasquale, "if we do not pay the ten dollars a month, a lot of people will starve. But I make ten dollars a week, and we will survive."

Guy put his arm around Pat and could only nod in agreement. His eyes teared up.

The next day Pasquale brought Mr. Smith a bottle of sauce, a bottle of homemade wine, and fresh Italian bread.

Betty treated him like a hero. His heart grew larger in love.

The slap on the back from Albert never came.

Acceptance from him was all Pasquale ever wanted and yearned for in his life, but it never came.
***

Life in Lawrence during the Depression was demoralizing. People clung together like glue. Mrs. Savastano, the restaurateur, distributed all the food left over from weddings and christenings. Squatrito, the baker, put out small sweet nuggets at the end of the day. Augustino, the barber, cut the price of haircuts to five cents and let in all kids for free.

Betty noticed that her husband was losing weight. "Pasquale, darling, please have more pasta, you are losing too much weight. The children are very satisfied—your mother made something special for them."

"Thank you, my sweet. I have so many things to be grateful for. You and the children are my life." He kissed her forehead and cried.

She hugged him. They were both afraid of the future.

"We do not hold any stock, like the wealthy people in Andover who are committing suicide." In her own way she was being positive. "Others, like your friend Kappy, have it tough."

Kap's Men's Store was in difficulties. Not many people in Lawrence could afford new clothes. He and others lowered their light to save on electricity, yet people still promenaded on Essex Street to look in his windows and dream about better days. Treat Hardware Store ran the Lionel Trains during Christmas-time. The Feast of the Three Martyrs was still a happy time, and the churches still collected nickels and dimes. Though times were bleak, the women of Lawrence still walked down Essex Street,

231

chatting and gossiping while they looked in windows and felt terrified to death about the future.

Sfascia Pepe ("pipe smasher") was the busiest man in The Plains because everyone's pipes kept freezing up in the winter. Elm Street was still busy. Every week a man came by with a tired-looking pony and snapped pictures of the children. The Pontiac Club was next to Pettoruto's. Down the street was Pittochelli's funeral home, a place to go on weekend afternoons to shoot the bull. Across from Pittochelli's, Mr. Arcidi hung thin chickens in his window, ready to be plucked. Candy shops, cigar stores, and Annie Basile's store of many things were all still open. Lots of bakeries remained open because everyone needed something sweet in those days.

The movie houses were dimming their lights. The ushers allowed kids in free when the cartoons were on. Tom Mix and Captain Marvel let the children of Lawrence forget they were hungry. Louie Pearl's candy store gave out free candy and popcorn on the weekends. When things are bad, people love to go to the movies to dwell in fantasy.

Now that Pat's mother lived with them, Betty slipped out to the matinees as often as she could. She picked up all her modern ideas from the movies. Pat got angry thinking about this and became controlling. He told his mother, "She is the opposite of you, Ma, and her own mother, and her sister, Rita. I do not want her turning into a flapper."

During the deepest deprivation any of them had ever endured, the Pontiac Club became an extension of Italian families and homes in Lawrence. Men who went to the club during these years were *"gente di nessuno"* (nobody's people). Thousands of men were out of work,

232

and many could not read. Pat's cooking brought some of them back to life, laughing, joking, and playing cards.

Phil DeFusco made it his mission to read and talk about the latest news. Phil was a World War I veteran and had been injured in Europe. He had a steel plate in his head, and he was tall and strong; no one would cross him.

During those nights and weekends, Ruffino, who was a caretaker at the Holy Rosary Church and a good eavesdropper, told them about something he had kept secret for years. "During the Bread and Roses strike, I let a man into the priest's home one night. I knew he was an owner of a mill because I'd seen his picture in the *Lawrence Tribune*. He had an appointment with Father Milanese. My wife, Sofia, God bless her, works in the office and also cooks for the priest. She told me she put a check in the church's account for fifty thousand dollars. *Male* (bad)—the bastard accepted fifty thousand dollars to dissuade the Italians from striking."

"How do you know this to be true?" Phil DeFusco's scalp was moving.

Pasquale went over to Phil. "I thought it was a rumor then and could not prove it, Phil. Now that we know the story is true, help us write a letter to Father Milanese, saying that we are aware of what happened and asking him to set up a free soup kitchen with at least half of the money he received from Mr. Wood."

Fifty men signed the letter. Phil DeFusco delivered it.

Father Milanese made a trip to the club the next night. Pasquale, Phil, and Guy Pettoruto were playing cards. "Well, boys, I got your letter, and it is a lie. And by the way, this club could be shut down anytime, you know.

233

Gambling is illegal. If I hear any more about this rumor, the club will be shut down." He walked out with his head in the air.

"The arrogant bastard—an Italian, can you believe it?" Phil was the first to open his mouth. "But we must keep this quiet for now, *capishe?* For now, anyway."

"We need money for food. The jackpots are not enough. We must find a way to open a food kitchen here now."

Pasquale agreed. The next day he asked, "What's going on today, Phil? The newspaper's first page is totally black."

"It's Black Tuesday, guys. Black for them on Wall Street. But it has been black for us for months now." Everyone stopped playing cards, and he went on, "That means that the stock market crashed today."

Guy Pettoruto, the spokesman for the group, always asked questions. Everyone listened because his brother Albert was a lawyer. Larry Pettoruto was present too, but he always seemed on another planet. Guy popped up now and said, "Thank God I do not have any stock—it will not affect me. Those guys have always lived a different life and have no idea how we as invisible Americans live in this invisible city of Lawrence."

Nunzio stood up next. "Guy, you are one of the lucky ones—you have your own business and can eat every day. I have been out of work for months and have to depend on charity for food for my family. I would use a pick and shovel if I had to, but I cannot get a job. Such a thing, eh? First the Roaring Twenties, when we thought we would be all right, and now this. *Messeria!*" (worse than miserable).

234

Guy did not defend himself; he looked over at Nunzio and said, "Come to the market tomorrow morning." He said nothing about the possibility that he might lose the market.

Phil, as usual, saved the day. "Listen, please listen: I heard that President Herbert Hoover said to expect more black Tuesdays, black Thursdays, and black Fridays. So let's talk about what we can do to save each other—our families and businesses."

Nunzio stood up, his bloodshot eyes glared, and he looked as if he were crazy. "Call the Mafia!" he shouted. "We are starving, and our children are malnourished."

Everyone started talking in Italian to each other. People had not spoken in their own dialects for years. Just when Pasquale was about to say something, Phil walked to the middle of the floor and, like the Statue of Liberty, raised his hand. "*Stupido, stupido!*" His voice was like thunder. "Just like a *chooch* (donkey). To beat this Depression, if it gets worse, you ask for the most *vergogna personie* (worst people in the world) for help? No mafia! No mafia! If you want their help, get out of the Pontiac Club and go to the club on Short Street. There the president knows who they are."

Nunzio started crying, repeating, "I am done with America! I want to go back to Italy! At least I could have my land and feed my children. But I do not have the money for the tickets."

Larry Pettoruto stood up. Larry was six feet tall, and his dark blue eyes were piercing when he focused them. He was a tough guy, but Albert kept him in line. "Okay, *basta*. Enough of this crazy talk. Phil, what should we do? Help us think straight. We are all starving for information, and

235

individually we mean nothing. Let's organize. Help us decide what we can do now—not next week or next month, now. We need ideas, ideas! Tough ones if we are to survive. Pat, you know these politicians; what can you do?"

Before Pasquale could speak, Phil said in a low voice, "First things first. Pat, Angelo, Larry, Guy, and Nunzio, I want you to meet me here tomorrow in the afternoon, at one o'clock; by night we will have a plan. Anyone can come, but we will get nowhere with too many ideas."

Pasquale said, "I will be at the bakery, Phil."

"Okay." Phil moved over to Nunzio's table and said, "How about five o'clock, everyone?"

"That is dinner-time at my house," Nunzio said more calmly, "but we do not have much food, so it will mean one less person to feed for Angelina."

"Spaghetti without meatballs," Pasquale chimed in, "for us all, tomorrow night, after we meet. *Capisci?* Be here."

The next night six men ate spaghetti and the meatballs that the Pettorutos donated, and some felt full for the first time in months. Crazy plans were disregarded. A carnival seemed like a good idea, but the thought of having fun was so foreign to them that they wanted to "think about it." Phil stood up and like an orator said, "Listen, guys, we can't wait. It's not for us, it's for the children of Lawrence. No one—I tell you, *no one*—can live without some hope and fun." They planned on meeting again in two weeks.
***

Busty Piazza went to the Morehouse Bakery the next day. Pasquale was in the garage. "Patsy, please, you must do me a big favor. My boy, Guido, came home today

236

from the fourth grade with two red patches on his culo. His teacher, Miss McSweeney, sent him down to the manual-training teacher, and two teachers took him into a closet and whacked him on his behind four times with a two-by-four pine board. Please, Pat, can you come with me to see Principal Hennessy? I don't speak good English."

Pasquale remembered when Miss McSweeney had sent Rita home crying many years ago. He thought, *Dio mio, my own son Anthony is no angel, and he's in the same grade.* He asked permission to go during his lunch hour.

Principal Hennessy took them into his office at the Oliver School. "Sit down, Pat, and you too, Mr. Piazza. I heard you are here to talk about Guido. What can I do for you?"

Busty was good at explaining what his kid had told him and about the red marks on his behind. He repeated what he told Pasquale.

Mr. Hennessey folded his hands and looked at Busty. "Guido was being disobedient again. Mr. Cariello and Miss McSweeney had to teach him and some of the other boys in the class a lesson."

Pasquale was thinking that Mr. Hennessey was not a cruel man. He asked him, "What had Guido done, sir?"

"He was disrupting the class by talking to Joey DiAdamo, and they were laughing. He has been told many times not to laugh in class and cause trouble. It was not the first time, Mr. Piazza."

Something about Miss McSweeney ticked Pasquale off, and he glanced up. "A laugh from a nine-year-old boy does not cause the kind of trouble that deserves beatings such as Guido got. This is called a misuse of power, Mr. Hennessy. Mr. Piazza does not want to cause trouble, but I

237

think you should look into Miss McSweeney's history of beating children. If I hear of any more beatings, I will report this to Governor Dever. What we need is a school committee, and I shall mention that to him when I see him."

Principal Hennessy nodded and walked them out.

That night at the club, Pasquale told Patsy Amante about a kid being beaten because he had laughed. Amante's response came as a surprise: "Children should be seen and not heard." His voice was angry. "Disciplining a kid is not such a big problem. We have other real worries here in Lawrence—the soup kitchens have long lines and not much food." He smelled of bleach as he shrugged his shoulders. "You are too sensitive, Pat. Smarten up. You will not live long. Forget about it."

Pasquale's voice quivered. "I will not forget about it, and if I hear of any more beatings, I will do something about it." He slammed the door and walked out.

He could not forget about it and told Betty. Betty held his sad face. "Maybe Amante was beaten himself and heard that from whoever brought him up. Anthony is in Guido's class and has never mentioned beatings."

Still Pasquale could not and would not forget about it.

***

One Friday night, Patsy Amante asked Pasquale to forget their disagreement and invited him to pick mushrooms on Saturday afternoon.

The next day was damp and misty. They were on their way in Amante's truck to pick mushrooms at a secret place in the woods. Pat recognized the place as Methuen, where his friend had a farm, but he did not say anything.

238

As they got closer to the spot, the truck came to a stop. "Listen to me, Pat." Amante pulled a red bandana out of his pocket. "You tell anyone about this spot, and I will break that hard head of yours. Turn around." He tied the large scarf around Pasquale's head. "You know what I mean? Everyone wants to know about this place. I tell no one."

Pasquale promised and noticed that today Amante did not smell of bleach.

"It is raining; we should have good luck."

As he started the engine, Pat thought, *The bastard is trying to distract me.* He felt the truck puff and crackle and knew they were going up and down hills. The wheels squeaked as the truck twisted and turned. Pasquale thought he could smell mushrooms. "Betty makes the best mushroom sauce," he said, "so if we are lucky, I will bring you some of it."

They came to a stop and got out. Pasquale felt the crushed leaves under his foot.

Amante whispered, "Take the blindfold off."

They were in a field with mushrooms as far as you could see. The aroma was intense, like a smoking meadow. Across the pasture stood some of the tallest trees that covered the sun. Amante's face took on the expression of a clown as he took his knife and cut into a white mushroom. He put it in front of Pasquale's face and said, "This is a porcini mushroom, but we must hurry to the gold ones behind those tall trees before the scavengers arrive."

He led Pasquale to another field, but this time it appeared as if the mushrooms were hiding under trees and moss—mushrooms as large as saucers, with smaller ones

239

attached.

Amante handed Pasquale a sharp machetti. "Start cutting the stems from the bottom. The big ones go in the huge basket, and the small ones go into the bushel. Waste no time. We are alone now, but soon they will arrive."

Pasquale lifted his head.

Amante was slicing like a machine, obsessed. "Fill one more basket. The vultures are starting to show up." The machetti flashed powerfully. Amante never looked up. He whispered, "I hope you change your mind about those teachers, Pat. We are friends forever, right?"

Pasquale deftly did not respond. After all, Amante had a machetti in his hand.

"Keep cutting, Pat. Whatever we do not want we'll sell to Bongi's."

"What if the mushrooms are poisonous, Amante?"

"Not these mushrooms, Pat. I am an expert. I learned the trade from my father in the old country. No one has ever died who ate my mushrooms."

Three doves hidden the forest watched them.

Pasquale pushed further. "What do you do to be sure?"

"It's no secret, Pat. When you go home, have Betty boil the mushrooms before she makes the sauce. Tell her to put in a twenty-five-cent silver coin in the water while they are boiling. If the coin turns black, tell her not use them. I have never had a coin turn black in the United States, only in Italy."

With their baskets and bushels filled, they covered the containers with burlap and jumped in the truck.

Once home, Pasquale turned to Amante. "Thank you, my friend, and I hope you can change your mind about

240

those teachers who abuse children."

"*Basta*, Pasquale, we are friends forever, and someday I will tell you my story."

Betty refused to cook the mushrooms until Pasquale told her he would taste them first, before she fed them to the children. She made the sweetest savory sauce. "Next time, Pat, I will not do this. You can buy the mushrooms from the Bongi's."

The truth was that Pasquale was terrified to eat them and never went mushrooming again.

***

One summer during the Depression, Mrs. Pettoruto announced to her family, "Mr. and Mrs. Balsamo, as a payment for what they owe us, have given us their summer place in Salisbury Beach for the summer."

Betty took a deep breath and went over to her. "I will be so happy to go, Mama. The children will be in fresh air, and I love the ocean. Everyone could come on the weekend."

They packed up the Pettoruto delivery truck, a 1931 Ford, for the month of July at Salisbury Beach and were soon on their way. Betty gave them a history lesson: "The Pawtucket Indians lived on Salisbury Beach before the people in the *Mayflower* came from England. Does anyone know what they ate and lived on?"

"Pasta and bread, Mama?"

Anthony burst out, "That's stupid, Lulu! Salisbury beach is on the Atlantic Ocean, so they ate fish."

"Well, that's right, but they also ate wild turkeys and other birds and lots of corn and plants. The Indians had trails that went right through Lawrence, kids."

"Mama," said Lucile, "where did you learn all

241

this?"

"I learned this history in high school. You, my dear, will go to college like your Uncles Al and Marco."

"Not me," said Anthony. "I'm going to work in the store like Uncle Guy and Uncle Larry and help Nona."

"When are we going to get there, Daddy?" Lucille started whining.

"In about one hour." Pasquale was thinking how resilient his son was and hoping he would change his mind.

On Beach Road, Betty opened the window. She took a deep breath and turned to Pasquale, who was at the wheel. "I have never had this feeling in my life, darling. My soul and body were thirsty for this salt air." She looked like the Madonna when she got excited.

He thought, *They are so happy. I will own a beach house someday.*

The beach cottage sat close to the ocean. Pasquale brought everyone to the mile-long jetties fifty feet away and made them promise that they would never go there alone.

"Oh, you worry too much, sweetheart. Mary will come to help me tomorrow. I feel free here!" Betty walked over to a Victrola and a radio. She pointed to a huge tin tub. "Look, Pat, a huge tub that we will bring to the ocean and fill for the baby to play in. Pat, darling, I feel so free here, and I do not feel trapped like I do on Elm Street. Let's open all the windows and sleep in this fresh air tonight. We can hear the waves, and won't that be romantic when we go to bed?"

He loved her for her deep romanticism. But he was worried about how she would manage when he and Glory left on Sunday night. "Betty, will you be okay when I leave

242

tomorrow? I could get my sister or my mother to stay with you."

"No, Pat, I want to be alone." She did not mind Mary the babysitter.

"You should be in the movies, Mona Lisa." Pasquale kissed her and the children.

She recognized his sadness. "After a few weeks I would reconsider, but for now let me be free, Pat. It is a free life here for me—less laundry, less housework, and you know how I love the ocean. The kids will be in bathing suits all day, and we will eat lots of fish. Mrs. Balsamo, who gave us the cottage, told my mother that every week at high tide the fish wash ashore on the beaches. Look over here—it is the basket everyone has for that occasion. 'Fish, fish!' is heard from one end of the shore to the other. They fill the baskets and have enough fish for a feast."

Every weekend Betty's family visited with food and toys. On hot days they stayed overnight, and the cottage was crammed. Some of the boys slept on the huge porch. One week all the guys from the club arrived and treated the children to rides on the dobby horses. Anthony loved the dodgems. Each time the guys came after that, they treated the kids to the dobby horses and dodgems at the Center. Betty cooked pizzas, corn, and pasta and experimented with dough for pizza. Mrs. Pettoruto and Glory always came on the weekends.

One week Pasquale took Friday off and went to Salisbury for a long weekend. Betty looked exhausted but tanned and beautiful.

'Betty, you've been running a camp here every weekend! You look tired." He imagined her cooking and exhausted.

243

"*Caro,*" she said, hugging him, "when my family comes they bring so much food that I don't have to cook for three days. Dearest, the children are brown as berries and healthy as horses."

She was wearing a taffeta bathing suit and, while he stood with the kids on shore, she dove into the water through a six-foot wave and swam to the jetties. Everyone ran up to her and was amazed at her strength, energy, and beauty.

"Let's fill up the tin bathing pan and put it in the hot sand and wait for the sun to warm the water for Joanne." She played, splashed, and laughed.

That day Pasquale told Betty how much he loved the beach house and what it stood for. "Here at Salisbury Beach, I know you are all happy. Best of all, Betty, I have not written any names or places in my notebook."

On his birthday, Glory wrote this poem, called "Salisbury Beach." He cherished this poem and wrote it on the first pages of a new book:

> *The ocean has a way of answering*
> *Thundering waves enter our souls*
> *They cry on those summer days*
> *Here I am not another thing*
>
> *Atlantic Avenue so full of dreams*
> *At night the calm sea is true*
> *True to everything that made juices run*
> *Worries and cares tossed in the sea and July sun*
>
> *It is now the summer of 1934*
> *And though my life has just begun*

And I do not know what it's all about
The names on Beach houses say it all
Bon Giorno, Patti, Little Italy, Ciao Bella
Names you love that have been stilled

The smells of red juicy roasted peppers
garlic and tomato sauce fill the air
Food cuts out the despair
All is forgotten to add another layer

Mrs. Battalato is partially blind
everyone helped her make it through
A heart attack at Eighty-two
She made it because neighbors
Were very kind

And did you know, Mama still cooks and cleans
And gets her swim in every day
After of course she checks us kids all
And waits for you and the others
to come on Sunday

And her friend Teresa who lives
just across the street
Can be counted on to offer
Anyone on her porch
The best of any treat

Porches filled with yellow and red tomatoes cans
with long-stemmed basil, tomatoes
and pepper pans
Our feet were always filled with sand

Oh, how happy to hear the band

Neighborhoods of friendly passion
That only a good gossip
would be in fashion
Clothes-lines filled with clothes
to bleach
Now this is really going to the beach

But most all, in spite of the fall
In nineteen thirty-four
We will never forget
that the days are filled
with those who loved
us all while the waves kissed the shore.

***

The mill owners were just waiting for the time to pay the workers back. It was the talk of the clubs in Lawrence.

Angelo arrived at the Pontiac Club early one day. He looked as if he had been up all night. "Bad news, guys." He stood up and waved his hands. "I just came from the Toilers Club, and another mill is going south to the Carolinas. Cheaper labor, and I hear they are building more factories all over the South. The Everett Mill is closing for good, and I would not be surprised if we see more mills go up in the South. We knew they were up to something, but not this."

"We should not have tried to strike again last year." Tony stood up. He had the floor now, and when he got the floor, it was hard to shut him down. He was screaming, "I was totally against it, and it was a dismal failure!"

246

"Pipe down," Guy said. "The point is what do we do now? In the first place, if the protesters hadn't been ignored, maybe we would not be in the situation we are in now."

Tony piped up: "The rich get richer, and the poor get poorer."

"Survive, that is what we do." Angelo took over again. He was wearing a bow-tie and had very nice black leather shoes. Being a lawyer must be pretty good. "The word is out." Angelo had everyone's attention. They stopped eating and listened. "President Roosevelt will pass the twenty-five cents an hour wage hike and the forty-hour work week soon. That will be good for the workers in Lawrence and all over the country. Mike Landers is our mayor, and he is doing his best to help, but the hard times are here, and his hands are tied. Did you hear that William White, who served a prison term, is running against him? Pat, Landers is a good man. Try to help him out. Last week he was standing on the corner of Essex and Broadway, handing out silk stockings to any woman who promised to vote for him."

"Yup." Pasquale added, "Patsy Amante, who is not here tonight, got the nylons from Filene's Basement and did not make a dime on them."

Guy stood up and said, "Amante had better watch his step. He was selling the clothes he bought from Filene's on the street the other day. As soon as he left, the cops came around looking for him."

DiAdamo told Pasquale that the cops were out to get Amante, so he sent one of the boys over to tell Amante to tell him to be careful. But, knowing how hard-headed he was, Pasquale also planned to talk to him directly.

247

Unfortunately they picked him up before he got a chance to and put him in jail for "loitering."

During his trial Patsy Amanto defended himself. Al Pettoruto said he would be in the background and encouraged this. Pasquale, Guy Pettoruto, and Phil DeFusco sat in the front of the court.

Amante began, "I went to school in Gaeta, Italy, and came in contact with both the poor and the aristocrats of that city. My father apprenticed me to a shoemaker, but I did not want to make shoes, so I fled to America. I was penniless when I came to New York. I worked as a boot-black, and I was called dago, wop, macaroni, and organ-grinder. I served in World War One and am an American citizen. I served with Phil DeFusco. I buy things in Boston because I want the women in Lawrence to have what is unavailable to them. Women in Lawrence work very hard, and some never leave the city. My things bring them joy. I only make five cents an item, and what I do not sell I give out free to those who have nothing. For that, you put me in jail for one month and treat me badly. I had no idea it was illegal to sell things on the street. The rag-man, the egg-woman, the ice-man—they and other peddlers come every day to sell their wares in Lawrence with their carts and mess up our streets, and they never get arrested."

Amante was acquitted, thanks to the advice of his lawyer, Albert Pettoruto.
***

One day Angelo brought a radio to the Pontiac. "I eat enough meals here, so I picked this up for you guys. The President is on tonight. It is his first fireside chat, so listen."

That night they were all glued to the radio. Franklin

248

Delano Roosevelt told them, "The only thing you have to fear is fear itself." Pasquale was to remember this all his life. He wrote in his notebook and also the word "Democrat."

On Sunday afternoons, while he was cooking spaghetti sauce, he would listen to Tony Brown's Orchestra on station WLAW and dream about singing.

The Pontiac Political Club was located in the empty store next to Pettoruto's Market. As soon as word spread, it gained over a hundred members. It was a place for Italian men, a safe place for them to come and play *La Briscola* and *La Scopa,* listen to forty-fives, and gamble. The Pontiac Club was a sanctuary for these men. They had seen Italian immigrants suffering not only from the prejudice tossed at them but from the lack of respect for their culture.

At 6:30 P.M., Archie Barsamian, the Armenian boy from Common Street, now a commentator, announced on the radio, "Grieco Brothers, who make some of the best suits for wealthy men in New York and all over the country, are slowing down, and hundreds of tailors and sewing girls are now out of work."

Guy stood up. "Pat, how about selling your sauce?" Amante volunteered to go to the North End and buy bushels of tomatoes from the pushcarts. There was enough money in the pot to buy some huge vats. So Pontiac Sauce was born. Children from Lawrence were each given a bottle so that they could climb the tenement stairs and deliver the sauce with other food.

No woman ever entered the Pontiac Club until Angie Soprano, the best pattern-maker at Grieco Brothers, banged at the door one night.

Phil DeFusco, who knew her, said, "Angie, *che surgeto?*" (what's the matter?).

She looked desperate; she was crying and about to faint. "Please, Phil," she said, "let me talk to Pat Foenia." Pasquale was making sauce for tomorrow's meatball and spaghetti supper, which he made for the children every week. "Please, Phil!" She kept sobbing and talking. "I heard he can help us. Sonny, he is only fourteen years old, he did not do anything wrong, and they took him bleeding to the police station."

"Slow down, Angie," Phil said. "Who took him to the police station?"

"The Irish cops. Sonny took some fruit that was outside of Tuffatore's grocery store on Common Street. Mr. Tuffatore came out yelling and told him to go back to Elm Street where he belonged, and the police grabbed him and hit him with a club and took him to the jail. Mrs. Barbagallo said he was bleeding from the head. Please, Phil, call Pat—I heard he could help."

"Angie, what do you want Pat to do? Sonny needs a good lesson; he should not have taken that fruit from the box and tried to run away."

"He was hungry, Phil! We have six kids, you know that. We cannot feed them enough. Please, Phil, call Pat. I already went to Mr. Grieco's, where I was laid off, and his son told me to let it go. He told me that when there is more work, he will call me. The police are after us all, Phil." She got down on her knees. "You should hear the stories from some of the mothers, women they call *putana*. We are afraid of the police, Phil, please. When I went to Father Milanese at the Holy Rosary, he said he would see what he could do. Then he said, 'Have you gone to see Pat Foenia?

250

He helps people like you.'" She wouldn't leave or give in and stayed on her knees as if she were praying. "Call him now," she said, "please, Phil!"

Phil said, "I will call him tomorrow."

"No, no, please, before they beat him up more. You know how angry he gets. If you do not get Pat now," she said, "I will call Betty. My sister-in-law knows her."

That was enough for Pat, and he walked out. She was slowly crumpling onto the floor.

"You're the club president, Mr. Foenia, and you help so many people in this city. Sonny is our only son—I have five girls and one boy—and he has a temper. My husband is out of work and is depressed and sees demons now. *Per favore,* Pasqualino. The Virgin Mary will bless you."

Guy, Pasquale, and Phil DeFusco, carrying Mrs. Soprano, walked over to the police station. Pasquale talked all the way. "Phil DiAdamo has helped me out many times and is a decent Italian cop. He has lots of guts and never takes anything except my sauce. He is not on the take, like many of the other cops in Lawrence."

Phil DiAdamo was one of the handsomest men in Lawrence. He looked like the statue of David. Lots of other men in Lawrence would have looked like him if they'd had enough food to eat, taken care of their bodies, and married Sicilian beauties. He was at the desk when they entered the police station. "Patsy, good to see you. Who is this, Patsy, a relative?"

"Phil, she is Sonny Soprano's mother. You have him locked up here. Can she see him? The kid was hungry. What kind of *frittata* (bullshit) is this? The kid took the fruit for his family, the father is sick, and there are five

251

other children who are hungry at home."

"Mrs. Soprano"—Phil DiAdamo took her by her arm—"come with me. Sonny is pretty beat up. He tried to get away, Mrs. Soprano. That boy has a temper; he needs to calm down."

Sonny was lying on a wooden bench in the cell. "Enough," Pasquale said to Phil. "What the hell are you guys doing? The kid has bruises all over his body! He is bleeding and has a split head. Did you call a doctor?"

"They tried to teach him a lesson, Patsy, but he fought back. He is known to the guys on the beat as a troublemaker. Not yet will we call Dr. Zanfagna."

"For three oranges and some grapes, a kid gets this? Who was it?" Pasquale's anger streamed out his whole body. Sonny was on the floor, and his face and arms were black and blue. The blood on his head had already scabbed over. "Who were they? I bet it was those three Irishers. We have been hearing that the three of them go around profiling Italian kids."

"That won't get you anywhere, Patsy. He shouldn't have fought back. You know that."

"Yeah, Phil, we all know what they think of us—we do not matter one damn!"

"Pat," Phil said, "I am only one, and I have to play their game and do what I can."

"Phil, how do we keep these poor souls like Sonny alive? You have to help us. Come to the club tomorrow, and maybe we can talk."

Angie, her voice hoarse from sobbing, was desperately trying to hold her son up. "Please let me take him home so I can take care of him. Oh, *Dio mio,* he is bleeding from his head! He can't walk!"

Guy picked him up and cradled him like a child. The blood of a child, unlike the blood of the meat he cut every day, made him sick.

Mrs. Soprano put a small handkerchief over the crack in Sonny's head.

Pasquale looked at her and was reminded of the Pieta (Mary holding Christ's body) he had seen in a church in Italy. He turned to the cop. "Thank God he still has a heartbeat, Phil, or I would go to Governor Dever for this one. I would go to Al Pettoruto, but he does not have the belly for this stuff. I want to take him to his own home, Phil. I will take responsibility for him. *Capisci?*"

This was the first time he had stood up to Phil DiAdamo, the cop, and he knew it would not be the last.

Phil DeFusco came over to see if they were okay. "*Dio mio,* what happened? How the hell did you get him out?"

Guy carried Sonny up three flights of dimly lit stairs. Five small girls with hungry brown eyes were huddled near the stove, sitting at a kitchen table and staring at the men. They were helpless and frightened to muteness. Mr. Soprano looked dead or drunk and barely raised his head. Pasquale thought of his own children, and then and there he made a promise in his soul, or maybe to the devil, to stop this abuse of innocent Italian people. He didn't know how, but he remembered his rage and wrote in his notebook the names of the three Irish cops.

Dr. DeCesare got Sonny all fixed up and helped get his father to Danvers State Hospital for treatment and medicine. Small donations of food for the family kept them alive. Mrs. Soprano was so grateful that she went over every week to 124 Elm Street and asked Betty if she could

253

help her with the children. Mrs. Pettoruto was always generous in giving her some food.

Sonny was never the same again—a broken human being, a bit scary, but very complacent. Pasquale hired him at the bakery, washing floors and killing rats in the basement.

Danvers State Hospital was a scary place from the outside, like a set of small castles attached together, with high peaked roofs and small windows that had iron bars, worse than any prison you could imagine. Pasquale drove the Sopranos there for an admittance. The eaves of the building had birds that looked like bats about to spring. He held up Mr. Soprano, and Mrs. Soprano followed. Once they got through the iron gates and were walking down the yellow-greenish halls, Pasquale wanted to run away. When Mr. Soprano had been admitted, Pasquale supported Angie until she could sit on a chair and get enough strength to walk back through the darkest, dirtiest hallways they had ever seen.

After two weeks, Pasquale drove Mrs. Soprano to the hospital again to visit her husband, and they took him back home.

Betty heard all about it that night. "They allowed us into his unit. All I could see were men who looked like scarecrows. The screams of despair and the moaning were haunting. I felt like we were being watched. When Mr. Soprano came out, we did not know who he was. He did not recognize his wife right away; he seemed drugged and barely able to hold up his head. He was as thin as a stripped chicken. 'Please, Angie, take me home,' he begged. Betty, I took full responsibility for him and signed paper after paper to get him out. I had to threaten the clerk and supervisor

254

that I would call Governor Dever if they did not let him go. How could something like this exist, Betty? Doesn't it matter to anyone that people in the Danvers State Hospital are living like a pack of wild dogs?" He began to cry, then added, "I couldn't do anything about it!"

"Yes, you can, my darling." Pasquale looked up at her blue eyes. "You can write the story in your notebook tonight before you go to bed."

Mrs. Soprano and all the women at 33 Oak Street brought Mr. Soprano back to health. With the permission of Mr. Morehouse, Pasquale hired him to wash the floors at the bakery, where he could keep an eye on him, and later he joined his son in killing rats.

On Thursday, Mrs. Morehouse's track day, Pasquale did the talking, and the story of Sonny horrified her.

"It is ironic that you are telling me this story, Pat, because Mrs. Stephens was just elected to the Board at the Danvers State Hospital. She is trying to do something about the horrible conditions. The women at my club have been raising money to help her out. She needs someone like you. I will bring her over to the bakery tomorrow, Pat. Would that be okay with you?"

Mrs. Stephens arrived, and Mr. Morehouse let her and Pasquale talk in one of the small offices. She had a sweet voice and a stout head. Pasquale thought that she had the courage of his mother back in 1912 during the strike, and he fell in love with this courage.

Mrs. Stephens spoke first: "I need someone to help me right a great wrong, Pat. Mrs. Morehouse told me all about you and Sonny Soprano. Will you help me and others make a change, to help people in that prison that is called a mental-health hospital?"

Mrs. Stephens gave Pasquale an opportunity he had never dreamed of. She brought him into a world of things that he had never known existed. She sponsored him to be on the Board of Directors at the Danvers State Hospital. Pasquale knew he would be taking a risk, but he jumped at the invitation.

Mrs. Stevens and the other eleven people on the Board approved of Pasquale, and he became Director Number 13, a number that became his lucky number all his life. Mrs. Stephens presented the first list of things that should be changed immediately. She had a lot of power on the Board because she told them that she would provide money for the changes. It also helped that her family owned the Stevens Mills in Andover. Kachadoor Barsamian, a man who worked there, said it was a good place to work. He planned to move to the new housing in Andover for immigrants who lived and worked at the mill.

The Board at the hospital presented the following list of changes:

1. The morning wash is not to be done with a hose on ten patients huddled together in a concrete cell with cold water. A plumber will install pipes for warm water. Only two men at a time will shower, with an aid to help.

2. Governor Dever will provide money for decent food. No more moldy bread will be served with meals. The Betsy Ross Bakery will provide fresh bread until a bakery can be set up at the hospital, where the patients can learn how to bake their own bread and pastries. (The Board members raised their eyebrows when they heard about the pastries.)

256

3. The patients will be allowed to work in the laundry, washing, drying, and folding.

4. The few women patients will be released to families who will be responsible for their care. A plan for these families to follow will be developed by Social Workers of Massachusetts.

Summers came and went, and the changes happened slowly. But, as the morning comes after the night without fail, so change came eventually to Danvers State Hospital.
***

The summers in the 1930s were hot, and children in Lawrence were suffering. At the Pontiac, Gus Salvetti said, "Maybe we could get a truck and bring the kids to Salisbury Beach some Sunday. Let's form a committee to make a plan. Let's put our heads together."

But Phil DeFusco, Patsy Amante, Phil DiAdamo, Tony Soprano, and Pasquale thought of another way. "Let's have a carnival right here in Lawrence."

The approval from the Parks Department to put equipment on the Common didn't come easily. Louie Scanlon, now the mayor of Lawrence, helped them get permits. Every business contributed, and the Traveling Carnival Company agreed to use their own men to bring in and remove the rides and stalls, in order to make the first carnival in Lawrence a success. Every penny from the Pontiac Club was used. Rocco asked all the other clubs in Lawrence to help. Pasquale promised Governor Dever that he would help him get the Italian vote when he ran next year if he helped them with the carnival.

Lawrence was lit up at night by the Ferris Wheel, a miniature railway, and a house of mirrors. The moon over the neighboring towns appeared to be smiling and brought in people from everywhere. Everyone forgot about the Depression for three days.

"Let's have a raffle to make money, Pasquale." Mrs. Morehouse was impressed by her own idea and offered to sell tickets for it at her club and through her people in Andover, Methuen, and North Andover. She even had the tickets printed.

"Mrs. Morehouse," Pasquale said, "this sounds wonderful, but what will we use for prizes? The only thing I can do is make sauce and ask some of the storekeepers to donate things. People in Lawrence do not have enough money to buy food, never mind raffle tickets. But I want so much to have this carnival. I will mention the raffle at a meeting tonight and we will come up with something, Mrs. Morehouse."

"Ask your members, Pat, and if they approve, we will figure it out."

In the end Mrs. Morehouse and the women of Andover came up with prizes: toys for the children, clothing from Andover's textile mills for the women, food baskets from Rita Pettoruto, kitchenware from the Racket Store, a suit from Kap's Men's Store, and Annie Basile's famous coffee pots. Every storekeeper in Lawrence gave something for the raffle.

The carnival drew Italians, Jews, Portuguese, Armenians, Polish, Lithuanians, Syrians, Lebanese, Irish, and even some of the people from Andover and the other neighboring towns, who wanted to see "what the wops were up to." They made over a thousand dollars because so many people from Andover bought raffle tickets. Owens Farm from North Andover donated a hundred chickens, which were all given away.

The carnival provided the people in Lawrence with fun and excitement, and in turn they offered Pasquale their full hearts on voting day. Governor Dever won big in Lawrence. Pasquale thought that knowing someone in a high place would help him with his own plan.

"Please, Daddy," Glory said happily one day, "can we make the carnival a Lawrence tradition?" And it did indeed become a yearly Pontiac tradition for Lawrence. Planning for it made people happy. For three days every year, Lawrence celebrated being Lawrence.

***

Pasquale's happiness ended when he received a letter with a wide black mark on the envelope. Betty was scared to open it and brought it to Mrs. Pettoruto, who read the letter, written in Italian. Pasquale's uncle Cosmos from Italy wrote that his father had been murdered by the Black Hand. Evidently he had refused to pay any ransom to keep his groceria running, so first the scoundrels wrecked the place, and then, because he fought back, they beat him up. He ran after them, fell, and cracked his skull. He died in the Naples hospital.

All Pasquale could do was think about his father dying alone, without him or his mother.

His mother and sister could not go back to Italy for his funeral. Pasquale wrote in his book of names, "Papa, I should have been there."

Betty and the children tried to console him, but all he said was "He died with the people who loved him still here in Lawrence. I offered my mother the money for a ticket to go to the funeral, but she said he would already be buried by the time she got there."

After that, Pasquale always carried the fear in his soul that he would die alone.

In the middle of his grief Betty and the children went to Salisbury beach, but Pasquale could not fight off depression.

Mrs. Morehouse knew how sad he had become and offered to set up an appointment with her "friend," as she called him—her psychiatrist. "He will give you some pills, Patsy, to help you out. You look like you are losing weight, and your eyes have black circles around them. Are you sleeping at night? What does Betty say? Do you want me to talk to her?"

To stop all these questions, Pasquale agreed to see her psychiatrist. Besides, Betty was at Salisbury with the children. He did not have the money to pay for the appointment, but it turned out that Dr. S. was doing it for nothing as a favor to Mrs. Morehouse.

"Betty," Pasquale said later, "Dr. S helped me understand that I could not have gone to see my father buried. I was angry at my mother, even though she now has diabetes and is partially blind, because she did not go to Italy and watch him being buried. I can't fathom how I could possibly be such a terrible son."

Betty shrugged it off. "Darling, all this will pass. Buck up—you still have us."

Pasquale woke up early one day before she went down to the ovens to bake. "I bought a two-family house on Prospect Hill," he told her, "and I want you to see it today. Now the kids can have a real sand box instead of a dough box."

Betty was shocked, happy, and sad.

That year the Pettorutos put a down payment on a

Salisbury Beach cottage on the Atlantic Ocean.

The years leading up to World War II were good for the Foenias and the Pettorutos. Betty was busy with her new house, Rita Pettoruto was running the store and developed the first baby-shower baskets, which sold like hotcakes, and Pasquale was still writing names down in his notebooks and seeing Dr. S.

Then Pasquale turned his attention to gambling and began working at the race track at night. He used the money from his gambling to pay Dr. S., who agreed to accept whatever he could afford. Pasquale deprived himself of all the joys of family and care that he deserved after a hard beginning.

On his last visit with Dr. S., the psychiatrist said, "Pat, you have a lot of life ahead of you. Be kind and good to yourself. Don't worry so much what other people say, and try to have a good life."

He told Pat that he had enlisted in the Army as America entered World War II. In some ways, Pat envied him.

"After initial success, the Allies were pinned down on the beachhead by a vastly superior German force. The Germans eventually committed 80,000 additional troops to the Italian campaign to 'push the Allies back into the sea.' Through sheer bravery and heroism, the Allies held the beachhead. Finally, with long awaited reinforcements, the Allies broke out in late May and ultimately marched victoriously into Rome, in June 1944."

— U.S. Navy Website

CHAPTER 14 – WORLD WAR II: THE SECRET MISSION

Pasquale was walking the streets in The Plains, checking on the windows to make sure no shades were open, wearing his Air-Raid Warden helmet and a yellow band on his sleeve. When the mock air-raid was over, he stopped in at his mother's apartment.

"Pasqualino, is it you? Come and talk to me. I've been so lonely since Josephine left to go home."

Maria was sitting in the middle of her kitchen on a wooden chair, with one forty-watt bulb hanging over her white hair, which was neatly wrapped in a pug. She was now partially blind and had diabetes. Her knitting needles did not stop as he came closer for a kiss. She had knitted hundreds of white woolen stockings for the war effort. She never missed a stitch. Maria's hands were still large, and the brown spots and blue veins danced up and down as she took a stitch, slipped a stitch. Those hands had touched thousands of things, and now the skin was thin and purple, but the hands still moved, the fingers working like puppets doing ballet.

"Pasqualino," she said, her voice soft and sweet, "is it you? Come and talk to me."

"It is me, Mama. How did you do today? Did you eat? Did you take the insulin that Dr. DeCesare gave you? Are you warm enough, Mama?"

She looked worn and older than her years from a life devoted to her family and all her causes. While in Italy, she had been involved in helping women get out of the kitchen and had been a strong supporter of women's rights. Here, she was just waiting for someone to come.

"So many questions, Pasqualino, you ask so many questions. *Caro,* one at a time. I am not as sharp as I was in 1912 during the strike. I ate well today: Josephine brought me some chicken soup, and for breakfast I had my usual milk and bread. Tell me, *caro,*" she went on, "what is happening with the war?" Without waiting for an answer, she went on, "Mussolini has allied himself with Adolf Hitler and Nazi Germany and is now considered our enemy. All Italian immigrants are now considered to be enemy aliens and are under watch. Some of the Italians are being held in prisoner-of-war camps across the country."

Pasquale told himself that it was good she was still interested in politics. He asked her how she had gotten all this information.

"Mr. Battalato gets the *Progresso* newspaper and reads it to me every week. That Mussolini and his prostitute, Claretta Petacci, should be hanged, both of them, by their feet."

Lately she had been lonely and missed conversation. Now she went into the Dominic story. Jospehine's husband, Dominic, has been very angry over

263

the fact that he was considered an enemy. He was basically a good man, but his anger had led to a drinking problem, and he had a temper when he drank too much. "I am worried about my Josephine and try not to ask too much of her. She works long hours, and Dominic cannot find work. You know, *caro,* I am so lucky to have Josephine, who is only my stepdaughter."

"Do not worry, Mama." He was cleaning up her sink and added more coal in the stove. "I will give him a job at the bakery soon. He has a *caba testa* (hard head). He just needs to learn a little more English. He is a fast learner."

"Good, Pasquale, that way you can keep an eye on him." She rose from her chair, and Pasquale noticed that she could barely walk. "Mrs. Romano, on the second floor, came to see me today with some escarole. Here, have some. Isn't Peter, her son, a friend of yours?"

"He is just a kid, Ma, only eighteen years old. Peter is in the 8th Army Air Force. Nunzio, Peter's father, is a member of the Pontiac. He is worried because last week his other son, Sully, got drafted."

"I am worried about you, Pasqualino—can they draft you?"

"Don't worry, Mama, they won't draft me. I am too old."

He did not tell her that he had received papers to register and would be leaving soon. He changed the subject. "What do you hear about the Campagnone boys, Ma?"

"Four of the boys enlisted together; poor Mrs. Campagnone goes to church every day. She sends packages to the troops every week. Last week I gave her woolen

264

stockings and woolen hats for our boys, and she brought them to the Red Cross. A brave family, those Campagnones, but not a family now." She got up to cover the water that was leaking from the refrigerator. "*Caro,*" she said, looking as if she were going to fall over, "when you come the next time, can you find me a piece of yeast? I would like to make bread one more time."

"Sure, Mama."

As he left, he found Mrs. Campagnone at the door with something warm that smelled like soup. Pasquale thought that his mother, sound of mind but blind and trapped in an ailing body, was the saddest thing in the world.

He never got a chance to bring her the yeast.

***

When the letter came from the draft board, Pasquale told Mr. Morehouse.

Mr. Morehouse was confident. "Do not worry, Pat, your job will always be here if you are drafted, but with an elderly mother and four children, I doubt very much that you will be." Pasquale was about to leave when he added, "Pasquale, I hear your son Anthony wants to be a State Police officer. Lieutenant Gerber is a good friend of mine. I will talk to him. He is a fine, strong, handsome boy. He has a job here for this summer. Let me know what happens at the Draft Board."

At the Draft Board, a special officer escorted Pasquale to a private room. Sitting behind a wooden desk, Colonel Burgess opened a folder. "I'm told you are a person of honor, Mr. Foenia. It is impressive that you speak both dialects of Naples and Sicily—is that correct?"

Pasquale was standing and did not know why he

was there. "I do, sir, but is that why I am being drafted?"

"You are not being drafted. The higher-ups need you for a special mission. It will look as if you were being drafted to everyone else. In fact, we want to send you on a special mission."

"Why me? I am not a specialist in anything."

The officer pointed to a chair and asked Pasquale to sit down. "We know you are fluent in many of the Italian dialects, and that is important in this mission. You will not be in active combat."

"But what will I be doing? And for how long?"

"This much I can tell you, Patsy: we are going to capture Rome from the Nazis. Right now, all you need to know is that it will be called Operation Shingle. You will be under cover with the journalists of the world. Your name will be Mark Anthony."

The whole thing was a mystery to Pasquale, but he asked again, "Doing what?"

"You will know once you get there, so be ready to leave next week." The Major wished him well and led him to the door.

Betty was expecting Pasquale to be deferred. When he arrived home, she was feeding the children. "Did you tell them you had four children and an aging mother? That my three brothers are overseas serving our country?"

They waited until the children were in bed. It was a night of love-making and fear of the future. Betty put her arms around him. "This is something you have to do." She knew she could not change his mind.

"It is only for six months, Betty." He tried to be brave.

The two new Air-Raid Wardens, Maria and Rose

266

DeFusco, Phil's wife, patrolled The Plains every night.
***

Pasquale and Huckleberry from *The New York Times* flew into Anzio and met the Italian journalist John DeVito, who was from the Italian newspaper *Il Progresso*. In preparation for the assignment, Pasquale learned that Mussolini had been placed under arrest by the Italian High Command and King Victor Emmanuel III, but that Nazi paratroopers had staged a commando raid and rescued him from the Apennine Mountains, where he was being held. Hitler then appointed him as head of the Social Republic of Italy, a puppet state in German-occupied Italy. While the Nazis were negotiating for an unconditional surrender, Mussolini and his mistress were waiting to take over Italy, somewhere near Lake Como. The Italian Partisans know where they were and planned an attack while the United States invaded Sicily.

January 22, 1944, was misty and foggy as the British 1st Infantry Division and the 46th Division, followed by the 504th Parachute Infantry Regiment and the 82nd Airborne Division, landed in Anzio, Sicily.

Pasquale was overwhelmed. DeVito, the most experienced, stood by him. "Let's call the landing The Anzio Beach Head." They all agreed and began sending messages.

Pasquale watched as troops swarmed the coast and beach. It was as if a beehive had exploded. "The Germans must be surprised." His voice shook.

DeVito said, "Those goddamn Germans are never surprised."

Things got quiet. Pasquale was glad he was there. The ship that had carried the journalists, under the command of U.S. Rear Admiral Frank J. Lowry, stood off shore. By early dawn, a Lieutenant Colonel reported the statistics: 36,000 men and 3,200 vehicles had gotten ashore, 44 men were missing, 13 soldiers had been killed, and 97 men were wounded. The Allied forces had captured 227 Germans. "Not so bad," he commented.

DeVito said, "Hold your horses. You Americans do not know the Germans. Be prepared for the worst payback you have ever seen. Those Germans have concentration camps where they are persecuting and burning the Jews. They will do the same to the Italians and Americans."

Pasquale thought about his family back home and wrote a letter to them in case he got captured.

The heavy attacks from the Germans came two days later. It was pandemonium. Luftwaffe aircraft swarmed all over the place. The United States hospital ship sank, and the stock of supplies piled on the beachhead was bombed to shreds. Yet 61,332 Allied soldiers had landed.

"How many casualties, Lieutenant? This looks pretty bad. We are in trouble."

Pasquale was taking notes; the journalists were ready to send reports in Morse code. The officer was unsteady as huge waves rocked the ship. "It is a living hell, and I do not know."

Pasquale rubbed the Saint medal on his neck. Before the Lieutenant walked away, Pasquale walked over to him. "I am really worried about my twenty-year-old cousin, Alphonse Pettoruto, who is on an English battleship preparing for the second landing here. Is there any way we could check on his whereabouts, Lieutenant?"

The Lieutenant was abrupt. "Not now, ask me later."

By February, the troops, after suffering 1,400 casualties, were so exposed that they were forced to retreat two and a half miles. The Germans continued attacking and destroyed a whole battalion. The deck of Pasquale's ship was covered with wounded marines, soldiers so wounded that some were being shipped to England and some all the way home. The pictures DeVito took and hid were confiscated by a Navy Seal. Every day Allied airplanes and artillery machine guns bombed and blasted. The sky looked like it was on fire. The Germans countered with a final five-day attack. The report given to the journalists was that 3,500 had been killed and wounded. One English tanker had been destroyed.

Pasquale was still worried about Alphonse. He wrote every day in a notebook that he called the War Book. The Italian journalist taught him about documenting events. The English guy kept figures and statistics.

By March 4th, there was a lull in the fighting. Pasquale was transferred to the warship with no explanation. When he arrived, some of the marines and soldiers who had been wounded were getting ready to go home. He located Alphonse right away. While they cried, kissed, and hugged each other, Alphonse told him that he would be going to the front in the morning.

Pasquale thanked the commanding officer because he thought he had been sent there to see Alphonse. Instead, he was taken to the Captain's quarters, where six German prisoners were being held. He learned from them that they were Italian men who had been drafted into the German army under duress by Mussolini, who had sold his men and their souls to the Germans.

"The Germans have sixty tanks and aircraft ready

to attack if the Allies try to take the factory near the Campoleone Cisterna Railroad. The railway travels straight to Rome, and the plan is to get German troops into Rome and take it over."

Pasquale had completed his first mission. The Italians offered information that helped the 91st Reconnaissance Squadron meet The Fifth Army with General Clark and abort the takeover.

Two correspondents came aboard that night and joined Pasquale the next morning with the 1st Armored Division and Clark's Fifth Army. Their destination was Rome.

***

It was the night before the invasion of Rome. Alphonse and Pasquale spent the night at a local bar. As he looked at Alphonse, Pasquale thought of his own two sons and said to himself, *He is only a boy, the jolliest, friendliest kid. God give me the gift of my own sons being like him.*

"I will be in a tank with three other guys," said Alphonse. "We are carrying oil. If you hear that something happens to me, give my mother these earrings that I bought today."

Pasquale felt the fear in Alphonse as he held onto him when they said good-bye.

Two correspondents, two infantry men, and Pasquale were in a tank farther down the line behind Alphonse's tank. It was a beautiful day, and even though it was dark in the tank they knew the sun was shining. Up ahead, Alphonse popped his head out of the top of his tank and gave the victory signal. Pasquale was looking for the sun and signaled back. He saw the bomb before it hit.

"Tank hit!" someone shouted. "Close the hatch!" It

270

was a direct hit by the Germans on Alphonse's tank.

The infantry guy said, "It's the oil tanker—roll her back!"

Balls of fire, torsos, arms, and legs were flying around. Pasquale thought he saw Alphonse's head fly through the air, and then arms and legs still attached to his body. "Let me out!" he yelled, and went to unlatch the door.

"You can't go out, Pat, it's hell out there."

"Please, Alphonse was on that tanker—I have to find him. Open the goddamn hatch!"

Someone said, "Okay, the tanks are stopped."

His legs sank down to the ground, and gunfire whizzed past him. He kept reaching for Alphonse's head. Amid all the dust, fire, and gunshots, someone knocked him out and carried him back to his tank.

Pasquale arrived in Rome and found out that the Germans were on the retreat. The base was totally disorganized, and no one knew who he was. He wandered around, found a bar, and drank as much as he could.

She was the most beautiful woman he had ever seen. Betty's eyes looked out of her face, as blue as the Italian sky. "*Caro.*" Now she had his mother's voice. "Why are you so sad?" She took his hands and kissed his palms. She ordered a drink from the bartender, who looked just like Alphonse, and he told her his story in English. He did not know if she understood. She treated him as though she understood his pain.

"Come, let us walk and get some air." She led the way. They stopped in front of a building that was still standing, with the remains of others all around it. She led him up one flight of stair and asked if she could make him

271

some espresso.

"Let me take your boots off," she said, and knelt on the floor. Gently she slipped the boots off and rubbed his toes. Still kneeling on the concrete floor, she kissed his feet. Then she went to make the coffee and asked, "Are you married?"

"Yes. I need some sleep."

She guided him to her bed. "Do you want to make love?"

He did not answer, just fell asleep.

He saw her in the night, opening the shutters of a window facing the bed. He was in his underwear and sweating. He started to cry. He remembered his dreams because he thought they were real.

He was following the tank that Alphonse had been in and praying that they would stay alive. Church bells from the nearby church mixed with the bells in Lawrence. Just as he flew through the top of the tank, it sounded like the end of the world. And yet there were fig trees that stood fast around them, on fire. As they burned, he knew they would rise again next year, here in Italy. His burned body, except his head, burned to ashes, and he was bringing Alphonse home in his backpack.

He looked around the tiny apartment and did not know where he was. He thought he was in Purgatory. *"Come ti chiami?"* (what is your name?) he asked.

She replied in English, "My name is Sophia," and she started rubbing his face and back and kissing his forehead. "There is a full moon tonight. Come and see." They went to the tiny window and opened the shutters.

"What time is it, and where am I?" He did not remember how he had gotten there.

272

"We are in Rome, and it is two o'clock in the morning."

She was making coffee, and her hair, which hung down to her shoulders, was red and shone in the moonlight. He thought of Angelica in Lawrence and quickly took the tiny white cup in his hands and drank the coffee. She brought over some small sweetbreads.

The red hair was all over his face. He did not want to see. Blinded by red, he thought, *No one in my life has ever said, "Come and look at the beautiful full moon."* She pressed her breasts to his face and lips.

She laughed as they dropped onto the bed. When an erection came, he was still kissing her breasts. He jumped out of her bed and ran behind the sheets hanging on a line in the kitchen, crying like a baby.

She handed him his clothes and said she understood. She told him that her brother had been killed by the Germans and that his name was Pasqualino too. They talked for hours about the dying, how the Germs (Italians called them "germs") had invaded by foot and by air. She hated them and said they had raped her sister and mother, who were now in Gaeta with their family. She talked about her faith in God but said that she could never forgive the Germans for what they had done to Italy. They wept together.

"I have some American coffee; would you like some?"

"Oh, please, yes. Sophia, do you know where the American Embassy is?"

"Yes, I work there during the day as a stenographer. Now, Pasqualino, tell me about your family in America."

She was dressing, and Pasquale became alive as he

273

talked about Betty, Lawrence, the Pettorutos, and his four children. She wore black clothes, her red hair wrapped in a black and white scarf. She looked like a nun and not the ravishing beauty he had met at the bar.

When they left the apartment, she reached down to her night table and gave him a silver medal of St. Christopher. "Here, take this and remember me when you look at it. St. Christopher is like you, Pasqualino; he carried the weight of the world on his shoulders, and his medal will protect you wherever you go."

"Thank you." He put all the money he had in his pockets on her night table as she turned the key to lock the door.

After they entered the American Embassy, she disappeared down a cool marble corridor, and he never saw her again.

***

In July 1943, over five hundred Allied planes bombed the hell out of Rome.

Pasquale spent the next six months working at the Embassy, translating, typing code, and interpreting radio broadcasts from Germany. Italian Partisans took Mussolini and Petacci from a convoy of Fascists and Germans trying to escape to Lake Como and hid them in a farmhouse. The next day Mussolini and his mistress were taken to the village of Giulino di Mezzegra on the shores of Lake Como, placed in front of a stone wall, and executed with machine guns. On April 29, their corpses were placed in a truck and dumped in the Square of the Fifteen Martyrs, and then the crowds, after kicking, beating, and spitting on them, hung them up by their feet. The people all over Italy celebrated. The heat in Rome was oppressive, but the people filled the streets, hugging, kissing, and dancing.

Pasquale was looking for Sophia. At the bar that night, he heard from the bartender that she had committed suicide. He asked his friend Richard Maloney, an English Intelligence officer, if he knew why Sophia had committed suicide, because he remembered Richard's name coming up in his conversation with her.

At the embassy, Richard was considered brilliant and something of a snob. "How the hell should I know, Pasquale? I did not know her."

Though he was usually drunk, Richard turned to Pasquale to help him with his Italian. Pasquale heard him say one day, "This is what happens to Italy when it declares war on us. The whole of Italy stinks because of the bodies under the rubble and bombed-out buildings. They are like niggers and have to be kept in their place."

"You spend too much time alone, Pat," he said another time, and took him to dinner in the Old Quarter. He liked his wine, so many a night Pasquale took him home drunk. At the Officers' Club and the Red Cross, tall and straight, with a crisp uniform and bright red hair, Richard was treated like a war hero.

A woman named Antonia rushed to hug Richard as he took Pasquale into the Red Cross station. She was from Naples, and as her lips slid across his, he took Pasquale's arm. "Pasquale, talk to Antonia; she loves Americans." He already had his eye out for a buxom blonde American who had just arrived from the States.

Antonia invited Pasquale to her apartment on Via Condotti one day. Pasquale declined because he had received news from the states that Vincieri from Methuen was in tough shape, suffering from VD that he had gotten

275

from one of those Italian "sluts."

"Can you take me to a store instead, so that I can buy a present for my wife, Antonia?" He purchased a bracelet for Glory, a ring for Betty, three gold medals of ten golden horns, and a pair of rosary beads. He included a ring that Antonia "could not take off."

Back in the Code Room, which was full of noise, Pasquale received a telegram: "Mother critically ill come soon." Richard Mahoney helped find him a seat on an ambulance plane returning to America the next day.

That same day, the British 8th Army Air Force was hit badly, and Mahoney was swearing to beat the band.

Pasquale turned to him. "What plane was hit, Richard? I have a friend named Peter Romano in that unit."

"No information until tomorrow," Mahoney said. "We have other things to worry about."

Peter was hit and became a prisoner of the Germans.

On the way to the airfield, the driver began talking to Pasquale in Italian. "I was studying for the priesthood in Tuscany when Mussolini ordered that all of us under twenty years of age be drafted to fight in the war. I was not ready or strong enough, but God gave me the strength to carry on. The Germans killed with no mercy, and I prayed, until at last I had to kill to save women and children from being raped." He went on, "The rape of the whole of Italy has been worse than death, and in the Italian way it is Purgatory: you know you are alive, but you live in sorrow, filth, and hunger. And the Germans like sponges, sucking it all in." He was driving slowly, with tears in his eyes. "This is what war does—destroy, murder, and ruin. My teachings say I should turn the other cheek and forgive, which is a

276

code for loving humanity. But how can I ever forgive?" Though tears, like raindrops, covered his boyish face, he continued. "My brother, Giorgio, is in America, at Fort Devens in Massachusetts. He is a prisoner of war. Do you know where that is?"

Pasquale did not know that America had any Italian prisoners of war and asked him what had happened.

"Il Duce was a very crazy man. First he invaded Ethiopia, and after that Hitler went to his defense. Then came France and Libya. Finally the British attacked Sidi Barrani in Egypt to stop him from seizing the Suez Canal, and he even tried to invade Tripoli. The British took over fifty thousand Italian prisoners. My brother was sent to America. He works on a farm during the day. He wrote to me last month and said he had met a very nice Italian-American woman from Lawrence, Massachusetts. Her name is Connie. Do you know her?"

"My wife has a very good friend named Connie." *This is too much of a coincidence,* he said to himself.

They arrived at the airport. "I will look into it, kid, and take it from there, okay? I promise." Pasquale ran to the plane.

He had a dream while flying home in the American B24 bomber. From his window, the world was full of shadows. Across the darkness the words of an Italian writer, written in neon script, moved with the day: "Strike a light, and it will cast a hundred shadows on the world." He was climbing a lighthouse, and when he reached the top, the roof was dripping with blood. A plane flew by, and he reached out touch it. A man was slumped over the wheel. The plane was smoking, with a wing missing. The plane exploded, and a body flew out. The olive trees stood fast

277

around Alphonse when the wind from the explosion went through them. Though the window of the plane he heard the velvet voice again: "The olives trees will rise again next spring."

Alphonse arose from the olive trees. "Alphonse," Pasquale said, "how come I never learned anything about this wonderful country in school? Italy is beautiful, art is everywhere, and our heritage is what no other country can boast about."

Alphonse said, "You did not want to know, or you would have asked questions, Pat."

Pasquale was crying. "That teacher made me and all of the other kids feel stupid, so we never asked anything that she would punish us for."

"Pat." Alphonse looked at him, and Pasquale noticed that he had one blue eye and one brown eye. "Do not let someone like that witch ever make you feel inferior."

"It is not true that I did not want to know. I just did not know how to know. Those teachers had only one thing in mind—to keep us ignorant, keep us Labor, and keep us down."

Then, in the dream, Alphonse became Peter Romano. He was dressed as a bombardier and said he had flown out of the plane before it crashed.

"You can fly?" Pat asked, looking at him.

"What do you think they teach you in bombardier school, Pat? Nothing. I flew by my soul."

He woke up crying as they reached America.
***

Pasquale slipped into Lawrence during a practice air-raid. Maria was lying in her hospital bed. She looked

278

peaceful. Josephine and Betty had been with her for three days. Dr. Calitri had said he did not know what was keeping her alive. Pasquale held her frail body close to his own in love and remembrance.

Josephine said to him, "Go home, Pat, and take Betty. You're exhausted."

The minute he left the hospital, his mother slipped away in peace.

Those who lived in America thought the war years were awful. That is because they were not in Italy. All over war-torn Europe during the war, the people understood that man is more than just a body of blood and bones. Their religion kept the Italians' spirit alive and believing in their faith.

Later on, while Pasquale was explaining his secret mission, he said to Betty, "Italians cry when they are sad; they cry in church; they cry after a sermon that touches their soul; they cry because they are grateful to be Italian. It is the principal thing for them, and often it is a survival instinct, so they do not break. They experience grief as a nation, a grief that is uncomplicated because they are proud to be Italian." He embraced Betty, and both of them started to cry. "I understand that because I am so proud to be American, my darling Americana."

CHAPTER 15 – TRANSITIONS

Pasquale arrived at Dr. S.'s office thinking to himself, *This is the last time.*

He started talking before he sat down. "Doc, I've decided to be an actor. I do not mean a stage actor, just a person—you know, a normal person who does not cry when I cannot find a name. The memories of Alphonse come to me every night. I am blessed with a wonderful, loving, smart family who love me, a good job, and lots of friends who have helped me though my grief. Tell me what to do, Dr. S.—I want to cry and write names in my books all the time. Lawrence is so different after the war. My children's faces when I get frustrated scare me."

"Pasquale," said Dr. S., "it is not up to me to make you happy. It is up to you. Time and time again you said you were happy. What has changed?"

Pasquale began to cry, and he cried until Dr. S led him to the door.

Then Dr. S. stopped. "Do something every day, Pasquale, no matter how small, that makes you happy. *Capisci?* Pasquale, there is a beautiful two-family house on Prospect Hill for sale. The second floor is already rented, so that could be an income for you. It is well-kept, and it has five garages that pay rent every month. The schools are much better up on the Hill than in The Plains. Betty will love it."

Pasquale left the office with a plan in mind. The following Saturday he went to the bank to see Mr. Murphy.

It had never occurred to him that people would not like his family because they had an Italian last name. When he talked to the renters who lived on the second floor of the house on Prospect Hill, he heard them whisper, "There goes the neighborhood. The dagos are coming."

Once the bank approved his loan, Pasquale asked the renters to move.

Betty did not want to leave her family and cried daily until she met a woman who became her closest friend ever, Mary Zolak. Mary sat at the counter in Betty's kitchen, eating a plate of spaghetti that Pasquale had put in front of her. "Betty, people on the Hill are very entitled. When Sam and I arrived on Prospect Street, I hated it. But when the word got around that Sam was a doctor, things changed. So, Pasquale, you should act like a politician."

"Will people begin waving to me and start being friendly to my children, Mary?" asked Pasquale. She was the most upfront woman he had ever met.

"You wait and see, Pat."

"If that is so, Mary, I will drive my children to school before I go to work every day, and they will be fine. They need to go to school with fresh, unafraid minds."

"You do not have to do that, Pat, but if you do drive, maybe my girls will join them."

So that was how it was. Pasquale loved driving the kids and dropping them off. He heard all their stories and the fun they had being friends, and not a word about bigoted teachers.

Mary and Betty cooked and shopped together, and Pasquale provided Mary and her family with his famous tomato sauce every week.

The Germans blew up a plane right on the runway…
The CQ woke me up one night and said we got two planes
needing a radio operator. What was I going to say? no?
So, I was the extra man on the crew. I didn't
have to go. I had flown thirty missions. We
dropped the bombs over Magdeburg, Germany.
There were only thirty-four guns there. Unlike
Brunswick on my last raid that had eleven
hundred. So, we dropped the bombs and started
making 180° to go home and we got hit.

Immigrant City Archives
— Peter Romano

Chapter 16 – EIGHTEEN PACKS OF LUCKY STRIKES

At the Pontiac Club they took advantage of the Columbus Day holiday to throw a welcome-home party for Peter Romano, and Pasquale thought, *It's my party too.* The whole of The Plains came. Peter had been a prisoner of the Germans for one year.

Surprised at the overflowing crowd, Peter sat shyly next to his brother and mother.

General Antonelli, wearing the Purple Heart, the Presidential Unit of Citation with the Bronze Star, the American Defense Medal, the American Campaign Medal, the Asiatic-Pacific Campaign Medal with three Bronze Stars, the World War II Victory Medal, and the Occupation Medal with the Asia clasp, stood up. He thanked everyone in perfect English, with no hint of a Sicilian accent.

Guido turned to Pasquale. "I guess you have to

speak the good English before you rise up to General, ha, Pat? His mother and father came from Calabria and lived on the fourth floor on Oak Street before the war. He was an only kid and got the best of everything. Now he abandons Lawrence and lives in Andover."

"Quiet." Guy Pettoruto poked him and said, "Hear him speak. Do not be a *disgratziato* (ignorant person)."

The General went on, "Peter Romano enlisted one year after Pearl Harbor was attacked. An eighteen-year-old, first-generation Italian boy, weighing one hundred and fifty-nine pounds. I mention his weight because it is part of his story. He trained in gunnery and became an expert in machine guns and the 47 and 45 Colt guns and ammunition. That led him to the B-24 Liberator as a top gunner and radioman for the American Air Force. He had to fix together the seventy-eight parts of his machine gun, and his final test was to take the gun apart and put it together with a hood on his head and blindfolded. For him, the pressure chamber during training was hell. When you are in the chamber, you have to wear an oxygen mask, and you spend three and a half hours at a simulated altitude of thirty-eight thousand feet. Peter was transferred to Ireland and then to England. He flew over thirty missions to Germany and France and was part of the squadron on D-Day. I hope you all remember D-Day. Peter was there."

Some of the guys were starting to squirm. Larry, under his breath, whispered, "Get on with it!"

The General spoke louder: "Peter completed his last mission and was getting ready to go home. But then the Captain came into where Peter was packing and announced that a German plane had shot one of the bombers that was to go out in the morning, right on the runway. Two planes were ready to go, and they needed a radio operator and an engineer. Peter and Richard Dorfman went on the last plane out.

"After dropping their bombs in Magdeburg, Germany, Peter's plane lost a section of the wing. The bomb bay was on fire, and he bailed out. He had never had any parachute training. On September 11, 1944, he landed in the middle of a big crowd of people. Richard Dorfman landed several yards away." The General stopped and beckoned to Peter. "I want Peter to tell you the rest of the story. But there's one more thing I want to leave with you with, something I learned from spending my adult life serving our country: we must keep our friendships to preserve our species and, you might say, our Italian heritage. Peter survived not only through his bravery; lots of guys were brave and lost their lives during the war. But he had a strong will too and is a man convinced of his principles. Peter endured humiliation, torture, and starvation for what he believed in. People in extreme situations endure better if they are not isolated. In spite of the stressful circumstances of solitary confinement, with no exercise, stripped naked, he kept in touch with his friend Dorfman. Both of them had a goal to survive and kept their loyalty not only to each other but to their country. Okay, you're on, Peter."

"I am not such a hero as the General wants you to think. I was only doing my job.
It was the luck of the draw when I decided to go on that run. The Germans must have known about this raid. It was pandemonium up there—firing came in all directions. Getting shot down was the scariest thing that has ever happened to me. My whole life went before me like a

movie.

My plane got multiple hits, we lost a section of the wing, and the whole bomb bay was on fire. The guys bailed, so I opened up the bomb bay, trying to get the fire out, and when I saw that the

co-pilot had been cut from here"—he pointed to his left ear—"all the way down his chest, I said, 'Let's get the hell out of here.' He died in my arms. I put the plane on automatic pilot, grabbed the co-pilot, and dumped the top gunner out. We all got out. We were up twenty-three thousand feet in the air. I remember in training they had said, 'When you break through the clouds, you bail out,' so I pulled my chute.

"In training, they repeat again and again, 'Bury your chute so that the enemy does not know where you are.' I'm down on my hands and knees, digging, trying to bury my chute. I looked up, and I was alone in a circle, and people were screaming, swearing, kicking, and spitting at me. I was dragged down to the local jail, and I see Dorfman, so I knew he was alive. They made us take off all our clothes and put us in a cell. The sergeant and the local police had the townies come to look at us like monkeys in a zoo.

"I was interrogated at Obertead, in a dark dingy cell. At night I did not know what was crawling over me— rats, insects, and who knows what else. I could not see my friend Dorfman, but I could hear him when he was beaten. The fact that he was alive kept me going. I was put on the uncooperative list because I would not sign the papers they put in front of me for five days in a row. They were written in German, so I could not understand what they were asking me to sign. From then on, I got one slice of dark bread a day in the morning, and if I did not eat it the guards would not bring me another thing until it was gone. Now I cannot even look at dark German bread, never mind eat it."

Peter was getting comfortable and relaxed, and the guys were listening to every word.

He went on, "I was sent with about ten other guys by bus to a transition camp, where we got de-loused with cold water and some kind of disinfectant spray. On the bus, Dorfman and I sat next to each other, and we made a plan to escape, which gave me hope even though I knew it would never happen. I was given a pair of pants, two pairs of underwear, two shirts, socks, a sweater, and one pair of boots.

"From the transition camp, we were transferred by train to a prison camp in Gross Tychow, on the border between Poland and Germany, where ten thousand prisoners were being held. Dorfman and I were separated, and I was sent to a room that was twenty-four by sixteen feet, with twenty-five prisoners, mostly Canadian and British men who looked as if they had suffered humiliation and starvation. They asked me how was Piccadilly Square. The day I had been shot down, I'd heard Winston Churchill give a big speech; he'd said the lights would be on in Piccadilly Square on Christmas. So I told them, and they started crying like babies. I slept on a bench on a straw mattress full of lice. There was a two-holed space for a latrine that was locked at night, and the doors and window were barred. Breakfast was a cup of *ersatz* (muddy coffee) and a slice of black bread. There was one pot-bellied stove in the room, and when October came it was cold.

"Dorfman told me that his room was close to a huge Red Cross warehouse full of boxes from the States. For weeks we waited and nothing came, so eventually we made

286

a plan to raid the place on a dark, moonless night. We were like bulls in a china shop, searching all over the place, looking for food to bring back to the other prisoners. I managed to sneak out two cartons of Lucky Strike cigarettes because I knew that the guards could be bribed with American cigarettes. They sure came in handy for me. Thanks to them I started writing a diary, which I have here." He took out a small book made of eighteen Lucky Strike covers and passed it around. It contained amazing drawings of the camp, along with the number of people killed, names, and places. It had been tied together with a leather bootlace.

"There was plenty of food stacked in the warehouse, only a skip and a hop from our barracks. To think, we never got any of it. The Germans did not want us eating better than they were. We took all we could carry that night and had a feast. I took the cartons of Luckys."

Tony Soprano spoke up: "Peter, did you and Dorfman get caught or punished for raiding the place?"

Peter smiled a shy, crooked grin. "Nope, no one squealed on us. If the guards knew, they did not say anything."

Soprano asked, "Why take the cigarettes when there was so much food stacked up?"

"We could barter for a little extra food with the cigarettes. Dorfman was looking for red pepper, and then we found out the Germans had stolen the red pepper. They planned to use it to pepper the dogs if we tried to escape.

"One day the commandant picked me up and started shaking me and screaming in German. I did not know what the hell he was saying, until someone yelled out, 'He wants your jacket.' I said, 'Why? It will never fit him. The guy is six feet tall and broad as a cow.' 'Just give it to him,' the other guy yelled. I took it off, and he kicked me in the groin, then threw the jacket on the floor and spit on it. From then on, I called him Sergeant Schultz—you know, like that guy in the movies.

"Dorfman and I were digging trenches next to each other. Hardly a whisper came out of his beaten body, and he whispered, "Peter, walk around do not sit or stay on your cot. We are going to get out, so we have to keep in shape." So, when I had the strength, I would march around the camp.

"In September of 1944, as the Russians were getting closer to the camp, we were told that everyone but the Americans were going to be shipped out. In January, we woke up and most of the people in the camp were gone, so we figured we were next. The next morning, we were told that we were leaving. 'You're going to be walking a long time,' a guard told us. I put on two pairs of socks, two pairs of underwear, two pairs of pants, and a jacket from an American who had been electrocuted while trying to escape. Believe it or not, I had knitted a woolen cap during my stay at the camp, because I had taken a ball of wool from the Red Cross."

Soprano asked, "So did you take the cigarettes with you?"

"Yeah, I hid them in my cap and boots." Peter sat down for a few minutes and took a deep breath. Then he went on. "As we passed the warehouses, the Germans told us we could take whatever we wanted. Thousands and thousands of boxes were piled high with goods, while we starved. I made a knapsack out of the pants I picked up and stuffed the legs with more cigarettes, a can of fat, milk

288

powder, and vitamin pills. I hid the Lucky Strike Diary in the cuff of my boot.

"After the first fifty miles in cold, snowy weather, I had to throw away a can of fat that I had taken from the Red Cross because it was getting too heavy. I kept the vitamin pills, though, and that was what kept me alive. We walked over five hundred miles and slept in barns, on the road, and in fields. When we first started, I began keeping the diary. As you can see, on the first page there is a sketch of the room we were in. Look on the other pages, and you will see how many miles we walked each day. Then I ran out of pencils and wrappers.

"On April 13, I woke up with gun butts hitting me and men telling me, 'Roosevelt kaput.' The Germans were happy that our President Roosevelt had died—they thought it meant that they would win the war.

"When we reached Hamburg, we were put on a train. No one told us where we were going. Some guys died in the train car. We went through the Polish corridor—I know that because Dorfman knew the place. When we reached Annenburg, all of us who had survived were thrown in an empty room they called a hospital. No beds, no blankets, no food. What kept me alive were the vitamin pills and the food I bought from the guards with cigarettes. One day I was walking around and spied some green leaves coming out of the ground. The Germans fed these greens to the cows, but to me they were Kohlrabi—you know, like our parents make. We ate them raw.

"I woke up and looked out of the window one morning. I saw a Russian soldier riding a jackass with a Thompson machine gun strapped to his back, and following him was the Russian army, all carrying machine guns.

Some of those Russian were nuts, trying to shoot the Germans hiding in the woods and raping the women in town, even though the people had white sheets flying on poles and wrapped around houses. The sons of bitches kept killing, even though the villagers had surrendered. I had locked us in the building, which was loaded with lice and bugs, and we could not get out.

"Finally, after five days, a convoy of American trucks came and opened the doors. A Lieutenant from the convoy asked for the highest-ranking guy, and of course that was me. He said to me, 'I want you to pick twelve men and go into the town and protect the Germans from those crazy Russians.' 'Me?' I said. 'Yes, you. You pick 'em.' I say to him, 'What the hell, are you crazy?' He comes up close to my face and says, 'How dare you call an officer crazy?' I knew I could bribe him, so I took off my watch and gave it to him, so I would not get shot. Then the Lieutenant said, 'This is what I want you to do. I want you to wear a white arm band.' I said, 'Where the hell am I going to get a white arm band?' He throws a sheet at me and says, 'Rip it up and get those twelve guys, and make sure you get them out first thing in morning, and make sure everything goes up. I have your name, rank, and serial number, so don't fuck up.'

"I picked out twelve American guys, mostly kids. I said to them, 'This is what the nut wants, but what he wants and what he gets are two different things. First, I want you to protect yourself. Do not get involved, walk together, smile at everybody, shake hands, and salute. Half of those Russians are drunk. And take the white arm bands off when we get out.'

"So we did all that, and a Russian officer came

290

over, and he spoke English. I gave him a big salute and said, 'What's happened here?' He says, 'By what authority are you here? This is Russian territory: we are in charge here.' So I say, 'No authority, General. We are just passing through. But what happened here? Some of those guys are Americans; they look like they are in trouble.' The guy goes back to his men. Then he strolls back. 'The men are telling me those Americans tried to stop the Russian soldiers from molesting these women. The idiots.' It seemed there had been two women on a bus, and the Russians had gone after them, and the women had started screaming, so two of my men had gone in. More Russians went in, threw our men out, and started pouncing on the Americans, but we got them out. So I said to the General, 'God, our officer is going to be mighty mad when he hears about the stupidity of these people.' He says, 'Stupidity, that's right, stupidity.' Then he says, 'Take these two back where they belong.'

"The next morning, the Looney did not like the report I gave him and said, 'You will go back in the morning,' and he turned around and walked out. The morning after that, he says, 'Why didn't you go?' I said to him, 'I am not going. I am not going back, no matter what you say.' He turned around and walked out again. The next day, a third American truck came through. I spoke to the Major and told him the story. He says to me, 'From the look of things, we are not getting out yet. The Russians are waiting for Marshall Zucof, and they want to make a big ceremony of releasing you prisoners.' Then he says to me, 'Look, the American lines are about thirty-five miles away. If you get across the Elbe River, American troops will be there. Just do not go all at once.'

"I took five guys: three infantry guys and two paratroopers. I was the highest rank, and the five guys were all privates, so they respected rank. The next morning, we go to the gate. I salute. The guard on duty was as crocked as a hoot owl. He says, 'You can't go.' So I say, 'Snaps,' and he says, 'Ah, schnapps,' and he opens the gate, and we got the hell out. We were on the road for ten days."

Joey stood up and asked, "How did you avoid the Russians?"

"Well," Peter went on, "if we ever saw them we would give them a big salute and smile. To make a long story short, guys, we kept going, looking for food, and we sometimes we holed up for a long while. Once we holed up in a farm and found a big fat pig. Sniper Chandler, who was from Maine, used a sledge hammer to kill the pig, and we found some potatoes too, and we ate and ate and ate. For three days, we ate and ate, and then we threw up. When I arrived at the American camp, I was under ninety-seven pounds with two pair of pants on, two pairs of underwear, and two shirts."

Angelo stood up. "Pete, how did you get across the Elbe River?"

Peter looked tired, but he said, "Well, there was a lot of shooting going on, so when the shooting slowed down, we kind of knew the war was over. When we finally crossed the Elbe, we just kept walking. There was a bridge there that had been bombed, but old ladies and kids trying to get away were crawling on their knees and getting over, so I said to the guys, 'If they can get over, so can we.' Once we got over the bridge, we found trucks there, picking up people. Being hungry all the time means that afterward you can never get rid of the hunger pains. Even today, I'd kill

292

for a loaf of bread."

     They all broke bread together, with spaghetti and meatballs and plenty of Betty's Italian bread and Pettoruto's wine.

For the thing which
I greatly feared is come to me,
and that which I was afraid of
Is come into me.
I was not in safety, neither
had I rest, neither was I quiet,
yet trouble came.

— Job

CHAPTER 17 – THE MAN WITH TEN THOUSAND NAMES

Lawrence after the war was invisible, disappearing into its own secret griefs. Pasquale wanted to be invisible too, because he was so ashamed of asking people for names. At first writing names in his notebooks had been a secret, but in time it seemed to him that everyone knew about him and his names. His obsession with people, names, and places grew stronger as he aged. Now, when he asked a guy for a specific spelling or a date, or who had been President Roosevelt's Vice-President, the answer would be "Forget about it, Pat. What does it matter to you? Don't get crazy."

"Maybe I am going crazy," he told Dr. S., who was back in his office in Andover. Pasquale had come to believe that his obsession had started when he was thirteen, when his father had died in Italy and no one in his family had gone back to Italy to see him buried.

"You're carrying your own burden plus your family's misfortunes," Dr. S. said. "How could your mother have gone back to Italy? You know you could not afford it

294

either. Even more significant is your experience in Italy during the war, when your cousin-in-law Alphonse was blown to bits. Your depression has taken over your life, Pat. You are not alone in that. President Abraham Lincoln suffered from depression most of his life, because his mother had died when he was nine. Dante, the Italian poet, was depressed. For people with feelings like yours, there sometimes comes a point when it just breaks your soul. Do not let depression break your soul, Pat. Continue listening to the music you love, and sing to your family and children. You tell me it makes you feel good. Well, find time every day to feel good."

Dr. S. had a book on his desk, and he picked it up and read a passage from it: "In the middle of the journey of our life I found myself in a dark wood, for I had lost the right path." Later Pasquale went to the library and read it.

In the next session with Dr. S., he cried and said, "I only went to school through the seventh grade, but I understand Dante's words in my bones and soul. I found them overwhelming, but I am proud that he was Italian."

With the help of his daughter Glory, who followed him through the dark path, he wrote this poem for Dr. S., written on the first page of a notebook:

This is My Belief

.

All life exists, but I refuse to exist at another person's expense
Me, sometimes I realized it was at my expense
I did not know
But in my soul, I did
I guessed it right

295

I paid the price
I rolled the dice
But that was trite
Compared to another one's life

So, I suffered and clothed myself in obsessions
Without the possessions
Yet no one knew
I could not live my life
At the expense of the other being.

***

"Come on, Pat," Betty said one day, "you and me, we will go to Salisbury Beach. I rented a beautiful room at the hotel right on the water. Maria Grazia will stay with the children. They love her. Please, Pat, I want to go with you. The salt air will help you get better. Rita will check in and mind the store."

Pasquale worried that he might tell her about the encounter with the Italian woman in Italy. Dr. S had told him, "If Betty asks, you should say something; do not lie." But Pasquale had heard through the grapevine that Betty and the girls from Elm Street had gone dancing at Fort Devens during the war, so he decided he would not ask her about that, and maybe she would not ask him about Italy.

While they were at Salisbury Beach, Pasquale tried to tell Betty about Dr. S. "I have an Obsessive Compulsive Disorder, and it is causing me lots of distress. I am not sure, but it probably started when I was in my teens and my father died. So, when I get a name, Betty, I have to know how to spell it and who the person is. It makes me feel better. Do you understand?"

"Well, Pat, is it hereditary? I mean, what about the

296

kids—are they going to get it?"

"No, Betty, it is not hereditary. It comes from my own thoughts."

"Can one get it from another person?"

She looked frightened, and he said, "Dr. S. told me you cannot catch it or inherit it."

"Will it get better, Pat?"

"Dr. S. was not sure, but he told me it comes and goes, and I know that to be true. It could turn into a major depression, so he is going to prescribe some medicine for me. But it is not hopeless, Lisa."

"Well, what did he tell you to do?"

"Sing."

"Sing? Sing to me, Pat. Oh, that is not so bad. We will get through it, Pat."

Pat felt a big pressure lift off of him once he had told her, and they had a good time at the beach. Frank Sinatra was singing "Fly Me to The Moon" and then "We Just Could Not Say Good Night."

Pasquale sang to the kids on Sunday mornings while everyone cuddled the bed, and then they ate lemon tarts.

***

When Mr. Pettoruto died, Rita took charge at the Market. She was the brains behind its success. Salesmen adored her. She knew how to wheel and deal and was known all over the city for her fruit baskets and baby baskets. She always dressed in a white blouse and black shirt, and her platinum hair, white skin, and blue eyes hid her shrewdness. She put Betty in charge of baking bread and pasta. Pettoruto's was making enough money for the whole family.

Meanwhile, Pasquale pretended to get better from his obsession. He became more critical of everyone, especially Betty. "Your sister is a big flirt," he told her. "She'd better watch out, or she is going to get a reputation. Someone asked me if she bleached her hair."

"Oh, Pat, you are so old-fashioned—it is just part of her style. She does not bleach her hair. Marco showed her how to keep it blonde by washing it with an egg yolk. She has been doing that for years."

"Talk to her, Betty. You know how some of these old gossips like to talk. I heard the olive-oil salesman tell her yesterday that she did not look like an Italian, and he asked where she came from. *Bella figura* if she gets pregnant like little Angelina." He looked at Betty, not expecting an answer. "Tell her not to wear too much lipstick in the store and to watch her step."

"No, Pat, not just yet." Betty's answer was alert and confident.

Since he had started his political activism, everyone had started calling him P.G. In his mind he tried to get better, but the names still came as he walked through his life.

Everyone's life went on, and he tried to follow in their happy footsteps. But things were going from bad to worse. Guy, Betty's brother, a common-sense, simple man, said to him, "Betty told me last night that you came home at midnight after cooking spaghetti and meatballs for all the people in the hospital who had no family. P.G., you did good things at the Danvers State Hospital with Mrs. Stephens. You stopped some of the savagery that went on there, with the help of Governor Paul Dever. What is wrong that you look so sad? What can I do to help?"

298

Mrs. Stephens was the sole benefactor at the hospital. Pat would have done anything for her. She had several club women volunteering to help the female patients. The idea of men volunteering to help the male inmates was written in his notebook, so Pasquale turned to Guy and said, "Yes, Guy, you can help. How about getting some of the guys in the club to volunteer to help the men in the hospital?"

It was not long before Guy and three other men were ready. Mrs. Stephens and her volunteers provided the training.

It was Mrs. Stephens who put the idea of shock treatments into Pat's head. "Pat," she said, "ask Dr. S. about the shock treatments. (You know I see him too, since my husband died.) The treatments helped my cousin, and she is fine now. She is not taking any medications. It is now 1951 and not the dark ages anymore."

She took him to the electric shock room at Danvers Hospital, so that he could try it out. Pat crunched over in severe pain and said, "The names are not as bad as the pain, Mrs. Stephens. Please, let's leave."

On the way home he turned to Mrs. Stephens and said, "I am not that brave. I could never submit myself to shock treatments."

"You would not have them here at this hospital, Pat," she said, comforting him. "It would be in a wonderful hospital in Belmont called McLean—that's where my cousin was treated."

But he didn't go and instead kept busy. At the Pontiac Club others joined him, and he plunged into charity and political life. "Wheelchairs for You" provided thousands of wheelchairs every year to children who were crippled. Some of the money came from the gambling pot, but when politicians began contributing, the fund grew by leaps and bounds.

The thought of a release from his names stayed with Pasquale. Betty suggested a physical examination. Dr. DeCesare gave him a thorough evaluation and said he was as fit as a fiddle. "Keep busy and happy, Pat," he said. "You have a beautiful wife, strong healthy children, and a lot to be grateful for." He took him to the door and said, "You do not need shock treatments. Stay away from them. You will be fine doing good deeds."

On the way home Pasquale began to wonder why Dr. DeCesare thought Betty was a beautiful wife.
***

Glory became Secretary of the Pontiac Women's Auxiliary.

Albert Pettoruto spearheaded the Scholarships for Education for children of Lawrence.

The United Cerebral Palsy Association of the Merrimack Valley honored Pasquale and selected him to be on its Board of Directors. The boys at the Pontiac held a banquet with fifteen hundred people in his honor, at two dollars a ticket. Pasquale donated the money to the Scholarship fund.

Pasquale was happy.

One afternoon Louie Scanlon appeared at the bakery. Mr. Smith was aware of the visit and led him and Pasquale to a small office. Louie took a seat behind the desk and asked Pat to sit across from him. "Patsy, I want you to help me with my campaign. I am going to run for mayor of Lawrence. This city has a large Italian population, and I want them to vote for me."

Pasquale looked puzzled and leaned close to the desk. "Louie, I have known you for a long time, and you have taught me so many things, but I am not qualified for politics. You once told me it is a dirty game."

"You're right, Patsy, politics is a dirty game, but we can make it clean—just trust me. You will be able to help the people who live in Lawrence, and I will show you how."

Over a handshake, a deal was made.

Pasquale found it thrilling, and the names lessened often because he forgot about them or was too busy. He carried a small notebook to write down the names of the people he wanted to know again. Betty and the children missed him, but she kept busy with the new house, collecting the rents from the garages, which she was allowed to keep.

Several weeks into the campaign, on Sunday morning, while everyone sat at the kitchen table having lemon tarts, coffee, and cocoa, Pasquale told his family, "A political campaign can be ruthless. I could never be a politician, Betty, mainly because I know the ins and outs."

Betty took a deep breath of relief but was not completely sure yet that her husband did not love politics.

Later they were alone, having a glass of Pettoruto wine. The children were at the movies. She sat at the window, the sun illuminating her face. She was about to cry and folded her hands as if in prayer. "Darling," she asked, "are you planning on going into politics?"

He reached out to her folded hands. "Never, I promise you." And she believed him.

He picked her up in his arms, and for a minute they felt peace and heard the bells from the churches all over

301

Lawrence.

Betty remembered her brother long ago, looking down at her and asking, "So what did you learn from that?" She took Pasquale's hands. "So what have you learned from politics?"

He looked up at the ceiling and put his hands on the back of his chair. "My sweet, I learned a lot during my political career, things I thought I did not know but actually did know. From the Irish people, I learned that with humor and a little drink there is no situation without a way out. The Jews taught me about moving forward and how education is important not only to remember history but also to learn that all situations are stages of change. Some lessons came from my Italian friends and enemies, some came through my own experience. I figured out that you cannot just wish for things; you have to plant a seed, and if you take good care of it, there will be growth. A few may fall along the way. Your father, God bless his soul, was a great model for me. Do you remember how every day he went out to his little patch, tilling, watering, pruning, and touching his plants?"

They made their way to the bedroom, and he whispered, "You harvest what you sow, my darling. This I want you to remember always. It's what Mr. Kapelson told me. Teach the children when the time is right." He whispered as if in prayer, "The whole wide world is a narrow bridge—the point is not to be afraid."
***

During the different campaigns for Louie, Pasquale met Charlie Hong and other people who changed his life forever. Charlie owned a laundry store on Essex Street. Charlie ironed, and his wife sewed. Every passer-by could see them every day and most of the night, ironing shirts, tablecloths, sheets, and silk blouses that the women from the Hills and Andover would bring down to him.

It was a month before election day, and Pat thought the window in the store would be a perfect place to display one of the signs he was putting up around Lawrence. When he went into the store not carrying laundry, Charlie looked frightened and his wife ran into the back room. After shaking Charlie's hand, Pasquale said, "Excuse me, Mr. Hong. Could you put a sign in your window for the next mayor of Lawrence?"

Charlie timidly agreed and put the sign up right where anyone passing could see it. Something about his slanting black eyes revealed something to Pasquale, and he said, "What is the word for 'thank you' in Chinese, Mr. Hong?"

"Ding how," said Charlie, and from behind the curtain appeared Mrs. Hong.

The Hongs became Pasquale's link with the Chinese community, in spite of many of the guys in the club calling Charlie a "yellow chink." Over Miville's Bakery, on the corner of Common and Hampshire Streets, his cousin owned the only Chinese restaurant in Lawrence. Pasquale had a sign made with red and yellow, and it almost glowed in the dark. One year, the Chinese vote for Louie Scanlon put him over the top.

The Chinese people were Confucians. Pasquale ate in their homes and learned that they had fled their country because of the Chinese Revolution, but when they got to Lawrence they could not find work because they looked and talked differently. So, they opened their own businesses. Whole families worked day and night to put

303

food on the table and send a small amount of their earnings back home. They exchanged food for their families.

Pasquale recorded those weeks as the happiest in a long time. When he went to see his therapist, Dr. S. said he looked happy and tired. "What's up, Pat?" Dr. S. led him to a chair.

Even before he sat down, he began talking. "I am overflowing with friends, Doc. Visiting the homes of the Syrians, the Lithuanians, the Armenians, and even some Sicilians has become a thing with me this month. It's sort of like the names—I had to make friends."

"Why is that?"

"Judge Bacigalupo told me one day, 'Pat, a seed may disappear, but an idea or wish, if planted in the ground and taken care of, will someday sprout and lead to the stars.' I had to write about the seed in my names book, and I thought I had to be the seed. What I mean is that, during this time in my life, I am totally submerged in politics, and I keep busy, I do not remember about the names; I just carry my notebooks in case. But the only way I could figure out how to deal with the tragic circumstances faced by all of the immigrants here in this town was to help them in the only way I knew, which was to give of myself. This country has been very good to me and my family, so I focused on helping other people. I resist the pull of my family, except on Sunday mornings, which are the best part of my life. On Sundays I make breakfast for everyone, sing to the kids in bed, and spend the afternoon with Betty while the kids go to the movies. Most of the men in Lawrence— my own friends—are lost in their own silence. Sometimes I notice their fear, disguised by a clown-like smile. I share the thread of their silences, but I do not smile much."

"Is that what you want to do, smile, Pat?"

"No, Doc, I just want to be happy and stop the names."

"How do you think you could stop the name-writing, Pat?"

Without a trace of tears, Pasquale said, "I don't know. Please tell me how, Doc."

On the way out, when they shook hands, the psychiatrist said, "You tell me how next month, Pat, but for now do something that pleases you every day."
***

Pasquale spent his nights at the Pontiac Club in the large kitchen. The large wooden table was bigger than some of the kitchens in the tenements. Mayor Scanlon donated all the plates, forks, and knives. Once Louie became mayor, glasses came from the Racket Store on Essex Street. Kappy, from Kap's Men's Store, played cards there several days a week and donated some of his winnings for dark green shades for the windows. There were also two round oak tables, several square tables, and more folding chairs. Tomato cans filled with beach sand were used for ash trays. Near the door, brass hooks held jackets.

It was time for a Women's Auxiliary. Just a few women came. They made white crocheted pulls for the shades. Phil said, "Don't make the place too frilly, girls, okay? No pink!"

The Great Attorney Angelo Rocco, though he lived in New York, visited often. He was still talking about how the entire bee-hive city of Lawrence had come to a stop after the strike. Talking to anyone who would listen, he said, "Never forget that Sacco and Vanzetti were innocent.

They were executed because they were Italians."

The men playing cards started squirming. "Enough already!" A whisper was heard, then Larry stood up. "I quote Phil DeFusco: 'Don't trouble trouble till trouble troubles you.'"

The New York attorney kept it up, and as he was leaving he turned and spoke as if he were in a court room. "Ask your children what they have learned in school about the history of the Italians in Lawrence." He told them he would be back next month.

Many of the members did go home and ask their children about what the teachers were telling them about the city's history. Pasquale asked his children, "Do your teachers ever teach you about the history of Lawrence? You know, about the strike, and your relatives, and the countries that Nona and Papa come from?"

"Daddy, every morning we repeat 'Lawrence is the greatest textile city in the world.' Sort of like a prayer." Young, strong, and handsome like his father, Young Pat got up from the dinner table and, as if giving a speech, waved his hand. "When I bring up other questions about Lawrence, the teacher just ignores me. All she talks about is Wood and how generous he is to us. Baloney! We guys want to get out of here. I am going to Italy."

Before anyone could say anything, Glory, now the peacemaker, spoke up. "We do not want to make enemies, Daddy. If we brought it up like you do, we would not have any friends."

Lulu, who followed and repeated everything, opened her green eyes wide as a kitten and cried out, "Daddy, we always say 'God bless Lawrence.' Do you ever feel lonely, Daddy?"

"Yes," he said, "sometimes I feel totally and utterly alone in my political work." He turned to Betty. "Some people call me Patsy. I wonder if it is a slip of the tongue, or if they really think I am a patsy. I know, though, that you cannot influence people unless you are a moral person, and that thought lives in my soul. If they think I am a patsy and I know I am not, then in my solitude I am proud. I have learned that maybe I am a lot like Vanzetti, who, like me, ran away from his father in Italy and came to Lawrence to chase an ideal."

"Oh, Daddy, that was so sweet!" Glory cleaned away the dishes.

At his monthly session, Dr. S. asked him how he was sleeping these days.

Pat folded his hands as if praying. "I sleep okay. But I have been dreaming a lot. I forget some of them, but I do remember this one very clearly. I was walking on all the streets of The Plains—Oak, Chestnut, Maple, and Elm Streets—and a velvet voice told me that my family were living in the stars of the sky because they could not understand me. Each star had a name: my family, my friends; a huge star had the name of Sacco, and the largest star's name was 'Bread and Roses.' All of a sudden, there was an explosion, and the family and friends I love the most disappeared into the heavens. I flew all over the sky looking for them. I caused the explosion, and I started to cry. My tears fell into the oceans below. The velvet voice like a falling star reached into my ear and whispered, 'Be faithful, Pat, because only in this way will you be admitted to the stars of your family.' End of dream."

Dr. S. looked up and asked, "What does that dream mean to you? You do not have to explain now, Pat. I just

307

want you to think about it for our next session."

The dream came to him in many different versions, until one Saturday on their usual trip to Filene's Basement, he told Patsy Amante about his dream.

"Listen Pat," said Amante, "you have to keep busy; we all have times when we feel down or depressed. Why do you think I do all the extra things I do? Working in the bleach factory is hell. All day long, I lift heavy vats of liquid that stink, and I go home smelling like a stinking donkey. I live in a boarding house, I have no family—be grateful that you have a wonderful wife and family."

Pasquale thought his friend assumed too much. "Thanks, Amante," he said, and changed the subject. "Are there any girls you like? How about Rita Scalera?"

"Listen, Pat, Rita Scalera goes to Mass every day. The girl is a saint. Saints are not for me. But that sister-in-law of yours, Pat! Rita is a looker, but she would never even give me a second look."

Pat dropped the subject and was happy when they arrived in the North End.

The wine-making season was in full swing. Like a painting, the grapes, in shades of purple, black, green, white, and red, filled the streets on pushcarts. The smells of bread and garlic filled the air. The pushcarts were loaded with food, and vendors making all kinds of sounds were urging people to get a bargain: "*Andiamo!*" and when a beauty walked by, "*Che bella!*"

Amante was in his glory. Salespeople tipped their hats or sent smiles of acknowledgment. "Been coming here five years, Pat, and no one here can smell me. Let's go to lunch."

Pasquale picked up a pamphlet lying on the

checked tablecloth and started reading aloud. "'The English were the first to arrive in the 1800s, then the Irish, then the Jews, and now the whole neighborhood is filled with Italians.' Did you know that, Amante?"

"Pat, we are in Little Italy, just like Lawrence. There are lots of bookies and some shady guys who try to run the place. But the people are happy and safe here. I will take you to the bathhouse and gym someday. Lawrence will never make it because of that Wood. The guy is a *farabutto* (scoundrel)."

Pasquale ordered tripe and asked for the recipe.

When they arrived back in Lawrence, Jenny Guisti ran out of her dry-goods store, holding onto her apron and waving, while they were unloading. "So, Pasqualino, you forgot me when you went to Boston. Next time bring me back nylons."

"Sure, Jenny, but you have to buy them from Amante—it is his business."

From then on, she would ask them to buy things like cotton bloomers, undershirts, and tablecloths, so she could sell them in her store.

It was June, and their mission was accomplished at Filene's. Amante waved two tickets. "Pat, you want to go to a baseball game? We could get a hot dog there. I got two tickets."

They sat in the last row in the bleachers.

Pat lit his Lucky Strike cigarette. "This is the life, Amante. I can't believe so many people are cheering and happy here."

The next day, at the club, Al Pettoruto, Emile Corrente, and Pasquale started gathering some guys together for the first Pontiac football team in Lawrence. Al

Pettoruto became Manager, and the team included Gus Salvetti, Al Zappala, Al Frasca, Emil Petralia, Cosmo Fiorello as the trainer, Nick Mancini, Sam Ferrara, Peter Grille, Nick Troianello as the Captain, Speedy Brown, Sam Brown, Paul Perrochi, Ray Simeone, Tony Piro, and Sully Petralia as the shortstop. Saunders Photo took the team's picture at the club, and the *Tribune* featured it.

Kappy bought and designed their first uniforms. Later on in his life Pat framed the picture, and it hung on Betty's wall; it was called "The Forgotten Days."

Between 1952 and 1972 Pat struggled daily with the names and could not shake the urge to write them down correctly and ask Betty how to spell them exactly. He thought she could answer correctly because she had graduated from high school. "Betty, how do you spell Enrico—you know, Maria Grazia's son?" Betty would say she did not know, but when she did answer, giving him any old spelling, he would respond, "No, that is not how you spell his name," and get angry. The urge to know was so severe, he started calling people until he got the right spelling. This compulsion waxed and waned, and sometimes he could no longer function. He told Dr. S. that in some part of his brain he knew it was not right. His whole life was ruled by the names.
***

Between 1952 and his death, Pasquale was admitted to McLean Psychiatric Hospital for what the psychiatrist called Obsessive Compulsive Disorder, with symptoms of depression and B12 deficiency. In the meeting with Pasquale's family, Dr. Z., a short, dark-haired man with a mustache, got up from his desk and sat next to Pasquale and daughter. He held the reports from Dr. S. "Tell me,

310

Pasquale, do you know why you are here?"

"Sure." Pat's hands had stopped shaking. "I have Obsessive Compulsive Disorder, which is making me depressed, and I want to feel better."

Dr. Z. took out a folder and a pen. "Tell me one of your happiest memories."

Without a blink of an eye, Pat said, "Winning first prize at the Palace Theater for singing 'I am a Yankee Doodle Dandy.' My daughter had been born three days before, and she was so beautiful that we named her Glory. The theater was packed with all the people from Lawrence, and they cheered for me. Everyone said I had good promise." He could not stop himself and went on, "My brother-in-law said I was another Mario Lanza. I dressed like James Cagney, and I practiced the song for weeks. I did not make any mistakes. But, Doc, while I was singing I thought I was James Cagney. I even lit a Lucky Strike cigarette and wore a checkered cap."

Dr. Z. smiled as if he approved. Then he asked, "So you loved the cheering. And what did you win, Pat?"

"It wasn't so much the cheering, it was being accepted. I won fifty dollars, and I brought it home to Betty. She was breast-feeding, and her eyes shone as if she was proud of me. None of the Pettorutos cheered except Little Rita, Lisa's sister."

"What did singing mean to you, Pat?" Dr. Z. put his chin on his hand.

"Singing for me always came from my heart, Doc. I sang at weddings, christenings, and birthday parties for free—well, maybe for a meal—and every Sunday morning in my bed with our babies. The song I sang for Betty and my firstborn was 'Roses Are Shining in Picardy.' Do you

311

know of it, Doc?"

"No. Can you sing the first few words for me, Pat?"

"I love the second verse: 'Roses are shining in Picardy, but there is never a Rose like you.'"

The Psychiatrist clapped him on the shoulder and said, "You have a beautiful voice. Keep on singing in your life."

Pat went on, "I knew all the words to the songs and did not have to worry about getting any names in my brain. I felt free from it, Doctor."

"You felt free from what?"

"The names, the names." Pasquale's eyes turned green and started to water.

"What else besides your family and singing do you find pleasure in, Pat?"

His tears disappeared. "Politics."

"Amazing, Pat. Did you collect any names during your political career?"

"Oh, not so many. I have those I want to remember in my books. Sometimes I call the library now in Lawrence, and Mrs. S. knows me and says, 'How are you, Pat? What do you want to know?' I tell her, and she finally gets the answer, and that makes me happy."

"Why?" Dr. Z. waited, and everyone stopped breathing for a moment.

"Because once I get the right answer, I feel better and can go on with my life."

"Give me an example, Pat."

"Hm. Well, one day I wanted to know which President had said, 'The only thing to fear is fear itself.' Mrs. C. at the library, who knows me now, laughed and said, 'Of course you know who it was, Pat—President

Roosevelt.' I like Mrs. C. because she did not say, like my wife, 'Don't you remember, Pat?' I felt so happy that day and remembered listening to President Roosevelt on the radio; he called them Fireside Chats. For most of the people in Lawrence, they were stove-side chats."

"Were you a happy kid? Who took care of you when your parents worked?" Dr. Z. waited patiently as Pasquale changed his demeanor.

"I took care of myself, since the age of seven. My mother and father had to work. Me and my sister, Josephine, stayed in our flat, once they went to work. Auntie Mary (she was not our Auntie, but we called her Auntie for respect) would come down once or twice to bring us upstairs to play with her kids. I did not like the *via vecchia*—the old way, Doc. But that is how it was then. Auntie Mary worked from 7 A.M. until 10 A.M. in Andover for the Woods, ironing and cleaning. They used to send a car for her. They provided an apartment on the third floor of our tenement for her and her family and her lazy husband." Pasquale squirmed in his chair. "I heard a lot of stories from Auntie Mary during the strike about how the other half lived. She was married to a lazy Sicilian man who told everyone he was an aristocrat and would not work in the mills. He never worked much and strutted around like he was the Pope."

"Did you want what the other half had, Pat?" Dr. Z. asked.

"Are you kidding? My firm answer is NO."

"Well, Pat, they lived well and had everything anyone could ever want."

"But you know, Doctor, they got it from the sweat, toil, and lives of all the immigrants in

313

Lawrence. I would rather starve. But, of course, my wife's family ran a grocery, and I worked in a bakery, so we never starved."

***

On his sixtieth birthday, at 8:00 P.M., Pat was admitted to McLean Hospital. Betty stayed home. She had attended several of the family meetings that had been held before his admission. She felt there was nothing more to say. "It's up to them."

It was still light as they drove into the grounds of McLean Hospital. The steel gate barricading the elevator door was locked. Everything was locked. Pasquale, Glory, and Anthony stood like statues. Once in the elevator they could hear keys and chains rattling. The elevator was dark, and then, when they arrived at the third floor, someone unlocked the door, and facing them was a well-lit yellow room.

For Pasquale, everything stopped, like a photograph. People were walking and talking, and there was a huge television. Once he was in the room, the photograph went into action.

Glory was bewildered and scared. She whispered, "This is not the same building where we were interviewed." Anthony's breath seemed to have been cut off.

An orderly brought them to Pasquale's room. After a few minutes a knock on the door startled them. "I am Dr. O'Loughlin." The interview lasted one and a half hours. They forgot they were in a locked unit. Then came another interview that lasted another hour.

Anthony asked, "Is my father getting dementia?"

Pasquale thought, *What the hell is that, cancer?*

The answer came quick and sharp. Dr. O'Loughlin

314

looked annoyed. "Your father is not demented, and I doubt if he has Alzheimer's, but he is severely depressed. I will recommend psychotherapy." Very softly he added, "And maybe ECT."

Pat heard ECT, and it stayed in his mind. When everyone left, he wrote the letters "ECT" in a notebook that Glory had left on the table. On the cover, in large black print, were the words "WHEN YOU VISIT, PLEASE WRITE SOMETHING. THANK YOU." A small pen lying next to the notebook was replaced by a pencil that night.

Once the door was shut and he heard a loud click, he realized that he was locked in. Before he had time to think, another click unlocked the door, and it opened to reveal a tall orderly. "Hello, Pat. My name is Santo, and I am here to give you some pills, so you can sleep."

When it came to pills, Pasquale was very sharp. "What are they, and what are they for?"

The orderly looked around, turned down his bed, and locked the door as he went out.

A sleeping pill helped Pasquale sleep, and when he woke up, he realized that he was in a small room with yellow walls striped by the shadows of the iron grates on the windows. He remembered visiting Congressman B., who was in jail for fraud; his window in prison had been the same. The shadows kept dancing on the walls. He focused on looking out toward the green grass as dusk approached. The street lights were still on, and as he looked out the window at the green grass, he was surprised that it was morning.

Pasquale heard a knock, and the door opened. "My name is Fred, Pat. I want you to take these pills, and then you can take a shower and dress up."

315

"What kind of pills are they, Fred?"

"Pat, the white one is for your high blood pressure, the green one is your vitamin B12, and this one is Prozac, for your anxiety about the names."

"So you know about the names? Will these help me forget them?"

"Well, you are in a safe place, and everyone is here to help you. How many kids do you have, Pat?"

Over the small desk next to the door was a bulletin board covered with pictures. In large black print a sign read, "WE LOVE YOU, DADDY."

"Five—two boys and three girls." Pat's eyes turned green. "Why is the door locked?"

"Well, Pat, it is for your own protection; we do not want anyone walking in on you here.
Head into the shower, Pat, and then you will go to breakfast."

Pat attended group therapy, one-to-one therapy, and physical therapy. He had time every night to sit in the Community Room, where a television was turned to the evening news. Every night, a woman named Rita would bounce in the room, head straight for the TV, and change the news to "The Price is Right." Most of the guys just got up and left the room, shaking their heads. Pat liked "The Price is Right" because it had spelling and words. Rita became his friend. Her red hair brought back to him the *putana* Angelica and that horrible night when some of the most respected women in Lawrence had broken her legs.

In group therapy one morning, while Rita was sitting next to him, he told everyone about the scene in the alley all those years ago.

Dr. Z. said, "Patty, how many years ago did this

316

happen?"

"I remember the year," he said. "It was 1921."

Dr. Z., looking very compassionate, said, "Patty, you probably saved her life, and that should make you feel good."

"I could not prevent it, and I should have been able to see what was coming." Pat's tears flowed enough to fill this small room at McLean. Rita put her arms around him and cried too.

He stopped looking in the rooms where people were lying like corpses, hooked up to tubes or machines. He felt better and wanted to get out of there before this happened to him.

On the way home, he told his children, "I felt like I was in another world, so distant from the one I love. I promise you I will never go back again."

It was a promise he could not keep.

***

From then on there was therapy once a month and drugs such as Zoloft, Prozac, Trazadone, Buspirone, Alprazolam, and many others. He felt like a zombie when he took them, and gradually he weaned himself off of them. He begged Betty for help.

"Pat, please calm down and stop this craziness. Take the drugs; they are good for you. You are making the children unhappy. They get frightened when they see you crying." Betty was at the end of her rope.

"Betty, you do not understand what is happening to me. If you did you would come with me to the psychiatrist."

"Pat," she said, "I have had enough. Spruce up and act like a man. Your children need a father, not a bumbling

317

cry-baby."

Over time Pasquale became abusive and very strict about his children's lives. He ordered the girls not to wear lipstick. "But Mom wears lipstick," Lucille would cry out. "Okay, then you will go to work after school." Lucille wanted to be a cheerleader and would say that she worked, but in fact she went to cheerleading practice. He was tough on the boys too, finding jobs for them after school so that they missed much of the sports they loved.

"Think about what you are doing to them, Pat." Betty never cried but talked on and on. "Forget about me, but the children, Pat, the children! They are so frightened." Time and time again Betty repeated, "Forget the names, Pat, forget the names. Maybe you should go to church and see Father Milanese."

Pasquale went to see Dr. S. instead. "I cannot forgive Betty for those words against the names, and for not coming with me to therapy, Doc. I know it is not right and the whole family is suffering. I want to go back to McLean Hospital and have shock treatments."

Dr. Z. said, "You are sure, Pat, that this is what you want? Why don't you go home one more time and think about this?"

After arranging to receive the shock treatments, Pasquale, who had wanted all his life to have a happy and safe home for his family, and who felt responsible for his home life, which was beginning to crumble, asked Betty for forgiveness. "My problem, according to the psychiatrists, was that I did not express anger for my obsessive names, because I liked them."

Betty and Glory looked frightened.

"When Dr. Z. asked me if I understood what I was

318

getting from having these obsessions, I thought I heard him say, 'Are you looking for attention'—or was that my mind, or that velvet voice in my head? Please do not despise me for my decision, and forgive me. I am not afraid."

Glory kept the notebooks from his times in McLean. In the beginning, the names and notes were many, but as the years rolled on, there were fewer and fewer names and notes. There were, however, dreams from Pasquale, Pasqualino, Patty, Patsy, Pat, and Patrick.

In his room at McClean Hospital, Pasquale Foenia started praying to a God that he had neglected for a long time. He dreamed of Moses from the Bible. Moses had to choose between two roads: one life and the other death. Geraniums were growing on the road to life, through the barred window. And then the velvet voice said, "It's okay, Pat, your mother and father are here in this room." His father was next to him holding pots of red geraniums, wearing his white apron and shiny leather shoes. He was older than Pat remembered him. His mother came in through the yellow wall; her eyes were still as blue as the ocean. She was carrying a basket filled with loaves of Italian bread. They merged and held hands.

"We are proud of you," his father said. His mother had tears in her blue eyes. The three of them were together in this yellow room.

He said to them, "Will you stay with me in my room until my treatment is over?"

My mother answered, "We will always be here beside you, *caro*."

"Papa, are you happy?"

"Now I am happy, that I am with your mother and you, Pasqualino." Tony went on, "It's your birthday, and

319

we want you to know that when you look up in the sky we will always be there as stars, looking after you, happy and laughing."

Then they disappeared into the yellow walls of the room.

There was a fortune cookie on the desk. The note read, "*Things that are done, it is needless to speak about… Things that are past, it is needless to blame.* — Confucius."

After that dream, Pasquale wrote, "I choose to have life and live to old age, so I can see my family do better than me."

The treatments worked for many years. Pasquale was in and out of McLean and a few times visited on an outpatient basis so that he could go home the same day. His treatments were what they call "bilateral"—the electrodes were on both sides of his head.

This was written in one of Pat's notebooks: "I lived my life of family, friends, work, and now retirement with oftentimes disastrous episodes of the names, but I got through it because I knew there was something I could turn to when the bad feeling came down upon me. But the most important part of my life now is the love and support from my family. Not that I love the treatment of The Electric Shocks. And let's face it, it is not because I want attention. It is just part of my life story now. You know, like David and Goliath."

Pasquale's pain was virtuous. He understood that for him undergoing the ECT twice a year would help him live to old age. He could not control his body, which kept punishing him for being right. When death came, it was understandable that Pat had a transformation.

The names of an entire community remained in his

notebooks forever. In his case I quote Gregory Bateson, who said, "The Map is not the Territory."

There is that in
me— I do not know what it is
but I know it is in me
Something it swings on more than the earth I swing
on awesome…
It is not chaos or death—it is form, union, plan—
it is eternal life—it is happiness

"Songs to Myself"
— Walt Whitman

BETTY'S DIARY

My brother Albert gave me this diary as a wedding present on my eighteenth birthday.

I am naming you Pasta, dear diary. Like pasta, I will measure you, knead you, and then with love turn you into a feast you will not forget. It is a fun name, don't you think? Sorry to say, but I will burn you before I die, in the hopes that like the Phoenix you might resurface again.

1930 – Pat and I got married in Lawrence on Thanksgiving Day. It made everyone happy. I should be happy. Everyone tells me I am a married woman. I went to Boston for my silk wedding dress and a white tulle veil that my sister Rita picked out. It is ten feet long. My uncle owns the flower shop and provided white lilies of the valley and stephanotis for my bouquet. All the girls from Elm Street wore pink gowns and beautiful hats as my bridesmaids.

My father looks like President Taft in the wedding pictures. My reception was at Savastano Hall. We had Italian Wedding Soup, raviolis, and chicken, and Amante went to Boston to buy the almonds from the North End.

When Pat proposed, I asked him to wait, but once my mother found out that we went out alone, she set the wedding date. It was my first kiss. I am only eighteen years old and have not seen the world.

My bridesmaids and ushers brought us to the Copley Plaza in Boston for our first night. My brothers arranged everything. I love them so much. We had a party in our room with Champagne and little sandwiches and cookies. I had a ball. My brothers really know how to throw a great party. Pat sulked the whole time.

We went to New York for our honeymoon. We stayed at my aunt's house in Brooklyn. My mother arranged it. We had a tiny room in their apartment, and the whole day people came, drank wine, and ate the fanciest food I ever saw in my life. Pat was happy to stay in the house. He can talk Sicilian to my aunt's husband, who is Sicilian, so lots of men came to talk to him about the strike and Lawrence. My God, all he talks about is Lawrence. We were in New York, I wanted to see New York! The Sicilians took Pat to Mulberry Street. I did not go because I wanted to go shopping and sightseeing. I wanted to stay in a hotel. Angelina Mancuso, one of my cousins, who is my age, took me to Central Park and Fifth Avenue. I wore my brown Chinese dress with pink peonies and a mandarin collar that Charlie's wife gave me for my shower present. Everyone said I looked beautiful. I went to the Empire State Building with Angela's sister in the afternoon. I would like to go by myself, but that is not the Italian way. I wonder if I will ever see New York again.

Pat says he loves me so much. But he checked to

see if I was a virgin. Good thing I was.

Maybe eventually I will feel the same way. What is love anyway?

I did not realize we were so different until our honeymoon. I made a decision never to expect anything of anyone while I was in New York on my honeymoon.

I will hide you in the hallway leading up to the attic in my father's tenement, where we will have an apartment soon. Please give me a good life, Mary, Mother of God, and I shall be faithful to you and Pasquale.

May Day, 1931
Dear Pasta,

I got out of bed today filled with hope.

I missed several periods and am pregnant. That witch Santa, with those beady eyes and hair coming out of her chin, came into the store today and without my knowledge (my mother must know something) asked to see my hands. Evidently if you show your palms the baby will be a boy, but if you show the top of your hands you will have a girl. So, when I flipped them over to show her, she said I was going to have a girl and that I was pregnant. That was not hard to figure out. I have only been married five months. Oh, by Jesus, they must be counting the months, those old hags with the beady eyes! (Not everyone, Pasta, because I know I will be old someday and will be called a hag, but I will not have beady eyes, I promise you that.)

Mary Angelica says I am lucky since I am not throwing up every morning. She is having her baby any day now and had a terrible time with throwing up. She made a mistake and had sex with that son of a bitch, who made her pregnant. He goes back to the Seabees without marrying her? Pat calls him a *disgratziato* (a bad human being), which he is. I will not give his name here in my diary or honor him in any way. His mother wanted Mary to go to the midwife and have an abortion. She said she would pay for it. She also said she would get rid of it. Mary Angelica went to see the priest at Holy Rosary, and the priest told her that she should have the baby and give it up for adoption. "No way! Let the priest have the baby and give it up," she told me. I agree with her. She is so brave and smart about things like this. I think it is because she works with lots of girls who are smart.

  We girls on Elm Street are planning a baby shower for her, and her own mother will take care of her and the baby when it comes. Mary is a pattern-designer at Grieco Brothers, where they make fine men's suits. Mr. Grieco said she would always have job at Grieco, but of course things are slow because of the Depression, and no one is buying suits. She is so worried that the *Disgratziato* who made her pregnant will show up. She has not heard from him in months. I think she still likes him. She told me she only went to bed with him once. She told him she was pregnant before he left, and he said, "Go get an abortion."

  Uh oh—I was staining a little today. I am still getting up at 4:30 A.M., going down to the bakery, and pounding out dough. Things are tough these days, with the Depression coming on. I am not sure I can bake the bread with my big belly, but I love mixing it. Rita came down today and said, "Are you crazy, Betty? I am going to get you some help, okay?" That sister of mine is a real flapper girl and a go-getter. Dr. DeCesare told me the staining was nothing but to take it easy. I did not tell Pat because he is such a worrywart.

June 1931

The whole country is in a bad way, Pasta. Pray for us. So many people are out of work. They opened a soup kitchen, and the Red Cross has people visiting the tenements, trying to help out. We are like a flock of birds going from day to day. Circling and watching sadness everywhere. People are hungry, and unlike in the 1920s all of us are scared.

I am adding more yeast to the dough to make it rise, and I do not like to do that, but it makes more bread. My father is giving too much stuff away, and our bills in the grocery store are piling up.

Pat got a job at the racetrack at night and on Saturdays and Sundays. Imagine people going to the horse races during these times. What do you make of it, Pasta?

Pat promises he will not bet any of his hard-earned money. One thing, he gives me his whole pay, and I am in charge of the money now. I gave him two dollars to bet with. After all, he is a man, and if I were him and working at a track I would try my luck.

I am praying to the Blessed Mother that these hard times won't last.

Oh, by the way, I went to the Rats Movie Theater (that's the Star spelled backwards) and saw *Platinum Blonde* with Jean Harlow and Loretta Young. I loved it and got a lot of ideas on how to fix my hair, and even though Pat will not allow me to wear lipstick, I bought a light pink one and a bright red one called Blonde, at the five-and-ten on Essex Street. Loretta's eyebrows were nice and thin, so I tweezed mine a little. Pat did not notice. I will tweeze a little more next week.

August 1931

Headlines in the *Progresso* paper: TENTH ANNIVERSARY OF SACCO AND VANZETTI. Pat is reliving the whole trial again. Those names, I am sure, are in his book. Like many guys in the clubs, Pat truly believes they were murdered and electrocuted because they were Italians. He keeps telling me about this Joe Morelli. Evidently Joe Morelli confessed to the murder. I told him today, "Pat, it is over, forget it." I asked my brother Al about it, and he told me to stay clear of the whole thing. He would not tell me if they were guilty or not. I love my brother, but I think he is buying into the whole idea of being American. I heard he is going out with an Irish girl. Rita told me she is blonde and a telephone operator. She went to college.

Enough with the whole thing about Sacco and Vanzetti. I told Pat, "There is nothing you can do about it." My brother Albert said to him yesterday, "Forget about it."

I asked Pat to take me to a matinee movie on Sunday to take his mind off those names. We went to see *The Public Enemy* with James Cagney. Jean Harlow was in the previews. I looked at Pat in the movie house and told him he looks like James Cagney. He liked that. The previews showed *Blonde Crazy* with James Cagney, so he said, "We will come and see it next week." Pat bought me popcorn. I love that Jean Harlow. If I put on lots of lipstick I could have lips like hers.

The movie took his mind off Sacco and Vanzetti, but who knows what is going on in his head about those stupid names and books. Outwardly he is handsome, thin, and very talented, but inwardly he is something I cannot

327

even name. I think he fights against eternal humiliation.

July 1931

Dr. DeCesare said I am at six months and that the baby is due in September or November. November 2 would be nice, since my brother Guy was born on that day. It is All Soul's Day. I am praying to Saint Anne, as she is the saint of motherhood, and Connie said she would protect me and the baby.

Pat is as happy as James Cagney dancing in *Yankee Doodle Dandy* and hopes we have a boy. My belly now gets in the way of my pounding the dough to make more and more bread. I go down even earlier because it is so hot, and with the ovens on it makes it hot as hell in the back room of the store, where I make the bread. My brothers Guy and Larry come down to help with lifting the flour sacks. I love my brothers a lot, Pasta. I hear them talking about the debt we are in with the store, and sometimes they let me in on some of their guy stories when they go to Salisbury Beach on the weekend.

Guy told me that after the baby comes he will take me to the beach and I can go swimming. He knows how much I love the ocean. I've got my bathing suit ready. It is like what Jean Harlow wore in the movie. I sent for it in the movie magazine I got in the doctor's office.

We are excited about our first baby. My mother is counting the months, but Dr. D. said the baby should arrive in November. Whew, that will stop the gossiping!

I haven't figured out how I am going to keep up my daily routine once the baby comes.

Connie is knitting things in pink because Mrs. Scuito said I am carrying all in the front and that is a sure

328

sign I am having a girl. She is such a superstitious woman. She wanted to do the *mal bocci* (evil eye) to me so that me and the baby will not get the evil eye. I let her do it to keep the peace. The woman is a nutcase, going around doing this stupid thing. And then my mother said I had to give her a loaf of bread for her service.

November 2 – All Souls Day

Glory came early in the morning. She weighed 8 lb. 4 ounces.

I did not have much labor, she sort of popped out. Dr. DeCesare said it was because I was an active young lady making all that bread. Glory was born at home because I did not have time to go to the hospital. Mrs. Buonaconti, the midwife, came over. I think the whole neighborhood heard me scream. I took a glass of wine before she came. My mother, who knows, told me to drink it. Glad I did.

Pat is delirious. And he sang to me and Glory. "Girl of My Dreams, I Love You." Can you believe he brought me a bouquet of flowers? The best roses, and then he sang, "Roses Are Shining in Picardy." Pat is very romantic with his songs.

He asked if he could bet two dollars at the racetrack for good luck. He is working so hard now. Two jobs, but he is happy. Thank God that Mrs. Morehouse is as old as my mother, or I would worry about him driving her around.

Thank God I have my family here. Living in the same place till my own apartment upstairs gets done is hard on Pat. Maybe that is why he is never home. Right now, I cannot complain because Glory has lots of aunts and uncles who love her and take good care of her. They know how much. I love going to the movies. The Capital Theater opened up today. Hello, Capital and Mr. Val Jean, the owner!

February 1932

I am pregnant again. Baby due in October. Dr. DeCesare told me I would not get pregnant again while I was nursing Glory, so I was not careful. Okay, Pasta, I need to be happy. Not easy these days, so I will think about next Christmas when I will have two babies. Hopefully it will be a boy. My mother, who is so stern these days and always thinking ahead, thought I was irresponsible. You know, Pasta, I think I married my mother sometimes, because sometimes Pat says the same thing. He does not say irresponsible, though, he says I am flighty.

I must have hope. There is sadness all over Lawrence because of the Depression.
Thank God Pat has a job. Mrs. Shuld the widow works in the mills. I saw her in the alley while I was baking the other day, and she was looking through the garbage. My father gave her bread and milk. She kissed his forehead. She has six children. Those Syrians are having it tough.

Pat said that he would find out for me how to make the flour and dough last to make more loaves of bread. The people come in and sometimes do not have the two cents to pay, so my father gives it to them for a penny.

Pat is worrying unnecessarily. He has a job at the Morehouse, and everyone has to have bread. Someone said, "Bread is the staff of life." For me it is, since I am a bread-maker.

Everyone is talking about hard times. Giorgio, that guy from California who sells us the olive oil, said it is just as bad in California and that people are hungry. He said people are committing suicide. Oh my god, Pasta, what is going to happen to us?

Giorgio has an eye for my sister Rita. He said she does not look Italian because she has blonde hair and blue eyes. He said to her, "Did your mother have a German boyfriend?" My father was behind the meat counter, and his look could have sent Giorgio flying down the street. Of course, Rita flipped those eyelashes and pursed her red lips. Giorgio is the kind of guy that Humphrey Bogart was in the movie *The Bad Sister,* who marries Bette Davis and then deserts her. I told Rita to be careful. She loves to flirt. I think she met him last weekend. Can you believe it? My mother will kill her if she finds out.

You know, my mother must have been a beautiful woman when she was eighteen and married my father. She is so stern now, but she still has those blue watery eyes. I wonder if she ever flirted with the sales guys of her day. Is this what happens when you have seven children, run a grocery store to feed everyone, and do not take care of yourself? Of course, she is always picking on almonds from her apron pocket.

She is a little tougher about not getting something for food from customers, but Daddy is so kind to the customers and truly feels for them. Some people only have two pennies, and he says, "Okay, you take this bread, it is yesterday's, so you have enough money." I am worried about him because he is always working, and now I know he is worrying about how we are going to pay the mortgage on the building. Things are tough, but I told him I would help because I have some money saved that no one knows about. I was saving it for a coat with a big fox collar like

Bette Davis wore in *The Bad Sister* with Zac Pitts.

1933

Pat is on a roll for Franklin Delano Roosevelt these days. Every night we listen by the radio to his Fireside Chats. Pat worked very hard in Lawrence to help him get elected. He got a good Italian vote, so Pat is now a devoted Democrat. He wants me to vote Democrat, but I am not sure yet. I do not know what Roosevelt means by a New Deal.

We are suffering in Lawrence because there is no work and most of the mills are shut down. Hundreds of people wait in line for a bowl of soup and a piece of bread at the soup kitchens. Thank God for them. Also, the people from the soup kitchens come in and buy bread. They even get the Betsy Ross Bread from the Morehouse.

President Roosevelt spoke the other night (we have a radio that Pat sometimes takes to the club, so the guys can listen, but we listen at home). I do not understand why the President of the United States said we should keep our money in the banks instead of under the mattress. How did he know that is where I keep mine? When I heard about Black Thursday, I decided to put the money I have right here, Pasta, in the book, where it is safe. Someday when things get better I will put the money in the bank, but I want to save it for my children and their education.

President Roosevelt said that six million people are out of work. As if we in Lawrence don't know that! It is a Black Friday all over the country. In Lawrence for us the whole year is like Black Friday.

Mr. Murphy came from the bank today and told my father that they would have to foreclose on the store. We are not the only ones they want to close down.

None of my college brothers could do anything. Even though they get some money from the school, my parents pay for the rest of their tuition. I take money from the register once in a while and send it to them. Pat keeps telling me that they should go to work in the summer.

Pat came through, AGAIN, for my family, so I hope they respect him more! Mr. Morehouse from the Betsy Ross Company took him and my mother to see Mr. Murphy at the bank.

Thank you, Saint Lucy, for answering all our prayers! The bank did not put up the white flag on our store, but Petrolia's on the corner has a white flag flying, signifying foreclosure. God bless Pat today. Pasta, I do not know why my brothers do not respect Pat, and I wonder what he has done to them. I guess he is not Wasp enough, like a lot of their friends. He is too much of a wop.

Pat told us that President Roosevelt said, "The only thing we have to fear is fear itself." That is unusual for him, because down deep I think he is always afraid. He wants us to be happy and not afraid.

I do not understand that, because if children do not have the right nourishment and warm homes to live in, how can they not be afraid? Is fear different from being afraid?

1938

I love having our own apartment. We stayed with my parents and five brothers until the attic on the second floor of the building was turned into a beautiful four-room apartment. Privacy at last! I have my very own kitchen, and Pat bought me a washing machine and a beautiful yellow and green stove. We went to the Racket Store to buy pots and pans and dishes. Only necessary things. You know how I like a little fancy and pretty stuff. I picked a beautiful cream, yellow, and red linoleum for the kitchen and pantry. I have my own sink and beautiful aluminum pans.

Maybe we can go out together as a married couple more often, because Rita will baby-sit.
Pat sometimes just does not realize how I miss going out with him. He spends a lot of time at the club. I said to him this morning, "Why can't you come home earlier, and we can go for a walk or go out?" He is always at the club.

I heard my brothers talking about it, and they are saying he is not home enough. My brothers bought us a radio for our wedding, and he takes it to the club. So what is the problem with him? He can listen at home. Oh well. I am glad I have so many friends. My best friend, Connie Pettinelli, is pregnant, and so all the girls are excited. My mother said she is a foolish girl, having a baby so early in her life. Wait till she hears I missed my period again.

1940

The Depression has lifted, so they say, but our bodies still hold onto the fear of not having enough food or work. People are coming out of it with scars that will last forever. Like, for instance, will I ever buy anything that is not on sale? Will I ever buy anything for myself? Will Pat ever get out of making sure we have enough food for our family? All of us have the scars imprinted on our souls. I've got to figure it out. I do not want to have the scars of anything remain on my body.

The only fun me and the girls from Elm Street have is going to Essex Street on Tuesday nights. Russem's Store has the most beautiful navy-blue dress with huge white

334

flowers in their window. I want that dress. Pasta, do you think I am selfish for wanting that dress? I am only wishing for it. It may be a sin because the priest said at confession that sometimes just thinking about something bad is a sin. Uh oh, I am in trouble.

1943

I have five children under seven years old. I have to spend my time and energy making our home nice and beautiful with what we have. The children right now are my first priority. My time will come, I am sure, when they grow up. I am writing with my whole soul.

I did skip out for a few hours this week. My father often gives me nickels and dimes. He knows I love the movies. I feel calmer and happy when I get out for a few hours. I told Pat the first time, and he seemed angry that I had left the kids and the house. I think he might be jealous. I went to see *George White's Scandals*. I love that Alice Faye. In the show her name was Kitty Donnelly. She sang "Oh, You Nasty Man." None of us women could ever say that to any man. But Alice Faye said it for us. I could have been like Alice Faye, if my mother hadn't insisted that I get married. I cried when I heard Alice Faye was going to stop making movies. That was the time I needed her most.

1944

I made one of the first pizzas here in Lawrence. I tried it because a thin slice of dough with fresh tomatoes from my father's garden and a little olive oil does not cost much and is nutritional. I was not supposed to sell it because my mother said it was for the family. I made enough, though, and it sold like hot cakes. My mother said

335

it was American Pizza and not what they make in Italy. Who cares—it is good.

My father and Pat were very proud of me. I bring the children down to the bakery now in the early morning if they are up, and they play with the dough in the dough box.

My mother and some of the women in the tenements make sauce now for the pizza, and we sell it in the store.

Some of the other stores want me to make it for them to sell, but I do not have enough help. I said to Pat today, "I want to open my own pizza shop. There are no pizza shops in Lawrence." He told me he thought there were some in Boston. He looked at me with those hazel eyes that turn green when he is mad and said, "No wife of mine is going to work."

WHAT DOES THE MAN THINK I DO EVERY MORNING?

I am going to open my own pizza shop someday. Right now, I am stashing away a few pennies and being very frugal with myself. Thank God the kids have everything they need from my sister Rita and my brothers. The boys have fun books, and the girls have lots of dolls. I will not give up the movies, Pasta.
***

Those sneaky Japs attacked Pearl Harbor in 1941.

Since we declared war, the mills are going strong, making khaki cloth and uniforms for the soldiers. People are working again. We are getting some money from all the debts that people owe us. It is not enough, though, and Rita is getting to be a tough cookie. She is a real businesswoman, and Al has a new word for her: *entrepreneur.* We are two sisters, one an entrepreneur and one a housewife.

That is me, a housewife, but I have an entrepreneur's mind. I am a mother now with four children. Yes, Joanne came after I thought I'd had a hysterectomy. But I guess they left something in, so I had her. Named her after St. John, since she was born on June 24. A gift for my old age, someone said. How ridiculous to put that on a baby, I thought to myself. Pasta, is that a sin? You know what the priest said: if you think something bad, it is a sin. How could it be a sin if you did not do anything? I won't argue with a priest, but he is way off. Well, some of my friends just have a different mindset, sort of old-fashioned.

Do we need a war, Pasta, to stay alive? Thousands of boys are being killed.

Larry and Guy enlisted to serve our country right away. Marco was drafted and is in India. Guy is in Germany. Larry is in England, and Albert got rejected because of his missing fingers. He did try to enlist, though.

We are glued to the radio, listening to Roosevelt. I saw a picture of Mrs. Roosevelt in the *Lawrence Eagle Tribune*. They do not match that well, but I understand she is very intelligent. I always wish I was intelligent, but I am just a mother and a bread-maker.

Cousin Alphonse, who lives next door, is leaving tomorrow with Peter Romano for a camp in the South. He came by to say good-bye. He is so young and just finished high school. He leaves poor Aunt Atilia, who is a widow, with seven children. She is dependent on him to help out since his father died at the Pemberton Mill in the fire. Alphonse Pettoruto's father was my father's brother. When he died, my father took responsibility for Aunt Atilia and all the kids.

337

1945

MY SADDEST DAY EVER—PAPA DIED TODAY FROM A MASSIVE STROKE.

I cannot tell anyone this, Pasta, but you: I refuse to wear all black like my mother. I will never be happy again. In a way, I am happy that he is not suffering. He could not talk, he could not walk. My independent Papa could not dress himself, bathe or feed himself. He sat in his worn-out wicker chair in the store, hour after hour, talking with his eyes. When I would stare into his eyes year after year, this is what he said to me: "I died of hard work." Every day since his first stroke, I saw his sad brown eyes that talked to me. Dr. DeCesare said there was nothing he could do.

What Papa's eyes said to me was this: "My body is dying, but my soul will love you and your brothers and sister all my life, alive or dead. We must all work hard to be respected as Americans—but never forget that you are Italian-American. Pat is a good man with a real soul. Stay with him; he needs you. Be good to him. He has sad eyes but a soul that will outlast all the hardships he must go through in life, because he is so proud of his Italian heritage. He feels what people feel. Help him. What really matters is living life with passion, with a sacred love that is revolted by talk that is vulgar and insulting. Never be vulgar, and if people insult you shun them. Do not mourn me; live on. Death is a proof that I lived and was here."

I pressed my face into my soaked pillow last night, and, in a way, I was glad that it was over for my father, who suffered so much because he loved so much. I shall miss him forever, even though I will not clothe myself in those dreadful black clothes forever. I will wear black for

338

one month.

Pasta, as I write this I am not crying because I can hear Pat practicing his song to sing at the funeral at Mass on Sunday. I love that song, "Mother, at Thy Feet I Am Kneeling." He also is practicing a song he will sing at the Rats theater next week, and it clenches my heart. He is singing "I am a Yankee Doodle Dandy." He sang it for us two weeks ago, and now it is perfect.

Look at him and help him, Papa, while you are in heaven. I do not know how to help him.

I am so tired.

March 12

Banks are open, and President Roosevelt told us to put our money in the bank again.

Our lives revolve around the war now. Please, God, help the Jewish people who Hitler is putting in concentration camps. They did nothing wrong. Mr. Kapelson talks to Pat about it. Hitler is a monster, but I think another monster is that idiot of a Mussolini. He is a traitor. The rat. The both of them, Hitler and Mussolini, should be hanged.

I have been driving the Delivery Wagon to Boston every other week to pick up canned food and cold cuts from the North End. I just love driving because I feel like a free bird. I tried to find a pizza store, but people looked at me like I was a nutcake.

The Toilers Women Club had a banquet to sell Bonds for the war effort, and we were invited. I personally bought four War Bonds. The kids can have them for college. I haven't been out to a big party for a long time without a baby in my body. I bought a non-pregnant dress.

339

It is five sizes smaller than the ones I have been wearing.

My dress is navy blue with huge gardenias printed everywhere. I bought it at Russem's on Essex Street. Mrs. Russem picked out a beautiful pin and earrings. I wore lipstick. Amazing that Pat did not say, "Take that off." Progress, huh.

When my brother Al came home from college this week, wearing his white flannel pants and white buck shoes (I am the one who sends him ten dollars from the cash register every week), he kept making all these comments like "Talk English, Ma." He seems to be ashamed of how my mother cooks and serves food. He pesters my mother to speak English and not Italian. He is in another world. He means well, and I love him, but if we did not understand Italian (I am not good at it), how could we wait on the customers in the store? I hope he is not ashamed of my mother, who has been a rock since my father died. She is still in black.

Pat says, "See what college does to you." He thinks my family and I are too close and do not have practical street sense.

Well, Pasta, I said if it was not for my brothers and mother to help me with the kids, there is no way I could continue baking the bread. Pat certainly does not make enough to save money.

No use arguing, he always wins that kind of argument. He dropped a bomb today and said he is sending for his mother to help with the kids. Woe is me! I do not think I will like that. We do not have room in our apartment.

"Where are we going to put her?" I asked Pat. "Do not worry," he said, "she and my stepsister can get jobs at

340

the mill and make enough money to live on their own eventually."

Now I hear his stepsister is coming also. Pasta, I must realize that there is nothing I can do about that, so I need to accept what I cannot change around here.

The War Years

Pat was called to duty. Not to fight but, I understand, to interpret in Italy. Now that Italy has joined Germany, that imbecile of a Mussolini has gone crazy.

When Pat left Lawrence, he told the kids he wanted to do something for his country and told them a made-up story.

So we all are proud of him. Except my mother, who said he is a selfish and foolish man and should stay home with us and, of course, help in the store.

Rita married Joe Coletta before he went to Fort Devens and shipped to New Orleans. Small wedding. She looked like Maureen O'Hara in the movie *How Green Was My Valley*, only Rita has blonde hair. Now that my brothers and Pat and her husband Joe are in the service, Rita is the real boss. Me, I am the bread-maker, but when I write in my diary, Pasta, I am a gorgeous flapper who is a writer.

I can dream, can't I?

Hey, why not a writer? I never thought of that. Okay, from now on I will try to write like a writer, like Richard Llewellyn, who wrote *How Green Was My Valley*, which I am now reading.

I have not heard from Pat. I am worried because I understand from my Auntie Atilia that her son is in Anzio and saw Pat and they all went out together.

I dreamed last night that Pat had an affair with a

beautiful slim Italian woman who looked like Sophia Loren. I saw her in a movie this week, *It Started in Naples*. She is gorgeous. She is proud of her boobs. Not like us Italian-American girls, who hide them under tight bras and corsets. Since I had the dream, I decided to go with all the women from Lawrence to Fort Devens on Saturday night, to the USO dance. I had a great time. No flirting. Just dancing.

Pat will kill me if he finds out. I did nothing wrong, by the way. After all, I saw a picture of Rosie the Riveter in a movie trailer last week. She is doing her bit to help the war effort, so I figured this was my little bit, to help the servicemen be happy. Thank God none of the men in my life are here to see me and watch over me. No doubt the gossips with their beady eyes will tell stories. By the way, Pasta, I have been driving since before the war, but last week I went to get my driver's license.

Oh, one more secret: since the kids are older now, some in high school, I add a little wine to their breakfast coffee and egg, so they have vitamins. And I have been smoking like Betty Grable. I tried a long thin one today and like smoking.

Many things have happened since Pat went away. The red stars are on every street here in the windows, because so many of our boys died in battle. My Aunt Atilia has never been the same since my cousin Alphonse was killed in action in Anzio. She sits by the window every day, praying for him to come home, dressed in black. We pray every day for God to watch over Larry, Guy, and Mark. My mother is still wearing black over my father's death. How many years now, I don't remember. The Comparones from

342

Oak Street lost five sons in the war. *Dio mio,* keep my brothers and Pat safe, so they can come home.

One Year Later

Pat is home after nine months away. He is changed. He is different. I went to see *Casablanca,* and since Pat would not come, I copied down a line from Humphrey Bogart: "I stick my neck out for nobody." Holy smoke, I think I am getting it from, Pat writing down these things.

Maybe he had an affair? He is not talking about anything, just filling his book with names. Our peaceful home has become a battleground for him. Nothing pleases him, and he does not sing to the children on Sunday morning anymore. The kids are afraid of him. My brothers keep telling me he needs to see a psychiatrist.

I am embarrassed when he yells and can be heard all the way down to Oak Street, but I cannot let it get me down. I must remember to keep my head high. My father always told me that. I wish now he had talked to me about the many things he went through as an immigrant.

I do not know what happened to Pat when he was in Italy. I told him that it is time to see a psychiatrist and that I will go with him. We cannot go on like this. Everyone is involved, including my family, who live downstairs and can hear everything.

Like today, he said the macaroni was not cooked right and did not eat supper and went to the club. The kids were frightened, and little Joanne ended up crying. I figured he probably cooked and ate at the club. Good. If he continues like this, I will cook just for the kids and me.

Dr. S. set up an appointment for Pat to see Dr. Z. at McLean Hospital on Wednesday, and he has agreed to go.

343

I think he had an affair in Italy. Sophia Loren did in the movies, so I see how easy it could have been.

I peeked in his book of names, and there were no women's names, only Alphonse. Next to his name was a gold star.

The War Is Still Going On—Therapy Days for Pat

Dr. Z. is very nice but does not talk much. He just keeps nodding. Pat cried when he told us the story about Alphonse and said that I keep harping on at him about an affair. I know something happened, but he cannot talk about it. His focus is on Alphonse.

This is serious, I realize, and I mentioned about the names and books since Pat never mentioned that issue. That did it—Pat blew up right in Dr. Z.'s office. Just like he has been doing since he came home from the war. He is so angry at me.

"She is wearing lipstick!" ("He finally noticed," I said.) Pat is boisterous now: "She thinks she is a big-shot because she drives." He said so many things that hurt me that Dr. Z. told him to stop. I decided then and there, that's it, I am not going any more.

Nothing pleases him. He has stopped singing, which is not a good sign.

I continue to go to the therapy sessions but will stop soon because it seems to me there are two against one. He needs to talk to the doctor alone.

I never realized how angry Pat is at my family. My brother Larry did come up to the apartment once when Pat had one of his episodes and told him to stop his yelling because the children were frightened. Once Guy came up with Rita and took the children out of the house. Pat is so

344

angry at them also.

The war is over, I thank God. Mussolini was hung upside down. Those Italians know how to kill someone in disgrace. Good for them.

Surprise of surprises: Pat bought a two-family house on Prospect Hill, and it has five garages that we can rent. He is so excited. I know that Dr. Z. put him up to this. Maybe it was good that I stopped going because really, Pasta, this is who Pat is, a guy who loves his family and would do anything for us.

I cannot believe he bought a house, though, without consulting me.

But, as they say, beggars can't be choosers. Who at my age has four beautiful children, a husband, and my own house? My sister Rita said, "What more do you want, Betty, for God's sake!"

I went to see *Moon over Miami* with Betty Grable and Don Amice. Don looks just like my brother Marco. I wish I could go to Miami Beach someday.

Pat is much happier away from my family.

Me, I am so lonely. In spite of having a home of our own and getting to keep the rent from the second-floor apartment and the five garages that are on our property. I have been putting away the money from the garages after I pay the insurance man, the milk man, and the oil man, so when the girls get married they can have beautiful weddings like the one my father gave me. Pat bought a new car from his cousin Angelo, who won it in a lottery. We used the money from the rent that I'd saved.

We live on Prospect Hill. Most of the people who

345

live here keep to themselves. I've only met one woman, named Mary, who came over to welcome us. She said the Hill is filled with German people who do not like Italians. She is Polish, married to a doctor, and lives in a beautiful large yellow house with a picket fence all around a beautiful lawn. The best thing is that Mary has two daughters who are Lucille's and Joanne's ages, and that means they will have good friends.

My mother told me before I moved that I must make a friend where I live, because sometimes a friend or neighbor will be there for you faster than your own family. Mary will be my friend up here on Prospect Hill.

Before we moved in, Pat's friend Joe Ferrara, who works for Romano Construction, remodeled our kitchen with beautiful pine cabinets and a pine hutch. We went to Sullivan's Furniture and bought a huge pine table and twelve chairs. I feel like I am rich.

Mary has been a frequent visitor, and when she comes over on the weekend she sits and talks to Pat. He makes her his famous *perpettas* (meatballs), and she always licks her plate. I think she is much too fat and should watch herself, but then I say to myself, "Mind your own business—her husband is a doctor, and if he doesn't say anything, why should I?" I really like Mary. Last week she showed me her new iron and said I could use it to press my sheets next week. Of course, when I do it, I will also iron some of her sheets and pillowcases.

I am getting used to Prospect Hill now that Mary and I go out once or twice a week.
She has been letting me drive her car once in a while. She said to me today, "Betty, you can drive. Go get a license." She was surprised that I already had a license.

346

Pat did not say a word, then or ever again, about me driving. I wish I had my own car because he uses ours. Once in a while I go out for a ride just to keep up and practice.

I love driving around in Pat's car because I feel free as a bird. I wish we had a better car, but now I can even drive to Salisbury Beach and go swimming. I have enough money to buy a second-hand car, but I am saving my money for a trip to Italy someday.

I got a letter from little Rita Grillo. You remember her—she had to go back to Italy with her father when she was thirteen years old, and it was so sad because she loved it here. Anyway, she is married, teaches English at the University of Caserta, and is begging me to come and visit with her mother, who is now a widow since Tony, Pat's brother, died.

Wow, Pasta, me going to Italy someday—could you believe it? I can't go now, but as they say, time will tell. I will make a novena for this wish of mine every Thursday night at Holy Rosary. I confessed that plan, with a lot of other thoughts I have, at Confession, and although novenas are not supposed to be for materialistic things, the priest forgave me, with five Hail Marys for my bad thoughts.

The Second Saddest Day of My Life

My mother died today. I sat by her coffin, filled with grief. She is laid out in the blue lace dress that she wore at my wedding. Rita and I decided to have her wear her velvet blue hat that brought out her watery blue eye. I thought I could see them. Mrs. Pettoruto, everyone called her. I do not remember her smiling very much, only when she came to the beach and stayed at the seashore with me.

347

My father was only fifty-six years old when he died, and she carried on. She never handed me cash like my father did, but other things I remember now, and I feel guilty.

While standing by her coffin I remembered Alice Faye because she had a hard life, coming from Hell's Kitchen—not too different from Lawrence during the Bread and Roses Strike. Did you know, Pasta, that she wrote a book called *Growing Older, Staying Younger*? Then there was that beautiful white satin gown that she wore in *George White's Scandals,* which my mother never would have dreamed of wearing.

Summertime in Salisbury Beach

Our dream came true: Pat bought a small cottage on the ocean at Salisbury Beach. In September, when everyone left for the summer after Labor Day, I stayed for two more weeks with Joannella. I feel the loneliness when everyone goes back home. I am feeling it now. I feel like my heart is broken. But what I do not understand, Pasta, is why I am so happy being alone. What is happiness? I have a dictionary that Al gave me, so I will look it up when I get home.

Happiness for me today is looking around and seeing all the colors we have chosen to put in this cottage by the sea, a happy place. The rooms are small, but I love the comfy blue sofa that I picked up at the second-hand store. Connie made beautiful yellow gingham pillows for it, for our cottage-warming. A rocker for Pat. A huge kitchen, small bedrooms. I have a garden of flowers and five tomato plants in memory of my father. And my mother's blue hat with the blue flowers on the bureau. Here I am happy.

I understand why I am here; though I hate to admit it, I needed a break from all of Pat's names and depression.

348

In spite of all that stuff, I love him. I feel guilty for not going to see him during his times at the hospital. Pasta, please understand, I needed a break. I've lived with the names and the depression twenty-four hours a day. Look, Pasta, I am happy about being happy, and since I cannot give you a dictionary definition of what it means, I will write my own list:

My family, when they are happy.

My brothers and sisters.

My children: Glory has her father's heart.

Pat Jr., who has my mother's blue eyes and my father's temperament.

Lucille, who is the picture of me and should be a nun like Saint Lucia.

Anthony, who is so kind and thoughtful. He wants to be a policeman.

Joanne, who holds us up and makes life worth living.

My memories and my love for baking bread.

My heritage.

Trying to be myself.

My girlfriends.

My own obsession about trying to be a good enough person, mother, and wife.

There is nothing wrong with that. I must remember to look up *happy*.

These will be the last few pages in this diary, Pasta. I want to end by telling you the truth. It took a movie and a look into my own future to make it a happy ending.

In the middle of an unhappy scene with Pat, I got in

the car and was on my way to see my family at the store, to complain about how mistreated I was. I was feeling sorry for myself. Why, I was thinking, and lo and behold—it was probably a wish from last night's novena—it came to me like a falling star: I WANTED TO CHANGE PAT FROM WHO HE WAS INTO MY BROTHERS OR JAMES CAGNEY. I got to the bottom of Prospect Street, and then the car made a screeching turn on Common Street and stopped in front of the Capital Theater on Jackson Street.

I said to myself, "Forget everything for two hours, or go over to the Market and cry your eyes out. If you go to the Market, it will give everyone lots of gossip for a month." So I sat alone and found you in my pocketbook with a pencil. I have no idea how you got there, but lately I have been keeping you close to me. There was no line, so I breezed right into the second row.

I cherish my time alone, so my mind can quiet down and think. Then, blasting from the screen, came some news clips and coming attractions. Then the sound of bells in the opening scene, just like the bells in Lawrence, sent me right into the movie. "Produced by Frank Capra." He must be Italian, so I wrote his name in the book, along with "James Stewart" and "Donna Reed." I said to myself, "What are you doing? You're copying names like Pat." But, like Pat, I could not help myself.

Bedford Falls is just like Lawrence. Jimmy Stuart (George Bailey) looks just like my brother Marco, but Donna Reed does not look like anyone in Lawrence. I wished I could be as sweet and nice as her, Pasta, but I am not. But when Mary (Donna) fell into the swimming pool, I became her. Pat became the whole movie, as I remembered how he had saved Mario from drowning when he jumped

350

into the canal in Lawrence. How Mario became deaf and dumb from that jump, and how Pat hired him at the Morehouse to clean up the bathrooms. And those hundreds of dollars he kept saving from gambling at the Pontiac Club to give to high-school kids, so that they might have a chance to go to college. How Pat helped hundreds of young men in Lawrence go to college by hiring them in the summer, so they could pay their tuitions. And those thousands of wheelchairs the Pontiac Club gave out to cerebral-palsy kids. And I thought, "If it hadn't been for Pat, Pettoruto's Market would have gone under." How about World War II, when he went to Italy even though he said he would never go back, to help our country? How Pat helped the people remember Alphonse and Peter by writing about their true stories.

And that is not all, Pasta. Pat is George, right on that screen, singing and helping the Martinis, who could be anyone in Lawrence, to have a wonderful life. And when George gets sick and depressed because all the good he has done to people passes him by, his daughter is like my own little Joanne, crying, "Please God, something is the matter with Daddy. Please make him better." I cried so hard when Pat (of course it was George) brought Giuseppe Martini to a new house and Mary presented the family with a loaf of Italian bread so that symbolically they would never go hungry, salt, so that life would always have flavor, and wine, so that joy and prosperity would reign forever.

I think in reality I've had lots of guardian angels like Clarence. but the closest person to Clarence in my life was my friend Mary. Not my family, but a friend. When she died, and now I know she is in heaven, I realized I had only myself to get myself to my end.

351

I sat in the Capital Theater for a long time after everyone left and realized how much of my life with Pat was my own love story, just like in the movie *An Affair to Remember,* with Irene Donne and Charles Boyer, or *Now, Voyager* with Bette Davis.

The truth is, Pasta, I never accompanied Pat on his journey because I was afraid. Afraid of what was facing me for the rest of my life. I did not have the courage, but he did. Pat knew that he had choices, so he held the demons by the horns and tried his very best to get away from them. I was not insensitive to his feelings, but I was tired. Pat did not have any physical ailments.
Not a one. Yet I failed to understand that emotional and psychological trauma is as heartbreaking as having a stroke or cancer.

So, Pasta, these are my last words, I promise. After I did a little research on Frank Capra and found out that he was born in Italy, I plodded on and found some of his last words: "There is a radiance and glory in the darkness, could we but see, and to see we only have to look. I beseech you to look." Not only with our eyes, Pasta, but with our souls—you know, like St. Theresa of Avila. Pasta, it took so long, and a movie is what brought me back to myself. (AND TO LOVE AGAIN, LIKE NOBODY'S BUSINESS.)

Betty's diary was never burned because her daughter Lucille found it.

Lightning Source UK Ltd.
Milton Keynes UK
UKHW021855170522
403141UK00007B/1563